THE MAKING OF HER

THE MAKING OF HER

BERNADETTE JIWA

A NOVEL

DUTTON

DUTTON
An imprint of Penguin Random House LLC
penguinrandomhouse.com

LIBRARY OF CONGRESS CATALOGING-IN-PUBLICATION DATA
has been applied for.

ISBN 9780593186138 (hardcover)
ISBN 9780593186145 (ebook)

Printed in the United States of America
1st Printing

BOOK DESIGN BY ELKE SIGAL

For Christine

In memory of my grandmothers,
Ellen Slevin and Mary O'Toole

Our future will become the past of other women.

—EAVAN BOLAND

THE MAKING OF HER

PART ONE

PROLOGUE

Dublin, 1966

People were forever telling her how lucky she was.

"You've landed on your feet there, Joan," they'd say, with a sideways nod in Martin's direction, all the while thinking of the family business he'd inherit, or the elegant house on Grove Square with its high ceilings and wide lawns.

"It's all right for some," the women in the queue at the butcher's would sniff, glancing in her direction as they grumbled about the shocking price of corned beef.

"Aren't you blessed?" Father Mac said, after the cutting of the cake at their wedding reception. "Imagine the life you'll be able to give your children. They'll want for nothing."

When she and Martin Egan took to the floor for their first waltz, Joan had believed it with her whole heart.

But what did people know?

CHAPTER 1

Dublin, 1996

The day started early. Joan had been up for hours. The roast was done, and the cake was cooling on the kitchen counter. One of the sponges had cracked when she was turning it out of the baking tin. Nothing a bit of buttercream wouldn't cover. Even though it was only the four of them for lunch, she was determined that Carmel would have a good birthday.

Joan eyed the kitchen clock. She should probably make the effort and go upstairs to change her blouse before Carmel arrived. She got as far as the first stair before Molly called out to her.

"Where are you going now?"

Joan thought about pretending she hadn't heard, but there was no use giving her mother-in-law something else to complain about, so she went and stood in the parlor doorway. "I thought I'd make myself presentable now the bulk of the cooking is done."

Molly patted the back of her freshly washed and set hair and gave her a withering look. "Well, don't be long."

Let it go, Joan thought, as she headed for the stairs, fists clenched at her sides. *Let it go.*

Back in the kitchen she put on a new apron over her clean blouse. Through the open kitchen window she heard Martin outside in the garden. He was humming to himself. Joan couldn't make out the tune but could tell he was in good form. The weather probably had something to do with it. You could never take a fine weekend for granted, Irish summers being as unreliable as they were. Today the forecast was for sunny intervals. They would eat outside—make more of an occasion of it. New potatoes. Cold roast beef. Linen napkins. The works.

Behind her, Martin stamped his feet on the mat by the back door. She didn't turn from the sink to greet him. She would have done, once. Not anymore.

"That's the patio chairs laid out. We're all set, apart from the wine."

Joan concentrated on the wooden spoon she was scrubbing under scalding water. He was waiting for her to say something. Let him wait.

"Don't tell me you're going to be like this all day, Joan."

"Like what?" she said, lifting her head to stare through the window at the fuchsia flowering in the side garden.

"Like a long streak of misery," Martin said. "Like someone getting ready for a funeral, not like a mother about to celebrate her only daughter's birthday."

Joan's shoulders stiffened. She spun to face him, gripping the spoon in her fist. Judging by the look of remorse on his face, he knew he'd slipped up. "That's just it, though," she said. "She's not my only daughter, is she?"

Martin came closer. "Keep your voice down," he whispered. "Mother's in the front parlor."

Joan shook her head and gripped the spoon harder. As if she wasn't well aware of Molly Egan's exact whereabouts every minute of the day and night. "I'm tired, Martin. Tired of keeping quiet for the sake of what other people will think."

Martin stood beside her and reached across to turn off the tap. "I thought we agreed there was no sense in dragging this up year in, year out."

"Did *we* now?" Joan said, failing to hide her irritation. Her husband's needless reminders to keep their secret safe grated on her more and more as the years passed. She supposed he had a point, though. What would it all have been for if word got out now?

"Why can't we leave the past where it belongs?" Martin said. "What's the use of dwelling on something that's behind us?"

"She turned thirty this year, you know." Her voice wavered, as though tears might come. "You might have forgotten her, Martin. But I haven't."

He couldn't look at her. "Ah, come on. Now isn't the time. Carmel will be here any minute." He paused, gauging the mood. "For Carmel's sake." His tone was gentler now.

"For Carmel?" Joan's eyes narrowed as she searched his. Those piercing blue eyes she had fallen for long ago.

"Yes, that's it. For Carmel," he repeated, resting his hand on her shoulder.

She nodded. He had a point. Spoiling Carmel's party wouldn't change anything.

"Come on. Let's just enjoy the day, eh?" he said, giving her shoulder a small squeeze. He waited. He knew her well enough to do that much at least.

She turned back to the sink, dropping the spoon into the basin of dirty water. "You're right. Now isn't the time. And this birthday cake won't ice itself, will it?" she said, forcing half a smile.

Martin exhaled. "Exactly! Right, I'll just nip down to the shops and leave you to finish up." He patted his trouser pockets, and loose change rattled against his thighs. "Have you seen my keys?"

"Over by the phone where you left them."

"That's right." He tutted and smiled. "I won't be long," he called over his shoulder as he left the room. The front door slammed in a light breeze behind him.

Joan opened the utensil drawer to look for the palette knife before turning her attention to the cake on the table. It was Carmel's day—definitely not the time for regrets. She dipped the palette knife into the chocolate buttercream, Carmel's favorite, and smoothed it onto the sponge in sure, swift strokes. What kind of mother would ruin her daughter's birthday by raking up the past?

Joan sighed. What kind of mother was she? That question had haunted her day and night for years. Carmel wanted for nothing, Joan consoled herself. She never had to worry about having enough food in her belly, money for schoolbooks, or a job that was made for her. Joan was glad of that.

She shouldn't have been surprised that her daughter settled for working in the family business—it was all she had known. Martin made sure of it. There were so many paths she could have chosen. Opportunities galore for girls these days. If Mary Robinson could be the Irish president, there was nothing to stop the young ones doing whatever they wanted. It was as if the country had only just woken up to the fact that half the population were women with minds of their own.

She stood back to admire her handiwork. "That'll do," she said, running her finger along the blade of the palette knife, licking off the last of the buttercream. You'd never know the sponge wasn't perfect underneath.

"Joan!" Molly called from the parlor.

She didn't answer immediately.

"It's half twelve," her mother-in-law shouted.

"I'll be there in a minute," Joan called back, running hot water into the icing bowl.

She took her time walking up the hall. "Yes, Molly?" she said, standing with one hand on the doorjamb. "What is it?"

Molly shifted in her chair by the bay window. Her lookout post, as Joan called it. "There you are. Are you not finished with the cake yet? Carmel will be here shortly."

Joan consciously relaxed her shoulders by inhaling and exhaling deeply, in through her nose and out through her mouth. Something she learned only recently to do. She'd read about it in a *Woman's Weekly* article for career women about combating stress. "I'm just doing the washing up. And I'm sure you'll keep Carmel entertained when she gets here."

Molly folded her arms across her chest and pursed her lips. "Well, I'm only saying it would be better if everything wasn't left till the last minute."

"Then the sooner I get back to the kitchen the better," Joan said, turning without waiting for a response. She didn't trust herself to say another word.

CHAPTER 2

Sometimes Carmel wondered why she stayed in Dublin. Or maybe, to be more accurate, why she'd never left. Now, here she was, at the "something and nothing" age of twenty-seven, alone in her flat, reluctantly getting ready to head out to a family gathering in her honor.

She stepped under the warm spray of the shower. The truth was, she had no time for birthdays, especially her own. She was far too pragmatic to enjoy the fuss people made of the occasion—a day that, if everyone was honest, didn't belong to her. All the bother wasn't for her. It was for her father and mother, and mostly for her grandmother, who life had dealt the unfortunate blow of a solitary son and then, to top it off, just one grandchild.

It was only natural they would want to pull out all the stops for her. She was all they had: their one and only. She turned the water off and dried quickly before wrapping herself in the towel. Shaking her wet hair loose, she toweled strands of it between her palms as she walked barefoot from the bathroom to the bedroom. She stood in front of the open wardrobe and flicked through the hangers, hunting for something suitable to wear to a birthday lunch other than the mostly blue jeans and black jumpers she always wore.

Surely there were times, she thought, as a kid, when she enjoyed being the center of attention—the cake, the presents, the fuss? No, she couldn't recall them. What she had been aware of, for as long as she could remember, was the need to be happy for the sake of the grown-ups. Mind you, nothing to that effect was ever said outright. It didn't have to be spoken aloud to be true. The weight of their expectations bore down on her.

Granny would like nothing better than to see her married and settled before she died—which could be any day now, as she kept reminding them. Carmel wondered whether it would be worse in Granny's eyes if she hooked up with a "waster" who was just after her money or, God forbid, she ended up a spinster. Left on the shelf like poor Miss Hannigan, Lord rest her soul, who'd had to content herself with teaching other people's children instead of having a family of her own.

Dad was happy as long as nothing changed and she continued on as his "right-hand girl." Nothing would please him more than Carmel working in the family business until the end of her days. And her mother? Well, she was a mystery. Who knew what Mam wanted—for herself, let alone for Carmel.

If Carmel smiled, Granny was in good form, or was a little less irritable with Mam. When Granny was more civil to Mam, her mother and father got along better. It was like a domino effect. Carmel had no idea when and why she'd become the first domino to fall. All she knew was she'd played this part in the family saga for as long as she could remember. Lately, it had begun to dawn on her that this role wasn't one she'd chosen. It had just fallen to her.

Behind their birthday-party smiles, though, there was always an undercurrent of sadness. Her birthdays were less a celebration of her life and more akin to a wake for what might have been: the brothers and sisters her mother never had because of "complications" after Carmel was born. The family didn't talk about Mam's "women's troubles." They didn't have to.

It was a crying shame, people around Harold's Cross gossiped, that Martin and Joan Egan had just the one. And them loaded with money, rattling around their big house on Grove Square. It just went to show money couldn't buy you everything.

The front door slamming shut downstairs drew Carmel to the window. She pulled back the net curtain a crack, just enough to see Lina, the medical student who lived in the basement flat, unlocking her bicycle from the railings. She was here alone, a long way from her family in Malaysia, but still making a go of things.

Carmel dropped the curtain, ducking back into the shadows out of sight, and watched through the nets as Lina adjusted the rucksack on her shoulders and rode off under the shade of the chestnut trees spanning Leinster Road. Carmel loved everything about the street she'd chosen to make her home. The tall Georgian mansions that lined both sides were once the homes of well-to-do families and their domestic help. They'd been snapped up by investors in the seventies and divided up into bedsits or flats. Now, twenty years on, they housed overseas students who were passing through or singles who couldn't afford the mortgage repayments on a place of their own.

Carmel could have rented a much bigger apartment. One of those new flashy ones over in Ballsbridge with its own entry and a balcony high up in the trees that gave the feel of having a garden. Rent was dead money, though, and she was saving for her future.

"You're not moving into that dog box," her father had protested, when she'd broached the subject of moving out. "You have a perfectly good room here at home."

"I know you want the best for me, Dad, but it's time I had my own place. I need to spread my wings a bit. You were married with a kid at my age."

His lips formed a thin line of displeasure. She needed to make her case before he shut the idea down completely. "And it's so handy for work. I can be there in ten minutes."

"I suppose," Dad conceded with a heavy sigh. "It's just that I'll miss having my little girl at home with me. It won't be the same without you."

"You'll see me at work all the time, Dad." Carmel smiled for him, sensing victory was within her grasp. She felt a fleeting guilt for using the business—the ace she always had up her sleeve—to smooth the path to getting what she wanted. She mustn't allow that guilt to deter her. "You probably won't even notice I'm gone," she said, resting a reassuring hand on his arm.

As luck would have it, the auctioneer who was leasing the flat was a friend of a friend of the family, so Carmel got first refusal on the place. "It's not what you know, Carmel." The auctioneer winked, as he handed her the lease agreement and his Bic biro with a flourish. His words unsettled her. She was sick and tired of people saying it was all right for her. This mantra had clung to her like secondhand smoke her entire life.

It was as if all her years of hard work and proving herself in the business counted for nothing because she'd been born into it. That was why she was determined to start something of her own—something nobody could take away from her. She didn't want special treatment because she was an Egan. But she'd spent weeks hunting for a half-decent place close to work, and this flat was perfect. So she signed on the dotted line.

Moving out of the big house on Grove Square had helped, even if it was only to a flat a mile away. It finally felt like she had room to breathe. She could go back to bed with the property section of the weekend papers on a Sunday morning, head out for a walk without having to tell anyone where she was going, and eat beans on toast for her dinner if she didn't feel like cooking.

Mind you, it had raised a few eyebrows around the neighborhood. A single woman leaving home before she was married, only to move down the road. What was the sense in that? It wasn't as if she was going to university in another county or leaving for England or America. Why pay rent when you had ample room at home?

If she had a pound for every time someone told her she must be mad to leave the family home, she could have bought the place itself twice over. She wasn't crazy—not yet anyway. That was exactly the point. She needed the sanity that only a bit of solitude could give her. And the time and space to dream—away from the nagging obligations of family and work.

Carmel checked the time on her watch; she'd better get a move on. Granny would be at the window looking out for her. She pulled on her good jeans, the only ones that were neither faded nor covered in paint, and the cream silk blouse Granny got her from Brown Thomas last Christmas. She debated whether to wear her black suede strappy sandals but decided to forgo the party heels that hadn't seen an outing in a long while and settled on her flat loafers. Better for walking.

Outside on the landing, she smiled at a couple of new students who'd moved into the flat below the week before. It was a minor miracle to exchange a polite greeting, and nothing more, with people who didn't know or care to know your life story. Some days she felt like packing a bag and skipping the country, fleeing the security and scrutiny that smothered her. She wouldn't, though. How could she do that to the three people who relied on her?

They'd never twisted her arm. She could have gone to university when she left school. She'd had the points for Trinity. But she'd chosen the family business, Egan & Son Builders Merchants & Suppliers, instead. Her father and grandmother were delighted. Oddly, her mother had been the one to question her decision, even before she got her exam results. "Are you positive this is what you want, Carmel?" she'd asked, frowning, as they stood next to each other, plating slices of Black Forest gateau in the kitchen the weekend of her eighteenth birthday party.

"Of course!" Carmel declared, brightened by her first legal glass of champagne. "Sure what else would I do?"

"Anything," Mam had said, eyes firmly fixed on the cake in front of them. "Anything you want."

Carmel wondered if she'd heard right. What an odd thing to say, especially since her mother had never taken much interest in her or anything she'd wanted her entire life. Mam hadn't even gone to the trouble of asking what she wanted for her eighteenth birthday. All she'd given her was Granny Quinn's old wedding band, the thin gold so worn it looked like brass.

Her mother had crept into her room in the small hours after the party guests left and perched on the edge of the mattress. Carmel could barely keep her eyes open.

"I have something for you," Mam whispered, switching on the bedside light.

"What is it?" Carmel mumbled, squinting against the brightness. Mam reached for her hand, uncurling her fingers, and pressed an envelope into her palm.

"It's my mammy's wedding ring. It was given to me after she died."

"Oh, right. Thanks, Mam," Carmel said, stretching across to put the envelope on her bedside table. "I'm knackered. Can I look at it tomorrow?" She yawned. She didn't remember hearing what her mother said next. Just the click of the light switch and the door closing softly behind her as she left the room.

The following day Carmel woke at noon and only recalled her mother's late-night visit when she saw the envelope next to her. She sat up and reached for it, then opened the flap and tipped the thin gold band into her hand. The ring was scratched and tarnished, more like a trinket you'd get in a Halloween barmbrack than a present for a special birthday. It had obviously been lying around in a drawer somewhere, no use to anyone. What was *she* supposed to do with it? She dropped the ring back into the envelope and stuffed it into the top drawer of her bedside table along with the used lip balm, dried-out nail polish, and old hair ties she kept but had no use for.

Downstairs over a plate of hot buttered toast, she thanked her mother for the ring all the same. "I'll keep it up," she said, spreading marmalade on her bread.

"Do what you like," Mam said, continuing to tie the black bin bag full of party napkins and streamers from the day before. And that was the last they'd spoken of it.

The business was in Carmel's blood, and she liked having her say in how it was run. She had grown up in Egans', helping out at weekends and during the summer holidays. Then work had consumed her twenties. Gobbled them up whole. She'd worked hard to expand their operations to meet the growing demand at the start of the property boom, even when the long hours, late nights, and weekends had seen off friends and boyfriends. Carmel cared more about what happened to the place than she liked to admit. She'd have the freedom to see the world once the boom waned, as it inevitably would. Now wasn't the time to let up.

Anyway, what was the sense in spending weekends getting wasted on overpriced Liebfraumilch in a club down Leeson Street, with people you'd grown apart from, or, worse, finding yourself in bed with a man you were too drunk to remember you didn't care about? No, she was better off building a solid career for herself. Everything else would fall into place when the timing was right.

Since moving out, she had more time to think about her future. The seed of a half-formed idea planted long ago had taken root. Carmel didn't just want to supply bricks and mortar to the men who built the new streets and suburbs springing up across Dublin. She wanted to have a hand in rebuilding the abandoned parts of the inner city—places passed over for the promise of an additional box room and patch of grass in what was now called the commuter belt.

What was to stop her building her own property development company? She could start small with a renovation of a couple of terraces off Portobello Road, down by the canal. Restore them to their former glory. She had enough savings behind her and plenty of contacts in the business. She was in the right place at the right time. And judging by what she'd seen happening in the building industry, this boom wasn't about to go bust any time soon. A new company would be her chance to prove she could succeed in her own right, not because, as the world seemed to think, everything had been handed to her on a silver platter. She hadn't breathed a word about her plans to the family yet. They would only worry about what she was getting herself into.

At the bottom of the stairs, Carmel stopped to check the post. There was nothing for her but a reminder about her dental appointment next month. She slid the card into her back pocket. A cool breeze wafted into the hall when she opened the door, and she wondered if she should go back up and get a jumper but decided against it. It was the first Sunday of summer, after all.

Leinster Road had the unhurried feeling of a lazy weekend about it. The hum of Flymos hovering across patches of lawn replaced the impatient honking of horns from the weekday traffic. She'd left in plenty of time and was in no rush to get to the house. The odd car passed her as she strolled under the dappled shade of the chestnut trees. At the junction on Kenilworth Square, the owner of the new café was on the path clearing outdoor tables. Inside, customers with the *Sunday World* folded under their arms lined up waiting for their orders to be taken.

Carmel peered longingly in at them, wishing she could spend a quiet hour there over a pot of Earl Grey and her copy of *Bridget Jones's Diary*, which was still sitting unread on her bedside table. But she couldn't keep the family waiting. She passed a couple of elderly neighbors out walking their dogs around Grove Square. Their conversation was the same one that was on everyone's lips—the only thing anyone could talk about for the past week—that divorce was finally legal in Ireland. People were either over the moon or up in arms about it. There was no middle ground.

As she walked up the gravel driveway, she noticed Granny sitting in the bay window facing the lawn, waving to her from the parlor. She waved back, mirroring her grandmother's smile, before climbing the stone steps to the front door and letting herself in with her key.

"Happy birthday, pet," Granny said, as Carmel bent to kiss her.

"Thanks, Granny. Where's Mam?"

"Oh, I don't know. Fussing about in the kitchen, I suppose," Granny replied, waving her hand dismissively in the direction of the door and tutting. "Your father's just gone to get a few extra bottles of wine." She patted the seat of the chintz armchair next to her. "I see you're wearing the blouse I bought you for Christmas," she gushed. "Wait till you see what I've got you for your birthday."

Carmel heard the rustle of plastic shopping bags and the clink of bottles. "I'm back!" called a voice from the hall. Dad marched across the room, arms outstretched. "There she is! The birthday girl! You're not too old for a hug from your dad now, are you?" He grinned, squeezing her against his chest.

"Is Mam in the kitchen?" Carmel asked when he let go of her.

"I think so. Probably. Anyway, I got a few more bottles in, so we're all set."

Carmel nodded. Exhausted already.

Her mother appeared in the doorway, wiping her hands on a tea towel. "I thought I heard you."

"Hi, Mam." Carmel smiled, taking a step in her direction.

"Happy birthday," her mother replied, holding out an arm—not for a hug but to give Carmel her post. "These came for you. There's one from Auntie Teresa."

"Oh, right. Thanks." Carmel took the colored envelopes from her. There was one from her old school friends, Aisling and Linda, who lived in New York. She'd lost touch with most of them, even her best friend, Rachel, who was married with two kids and living out in Lucan. The past was all they had in common, and they rarely even spoke on the phone anymore. The others had fled Dublin for greener pastures, clutching their degrees or husbands, sometimes both. Carmel had acquired neither. There had been teenage crushes before steady boyfriends and a few good-enough men over the years—plenty who were interested until it dawned on them that she wasn't going to cook, clean, and pick up after them like their mothers did. "I want a wife, not a career girl," Niall O'Sullivan, the last of them, had argued with her over a chow mein at the Fortune Cookie one weekend. Apparently, she couldn't be both.

"Well, then," she said, gathering her coat and her handbag from the back of the chair. "I'm clearly not the woman you're after." She stood, picking up the docket the waiter had propped against a bottle of soy sauce. "Don't worry about the bill. I'll get it," she said, and she left without looking back. There would be no birthday card from Niall this year.

"I'll look at them later, Mam," she said, crossing the room to put the envelopes on the coffee table.

"Now, what about my card?" Granny demanded behind her. "I haven't even had a chance to give it to you yet."

Carmel suppressed a sigh. This was not the day she'd have planned if she'd had her way. Not at all. She hitched a smile on her face and waited for her party to begin.

CHAPTER 3

It was his snoring that woke her. The same rude awakening Joan had every morning. There was nothing to be done about it, the doctor had said, when Martin finally went to see him about the problem. Snoring was perfectly normal in middle-aged men. She elbowed her husband in the side. He shifted but hardly stirred.

Joan envied the way he could sleep through anything. No, "envy" was too benign a word for what she felt. Fury was more like it. Despite their Egyptian-cotton sheets and goose-down pillows, she woke exhausted every morning with a dull ache behind her temples, knowing she'd been asleep for hours but feeling she'd barely closed her eyes at all.

The red numbers on her digital bedside clock blinked from 5:29 to 5:30. Too early to get up yet. Too late to go back to sleep. She turned onto her back, wide awake now, seeing the first sliver of daylight creep through a crack in the curtains. She'd get up shortly, as soon as the central-heating timer kicked on. Summer had left abruptly, and she could feel that September chill in the air on the tip of her nose.

She pulled the covers to her chin and tried to shake off her darkening mood. It wasn't as if she minded being the first up every morning. She'd always been an early riser—ever since she started work at the Royal Candy factory when she was fourteen, years before she met Martin. Mornings were the best time to be alone with your thoughts, the only bit of peace and quiet you might have all day.

There was no sense just lying there. She slid from beneath the sheets, pushed her feet into slippers, and pulled on her dressing gown, tiptoeing past her mother-in-law's bedroom as she made her way down the thickly carpeted stairs to the hall. In the kitchen, she flicked the switch on the kettle, then padded across the tiled floor into the conservatory while she waited for it to boil. She loved standing there, in the half-light of the early morning, looking across the expanse of lawn to the birds at the feeder that hung from the cherry tree.

She and Martin had added the conservatory about ten years after they were married—with his mother's blessing, of course. Nothing ever happened within these four walls without Molly's say-so. It was Joan's favorite room in the house, probably because it was the only place in the whole grand Georgian property that felt like it contained any part of her. "It's far from chintz and conservatories you were raised," her granny would have chided her if she'd been alive to see it all.

Joan didn't take the luxury of their quarter acre of lush garden and this one solitary hour in her day for granted. Once upon a time she would have busied herself in the kitchen buttering bread or steeping oats for everyone's breakfast. Not now. Not since Carmel had left home. Now she made herself a strong cup of tea before settling in her favorite armchair, feet tucked under her, letting her mind wander. This hour was her little piece of heaven. If it was up to her she would have bottled this feeling and made it last all day. But it wasn't up to her. Nothing had been, not for a very long time.

The sound of the toilet flushing upstairs meant it was seven o'clock and time to get the rashers and eggs on for Martin's breakfast.

He came into the kitchen reeking of Old Spice, sniffing the air and rubbing his hands together, pecking her on the cheek as he passed. "Lovely," he said into the pan.

He had his plate cleared in minutes, and before she knew it, he was halfway out the kitchen door, draining his mug as he went.

"Don't forget to give Liam Walsh a ring when you get down to the yard," Joan reminded him. "That invoice needs to be paid, and I'm sick and tired of chasing him."

"Will do," Martin said, doing up the zip of his jacket, a piece of toast wedged between his teeth. "What time will you be in?"

"As soon as I can, Martin. As soon as your mother is up and sorted."

"See you later, then," he called over his shoulder as he left. The smell of his aftershave lingered.

Joan scraped the remains of his rasher rind into the bin and rinsed the plate, like she'd done a thousand times since she'd moved into Martin's childhood home. Then she left the dishes in the sink and made her way back upstairs to get dressed.

The hinges on the antique rosewood wardrobe creaked when she opened it, revealing the regimented assortment of skirts, dresses, and cardigans. The sweet scent of the dried lavender sachets inside the wardrobe tickled her nostrils. Outside, in front of the orderly row of three-story terraced houses on Grove Square, cars and snippets of conversation were starting up.

Joan knew from the voices below the open bedroom window that Des Ryan, the postman, had found a reason to knock on their neighbor's door. *Nothing new there*, she thought, as she slid a navy cardigan off its hanger. A package that was only slightly too bulky or too wide to fit through a letterbox was all the invitation Des needed—any excuse to strike up a conversation that might yield a juicy bit of gossip.

Des had been delivering the post around Harold's Cross for years. He was used to being greeted with open arms by mothers waiting for news or even better a few shillings from their sons and daughters in Liverpool or Boston. Being acquainted with everybody's business was another perk of the job. You'd be amazed the amount of information a trained eye could get from the outside of a little four-by-six envelope. Even bad news was better than no news in Des Ryan's book—sometimes the worse the better.

It was a wonder he held on to his job at all, the way people's business slipped off his tongue and into casual conversation. Des had a knack for saying just enough to damage a reputation without delivering the fatal blow that brought it down. He only had to plant the seed of a scandal and the whispers would take hold, spreading and strangling like bindweed. Like the time Mary Farley got a letter from her brother Mick in Glasgow, with a faint Scottish Prison Service watermark on the envelope. Before long, every Tom, Dick, and Harry in Harold's Cross knew that Mick was serving ten years in Barlinnie for glassing a fella in a bar on Sauchiehall Street one Friday evening.

The letterbox clacked shut, and the letters landed on the polished mahogany floor of the hall as Joan reached the last stair. She bent to pick them up, expecting the usual brown envelopes—the gas bill or Martin's bank statement.

The letter on the top of the pile caught her off-guard. The pale-cream envelope with the handwritten address stuck out among the brown windowed ones, but it was the English postmark and purple stamp with the unmistakable profile of Queen Elizabeth that knocked the wind right out of her. The room swayed. She squinted at the handwriting on the front, trying to focus.

There was only one person who could be contacting her and Martin from England, since neither of them, unlike half the country, had close friends or relatives there. She steadied herself, leaning on the hall table, closing her eyes until her heart stopped racing, before daring to look at the envelope in her hand more closely. She imagined the daughter she hadn't seen in thirty years standing in front of a revolving rack of notepaper and cards, trying to make a choice. Something neutral. Nothing too decorative or symbolic. Cream, not mauve. Flowers, not hearts. A card that wasn't so small it looked like you were only going through the motions. One that was big enough to convey the bare bones but not so big you were left with a lot of white space in the margins—blankness that would make it look like you hadn't enough to say.

Joan had the sudden and odd realization that the letter was twelve years late. The truth was she'd been more prepared for it when April turned eighteen and would legally have been allowed to access her adoption file. Joan had been ready for a letter back then. She'd checked the post every morning for months. Hoping. She even secretly bought April a present for her eighteenth birthday. A locket. She kept it hidden in a corner of the bottom drawer of her dressing table, unopened all this time.

Now, finally, here was that long-awaited letter from her daughter searching for her birth parents. Birth parents. Two words you wouldn't put together unless you had no choice in the matter. Joan and Martin hadn't ever needed to say them. They didn't have to explain their relationship to April to anybody because nobody in Dublin knew she existed. Martin had been determined to keep it that way. The few occasions over the years when Joan had voiced her doubts about guarding their secret had sent him into such a frenzy that she'd stopped raising the subject.

Like that day right before Carmel was born. They'd been doing up the room that was to be the new baby's nursery. Joan stood in one of Martin's old shirts with a paintbrush in her hand, applying buttercup-yellow emulsion to the walls in even up-and-down strokes. Martin was in charge of painting the high ceiling. The scent of lilac wafted through the open window on an almost-summer breeze.

"I can't wait for us to be a family," he said, turning to Joan and looking into her eyes. Something about hearing him say the word "family" made her freeze. It was a word he hadn't uttered since their time in England. Since before April was born.

Her smile slipped as the baby kicked at her insides and she rubbed her palm in circles over her enormous belly. "What will we tell this little one about their big sister?" she said.

Martin shook his head. "We'll tell them nothing. We'll tell nobody anything. We can't let a word of what went on in London get out, Joan. You see that, don't you?" His smile was gone now too, and in its place was a worried frown.

"But why, Martin? Why not?"

"Do you really want to give people another reason to gossip about us, Joan?" He was pacing in circles around the empty room.

"You'll wear a hole in that carpet," she said in an attempt to rescue the afternoon. Martin ignored her. "So what exactly are they saying?" she continued, hardly daring to breathe.

"I've lost count of the number of times the fellas down at the pub have asked me if I married you because I wanted a 'bit of rough.'"

Joan gaped at him.

"They were expecting you to pop a baby out six months after our wedding. The whole lot of them are convinced you're a gold digger, and I won't give them the satisfaction of tearing us both down like that."

"It's just talk, that's all," Joan said. But a flutter of anxiety flared in her chest. "I suppose, because I grew up on the estate, they think I'm not good enough for the likes of you," she continued, her face hot with anger. "What we do with our lives is none of their business."

She was expecting Martin to nod in agreement or come and put his arms around her. But he just stood there, hands by his sides, still holding the paint roller. "All the same, we can't give them an excuse to drag our good name through the mud, Joan," he said in a low voice. "Besides, we made our decision back then, and we have to move on. We have another little one to consider now."

Joan swallowed and shivered, suddenly cold. The evening was

drawing in, and the shadows lengthened, sucking every bit of warmth from the room.

They'd barely even talked about April in the years since giving her up for adoption. It was less painful to believe they had given her up for *her* sake than to admit they'd chosen to give her away for theirs. But give her away was exactly what they'd done. They had put pen to paper, promising her to strangers. They had signed their names in indelible ink on legal documents that allowed her to be taken from them. And then they had pretended to forget.

Every now and then, they made the vaguest of plans about what would happen if she finally got in touch, but precisely what they would do when she did was never discussed. Whatever Martin said, Joan clung to the belief that when the time came, when April did finally contact them, he would be as overjoyed as she was now.

The envelope felt lighter in Joan's hand than she'd imagined it would. Much lighter than it should, she thought, given the weight of the words inside. She walked back through the hall into the kitchen on autopilot, switching on the radio on the windowsill so *The Gay Byrne Show* would drown out the silence. She took her reading glasses from the top of the pile of recipe books she'd been thumbing through the evening before and put them on, then tried to make out the postmark. The letter had been posted in London the previous week, on September 20, 1996.

She sat down on the pinewood chair at the head of the kitchen table and, hands shaking, slid her thumb under the corner of the envelope, unfolded the single sheet of plain, cream notepaper, and began to read.

CHAPTER 4

Dear Martin and Joan,

My name is Emma Hudson. I was born April Egan on 1st April 1966. I was adopted six weeks after my birth. I've known for certain that I was adopted since I was eighteen. I discovered from the paperwork in my adoption file that you are my birth parents.

I believe that following my birth you returned to Ireland and that you married a year later. I'm hoping the intervening years have been kind to you, as they have been to me.

I happen to be coming to Dublin in a couple of weeks, and I thought this visit would be a good opportunity for us to meet. You can reach me at this number, 0171 669141, to arrange a time and a place.

Looking forward to hearing from you.

Best wishes,

Emma

Joan couldn't steady her hands as she read and reread the letter. She checked the date it had been posted again, and her eyes darted to the calendar pinned on the corkboard next to the fridge. April, who she now knew had lived her life as Emma, would be arriving in a week or so. Sweet Jesus.

She took off her glasses, still keeping a hold of Emma's note in her trembling hand. Then she closed her eyes and tried to imagine Emma standing in her kitchen in London, licking the envelope flap before pressing it down, making sure the secret was firmly sealed inside.

Tears sprang from nowhere, filling Joan's eyes. What now? You'd think with thirty years to plan for something you'd have an idea what your next move should be. It wasn't as if there was a decision to weigh up—she hadn't much choice in the matter. Emma knew where they lived. She could turn up out of the blue at any time. Joan couldn't risk that, no matter how much she longed to see her. If only she had more time.

She glanced at the clock. Martin would be up to his eyes at work by now, punching the prices of liters of Dulux paint, boxes of screws, and lengths of skirting board into the till. She should phone him. Tell him he was wanted back home right away. But as she reached for the phone she realized this was a bad idea. If she called the yard in a panic, Carmel would know immediately something was up.

What a bloody fool Joan had been. Why had she not said something to Carmel before now? How had she let it come to this? This wasn't how she had meant for things to turn out all those years ago.

She jumped at the sound of her mother-in-law's walking stick banging on the bedroom floor above her. "Joan! Joan! It's after half eight. Where's my tea?"

Joan folded the letter, across the crease Emma had made in the notepaper, and shoved the envelope into her handbag. Then she stood up and flicked the switch on the kettle. "The kettle's on!" she heard herself call out in her normal voice, as if it was just any old day.

JOAN SET MOLLY'S TEA DOWN on the bedside table without receiving a word of thanks. "Have you taken your tablets this morning?" she asked, as Molly took her first sip.

"This is as weak as dishwater." Molly scowled. "Just as well Betty will be here shortly to make me a proper cup."

"Just as well," Joan said. She too would be glad when Betty, the home help, arrived for her shift at nine. "So you don't need anything else before I go?" she asked before she left the room.

"She's in foul form today. I was late up with her tea," Joan said, rolling her eyes, when she answered the door to Betty.

"Don't you be worrying, Joan. You go on. I'll have her sorted out in no time," Betty said with a reassuring smile. "We'll have no shortage of things to talk about what with your one Princess Diana's divorce still splashed all over the papers." She waved Molly's morning newspaper in front of her.

"Thanks a million," Joan said, still standing in the doorway.

"Can I come in now?" Betty asked.

"Oh, God, of course. I don't know where my head is this morning," Joan replied, stepping aside to let her in.

"Are you sure you're all right, Joan? You don't look yourself."

Joan scrambled for something normal to say. "Ah, I'm just a bit tired. I was awake early."

"As long as there's nothing wrong," Betty said, removing a freshly laundered apron from her bag, then double-knotting it firmly around her ample middle.

Joan grabbed her coat from the stand and dropped an umbrella into her bag. The walk to the yard would do her good. When she reached the gate at the end of the driveway, she surprised herself. Instead of turning right, toward the yard, she turned in the opposite direction, away from the village and the need to exchange pleasantries with whoever she met on the way.

Where was she going? She wasn't sure. But she wasn't ready to face Martin, or Carmel, or anyone else for that matter, if Betty's reaction at the door was anything to go by. Not yet. Not this morning, with her mind only on the letter she'd longed for now zipped into the back pocket of her handbag. She shoved her hands into her coat pockets and her chin down into the collar, keeping her eyes fixed on the footpath in front of her.

Apr— . . . *Emma*'s letter—would she ever get used to thinking of her as Emma? How could she be anything but April?—had been the only thing on her mind since the post arrived. She was surprised she'd managed to hold it together long enough to get out of the house. The beginnings of a headache threatened. She needed time to think. To breathe.

She looked up when she reached the traffic lights and realized she was standing outside the smooth granite façade of St. Jude's. She had the sudden urge to rest her forehead against the cool stone walls. This wouldn't be the first time she'd escaped to the sanctuary of the local church—not to find God but to search inside herself.

The car park was deserted. Weekday Masses weren't well attended anymore—not like the old days when the devout would mark the start of their day by offering up prayers to God. Joan remembered a time when it had been standing room only at eleven o'clock Mass on a Sunday. Not nowadays, though. People just didn't seem to need religion anymore. Not since the shops started opening on Sundays. You'd be lucky to get a seat in the pub on a Sunday lunchtime. The McDonald's drive-through at Nutgrove would be bumper to bumper the entire day. Yet half the pews at St. Jude's would sit empty.

On weekday mornings, a few devout parishioners came to pray or light a candle for an intention. Joan wasn't devout by any stretch of the imagination, and she didn't know if her dilemma counted as "an intention." But the church, one of the last quiet spaces, had always been a good place to come and think.

Inside the church porch, she dipped the tips of her fingers into the cool water and made the sign of the cross, touching her brow, then her breastbone, before pushing open the heavy door. The familiar smell hit her: furniture polish mingled with candle wax and fresh chrysanthemums. She breathed it in and genuflected, before sliding into one of the pews to the right of the altar.

Graying and balding parishioners were dotted around the pews, and a disheveled homeless man sat three rows in front of her, his head lolling then jerking every now and then as he dozed.

It was hard to believe, she thought, as she gazed at the clouds painted on the soft-pink sky of the ornate ceiling, that this place would be closing its doors forever in a few weeks. Throughout her childhood, that sky had propped up the promise of eternal life in heaven. Soon the bulldozers would be here to tear it down and the dwindling congregation would flock to neighboring Holy Trinity.

St. Jude's had always seemed so permanent when she was growing up. It had been the heart of the parish for over a hundred years, a touchstone for the entire community. This place, where life and death were marked and acted out, was to be demolished. The land on which it stood would be sold off to the highest bidder.

Joan knelt where thousands of good Catholics before her had whispered their half-told sins and rested her head in her hands. She let out a weary sigh as she too prayed for guidance and forgiveness—from God or her daughters, she wasn't sure.

She checked her watch. It was almost ten. She blessed herself again, then slid out of the pew, back down the nave and past the curtained confession boxes near the entrance. The rows of votive candles burning brightly in the dimly lit corner near the entrance caught her eye, and she pulled her coin purse from her pocket, emptying her loose change into her hand. Her ten- and fifty-pence pieces clattered into the brass donations box. Then she took a fresh candle, held it to the flame of another until the wick began to burn, and placed it between two others—more prayers waiting to be answered.

"How-ye, Joan?" Tommy Cafferty, who lived a few doors up

from where Joan was reared, came over and stood next to her. "It's not like you to be here during the week. Is everything—"

"Everything's fine," Joan replied, in hushed tones, cutting him off. "Thanks, Tommy. Just fine."

"Glad to hear it," he said, patting her arm. He took a shallow wheezy breath as if he was about to continue the conversation.

"I'd better get to work before they send out a search party for me," Joan said, backing away.

"Nice to see you," Tommy called after her as he hobbled up the aisle. She wondered if she was acting normally or if anything she'd said or done would give her away. Even here, she thought—especially here—the eyes of the parish were always on you.

As Joan left the building and stepped out into the tiled porch, the heavens opened: a steady reliable shower, the kind that would do a garden good. Fat raindrops made deep puddles in the uneven tarmac of the church car park, and thunder rumbled in the distance. Maybe she was better staying put and waiting until it eased off a bit.

She saw Father Mac making a run for it from his car to the parish house. He'd be heading home to return a few phone calls, followed by a bit of lunch laid out by Mrs. Sullivan, his housekeeper. Some people said priests had it easy, that they lived in the lap of luxury, waited on hand and foot while many of their parishioners could barely make ends meet. But what did anyone know about living someone else's life? What had Father Mac sacrificed for his life of convenience? She watched him wipe the soles of his black leather brogues on the welcome mat as the front door opened magically for him, and caught a glimpse of Mrs. Sullivan's yellow rubber glove before the door closed again.

The only time Joan had ever set foot anywhere near the parish house was the day of Ma's funeral. Da had asked her to deliver the priest's dues for saying the funeral Mass. She had clutched the folded brown envelope in her hand as she hurried around the side of the church. Blinded by tears, she'd collided with the housekeeper, a thin-faced woman long since dead, whose name Joan had forgotten, sending her shopping basket flying. "Jesus, Mary, and Joseph! Stupid child!" the woman yelled at her. "Your mother should put some manners on you!" She bent to pick up a perfect red apple that had rolled away from her into the grass.

Joan was so scared she turned and ran in the opposite direction, angry tears stinging her face. "My ma is gone," she sobbed, stopping to lean against the gable wall of the church. "My ma is gone."

The churchyard felt as cold and lonely a place today as it did then, Joan thought, while she stood sheltering from the storm.

CHAPTER 5

Emma massaged the tense muscles at the back of her neck, tilting her head one way, then the other. She didn't need to hear the beeps from the cardiac monitor or watch the rise and fall of his chest to know her son was still breathing. She'd learned to listen for the cadence of his breath since the very first night he was born: him sleeping soundly next to her hospital bed, cocooned by the Perspex walls of his rectangular crib; her, wide awake, mesmerized by him.

She hadn't been able to take her eyes off the tiny nails on the fingers of his scrunched fists as she stroked the back of his hand with a single finger. "I can't believe you're mine," she'd whispered to him in the dark. By the time she and Matt brought him home and laid him in the new Moses basket next to their bed, she'd gotten into the habit of holding her breath in the dead of night so she could listen for his.

When Ben was six months old, they moved him to his own room, its ceiling decorated with luminous stars. Still they slept with the baby monitor on and the door open for peace of mind. She never got out of the habit of listening for him, even after his third birthday, when they bought him a proper bed and he could dart across the landing to their bedroom if he woke in the night. It was an instinct she had developed—that always-on acute awareness—something that wasn't talked about in the parenting books, the impulse a mother had to do everything in her power to keep her small human alive.

And now Ben had made it through another night. "Thank God," Emma said, surprising herself. All her life, she'd resisted believing in an almighty God. Now look at her: a hypocrite clinging to gratitude.

She stared out the window. Her reflection, illuminated by the artificially bright backdrop of the hospital ward, stared back. She had the look of someone who'd been sleeping rough on a bench outside the Tube station. Ruffled dark hair framed a pale, pinched face, and her eyes were sunken and ringed with dark circles. "Bedraggled" was the word that came to mind, she thought, trying to comb her hair into some kind of order with her fingers.

The comings and goings from beyond the four walls of Ben's room gave her days rhythm. It must have been around seven because the staff arriving for the early shift were parking in the lined bays five floors below. From where she stood at the window she could see them gathering bags, stethoscopes, and packed lunches from the back seats of their cars. Had it only been three months since she was one of them, arriving for her shift on the maternity ward, ready to take on the day? They waved to one another, smiling in the bleary-eyed solidarity of shift workers, shouting greetings she couldn't hear from behind the double glazing in the isolated room. Other people's air had become Ben's enemy.

Emma sighed, picking up the rough hospital blanket from the reclining chair next to her son's bed where she'd been sleeping for weeks. She folded it from corner to corner, then draped it over the back of the chair. The question that haunted her every waking moment was would Ben make it through another week? She turned expectantly to the door as Joe, one of the staff nurses, entered.

"Any news?" Even as she blurted the words, she knew from the look in his averted eyes that there was no new lifeline for Ben. Not today. Joe shook his head. Emma pulled her cardigan closer to her body and tried to read the expression behind Joe's practiced smile.

"I'll be looking after Ben this morning." His kind gray eyes finally met hers. "How's he doing?"

"He had a good night," Emma said, a little too brightly. There she was, doing it again—what she'd learned to do over the past months: squeezing hope out of every insignificant thing, wringing it dry. The nursing and medical staff played along, administering that hope in the tiny titrated doses she needed to keep going. She wasn't kidding anybody, least of all herself. Let's face it, there wasn't a great deal of hope with this type of leukemia when chemotherapy didn't work, unless a bone marrow donor could be found.

Joe washed his hands before picking up the charts from the end of the bed, glancing at the peaks and troughs of Ben's observations—the warning signs plotted in red pen, a collection of connected dots that showed all was not well. "That's good," he said, placing two fingers on Ben's thin wrist, feeling for his pulse.

Ben didn't stir. He lay pale and motionless, as no three-year-old ever should. "His obs are fine. Looks like we've finally got that temperature under control." Emma gave him a weary smile. "You look exhausted. Why don't you go get a cuppa or some fresh air while he's sleeping? We'll keep an eye on him."

"Yeah, you're right," Emma said. "I should take a break now so I can be here when he wakes up. Won't be long. I'll try to get some breakfast into him when I get back." Joe replaced the charts and gave her a thumbs-up. She bent to kiss Ben's forehead, smoothing the downy fuzz on his balding scalp. "See you later, buddy," she whispered. Ben's eyelids flickered but didn't open.

Emma picked up her handbag and crumpled trench coat, then made her way out of the ward, past the side rooms where other terrified parents were waiting for their miracles. Down in the hospital canteen she sat clinging to a mug of stewed black tea, next to some interns, stethoscopes slung around their necks, who were bolting breakfast before the emergency pagers they seemed too young to carry went off.

She sipped at the lukewarm liquid, trying to halt the panic that crept through her whenever she had more than a few minutes alone with her thoughts. Someone planted a kiss on the top of her head, and she turned, surprised to see Matt in his white coat, ready for work.

"They told me you were down here," he said, pulling up one of the plastic chairs opposite. "I thought I'd catch you before my ward round."

Emma nodded, then remembered to smile. "He had a good night."

"How'd *you* sleep?" Matt reached across the table to take her hand in both of his.

"Oh, you know," Emma said. "I dozed on and off. You?"

"Same. I'm used to it, though. I knew all those sleepless nights I clocked up as an intern would come in handy one day."

"I wish they hadn't," Emma said, looking away.

"Me too. I'm sorry, love, that wasn't funny. This . . . I just want us to wake up from this bloody nightmare."

"I know, love." Emma gave his hand a gentle squeeze. "We'll get through this."

"I don't know how people without a medical background cope," Matt said.

"Maybe they're better off—not knowing, I mean."

"Yeah, ignorance is bliss, all right. Speaking of . . ." He shifted in his chair. "The Egans will probably have the letter by now."

"Probably. It's been a week since I posted it," Emma said.

Matt didn't need to remind her about the letter she'd written, stamped, and addressed but had kept in her handbag for days before she'd finally posted it. "I wish I hadn't held off posting it. I was hoping . . . just in case he . . ." Emma trailed off.

"I know. I don't blame you." Matt spoke in a whisper now, stroking the back of her hand. "It was time, though. We were running out of options."

Emma looked into the depths of her husband's sad brown eyes. It was that same look that had finally convinced her to walk down to the postbox a week ago before she could change her mind.

The morning she'd posted the letter, she'd found the smooth cream envelope at the bottom of her bag among the unused tissues, hairgrips, and a forgotten packet of Wrigley's chewing gum. The Irish names on the front were so familiar and yet so alien to her. It wasn't a letter she'd ever imagined sending. But what choice did she have?

She didn't want to admit, even to herself, how desperate she was. In the twelve years she'd known about her birth parents, she hadn't once been tempted to contact them. She wasn't interested in hearing their reasons for parting with her. Emma hadn't spent years in counseling, coaxed to name her feelings by sympathetic professionals in private rooms, strategically accessorized with boxes of Kleenex, only to let those unspeakable feelings rear their ugly heads again.

All that had changed since Ben's diagnosis and the chemotherapy that had left him weaker but not cured. Unless they could find a suitable bone marrow donor, he would die. So far, every avenue the medical team had been down had drawn a blank. Matt's family had already been ruled out. The Egans might be Ben's last hope. She had to do it for him. And Matt was right: they didn't have time to hang about.

She was flushed and breathless when she reached the postbox on Newport Street, the nearest one to the hospital. She leaned against it for a moment to catch her breath and rummaged in her bag. The morning traffic was building, and diesel fumes caught in the back of her throat. A couple of cyclists raced past her at the junction when the light turned green. A young mother dressed in an orange sari, bright against the murk of the London street, held tight to her daughter's hand as they crossed the road on their way to school. Emma envied her the predictability of an ordinary day.

Emma took the letter from her bag, turning it over in her hand, staring at her neat handwriting on the front, remembering how she'd weighed and measured every word inside. Suddenly she slammed the heel of her other hand against the letterbox in protest. The stinging pain of the impact was comforting. She held the envelope at the mouth of the letterbox, then—"Fuck it," she swore under her breath—she let go of it before she could change her mind. The letter slid silently down, landing on a pile of envelopes. In limbo.

That was that. There was no going back.

"Shit!" One of the interns at the table next to them swore at the sound of his pager. He abandoned a half-eaten sausage sandwich and started running as though a life depended upon it, white coat billowing behind him.

Emma pushed back her chair. "I'd better head back up and see if Ben's awake. I might be able to get some breakfast into him."

Matt stood facing her. "We'll get through this. Whatever happens," he said.

"I know," Emma replied, stroking the dark stubble on his chin with her thumb. "Now, go on. Don't be late for your ward round. I'll see you at lunchtime."

"It's a date," Matt said. "Same time, same place?"

"See you later," Emma replied, as they parted ways in the corridor outside. If Ben could go through the pain of these past few weeks, she could swallow her pride and ask these people who had tossed her aside long ago for help. All she needed from them for now was a reply.

CHAPTER 6

The rain had eased, and the sun was trying to break through a gap in the clouds. Joan pulled her hood up before tiptoeing around the puddles in the rain-soaked car park. The ground was strewn with fallen conkers, and the autumn air smelled of damp leaves. She stood for a moment to breathe it all in before leaving the church grounds and turning onto Harold's Cross Road. It was already after ten—Martin and Carmel would be wondering where she'd got to.

As she passed Concannon's Bakery she decided on impulse to go in. The waft of warm bakery air hit her when she stepped inside. "Looks like we're in for more rain," Mrs. Concannon said, while removing the half-dozen iced finger buns Joan had asked for from the front window. She placed them between pieces of greaseproof paper and then into a brown paper bag. "Please God it'll brighten up later or I'll be twiddling my thumbs here all day."

"Please God," Joan agreed, peering into the cake cabinet.

"Something else for the lads down at the yard, Joan? Unless you're not at work today," Mrs. Concannon said, eyeing the clock hanging on the opposite wall.

"Oh, no. I just had a couple of errands to run," Joan said, too quickly. "Go on, then. I'll have one of your lovely fruit loaves, Mrs. Concannon." She opened her handbag to get her purse and remembered Emma's letter. Mrs. Concannon's chatter faded into the background, and Joan didn't hear a word she said until she'd finished ringing everything up on the old cash register.

Joan handed over a ten-pound note, and when Mrs. Concannon counted out her change she stuffed the coins into her coat pocket. "Thanks a million, Mrs. Concannon. I'd better get going while there's a break in those clouds."

She checked her watch again as the bakery door closed behind her. It would be half past ten by the time she got to the yard. She thought about Emma's letter while she waited for the lights at Rathgar junction to change. Her mood brightened, and her mind calmed. *It'll be okay*, she told herself. *Isn't this the day we've been waiting for all these years?*

She walked up the hill, past the deserted factory where she'd once worked. The site had been sold and was earmarked for yet another housing development. The builders would have fifty flash new apartments up in no time. Finally she rounded the last corner before the yard. As she passed in front of the shop window, she caught sight of Carmel, laughing with a customer at the checkout, her long blond hair pulled back off her face in a practical ponytail.

Carmel looked up just then and met Joan's eyes for a split second. She tilted her head, her brow furrowed. Joan broke eye contact and kept walking. She went into the warehouse by the back gate and hung her coat in the staff kitchen before putting on her blue shop overall. Then she boiled the kettle and sliced the fruit loaf. "Help yourselves, lads," she called out to the men working in the warehouse. She'd save an iced finger or two for Martin. A little something with his tea was always guaranteed to put him in a good mood.

Martin was in his office across the corridor, on the phone. His thick brows were knitted in a frown, his free hand gesticulating wildly. When the tea was ready, Joan picked up her handbag and a mug of tea and made her way over to him.

He swiveled his chair around when she slipped through the door. *I'm on the phone*, he mouthed, pointing to the receiver in his hand. Joan placed the mug of tea on the desk in front of him and closed the door behind her. She leaned against the door, folded her arms, and waited.

"Look, Noel, we're not getting anywhere. We'll never get this sorted over the phone. You'll have to come down and bring all the receipts with you," Martin said, rolling his eyes. "We'll go over everything with you then. All right? Okay. Okay. Yeah. See you later then. Bye. Bye now." He shook his head as he hung up. "I could do without Noel Carmody giving me earache about his receipts," he grumbled. "Where've you been? It's been bedlam here since we opened."

"I know. Sorry I'm late. I got held up at—"

Martin ignored her, picked up his mug, and took a loud gulp. "Is there anything with this tea?"

"I got iced fingers and a fruit loaf at Concannon's on the way here. I'll get you some in a minute if you like."

Martin took another slurp of his tea, then turned away to attend to the paperwork on his desk. Joan caught a glimpse of the shiny patch on the back of his head where his hair was thinning. She moved toward him, placing a hand on his shoulder. "Martin, we need to talk."

"This isn't a good time, Joan." He pointed to the pile of papers on his desk. "Can't it wait until this evening?"

"It's important, Martin. I think you'll want to know sooner rather than later."

He sighed, swiveling around in his high-backed office chair to face her. "Go on, then."

Joan set her handbag down on the desk, took out Emma's letter, and offered it to him. "Here."

"What's this?" He frowned.

"Read it."

She watched as he unfolded the letter and didn't take her eyes off him as he scanned the lines of Emma's handwriting. After a few moments, he stopped to look up at her. He tried to say something, but the words forming on his lips didn't leave them. He returned to the letter, then dropped both hands, still holding the piece of paper in his lap. His face was ashen, his lips a thin tight line. "Good God. After all this time."

"I know," Joan said.

Martin shook his head, barely glancing at the letter before handing it back to her. "What could she want from us after all these years, Joan? We're nothing to her. Strangers."

"What do you mean, Martin? She's our daughter—our own flesh and blood," Joan said, her voice rising.

Martin took a second too long to answer, and when he did, he avoided her eyes. "There's too much water under the bridge, Joan," he said. "Maybe if she'd shown up when she turned eighteen things would've been different. The timing just isn't right." Joan stared at him in disbelief. "We're up to our eyes in work at the moment," Martin continued. "Who knows what damage it would do to our reputation if this got out. We've worked hard for all of this." His arm gestured around the room, then beyond it to the men stacking boxes in the warehouse and their daughter serving customers in the shop.

Joan recognized the flicker of agitation in Martin's eyes. He was useless at hiding what he was thinking. His mind was clearly racing. "And what about my mother? The shock would kill her." Of course! Joan was wondering when he'd bring his mother into it. "And Carmel. We can't do this to her." He leaned forward in his chair, taking Joan's hand in his. She stood motionless next to him, arms locked by her side. "We can't meet her, Joan. Not now."

Joan wrenched free of his grasp. A feeling of déjà vu swept over her as she stood staring at him. He sat slumped, head in his hands, in exactly the same way he had all those years ago on the bench in St. Stephen's Green when she told him she was pregnant.

"You promised me!" Joan could hear the desperation in her own voice. "You said we'd see her again one day. This is our chance, Martin."

He threw his hands in the air. "For God's sake, Joan, I was a bloody kid! Wet behind the ears. What did I know back then? We've built a life for ourselves, a good life. We're doing well." He was on a roll. "And we have our good name to consider. Don't forget I'm up for reelection as president of the Chamber of Commerce." He straightened now, leaning back against the smooth leather of the chair with his hands clasped behind his head. "I won't let anything get in the way of everything we've worked for. It's too late."

Joan balled her hands into tight fists. "You're spineless. You know that?" she said softly but with such bitterness that Martin was taken aback.

"Well, at least I'm not a bloody fool." He pushed his chair back and stormed out, yanking the door open but taking care not to slam it as he left the room. It wouldn't do to let everyone know they'd been arguing.

Joan leaned against the side of the desk, fighting tears with small shallow breaths. She examined Emma's letter, still in her hand, tracing her fingers over the letters of her daughter's name in the signature. "My baby girl," she whispered. "Who are you?" It was then that she understood once and for all that she had to know the answer to that question. *To hell with you, Martin Egan*, she thought.

Carmel breezed into the office. "I wondered why you were late, Mam. I thought it must be something to do with Granny?"

"She's fine," Joan said, stuffing the letter back into her bag.

"What's up with Dad?"

"Oh, some issue with Noel Carmody's receipts. He'll get over it."

"Ah, right. Well, could you give me a hand out front? I'm busy serving and someone needs to man the till."

Joan cut her off. "Give me a minute, will you? I've only just got in!" She heard the sharp edge in her voice, snapping as it often did when she spoke to her daughter.

"Sure," Carmel said with a shrug as she left the room.

Joan cursed herself for being such a bitch. Anger flared—at Martin, at Molly, at the whole world, dead set on keeping her from being the mother she always wanted to be. And at herself, for letting it happen. She should have stood up to the pair of them. She should have put her foot down, made sure she and Carmel had more time together when Carmel was younger—just the two of them. She shouldn't have allowed this distance to open up between them. And now it was too late. Too late to say everything that had gone unsaid. Too late to undo what was done.

Martin went back to his office and stayed there with the door shut all afternoon. Joan remained quiet and watchful, going through the motions of serving customers—smiling politely, directing them to the shelves where they'd find boxes of nails or sheets of sandpaper, taking their money. She watched Carmel's easy way with her customers and couldn't help but wonder if Emma was anything like her. Would she be as good with people as Carmel was?

"How's our Madonna today?" Joe Byrne winked at Carmel as he stacked his purchases on the counter.

"Getting into the groove, Joe, getting into the groove," Carmel replied, smiling back at him. She was well able for the likes of Joe Byrne, Joan thought. She admired the way Carmel could hold her own with every customer who set foot in the shop. *No thanks to you*, said the voice in her head.

At the end of the day, Carmel cashed up, and Martin finally emerged to lock up and set the alarm.

"I'm off," Joan said, without looking at him.

"Don't you want a lift home?" he asked.

"I'll walk."

Carmel stopped tallying the pile of notes she was counting and glanced from her mother to her father. There was no doubt she'd worked out that the foul mood that had descended on Egan & Son had nothing to do with Noel Carmody's receipts.

As far as Joan was concerned, Martin could deal with any questions Carmel had about it. She left the yard through the back gate, but instead of heading home she walked purposefully toward the village. The rain had dried up, and the sky was clear. Buses packed with evening commuters sped along the main road. Young office workers, heading home, waltzed past her plugged into their Walkmans. As she walked, her hand jangled the change in her pocket that Mrs. Concannon had given her that morning.

She carried on until she reached the phone box at the junction outside the library. Inside it smelled of urine and last night's fish and chips. She made sure the door was shut, then propped Emma's letter on the small metal shelf in front of her. Cradling the receiver between her neck and her right ear, she fed the coins one by one into the slot. When there were no coins left, she took a breath and tapped the receiver against her forehead. "You're wrong, Martin," she heard herself say aloud. "Dead wrong."

And she dialed.

CHAPTER 7

Emma sat on the edge of the bath, soaping Ben's back. She felt each jagged vertebra jut out along his spine through the sponge and winced. She mustn't waste this precious time they had together fretting about how frail and ill he was. Having him home this weekend was their chance to feel like a normal family again, even if it was only for a day or two before his treatment continued next week, and even if Matt was still on call tomorrow.

"Okay, love, it's time to come out now," she said. "The water's getting cold."

"Aw, just one more minute, Mummy, please!" Ben pleaded, tipping water from the blue bucket in his right hand to the red one in his left. He smiled to himself, watching the water trickle through the holes in the bottom of the red bucket back into the bath.

Sighing, Emma watched her son refill the blue bucket, then the red one. That was exactly what her life felt like now: a scramble to fill a leaky bucket. "All right, just one last turn, Ben, and then we'll get you dried, okay?"

"Okay," Ben agreed, smiling back at her through chapped lips.

Emma stacked the buckets on the corner of the bath and was

pulling the plug when the phone rang. "Will you get that?" she called downstairs to Matt. She heard him cross the kitchen into the hall and the ringing stop.

Ben reached his wet arms out to her. As she wrapped him in a warm, fluffy towel, she pressed her nose against his scalp, breathing in the sweet, bubble-bath smell of him. "There," she said, placing him onto the bath mat and hugging him close.

Matt's feet thumped up the stairs, and Emma turned expectantly toward the door, smiling as she knelt on the floor, toweling Ben's arms dry. "It's for you, love," he said, touching her on the shoulder.

"Who is it?"

"Joan. Joan Egan. Calling from a phone box by the sound of it."

Emma jumped up, thrusting the towel at him. "Can you get him dried?" She didn't wait for an answer before racing down the stairs. Breathless, her hand shaking, she picked up the receiver. "Hello . . . Joan?"

"Eh, hello, yes."

The line went quiet, the static of the distant connection echoing in Emma's ear. "Are you still there?" she said, heart accelerating.

"Is that you? Emma?" The hesitant, halting voice sounded foreign and unfamiliar.

Emma sensed Joan floundering like a hooked trout on the other end of the line. For a split second she was glad to hear her scramble for words to fill the silences. Glad the mother who abandoned her without a second thought was struggling. Jesus, what kind of hard-hearted bitch was she? Maybe that was why she'd buried all thoughts of Joan. They brought out the very worst in her. Their brief conversation went well, though, better than she could have hoped. Joan agreed to meet her, and right now that was all Emma cared about.

"I'll let you go, then," Joan said, once their arrangements to meet in Dublin the following weekend were made.

"Goodbye, Joan. And thanks for calling," Emma said. "Bye," she added, just as the line went dead. She replaced the receiver, sank onto the bottom stair, and let out a long breath. She could hardly believe she'd be meeting her birth mother next week.

She turned to the sound of Matt coming down the stairs behind her. He was carrying Ben in the crook of one arm as if he weighed nothing. Matt had dressed him in his *Thomas the Tank Engine* pajamas and smoothed Vaseline onto his dry lips. When he reached the bottom, he put his other arm around her. "You okay?" he whispered, kissing her hair.

She nodded. "I'll tell you later."

"Pasta okay for dinner, buddy?" Matt asked.

"I'm not hungry," Ben replied, sticking out his bottom lip.

"Pasta would be lovely," Emma said, with a grateful look. "You okay if I give Mum a quick call to let her know what's happening?"

"Sure," Matt said. "Ben can watch *Thomas the Tank Engine* while I get the dinner going."

She lifted the receiver again and punched the numbers in before settling herself on the bottom stair. Her mother picked up on the third ring. "Hello, Mum."

"Emma! Is everything okay? How's Ben?"

"Yes, yes, everything's all right. He's fine. Dr. George checked his bloods and examined him before she discharged us. Besides—"

"And what did she say?" her mother interrupted, something she'd never normally do. They'd all been doing things they would never normally do since Ben's diagnosis.

"She was happy to let him out for the weekend as long as we keep to ourselves. And the hospital is only down the road," Emma said, stating the obvious. "So there's nothing to worry about."

"Good. That's a relief. We're praying for him. Has there been any news of a donor?"

"No, no news yet." Emma sighed. This was how every conversation began since Ben got sick. Everyone was on high alert.

"Oh, well, maybe after the weekend—"

"Mum, there's something I need to tell you," Emma cut in. "Remember I told you about writing to the Egans?"

"Yes?"

Emma could hear her mother's steady breathing through the receiver. She imagined her fidgeting with the gold cross and chain she always wore around her neck. "Well, Joan called."

"Did she really? That's wonderful news, darling! Are you okay?"

"I'm fine, Mum. Really."

"Did you tell her about Ben?"

"God no—and frighten her off completely?!" She could picture her mother smiling on the other end of the line.

"You're right. It must have been a shock for her, getting the letter out of the blue."

"I know. Anyway, I'm going to meet her in Dublin next week."

"And you'll tell her then?"

"Yes. I'll ask her to be tested."

"Good. That sounds like a good plan, Emma. Why don't Dad and I come down and help Matt while you're away?"

"Could you, Mum? That would be a weight off my mind. Are you sure?"

"Of course I'm sure. We want to see Ben anyway. It's at times like these I wish we hadn't retired to Scotland. We should be there for you."

"You've always been there for me, Mum. Always," Emma said, closing her eyes and resting her head against the wall. They were both quiet for a moment.

"Emma, are you still there?"

"Yes, Mum. I'm still here."

They hung up five minutes later. Emma promised to call again if there was any change in Ben.

Ben barely touched his food. They tried not to make a big deal of it, which they would have done before. Emma remembered the times before he was sick, how they'd coax him to eat when all he wanted to do was get down on the floor and play. Now he didn't have the energy for that. And neither did they. "Before" didn't matter a damn. All they had was now, and they were grateful for each small bite.

"What story will we read?" Emma asked Ben as they lay next to each other on his bed after dinner. "*Where the Wild Things Are*?"

"Yes, please."

Ben's eyes were closing before she finished. She longed for those times when one story was never enough. When he would pester her for another. When she would be firm and refuse because there were lunches to pack for tomorrow and laundry to fold. Stuff that now seemed like the least important thing in the world to worry about.

She pulled the covers up under Ben's chin and turned out the bedside light. Then she sat on the side of the bed, looking down at the book in her hands, remembering. When she was growing up, bedtime stories with her mum had been an anchor in her life. Would that have been true, she wondered, if Joan had been her mother? She frowned. Wasn't Joan her mother? Weren't they tethered anyway? Would they want to be? Just thinking about it did her head in.

Down in the kitchen, Matt was at the sink, drying the last of the dishes. Seeing his broad shoulders and strong back steadied Emma. She went behind him and wrapped her arms around his waist, pressing her cheek into his sweatshirt. "Want a hand?" she asked, letting go.

"No, I'm almost there. You just relax," Matt said, opening the cutlery drawer. "You must be shattered."

"I can't believe she actually called," Emma said.

Matt put down the tea towel and turned to face her, resting his hands on her shoulders. "Are you ready to talk about it?"

Her eyes met his and she nodded.

"What did she say?"

"Not much." Emma stepped back, leaning against the kitchen counter. "It was all pretty awkward, to be honest."

"It was bound to be," Matt said. "I don't suppose you told her about Ben?"

Emma frowned and shook her head.

"Yeah, you're right. It's too soon," he agreed. "You'll have a better chance of convincing her face-to-face."

"Exactly." Emma picked up the dishcloth and started wiping the table. "The good news is she's agreed to meet me. I said I'd be there next weekend." She swept the stray crumbs into a neat pile. "She was fine with that. She'll call again during the week with the details about when and where to meet."

It was Matt's turn to frown. "Wait a second. You mean you're not meeting at their place? That's odd."

Emma stacked the clean table mats. "Not that strange when you think about it. I'm their dirty little secret, remember?"

Matt moved toward her, tucking a strand of dark hair that had fallen across her face behind her ear. "They don't know what they've been missing," he said, kissing her forehead.

She smiled. "You know, she didn't mention him at all. Martin, I mean . . . Not once."

"She was probably just nervous speaking to you for the first time, Em. Maybe she just forgot."

"Maybe," Emma said. "Maybe."

"You'll know more when she calls again. And she might open up a bit when you meet her," Matt said.

"I guess so . . ." Emma hesitated. "You know, hearing her voice . . . I almost felt sorry for her."

"How do you mean?"

Emma sighed. "I've always been determined to despise her for what she did." She was quiet again, fearful of the words she was about to say. "Writing her off as heartless made it easier to disown her."

"Go on," Matt said.

"But hearing how small and scared she sounded . . . she didn't match the story I'd told myself about her." Emma looked into Matt's eyes. "I guess I never thought of her as my mother until I heard her speak. She was never real, until now."

"And you're confused because you don't know how to feel about her anymore?" he asked.

She nodded. "It's not just that, though. I feel like I might be ready to hear her side of the story."

"That makes sense," Matt said, putting his arms around her. "Maybe now's your chance."

PART TWO

CHAPTER 8

Dublin, 1960

Joan stood barefoot by the window in her flannel nightdress, watching her mother pacing in slow halting steps between the front room and the scullery. She'd been at it since early morning, stopping now and then, hands either side of the sink, to lean over and catch her breath. The baby was coming.

"Can I rub your back for ye, Ma?" Joan asked.

"Thanks, love. You're a good girl," Ma said between breaths. "But I'm best left to me own devices." She smiled weakly. "All this will be forgotten as soon as the baby is here." She planted a kiss on Joan's forehead before her face contorted as another contraction took hold.

Joan knew what would happen next. She was thirteen, the oldest of the five of them, nearly two years older than Teresa. Old enough to remember when her younger sisters Eileen and the twins Mary and Margaret were born, a little more than a year apart. Soon one of the neighbors would send for the midwife and Granny. The midwife would arrive with her brown leather bag, and she and Ma would go upstairs. Joan would stay downstairs with Granny to mind the little ones, or they'd be sent outside to play if the weather wasn't too miserable.

And when it was all over, even if it was another girl, Da would wet the baby's head down at O'Grady's bar. Nothing much would change for Ma. The laundry pile would climb higher. The slices of bread she'd cut from the loaf for breakfast would get thinner. The tired circles under her eyes would grow darker. And she wouldn't seem to mind any of it.

This time was different, though. Joan knew something was wrong as soon as the midwife started helping Ma, her belly still swollen tight, back down the stairs.

"Where are you going, Ma?"

"Don't worry, love," Ma said. "The baby's just turned the wrong way around. We're going to the hospital to get her sorted out. We'll both be back before you know it." She winked, and that wink made Joan believe everything would be all right.

She helped get the little ones into bed that night, then lay wide awake next to Teresa, who was sleeping soundly, waiting for Ma to bring the baby home. She listened to the sounds outside on the street. The songs of drunks coming back from the pub. The clink of milk bottles being put out for the morning. Cat fights. She woke to the sound of the front door closing. The sun had barely risen, and none of the others were up.

Joan ran downstairs to see Da filling the kettle in the scullery. He never filled the kettle. That was Ma's job. Da didn't turn to smile at her or to tell her to get the fire going. He didn't say a word. He stood, with his back to her, still in his overcoat. She watched his slanted shoulders rise and fall on a wave of quiet sobs.

It dawned on Joan that he'd come home alone. She held her breath, waiting, the cold creeping into her bare feet through the concrete floor. Da wiped his nose on the back of his overcoat sleeve. "What are we going to do now, Joanie?"

He seemed to be speaking to himself and not to Joan at all.

He lit a match and held it to the gas, igniting the blue flame, and then, as if remembering something important, turned to look at her. His red eyes and tear-stained face made Joan's stomach lurch. Da reached a hand into his jacket pocket, took out a crumpled envelope, and held it out. "She'd want you to have this, Joanie." Inside, in a corner of the envelope, was her mother's gold wedding band, scratched and worn thin by the years of scrubbing and cleaning and caring for them all. It was the only thing of value Da had ever been able to give her. Something Ma would never have taken off her finger of her own accord.

Joan wanted Da to put his arms around her. She wanted to wail. Da stood, arms by his sides, fists balled, looking down at the floor, while the tears that had welled up in Joan's eyes rolled down her cheeks.

"You'll have to be a big girl now your ma is gone."

As the disaster of a day wore on, nobody mentioned the word "dead." They talked about Ma having passed away, being in a better place, at peace in heaven with the angels. Thank God, they said, the baby—a little girl, six pounds thirteen ounces—had been spared.

Granny didn't move from her chair by the fire all day. She stared into the flames, her eyes raw from crying, cardigan pulled tight around her. Who had lit the fire? Joan wasn't sure. There were too many people in and out of the house to know. There was a purposeful energy about the place—a strange, party-like atmosphere, people wanting to make themselves useful. Nothing like a good tragedy for bringing people together. "There but for the grace of God go I," they murmured to one another.

Mrs. Flanagan from across the road took Joan's little sisters to her house to mind them for the day. Another neighbor, someone she didn't know, brought a pot of soup and a loaf of bread for supper. There were knocks on the door, offerings left on the front step: pink roses picked from someone's garden and a plastic bottle of holy water in the shape of the Virgin Mary, sealed tight with a blue crown lid. Gifts her mother had never been given when she was alive, arriving in abundance now she was dead.

In the evening, Mr. Hanlon, who lived in the gray pebble-dashed semi attached to theirs, took Da to the pub for a quick one to drown his sorrows. Mrs. Hanlon was so sorry for their troubles she brought a miniature bottle of Jameson to help Granny get over the shock. "Those poor little . . ." she half whispered, looking in at Joan and her sisters. "You know where we are if you need us." She patted the slack skin on Granny's hand.

Joan sat cross-legged at Granny's feet on the linoleum floor late into the evening, neither of them saying very much. As Granny sipped the whiskey, the heartbreak that had been building up inside her all day tumbled out of her. "Your ma was a good daughter, Joan, despite what a lot of people around here said about her." She sniffed. "She wasn't the kind of girl they made her out to be. She made one mistake her entire life."

Joan shifted uncomfortably to her knees in front of the hearth. She wished Granny would stop talking. She wanted to put her fingers in her ears, to change the subject, to scream, but she was too afraid to speak.

"The only wrong move she ever made was getting into trouble before she was married, and sure isn't she paying for her sins now?"

Joan jumped up and made for the door. She ran upstairs and buried her head in Ma's pillow and, finally, sobbed. Had Ma just pretended not to care what people thought of her? Deep down, had she regretted having Joan? Did she mind the snide remarks about the cut of her girls in their battered shoes and hand-me-down dresses that were always slightly too short for them? Had she ever grown tired of holding her tongue?

Joan had never once seen Ma's smile fade when one of the neighbors chided her for her swollen belly. "Jesus, Mary, and Joseph! Don't tell me you're up the spout again?! Would you ever tell that fella of yours to tie a knot in it, Anne." If Ma had been ashamed, she'd never let on. She had a way of making believe she wanted for nothing, even though Joan knew that wasn't true, especially on Fridays when Da brought his brown pay packet home after the barman at O'Grady's had seen more than his fair share of it.

In the days and weeks that followed, it was the things Ma did that no one knew needed doing, the things money couldn't buy, that they missed most of all. There was no fire burning in the grate when they got up in the morning. The house felt cold, dark, and empty. The girls' hair was always matted and tangled without Ma there to comb the knots out after their baths in the battered zinc tub by the fire on Saturday evening. They were all adrift. Lost.

Joan helped Granny fill the void as best she could. Making the tea in the morning before school. Buttering the bread for supper. Trying to get the little ones to wash their faces at night. But no matter how hard Joan tried, they always looked scruffy, with tidemarks around their necks and socks down around their ankles. There wasn't enough of anything to go around. She lost count of the number of times one of them said the words she thought she was too big now to say: "I want Mammy."

The baby came home from the hospital the day after they buried Ma. "We'll call her Anne after your mammy," Da said, sliding the baby, swaddled in a rough wool blanket, into Joan's arms. Baby Anne stirred in her sleep as her weight shifted from the warm crook of Da's muscular arms to Joan's cold bony ones. Joan stiffened, afraid she'd drop her, but she relaxed as Anne snuggled against the warmth of her belly. "I'll look after you, Anne. Don't worry." She breathed the words against her baby sister's cheek.

And she'd tried her best. But her best hadn't been good enough. When Anne was two months old, the nuns from St. Rita's convent, who'd been keeping an eye on them, said it was obvious they weren't managing. Granny Riley couldn't be expected to take care of them with her bad heart, and Da needed to earn a living, so he couldn't mind them.

Baby Anne was first to go, taken to a farming family somewhere down the country who could give her a decent life, or so they said. One by one, each of Joan's sisters was taken away, until it was just herself and Teresa left. They'd both be old enough to leave school and get a job soon. It was for the best, Da said. How could he have been so sure?

One winter evening, months after the little ones were taken, Joan was sitting next to the fire cutting up sheets of old newspaper to line her shoes. She squinted at the "Lost and Found" ads in the firelight. A memory of Da reading them out to Ma came to her—the pair of them bewildered by the things people would pay good money for an ad in the *Evening Herald* to recover.

"Would you listen to this, Anne?!" Da called from his seat at the table. Ma came in from the scullery, wiping her hands on her apron, and stood next to him, peering over his shoulder. Joan couldn't remember what they'd been laughing at. She was too young at the time to get the joke, but even so warmth spread through her as she hunkered down on the hearth watching them together.

Now, she ran her finger under the closely set lines of print.

FOUND a marcasite brooch, vicinity
Rathmines. Box 2022.

STRAYED from Terenure Road North, Friday,
Irish Terrier. Reward. Box 1440.

WANTED good Catholic home for lovely boy,
2 years of age. Fully surrendered, no fee. Apply,
St. Rita's, Abbey Street.

Her heart was suddenly in her mouth. Maybe this was how the nuns found new homes for her sisters. She continued reading, urgently mouthing each word under her breath, like an incantation that might conjure some small detail about her sisters' whereabouts.

> FOUND a pigeon, rubber ring with number 88 on leg, in Ballsbridge. Box 3190.
>
> WILL childless couple adopt Edward? Aged 3 years, 2 months, healthy, fair, very intelligent. Priest's reference essential. Full surrender. No fee. Apply, St. Rita's, Abbey Street.

Bile rose in her throat. She scrunched the page into a tight ball and flung it into the fire, watching the flames engulf it until nothing but the flakes of white ash and the dark stain from the newsprint on her fingers remained.

Da and the nuns had been right about one thing: Granny Riley's heart wouldn't have stood up to looking after all of them. As it was, it didn't stand up to losing most of them. They buried her the following winter, and Joan hadn't seen or heard of her little sisters since.

CHAPTER 9

Four years later

Joan pulled the threadbare flannelette sheet over her head. Teresa stirred in the bed next to her, taking half the sheet with her. It didn't matter—the sheet did nothing to block out Da's drunken snores on the other side of the paper-thin plasterboard wall. Da always slept like a baby after a few jars. He wouldn't be awake for an hour yet, not until long after both the girls had left for work. It was a miracle he held down the few laboring jobs he managed to get.

Joan knew by the angle of the light outside the window that it was time to get up anyway. She reached over, poking her younger sister playfully in the ribs. "Hey, time to get up, sleepyhead," she whispered.

Teresa groaned. "No way. It can't be morning yet."

"Shush! Da's still asleep." Joan swung her legs out of the bed in one swift move. No point putting off the inevitable. The cold numbed her feet. She dressed in a hurry, pulling on the work overalls she'd left on the chair in the corner the night before. "Come on,

Teresa. You'll be late for work if you don't get a move on. I'll get the kettle on."

Downstairs in the scullery, she and Teresa huddled next to the stove, hands stretched out toward the flame, waiting for the kettle to boil. Teresa had to leave the house before Joan to catch a bus into Bishop Street and the Jacob's biscuit factory where she'd worked since she was fourteen. Teresa rubbed the sleep from her eyes while Joan filled the mugs, and Joan watched her sister as she sipped from the mug of sweet milky tea.

She tried to ignore how pinched Teresa's face was and the sharp angles of her shoulder blades under her loose factory overalls. There was nothing to her. Joan worried she wasn't getting enough to eat—well, enough of the right things to sustain a teenage girl anyway.

"Joan?" Teresa said, as they stood shoulder to shoulder, their backsides against the cooker. "Will you do something for me?"

Joan put her mug down. "What?" she said, curious.

"Let me warm my hands, just for a minute." Teresa laughed, thrusting her freezing hands inside Joan's cardigan and under her arms.

"No! Get away from me, you!" Joan squealed, wriggling free. "You're freezing!"

"Not now!" Teresa giggled, picking up her tea.

"Look at the time! You'd better get going," Joan said, taking her sister's mug from her. Within five minutes Teresa was out the door, pulling on her hat and coat as she went. "Mind yourself," Joan called after her as the door slammed closed.

She rinsed the cups in the sink and had a look in the kitchen cupboards to see what there was. Nothing she could make a dinner with. The jam jar they kept the coins in for the messages and the meter was empty. Da had been dipping into it again. Who was she kidding that keeping it out of sight on the highest shelf would stop him drinking their last penny? Her jaw clenched. She wished she had enough money to give Teresa a decent meal seven nights a week.

Soon it was time to head off to work herself. Eight hours standing on the assembly line at the Royal Candy factory lay ahead of her, dipping squares of caramel into pink and white icing. She sighed as she pulled the hall door shut behind her. "Another day, another dollar," as Da would say. Each one the same as the last.

She didn't mind the walk to work through the Cranmore housing estate as long as it wasn't raining. The estate where she'd been raised was bookended by two churches and sustained by a single factory and three pubs. The people she met all knew her by name. Flat-capped men, the first fag of the day dangling from their lips. Stooped aul' ones leaning on their sweeping brushes and gossiping at their garden gates. Kids too young for school whose mothers were already sick of them sent out to play and told not to come back until lunchtime. "Off to work, Joan?" they'd say, stating the obvious, as if they'd been looking out for her.

Mostly Joan kept herself to herself at work, doing her best to avoid the roving eyes and hands of her supervisor, Jim Brophy. She couldn't understand what her friend Esther Molloy, who stood beside her on the assembly line, saw in him. She was welcome to him—and any other fella who was only after what he could get.

Midmorning, the sun finally poked through the clouds. It was a fine day now, warm enough for herself and Esther to take their lunch break outside. They sat on the concrete, backs to the factory wall, bread-and-butter sandwiches balanced on their knees. A few feet away, the other girls congregated to gossip in a halo of cigarette smoke near the back door of the factory.

Mary McBride held out her left hand to show off her five-stone twist engagement ring. The girls cooed and clucked around her, asking about the wedding plans. It wouldn't be a long engagement, judging by the buttons straining across the front of Mary's factory overalls. She'd be walking down the aisle from the side altar of St. Jude's on Larry Murphy's arm in no time.

"I wonder what it was like," Esther said, elbowing Joan.

"What?" Joan replied, biting into her bread.

Esther's face flushed. "You know . . . *it. Doing it.*" She giggled. "I'd love to ask Mary. But I wouldn't dare."

Joan stopped chewing and swallowed. "I wouldn't have a clue," she said, brushing crumbs off her lap. "I don't suppose your ma has ever let anything slip, about the mechanics like," she said, blushing.

Esther gawped at Joan, and laughed. "You must be joking! The nearest Mammy gets to telling us girls about it is doling out dire warnings about keeping our legs crossed and our knickers on."

"It must be nice but," Joan mused. "Otherwise, why would a girl risk it?"

Esther cocked her head. "You're right. I never thought of it like that." She bit into her own sandwich. "Yeah, it must be nice all right." They didn't say another word to each other until the siren signaling the end of the lunch break pierced the silence.

Afternoons were the worst, with several more monotonous hours rooted to one spot on the assembly line still ahead. The constant hum of machinery. The sickly sweet smell of warm sugar. The ache in her shoulders and calves. That evening, Joan clocked out bang on time. Another day over, and the chance of some fresh air at last. She stood at the factory gates at the bottom of Ardeer Avenue, next to one of the granite pillars, and breathed in the cut-grass smell of the suburban summer evening.

A broad young fella she didn't recognize was wrestling a bulky messenger bike up the steep hill. His shirtsleeves were rolled up, and the taut muscles in his forearms flexed as he pulled on the handlebars, moving his body from side to side, his long legs strained with the effort of pushing the pedals around. It would have been easier to get off and walk, but this fella seemed determined not to let the incline beat him. She liked that.

She couldn't see his face under the charcoal-gray cap he wore until he'd almost passed her, and even then she could only see his profile because his eyes were fixed on the road ahead. The sign on the side of his bike read *Egan & Son Builders Merchants & Suppliers.* He must be the new messenger boy from Egans' builders' yard. Joan immediately felt sorry for him. Although her own job was a drag, at least the factory was big enough that you could lose yourself among the hundreds of interchangeable workers, all dressed in hairnets and identical white overalls. There was never any need to draw attention to yourself. If you had to be a cog, you might as well be an anonymous one.

Egans' wasn't a small business, and they seemed to be taking on new people every year, but it was still run by the family. The poor messenger boy would have to answer to Mrs. Egan, who had taken over the running of the business since her husband died in his sleep a couple of years back. Heart trouble, they said. Word was she ruled the place with a rod of iron and was never off the backs of the poor unfortunates who worked for her. Joan imagined the new messenger boy had already had his fair share of earache from her.

She watched him disappear up the road and out of sight and continued on home. There was plenty to do before Da got back from the pub. The dinner to make, for starters, never mind the washing and ironing to sort out.

Teresa got in the door shortly after her, lamenting the tragic day she'd had. "And to top it off I laddered my tights on my handbag buckle getting off the bus." She grimaced.

"Maybe they'll mend," Joan consoled her. "We can give it a go tonight after dinner."

She didn't give Egans' messenger boy a second thought until she left work the following evening and saw him battling the hill once more, and again the evening after that. On the fourth evening she found herself looking out for him, and every evening after. June became July, and she began to imagine the sound of his voice. His smile. The exact color of his eyes.

She replayed all kinds of scenarios over and over in her head where he would have to stop and get off his bike: a puncture, a load that was too heavy, some eejit walking out in front of him. Before long she was fantasizing about the first time she would look into his eyes, and he into hers. In her fantasy they would fall for each other without saying a word.

More than once she told herself how ridiculous she was being. *For God's sake, Joan, get a grip. You're standing here, wearing factory overalls, caked in icing sugar, at the bottom of Ardeer Avenue—not on some Hollywood film set with Burt Lancaster.* But as the summer passed she found herself making excuses not to hang back gossiping with her workmates as they fumbled in their bags for lipstick or cigarettes and matches in the changing rooms.

She always stood in the same spot, five nights a week, just out of sight in the shadow of the stone pillar to watch him fight the hill. Sometimes she was breathless when she arrived at the gates, fearful that she'd missed him. At first, watching him was a bit of amusement at the end of a long day. Then it became a game—seeing if she could synchronize with his arrival. Over time—she didn't know quite when—catching a glimpse of him became the highlight of her day. Knowing he would be there, like clockwork, was somehow thrilling. Little by little, a place was carved out for the messenger boy in her mind—and then in her heart.

Joan wasn't used to this feeling, especially where boys were concerned. Getting too close to boys, or, worse, letting any one boy get too close to you, was risky. When she'd turned fourteen, her skinny frame had softened into curves where the eyes of every man and boy she encountered lingered, or tried not to linger. The unwelcome attention brought her no joy. Far from it. It was one more thing to worry about.

Every one of the fellas she knew was the same as the next. They all came from the cramped, pebble-dashed houses, built back-to-back on the crowded streets of the estate, with no education and few prospects of ever becoming anything other than who they already were. Joan started wearing thick woolen cardigans buttoned up to her neck and developed a habit of folding her arms across her chest whenever she was standing. She began to avoid the Friday night dances, where fellas thought they could buy you for the price of a Club Orange. Every Friday night followed the same predictable pattern. As the night wore on, couples abandoned the lights of the dance floor for the shadows of nearby lanes and doorways.

One Friday afternoon, Esther and their friend Imelda asked Joan to come to the dance at the Crystal Ballroom that night. "Come on, Joan. It'll be a laugh," Esther said, linking arms with her as they skipped out the factory gates.

"Who knows, you might get lucky." Imelda laughed.

In a moment of weakness, Joan agreed. Maybe she was secretly hoping the boy from Egans' would be there. "Okay," she said, rolling her eyes. "I give in. But I'm warning you, I'll be leaving early if there's nothing doing."

"That makes three of us!" Imelda cackled.

On her way home, Joan thought about what she might wear to the dance. She could borrow a scarf from Teresa that would add a splash of color to her outfit. Maybe tonight would be her night?

CHAPTER 10

Joan sat at the edge of the dance floor with her candy-striped swing skirt tucked under her knees, trying to imagine the couples moving their hips in time to the music into other lives. It was impossible. They, like herself, would end up carbon copies of their mothers and fathers, just as their mothers and fathers had done before them. Holding their breath for Friday and the payday brown envelope. Delighted with the few shillings that would barely last until Tuesday the following week if they were lucky. Eking out a day-to-day existence, like hamsters on a wheel they could neither stop nor get off.

"Are ye dancin'?" George O'Brien, a wiry little fella from the estate, asked, grinning down at her, showing the prominent white teeth that had earned him the nickname "Tombstones."

"Not tonight, George. But thanks anyway," Joan said, adjusting the red chiffon scarf she'd knotted around her neck just a few hopeful hours ago. Nothing much had changed since the last time she'd been at the dance hall, months before. Beneath the beat of the music and behind the bright lights reflected in the disco ball, the place was as jaded as ever. Paint peeled in the far corners of the damp walls—the faded velvet curtains framing the stage frayed at the edges. The crowd was full of the faces she'd see back at the factory on Monday, without lipstick, eyeliner, and back-combed hair.

To make matters worse, there was no sign of the messenger boy. She wondered what she was doing there. She already knew she wasn't going to find the man of her dreams at the Friday night dance. And she remembered the exact moment when she had given up trying. It was nearly two years ago, the week after her sixteenth birthday, the night Jim Brophy had almost overpowered her against the high ivy-covered walls surrounding the convent grounds.

She was on her way home from the dance. They'd had a laugh that night, a group from the factory, jiving to "Let's Twist Again." Jim was a few years older than her and seemed nice enough. He bought her a lemonade, and they had a couple of slow dances earlier in the evening. She liked the clean-shaven smell of him and his dark hair slicked back—for the night that was in it. She was flattered by his attention. When he asked if he could walk her home, she shrugged. Where was the harm? But as they passed the convent gates, Jim playfully grabbed hold of her wrist.

"C'mere to me," he slurred. How had she not realized he'd had so much to drink after they'd danced? At first she thought he was only messing. It was just the drink talking, making him giddy. She was mistaken. Jim's intentions became clear as he dug the tips of his fingers into her shoulders and thrust his tongue into her mouth. Her first kiss. Sweet sixteen.

She gagged against the bulk and the feeling of it. The stale-beer-and-fags taste of him. She tried closing her lips and pulling away, but Jim tightened his grip, teeth clashing with hers. She turned her head and opened her mouth to scream. But no sound came out. Jim's hands groped her breasts through the thin satin of her good blouse. He moved urgently, shifting a hand to hold fast to her upper arm, the other reaching under her skirt and between her legs, thick fingers probing her knickers. Joan pummeled his back with her fists and tried to break free.

"Playing hard to get, are we?" He laughed, loosening his grip to undo his belt buckle. Joan saw her chance. She jerked her knee up and into his groin. Jim doubled over. Free from his grasp, she fled, heart hammering, glad she wasn't wearing heels. Jim called after her, "You frigid little bitch!" She didn't stop to listen or dare to look back.

Jim avoided her eye the following Monday when he passed her assembly line in his white factory coat—and every day for weeks after. And he wasted no time telling anyone who would listen that Joan Quinn thought far too highly of herself.

Joan smoothed her skirt, shuddering at the memory of Jim Brophy's hands groping her. She hadn't been back to the dance hall since then—until tonight. She stood up and walked to where Esther was talking to some new girls from the factory she didn't know well. *I'm off, Esther*, she mouthed, and waved as the guitarist strummed the opening chords of an old Elvis number.

Esther beckoned her over, but Joan waved and shook her head, then headed to the cloakroom to collect her coat. The night hadn't been a total waste of time. She'd made up her mind about the man she wanted and had thought of a way to get him to notice her the next time he cycled past the factory.

THE FOLLOWING MONDAY, SHE WAITED so long outside the factory gates that her hands and feet were numb from the cold. She was still there when the security guards came to lock up. The messenger boy never showed. Every night for the next two weeks she waited, but there was no sign of him. He had vanished off the face of the earth.

It was strange that the absence of a fella she'd never met made her days at the factory drag more than usual. The nights drew in, and the days grew shorter. Joan still glanced left when she reached the gates each evening. Looking for the messenger boy had become a reflex, but now, after a month of nothing, she had given up hope of seeing him again. She kicked herself for not having the guts to say something to him when she had the chance—one evening, any evening, that summer gone.

At home, before Da and Teresa got back from work, Joan hunkered down next to the fire and cleaned out yesterday's spent ashes into a bucket. She twisted some pages of old newspaper, laying them on the grate under a few lumps of coal, then put a lit match to the paper and watched the orange flame lick the corners of it. There was no warmth in it yet, but Joan put her hands out toward the fire anyway, trying to thaw her fingers.

She thought back to her messenger boy and wondered why she'd put so much stock into seeing him. "Silly," she scolded herself, shaking her head. She'd conjured up some story in her mind. Fooled herself with some romantic notion she'd seen played out on the film screen during Saturday matinees. A notion about true love triumphing against all the odds.

She sat back on her heels, staring into the flames. Maybe it was for the best in the long run. Love, or, more precisely, the act of loving itself, could land you in trouble. It wasn't just your heart that could be broken. It was your whole life.

Nobody had ever warned Joan of this fact. They didn't have to. She'd seen with her own eyes how her mother's life had panned out. Where had love got Ma in the end? Shackled to a drunk who could barely support her. Saddled with five kids and pregnant again. Whispered about behind her back by people on the housing estate and beyond who barely knew her by name. Buried by thirty.

That night, as Joan lay next to Teresa, she tried to picture Ma's face. It was a ritual she went through, like a complicated prayer she had to keep reciting so she wouldn't forget it. She was terrified that if she didn't, the few memories she had of Ma would be wiped away. If she was honest, they'd already faded, but she didn't want to admit that, even to herself.

CHAPTER 11

December was hectic at the factory. There was always more demand for sweets and chocolate coming up to Christmas. Joan was looking forward to the two days' holiday. Then, out of the blue, on a Monday evening two weeks before Christmas, she saw her messenger boy again. She hadn't been looking for him and only noticed him because he was walking beside his bike, pushing it up the hill, beaten at last by the ice that made it too hard to pedal without risking his neck.

This was her moment, and Joan knew she'd be a fool not to take it. She stepped onto the road right in front of the messenger boy. The front wheel of the bicycle skidded on the ice, then slammed into her shin. Her knees buckled as she slipped and fell into the road.

"Oh, Jesus. I'm sorry," the messenger boy said, a look of horror on his face. "I didn't see you there."

Joan didn't get up. She stayed right where she was, sitting in the middle of the road and brushing dirt off her coat.

"Here, let me help you," he offered, steadying the bike with one hand and extending the other out to Joan. She reached up and took it, looking directly into his brilliant blue eyes for the first time. "Are you hurt?" he said.

Joan shook her head. "You're all right," she said. "Nothing's broken. I should have been looking where I was going."

He seemed caught off-guard for a second—like many a man before him when he saw Joan for the first time. The striking combination of her long dark hair pulled back from her face, her flawless pale skin, and vivid green eyes rarely went unnoticed. Joan could see the heat rising in his face. She was used to the silent stares of men and boys and did nothing to encourage them, but this fella was different. She felt it in her bones.

She didn't want to let go of the gloved hand she was still holding in hers. "I'm Joan. Nice to meet you," she said, as if this was the very first time she'd clapped eyes on him.

"Martin. Pleased to meet you, Joan." His expression changed abruptly. "Oh, God. Look at the state of your coat. Let me get that cleaned for you."

"Not at all. It's only a bit of mud. It will brush off when it's dry."

"Well, if you're sure you're all right. I'm already late and there'll be hell to pay if I'm not at the yard by six."

"Go on. I'm grand."

Martin threw his leg over the crossbar and wobbled as the bike wheels spun on the ice. Joan suppressed a smile, pretending not to notice. "See you around!" he called, and waved to her. She waved back, watching until he was out of sight, then practically skipped the rest of the way home, ignoring the soreness in her scraped knees that would be black and blue by morning.

For the next three nights, Martin waved to her as he passed on his way to the builders' yard. On Friday, she saw him waiting at the gates before she reached them. She wanted to run to him but slowed down instead. It would be better if she took her time getting there.

He grinned. "Thank God it's Friday, eh?"

"Are you waiting for someone?" she said.

"I might be," he replied, with a shy smile, making it clear he was there to see her. "Where are you headed?" He brushed his thick blond fringe self-consciously from his eyes.

"Just off home," she said, catching his eye.

"Do you have far to go?"

"No. I only live up the road, at the top of Ardeer Avenue."

"Can I walk with you for a bit?" he asked warily, as if he was afraid of the answer he might get.

"As long as you keep the wheels of that thing away from me." Joan smiled and pointed at his bike.

"All right." Martin grinned, and they fell into step with each other. The icy path sparkled under the streetlights.

Half a mile to home, Joan thought, as she sneaked a sideways glance at Martin. For the first time in her life, she wished it were farther. Despite the bitter cold, she was in no hurry to get there. Those imagined moments she'd only dared dream about over the past few months were coming true.

Martin was taller than she was, Joan noticed, but not so tall as to be lanky. She veered over to the edge of the path, getting as close to him as she could, their elbows almost touching as they walked. She hardly noticed the people hurrying past them on the opposite side of the road.

"Are you sure you're all right?" Martin asked, when they'd gone a little way. "After the fall the other day, I mean."

"I'm grand," Joan reassured him. "It was my fault. I wasn't looking where I was going."

Martin slowed, turning his head toward her. "I'd hate to think I hurt you," he said softly.

Joan held his gaze. "I know," she said.

The bicycle wheel bumped the curb and Martin adjusted his grip on the handlebars. "So, how long have you worked at the factory?"

"Too long!" Joan replied, rolling her eyes. "You?" She pointed to his bicycle.

"Same." He smiled. They were both laughing as they carried on up the road.

Every evening the following week they met at the factory entrance, walked up past Egans' yard, and parted ways under the tall chestnut tree that marked the entrance to the Cranmore estate. Martin wasn't from the Cranmore. They'd have met long ago if he had been. Joan knew every last one of the snotty-nosed, arses-out-of-their-trousers young fellas she'd grown up around. It was as if he had landed in her life from some distant planet, bringing color and light with him.

She liked the fact that they knew almost nothing about each other. They were two blank slates, making it up as they went along. "I've never seen you at the Friday dances," Joan said, one evening.

"I'm not much of a dancer"—Martin blushed—"although I'd have gone if I'd known you'd be there."

Joan tossed her ponytail over her shoulder. "Flattery won't get you anywhere," she said, beaming. "You didn't miss much. The music leaves a lot to be desired."

"Who do you prefer? The Stones or the Beatles?" Martin asked.

"The Beatles, of course!" Joan replied. "My turn. Now let me see . . . I know. Elvis or Cliff Richard?"

"It has to be Elvis," he said. "How about actors? Gregory Peck or Paul Newman?"

"Paul Newman," she said. "I loved him in *The Hustler*. Okay, let's see now . . . Elizabeth Taylor or Doris Day?"

Martin cleared his throat, like someone who wasn't sure he had permission to speak. "No contest. Elizabeth Taylor, every time." He blushed again. "You're the image of her, you know," he said, looking down at his feet. Joan's heart soared.

She was offered overtime the following week in the packing department for the run-up to Christmas. Any other time she would have jumped at it. Most families used the money to buy a few little extras—a nice bit of ham or a bottle of Jameson. Since the bulk of their wages was handed over O'Grady's bar, Joan's family would have used it for essentials: potatoes and butter. But for the first time in the years she'd been working at the factory, she turned down the extra hours.

Walking home with Martin became the brightest spot in every day. Joan couldn't always remember what they talked about on those short walks home. Nothing out of the ordinary, just everyday stuff. It didn't matter one iota to her what words passed between them, only that they were together, easy in each other's company. Martin seemed to hang on her every word.

There was something else too: the way he looked at her in the comfortable silences that passed between them and the awareness she had of his body in space and time as he walked alongside her, though they'd never done more than accidentally brush hands. Joan felt his presence even when he wasn't with her. It was as if her mind was signaling her senses to take all of it in. She was giddy, lighter, and more hopeful than she had been for a very long time.

Two days before Christmas, on their walk home together, Martin stopped at the side of the path to face her. "Joan." He cleared his throat. She was about to smile, but a frown creased her brow when she saw the serious look in his eyes. "Eh, I don't think I told you . . . I'm finishing up work today. I won't be doing deliveries in January."

Her heart missed a beat.

"I'm back at school after the holidays, worse luck," he said, pulling at the tassels on his scarf. "Still, only one more term to go until it's all over and done with, thank God."

Everything started to fall into place—but not in the way she'd hoped. So that was why she hadn't seen him working between September and now. "It's well for you, still being able to go to school," she teased.

Martin bowed his head. She immediately regretted her words. "I know it's not a luxury everyone can afford," he replied. "That's why I want to do as well as I can in the exams."

Joan didn't know another eighteen-year-old who was still at school. All the kids from the housing estate left by the time they were thirteen or fourteen, taking whatever manual job they could get. Some, like her, got on the assembly line in the factory. Others did piecework, if they could sew, or labored on building sites. The rest headed off on the boat from Dun Laoghaire to Holyhead to find work in one English city or another. Beggars couldn't be choosers. Martin, it turned out, was a chooser, a cut above, and by the sound of things, out of Joan's league. She hid her disappointment by keeping the conversation going.

"Don't they mind you doing a vanishing trick every few months?" Joan asked as they neared Egans' yard.

"I'm sure they would"—he hesitated—"except it's my father's business, so they kind of have to put up with me."

Jesus! The penny finally dropped. The real reason she hadn't met Martin before dawned on Joan. She'd only gone and fallen for Molly Egan's son and heir, the young fella everyone in the neighborhood knew would one day take his father's place at the helm of the family business. He didn't live on any Dublin Corporation housing estate—he lived in one of the big Georgian houses on Grove Square.

Martin must have seen the color drain from her face. "I thought you knew."

"I hadn't a clue." It was Joan's turn to look him in the eye. She wanted him to see she was telling the truth.

"Right. Right." He looked down, scuffing the toe of his work boot as he tapped a foot against the edge of the curb. "I'm sorry. Maybe I should have told you sooner."

"You're all right." She didn't know what else to say. "I'm really sorry about your da."

"Thanks. It hasn't been easy since he died." Martin turned to face her, his expression serious. She held her breath and her tongue and waited until the words tumbled out of him. "Look, Joan, I realize I barely know you. And it's only been a couple of weeks. But I don't want to stop seeing you."

She exhaled. They walked on in silence, Joan's mind swirling.

As they passed the entrance to Egans' yard, she noticed someone hovering on the front steps outside the office and recognized Mrs. Egan, standing on tiptoe and craning her neck to get a better view of the street.

"There you are," Mrs. Egan snapped. "You're late, Martin." Only it wasn't Martin she was glaring at but Joan: looking her up and down, taking her in with a single hostile stare. Joan squirmed, tugging at the collar of her coat. "We're up to our eyes in last-minute orders, and here's you out gallivanting. What were you thinking?"

Martin's cheeks burned. Even though he was more than a foot taller than his mother, he seemed to shrink in her presence. Joan backed away to continue on up the road. "Happy Christmas, Martin."

"See you, Joan," Martin said, without looking at her. He turned into the yard, head down, dragging his feet behind him. Joan walked away, crushed. Then Martin's voice called out, "And Happy Christmas!"

Joan turned back, buoyed by his smile, and was caught in the crossfire of Mrs. Egan's scowl. She ducked her head and kept walking. After a few steps, she stole a glance over her shoulder and spied Mrs. Egan still watching from the front steps, making sure Joan was well on her way up the road to where she belonged.

CHAPTER 12

As she continued on home along Ardeer Avenue, Joan didn't know which way was up. She couldn't pretend nothing had changed. This friendship, or whatever more she hoped it would be, would go nowhere if Molly Egan had anything to do with it, despite what Joan hoped Martin felt for her. There was no way someone like Martin Egan could ever be serious about a girl from the Cranmore estate, even if he wanted to be.

She knew his mother would put her foot down and make it impossible for them to be together. Soon he would find himself being introduced to the right kind of girls. Girls with an education, who might go to the secretarial college and learn to type or get a job in the bank. Girls from respectable homes who had the newspaper delivered every day—so they could read it, not line the soles of their shoes with it. Joan wasn't about to make a fool of herself. She would not be a bit of a diversion on the way home from work of an evening. She did not want to be some other girl's warm-up act.

The estate felt eerily quiet as she walked back to the house. Men lucky enough to have work in the factories or on the building sites of Dublin's new housing schemes cycled wearily past her, heading home after their day's hard graft. Cheerful coal fires glowed through people's windows, and she could smell smoke rising from the twinned chimneys of semi-detached houses on either side of the street. When she unlocked the front door, a blast of cool air hit her, and she shivered. "Jesus, it's colder in than out," she muttered to herself, switching on the light and hanging her coat in the hall before going in search of kindling.

She and Teresa were glad of the break over Christmas. With no work to go to, they could have a lie-in every morning, which saved having to light the fire until later in the day. When Da wasn't in the pub, cadging as many goodwill drinks as were bought for him, he was in bed sleeping them off.

On New Year's Eve, Joan sat watching Teresa backcomb her hair in front of the mirror over the fireplace. She was meeting a couple of girls from work in town. The pillarbox-red lipstick and miniskirt made her look older than her sixteen years. Teresa hummed the chorus of "Oh, Pretty Woman" as she worked her hair through the comb.

"Who is all this in aid of?" Joan teased.

"Never you mind, Saint Joan!" Her sister laughed back at her.

"Well, he's a lucky man. You're going to knock him dead looking like that. But mind yourself, won't you?" Teresa turned from the mirror, comb in hand, and stuck out her tongue. "I'm serious."

"You worry too much, Joan. I'll be absolutely fine. You should come with us!"

"I can't. Not in this state," Joan said, smoothing a wrinkle in her dark woolen tights. "I haven't a thing to wear." The truth was, her heart wasn't in it. The only person she wanted to be with was Martin.

Outside, the front gate squeaked on its rusty hinges. Da was home. He swore, his key missing the lock as usual, adding another scratch to the door's peeling paintwork. The girls exchanged a look.

"For fuck's sake!" Da swore again, slurring his words.

Teresa opened the front door, and Da steadied himself on the doorstep, then took one careful step into the small square hall. He squinted, looking at Teresa as if he were seeing her for the first time. "Do you mind telling me what the fuck you think you're wearing?" he said, eyes narrowing, spittle flying from his mouth. "You look like a bloody hoor."

Teresa bristled, then straightened herself. Joan inched forward on her seat next to the fireplace. On alert now. "Ah, Da, don't be like that. I'm just meeting a few of the girls from work. We're off out dancing."

Da swayed while trying to extract an arm from his coat sleeve, then stuck his face menacingly close to Teresa's. "Don't tell me what I can and can't be like in my own house," he snarled. "And you needn't think you're going anywhere in that getup!"

Teresa sidestepped to the left of him, grabbing her coat from the brass hook behind the door. "I'm sixteen, Da, old enough to hold down a decent job, which is more than can be said for you. You can't tell me what I can and can't wear."

"Now, that's enough, T," Joan said, her eyes widening as she gave her sister a warning shake of the head.

Da swung his arm and made a swipe at Teresa. She ducked away from his fist, and he staggered forward in the narrow hall, hitting his head on the wall. "Jesus bloody Christ!" he roared, holding on to his head with one hand and taking another swipe at Teresa with the other. "If I get my fucking hands on you, you little bitch . . . I'll burst you."

Joan jumped up from where she'd been sitting and pushed herself between them, grabbing Da's sleeve. "Don't, Da, don't. You're tired. Let her go," she pleaded. "Go on, Teresa. Go on!"

Da shook his arm loose from Joan's grip. "I'm sick and tired of people telling me what to do," he spat. His face was so close now Joan could see every red vessel in his bloodshot eyes.

"I know, Da," she soothed. "You must be tired. Sit yourself down. Take the weight off your feet. I'll put the kettle on, and we'll have a nice cup of tea." She helped him ease into the chair. Teresa watched her, one hand on the latch of the door. Joan nodded to her. *Go*, she mouthed. *I'm fine.*

Teresa returned a grateful but equally silent *Thank you* and escaped into the bitter night.

Da was asleep in the armchair before Joan lit the match under the gas. She knelt to take his shoes off, then slumped in the chair opposite him. He'd always been fond of the drink, but now his drinking was out of control. It was only a matter of time before this powder keg of a man he'd become did more than just raise a hand to one of them.

When she saw Martin, standing awkwardly in his school uniform by the factory gates the first Monday back at work, Joan's heart turned over. She had been positive he'd give up on her after their run-in with his mother before Christmas. He had good reason not to be there, she knew that. "Hello," she said when she reached him, smiling and searching his eyes.

Martin didn't say a word. He stepped out from behind the stone pillar, lifted her chin between his thumb and forefinger, then kissed her lightly on the lips. "I missed you."

Joan felt like a tiny figure in a snow globe that had just been upended. Her feet were still firmly planted on the ground, but her head was swirling, giddy with happiness. She'd never been kissed like this before. It felt more like a promise than a kiss, and it left Joan even more terrified of losing Martin.

As the weeks passed, she alternated between dark thoughts about why it wouldn't last and bright ones imagining their future together. Maybe they could keep things to themselves. Maybe if Mrs. Egan didn't find out they were still seeing each other, then they would have a chance.

Whenever thoughts of Mrs. Egan's plans for Martin's future

loomed too large, Joan would mentally cross off the number of weeks they'd been together and use every day as evidence of his love for her. She knew that despite what Da said when he had a few jars in him about her being a stunner and a great catch for any man, he, like everyone else, would say that Martin was out of her league and was only after what he could get.

Joan didn't want to hear those words spoken out loud before she had time to prove them all wrong. She didn't even tell Teresa—not that her sister had time to notice what was going on in Joan's life anyway. She was always off out somewhere these days, steering clear of Da whenever she could.

Joan and Martin agreed it was too risky for him to be seen walking her home after work. If word got back to his mother, she would put a stop to it. She'd warned Martin against having anything to do with Joan, so Saturday afternoon became their time. It was the only time in the week when Martin could find an excuse to be out of the house by pretending he was a sub for his school rugby team. He hated rugby with a passion, but his mother was in favor of him playing it on the grounds that it would make a man of him and get him in with the right crowd. Joan wondered if Mrs. Egan ever questioned why, week after week, even long after rugby season was over, the white shorts in the duffle bag returned home spotlessly clean.

They always met at the same spot in Bushy Park—on the bench under the poplar tree near the children's playground, where they would be anonymous among the dog walkers and the families having a bit of a day out. Joan made sure to always be there before Martin. She liked to watch him walking across the rugby field, duffle bag slung over his shoulder. As he skirted the edge of the pitch, she would let herself take him in—all of him, in a way she couldn't when he was sitting just a few inches from her on the bench.

He greeted her in the same way each time, taking her hands in both of his and kissing the tips of her fingers lightly before folding them in his hand and placing them in his lap, their knees touching.

The first two Saturdays, they just talked. Him mostly. Telling her what it was like to be an only child, even more lonely now with his father gone. And there she was, thinking people with plenty of money didn't have a bother on them.

"What would you do if your da was still alive and you could do anything you wanted?" Joan asked him.

Martin shook his head. "That's just it, you see—I don't know. The builders' yard is all I've ever known." He looked up at her, then back down at her hand in his. "Taking over the business is the only dream I've ever been allowed to have. I promised Da I'd keep it going when he got sick and that I'd do right by my mother. I'm all she has."

"Of course, you want to do right by your family," she said, squeezing his hand.

"I'm determined to make the best of it," he said, sticking his chin out defiantly. "I don't want to spend my entire life listening to people saying I had everything handed to me on a silver platter. I want to put my mark on the business, Joan."

"That's only natural," she replied.

"What about you, Joan?"

She stayed quiet for a moment. "Dreams are off-limits for some of us," she said eventually. "Sometimes it's as much as we can do to cope with reality."

Joan liked it when Martin talked. It gave her the chance to look at him squarely instead of sidelong. She had memorized every inch of his face. The thin upper lip that didn't seem to quite belong to the thicker lower one. The brilliant blue eyes, framed by serious dark brows and that thick blond fringe he kept pushing off his forehead. He was nothing like the grabbing men she knew from the factory or the Friday dances who were only after the one thing.

The second time he kissed her was the Saturday she told him about Ma dying and the hole that had left in her life. Her voice wavered as she recounted the story of the nuns coming to take her little sisters away. How the baby had been taken out, swaddled in an old blanket, to a waiting car. How she had screamed at Da afterwards. How all the accusations in the world wouldn't bring them back. And nothing would stop her missing them.

Martin shook his head, looked into her eyes, and tucked behind her ear a strand of hair that had come loose from the ribbon that had held it. "How could he have let it happen?"

"I suppose he couldn't see any other way," Joan said, burying her cheek in his chest.

"There's always another way," Martin replied, stroking her hair. "You've got *me* now, Joan. I'll take care of you. I'm not going anywhere." And then he took her face in both his hands and kissed her. "I don't know how to say this," he began in a whisper, when they finally broke apart.

"What?"

"Well, it's like . . . I've never been able to talk to anyone the way I can talk to you."

Joan touched his hand. "What do you mean?"

"Everyone else expects me to be what they want me to be. Mother wants the dutiful son. All the relatives expect me to keep living my father's dream—with the business and everything, I mean." He paused, absent-mindedly kicking at the worn patch of grass beneath the bench.

"Go on," Joan encouraged.

"You like me just as I am," he finished, drawing Joan close again.

Her head rested against Martin's chest, and as it rose and fell with his breathing, Joan thought about what he'd said. He didn't just like her. He liked who he could be when he was with her. The same was true for her. When she was with Martin, she could be the kind of woman she wanted to be.

CHAPTER 13

One Sunday, Joan and Teresa were walking arm in arm to ten o'clock Mass when they passed Martin and his mother coming back from the earlier one. Joan, who was well used to recognizing Martin from a distance, saw them walking up the road toward them. Teresa was chatting away, oblivious to her sister's panic.

"Let's cross over," Joan said, dragging her sister to the opposite side of the road.

Teresa frowned. "Why?"

Joan scrambled for an excuse. "I've been meaning to look at the roses in Mrs. Kane's garden since I saw them on the way home from work the other day."

Teresa shrugged. "All right, then."

Martin spotted them as they began crossing the road. Joan watched him strike up a conversation to distract his mother. She put her head down and kept walking.

They became even warier and began to seek out quiet corners of the park farther from the playing fields. One Saturday, Martin pulled her off the bench. "Come with me," he said, grinning. "I've got a surprise for you."

He took her to a clearing in the shade of the tall rhododendron bushes at the edge of the park. "Close your eyes," he said, leading her by the hand through a gap in the foliage.

"You can open them now."

When she did, Joan saw that Martin had laid out a picnic blanket and a punnet of the first summer strawberries. He sat down and patted the blanket next to him. Joan knelt beside him, leaned forward, and kissed him. "How did you find this place?"

"It took some doing!" Martin replied. Then he was serious for a second. "Will you do something for me, Joan?"

"That depends."

"Can I see your hair down?"

Joan said nothing, she just pulled at the green satin ribbon and shook her hair loose, without looking away.

"It's even more beautiful than I thought," Martin whispered, reaching out a hand and running his palm from the crown of her head to the small of her back. Joan leaned into him, and they lay back together on the blanket. His kisses, tender at first, became more urgent.

"Maybe we should slow down, Martin."

"Of course, of course," he said, flustered. "But you're not making this easy looking like that, Joan Quinn."

They lay, holding each other, until long after they heard the sound of a referee's full-time whistle in the distance. Then Martin rolled up the picnic blanket and threw the last of the strawberries into the bushes for the birds. They walked out from behind the undergrowth, hand in hand, nearly colliding with a woman walking a couple of lively Labradors.

"Sorry about that. They can't wait to get going today." The woman pulled on the leads to make the dogs heel, then looked up, smiling. "Oh, it's you, Martin!" Her eyes moved to Joan, and to the dried grass caught in her long dark hair. "Lovely day, isn't it?"

Martin dropped Joan's hand. "Yes, yes, lovely day for a walk,

Mrs. O'Rourke," he shot back, a little too quickly, his face scarlet. "Cheerio now." His pace quickened as he hurried away.

Joan struggled to keep up with him. "Who was that?" she whispered under her breath, though the woman was out of earshot.

A pained look crossed his face. "Our next-door neighbor, Mrs. O'Rourke."

"Maybe she'll forget she saw us and say nothing." Even as the words left Joan's mouth they both knew that would never be true.

The following Saturday, Martin sat down on the bench next to Joan with a thump. Joan shivered against the cloudy day and his chilly mood. "She knows, then."

He nodded. "She went berserk. Apparently, my father would turn in his grave if he knew I'd disobeyed her. She's sending me away at the end of the summer, Joan."

Joan's heart raced.

"It's all arranged. I'm off to London for a year in September to study accountancy," he continued, through gritted teeth. "But it's really to get you out of my system. And she's put her foot down. I'm not to go anywhere near you or this park in the meantime."

Joan's eyes were wide with disbelief. Her stomach twisted into an anxious knot as her hopes for a future with Martin evaporated into the ether.

"I wouldn't put it past her to have followed me here," he complained, slamming his fist into his thigh.

Joan watched a lone sparrow hopping along the edge of the field. "Is that what you want?"

Martin took hold of both her shoulders and spun her to face him. "Of course not. You know I'm mad about you, Joan. But what option do I have?"

Joan stayed quiet. Despite everything, Martin was as trapped by his sense of duty to his widowed mother as she was on the Cranmore estate. A gilded cage still had bars. Could this really be how it was going to end?

Martin's eyes pleaded with her. "I'll write to you from London, Joan, and once I'm back home . . ." He didn't finish the sentence. Joan shook her head in disbelief. "And we still have next week," he said.

She frowned. "What do you mean? I thought you said—"

"Mother is off to a wedding in Kilkenny next Saturday," Martin interrupted. "She'll be gone all day, and she's staying with her cousins overnight."

Joan didn't know what to say, let alone think or feel.

"Promise me you'll be here next week, Joan."

"I'm not sure," Joan said, looking down at her feet, not knowing if her heart was angry or just aching. They walked in silence to the edge of the playing fields without touching and parted ways before reaching the empty expanse of grass.

Joan kept her eyes firmly fixed on the path ahead of her as she walked home, her mind still on the conversation with Martin. She was home earlier than usual and found Teresa sitting in the armchair sewing a button on her good coat.

"Did he stand you up?" Teresa said, laughing.

Joan's heart leaped. "What are you talking about?" she snapped.

Teresa flinched. "Just joking," she said warily.

Of course she was, Joan realized. Teresa hadn't a clue about Martin. "Sorry," she said. "My mind was elsewhere. I had no idea what you were on about. Where's Da?"

"Still sleeping it off upstairs." Teresa rolled her eyes.

"Bed is the best place for him, then," Joan said. "Fancy some soup before you go out?"

"As long as you're making it, I'm happy to eat it," Teresa said.

After they'd eaten, Joan poured hot water onto their dirty bowls and tossed a tea towel in her sister's direction. "I'll wash, you dry."

Teresa hummed while they worked.

"Looking forward to your night out, then?" Joan asked.

"How can you tell?" Teresa said, elbowing her in the ribs.

They heard a squeak of bedsprings and the thud of feet on floorboards, and stopped talking, exchanged a wary look, and listened out for Da's footsteps on the stairs. Moments later, he stumbled into the scullery, bleary-eyed, in stockinged feet, reeking of sweat and stale beer.

"What's for dinner?"

"We left you some soup," Joan said, gingerly.

Da lifted the lid on the pan and sniffed. His face soured. "I suppose it'll have to do," he grumbled.

Joan's insides contracted as she ladled soup into Da's bowl. "Come on now, Da. We're all doing our best." The hour in bed hadn't improved his mood. She set the bowl of steaming soup and a clean spoon on the table.

Da pulled out the chair and sat down with a thump, staring at the bowl. "What's this?" he glowered, stirring the diced turnip and carrots.

"Vegetable—"

"I can't eat this," he protested, flinging his spoon down. "It's not enough to keep a grown man going."

Teresa folded the tea towel at the sink. "Beggars can't be choosers," she muttered under her breath.

"What did you say?" Da was on his feet so fast he almost sent the chair flying. "Who the fuck are you calling a beggar, you cheeky little bitch?!"

Teresa stepped back while Joan moved a step closer to Da. The smell of drink off him was overpowering. "She didn't mean anything by it, Da," Joan said, putting a steadying hand on his shoulder. "Here, sit down now and get this into you. Would you like a bit of bread with it?" She kept her eyes on both Da and Teresa as she backed into the scullery to get the bread.

"I know exactly what she meant," he said, as he lowered himself into his chair. "And I've had enough of her back chat. Do you hear me?"

Teresa inched toward the door. Suddenly, Da sprang to his feet and hurled the bowl at her. She ducked in time for it to smash against the wall behind her head, then screamed and clutched her arm. Shattered pottery and molten soup splattered the walls and the concrete floor.

Joan covered her mouth with her hands.

"Shut up, will you? And get this bloody mess cleaned up." Da shoved past Joan and stormed through the sitting room and toward the stairs.

Teresa crunched through the broken shards of pottery and turned on the tap, running cold water over her scalded arm. Joan rushed to her. "Jesus, Teresa! Are you okay? Let me see." Her heart hammered as she examined the red skin on her sister's arm.

Teresa winced. "It'll be okay." Despite her attempt to play it down, she was still shaking, and Joan saw terror in her eyes. Neither sister wanted to admit to the other their darkest fear: that one day Da might do worse than they dared imagine even now.

"Come on," Joan said. "I'll help you get ready. Don't let him spoil your night out."

When Teresa was gone, Joan swept up the remnants of the broken bowl, mopped the floor, and wiped down the wall. Da would be all apologies in the morning, like always. Voice rasping in his parched throat, elbows planted on the Formica table, head hung in hands. But words alone changed nothing. Promises were broken as easily as they were made. The worry was that he wouldn't stop at breaking bowls.

Joan stood in the kitchen, staring at her reflection in the window, the dark night beyond. This life, tiptoeing around Da, scraping to make ends meet, never having enough—it wasn't what she wanted for herself, or for Teresa. It wasn't the life she had imagined on those glorious Saturday afternoons with Martin, before Molly Egan trespassed on their dreams.

There was no way on God's earth Joan was going to let herself end up with some drunk who couldn't put food in the mouths of the children he would happily put in her belly. She wasn't about to allow Martin to get on that boat to England without showing him how much she loved him. He wanted her, and she wanted him. That was what mattered. They didn't have to give up on their dream of a life together. They just needed to follow their hearts.

CHAPTER 14

Granny's words about Ma's "only mistake" had stayed with Joan. But in time, as she turned those words over and over in her mind, she came to believe that Granny had it all wrong. She said that Ma's only blunder had been getting into trouble before she was married.

But it was more than that. Ma hadn't stopped to think about *who* she got into trouble with. She'd fallen for the wrong man. That was a mistake Joan wasn't about to make. Martin was different, nothing like any of the fellas she knew. He was mad about her too. She couldn't let his mother come between them. *We still have next week*, he'd said. One last Saturday. It was Joan's last chance to help him see they were meant for each other.

The following Monday morning, she waited at the corner of Grove Square until she saw Martin dawdling up the street, his head down and schoolbag draped across his body. She stepped from behind the hedge that shielded her from view. "Martin!"

He hurried across to her, looking over his shoulder. "What are you doing, Joan? God knows what my mother will do if she finds out."

Joan put a finger to his lips. "It's okay," she soothed. "It'll only take a minute." She scanned the street before going on. "It's about

Saturday. Why don't we meet at your place? Instead of at the park, I mean." Martin seemed confused. "You can show me that view of the factory you're always going on about."

Martin hesitated. Joan took his hand in hers and waited.

"What if the neighbors see you?" he said.

Joan was two steps ahead of him. "I could come through the back gate. That way, nobody would see me. Nobody would ever have to know."

The following Saturday, Joan took her time buttoning her red sleeveless summer dress in front of the bedroom mirror and stood with hands on her hips, examining her reflection. The dress hugged her figure in all the right places; its wide skirt swung as she moved one way, then the other, and it went well with the sandals she'd bought on tick from Sloan's that morning. She left her hair loose, flowing over her bare shoulders. "You'll do," she said, looking at her reflection. This was her one and only chance to make sure Martin wouldn't forget her before he set foot on that boat to England. She wanted to leave him in no doubt that she was his girl.

As she approached the back gate of the big house on Grove Square, she heard Martin's footsteps on the other side of the high stone wall, pacing the path, waiting for her. She allowed herself a half smile as she opened the top two buttons of her dress, exposing a hint of the lace on her bra, before she tapped on the back gate.

When Martin appeared, he couldn't take his eyes off her. As soon as he closed the gate behind them, she kissed him hard on the mouth. She felt his surprise when her tongue searched for his, but he did not pull away.

Joan let him lead her by the hand up the garden, past the flower beds where sweet peas had just come into bloom, and into the house. He turned to her as they entered the kitchen. "Can I get you anything? I mean, a drink or something?" He blushed. "We have red lemonade."

"That would be lovely," Joan said.

His hands were shaking as he poured the fizzy liquid into two tall glasses. "Would you like to sit down?" he said, pointing to a pinewood chair at the table.

Joan walked toward him and took one of the glasses from his hand. She put it to her lips, sipping her drink while he watched her. "I don't want to sit down," she said, taking the other glass of lemonade from him and setting it down on the table.

Martin pulled her to him. His lips were on hers, her fingers in his hair. He was breathing hard.

"Now, how about showing me that view from your room?" Joan said when they finally broke apart.

"Do you want to?" Martin asked. Joan nodded.

Her heels struck the hall's mahogany floor as she crossed to the staircase, which wound up one flight, then another to Martin's room. He led her by the hand to the window. "There," he said, standing behind her, pointing over the treetops to the factory chimneys in the distance. "Can you see it?"

"You can't miss it," Joan said.

"True," he replied. "No wonder I can't get you out of my mind. Whenever I look out this window, all I can think of is being with you."

She leaned against him, drawing both his arms around her. He planted a kiss on her bare shoulder. "Is that what you want?" she asked. "To be with me, I mean?"

"More than anything I've ever wanted," he said.

She turned to face him. "But look at us, Martin. We're from two different worlds." She gestured at his room.

"You don't belong there," he replied, nodding toward the window to the factory and the housing estate beyond. "You belong with me."

Joan lay back on the blue candlewick bedspread, and Martin lay down beside her. He kissed her impatiently, the soft stubble on his chin scratching her cheek. She shifted into him. His breath quickened as he rolled onto her, fumbling with his belt buckle. The sharp edge of it grazed her hip through the fine fabric of her dress, but she didn't flinch; instead she reached down to help him undo the belt and kissed him harder. Wordlessly, she pushed her white cotton knickers down over her ankles and pulled him closer. He hesitated for a split second. "It'll be all right," she said. "It's just the once."

"You're sure?" he asked, searching her face.

"Yes," she whispered, then closed her eyes, not knowing what to expect. She held still and squeezed her eyes tight when he entered her. She wanted him to feel with his entire being that she was the one, despite everything she was not. If she could have breathed a word of what happened that afternoon to anyone, she'd have told Esther Molloy that what she'd suspected was true. It *was* nice. Nice to feel wanted and to be held afterwards, safe in the crook of the arm of a man who loved you above all else.

If she got pregnant, people would blame her and her alone. They'd have no sympathy for a floozy who got caught out with a respectable young man. Nobody would blame Martin in the slightest if he chose not to stand by the young wan who dropped her knickers for him. No, they would blame—not pity—her.

None of this troubled Joan as she lay there under him when he stopped pushing into her and his breathing slowed. She would never again have to give a damn about what anyone thought of her once Martin Egan came back to her from London and put a wedding ring on her finger. She nuzzled into his neck, kissing him behind the ear as he dozed next to her.

Joan slid out of the bed and across the landing to the bathroom. She checked herself in the mirror. Her face bore no clues as to the events of the past half hour. Her eyes did not betray her secret. There had been no lipstick to smudge or mascara to run. She had never needed war paint. She leaned forward to examine a small frown between her eyebrows. It was only when she stood back to smooth the rumpled skirt of her dress that she caught sight of her feet, still strapped into the red patent-leather sandals she'd be paying for by the week long after Martin had left for England.

The floorboards creaked as Martin moved around the bedroom opposite then headed down the stairs. She splashed cool water on her face and dabbed it dry with the freshly laundered towel Mrs. Egan would have folded over the rail the night before. It smelled of lily of the valley.

She could hear Martin down in the kitchen, whistling. Maybe he was drinking his glass of red lemonade. She tucked her hair behind her ears. *Breathe, Joan, breathe,* she told herself as she opened the bathroom door. She scanned the bedroom, straightening Martin's bedspread and making sure to leave no trace of herself there for Mrs. Egan, who would be halfway through a turkey and ham dinner at the hotel in Kilkenny, to find.

It was gone dark when Martin undid the bolt on the back gate to let her sneak out into the night. He pulled her back, pressing her against him for a last kiss.

"I don't want you to go," he murmured into the shadows.

"Me neither," Joan said, trying to read the expression on his face in the moonlight. "Do you wish we hadn't?" she asked, knowing the answer full well.

"No. Do you?" he said, running his hand through her hair.

"Course not," she replied, bringing the tips of her fingers to his lips. He kissed them, then took her hand, shaking his head. "This isn't right," he said. "Why shouldn't we be together?"

"What do you want to do?" Joan said.

Martin hesitated. "I want you to wait for me until I get back from London," he said, his eyes searching hers. "And I want to keep seeing you before I go. Will you meet me on Saturday in St. Stephen's Green?"

"Yes, you know I will. Are you sure you'll be able to get away, though?"

"I'll think up some excuse."

Her heart was suddenly lighter. Things were going to work out after all.

CHAPTER 15

Sometimes Joan woke in the early hours, tormented by the same bad dream. Martin, all decked out in a dress suit and dickie bow, standing at the altar of St. Jude's. Mrs. Egan in the front pew, beaming as the congregation turned to see her son's bride appearing in the church doorway. The organist playing the "Wedding March." The bridesmaid straightening the hem of the bride's dress. The nightmare always ended the same way: with the red lipsticked smile of a stranger appearing from under the veil. Martin wasn't marrying Joan after all.

The days at the factory dragged more than she ever thought possible. The laughter of the other girls on their smoke breaks grated on her nerves. The smell of the sugar warming turned her stomach. She'd never said so many prayers in her entire life—if you could call them prayers. They were more like silent bargains with Our Lady, imploring her to intercede on Joan's behalf to God the Father, the Son, and the Holy Spirit. And pleading for her period to come.

Weeks passed, and there was still no sign of it. She didn't need a doctor or a test to confirm what she already knew. She was pregnant with Martin Egan's child. On the way home from work each day, she went to the church to light a candle to St. Anne, the mother of Mary and her own mother's namesake. She got down on her knees and prayed for forgiveness and for Martin's willingness to stand by her. At night in bed, curled up next to Teresa, she imagined the little life growing inside her. Time was running out. She had to tell Martin before he left for London. Surely he wouldn't leave now. He'd want to stay and do the right thing by her and the baby.

JOAN WAITED ALONE ON THE BENCH in St. Stephen's Green where she and Martin had been meeting lately, far from the prying eyes of Harold's Cross. Her fingers fiddled with one of her coat buttons as she watched couples holding hands passing by on their way to Grafton Street. Bloated ducks bobbed about on the surface of the pond, ignoring the crusts thrown for them earlier by children who'd arrived too late in the day.

Vaguely, Joan remembered an August afternoon long ago when she was brought as a child by her mother to do the same—clutching the scraps of stale bread wrapped in wax paper with one hand while Ma gripped her other hand for dear life.

"Be careful, love. Don't fall in."

Joan was so lost in the memory that she didn't see Martin walking across the park toward her. He sat down heavily next to her and let out a long sigh, his hands clasped between his knees, eyes glued to the ripples on the duck pond.

"It'll be September before we know it," he said, looking across at her. "I don't want to go to England without you."

Joan stalled for a second, trying to form the words she needed to say. "Martin"—she couldn't look at him—"I have something to tell you."

"What is it?" he said, picking the peeling green paint on the bench with his thumbnail.

Joan's throat tightened and her voice was little more than a whisper. "I'm pregnant." She waited for the words to sink in.

Martin whipped his head around to face her. "Are you sure?" he stammered.

She lowered her eyes. "It's been too long, Martin. Weeks and weeks."

"Shit!" His head was in his hands now, fingers running through his hair, the color rising in his cheeks. His movements were jerky, panicked even.

"I'm sorry," Joan said, hands gripped so tight in her lap her knuckles grew white. Then she waited, hoping he'd say something, before continuing. "What are we going to do?" She had rehearsed the question over and over in her mind for days: What are we going to do? What are *we* going to do? Now, sitting on the park bench next to Martin in the fading summer light, she realized that he didn't have to do a thing. He was free to get up and walk away, if that was what he chose to do. He didn't have to live with the answer to her question. He could make it go away at a moment's notice, by simply standing up and walking back the way he had come—over the little stone bridge, past the tidy flower beds toward Leeson Street, up the Grand Canal and home again to the even keel of his life on Grove Square. Nothing was inevitable for the child's father. Nothing need change for him.

As much as she believed Martin loved her, as much as she hoped against hope he would support her, she still wasn't sure he would do the right thing. No girl could take it for granted that the man who'd got her in trouble would stand by her. But on that Saturday, when they lay down on Martin's bed together, Joan had been willing to take the risk. It was another Joan entirely who sat on this park bench today, too afraid to meet his eyes.

Despite the warmth of the summer evening, a fearful chill worked its way down her spine. Was this the panic Ma had felt as Joan grew inside her? A sense that she was hemmed in on all sides? That her life from now until the day she died would be defined by a single decision? Watching Martin, she knew that the direction of her life, which had seemed hopeless before meeting him, was completely in his hands.

Martin's foot tapped against the concrete, and she could see his mind working behind that troubled furrow of a brow she knew so well. She was at the mercy of his decision. If he didn't stand by her, she would have no choice but to face Da and beg for his help. Martin's hand on her shoulder brought her back to reality.

"You don't need to worry. You'll be all right, Joan." He cleared his throat and corrected himself: "We'll be all right. I think I know a way we can fix this."

Joan's eyes widened. "I'm keeping the baby, Martin. I wouldn't. I can't."

He shook his head. "Our baby," he said, his expression softening. "And that's not what I meant." He gave her a long look. "Come with me to London."

Relief flooded through her as his plans spilled out: he had money saved, he'd buy her a ticket for the boat, he'd find her a place to live, they'd be a family. She flung her arms around him and buried her face in his neck. She knew now she'd been right to trust in him and their love all along.

PART THREE

CHAPTER 16

Dublin, 1996

Joan was glad of the walk home from the pay phone. She wanted time to go over the conversation with Emma, to cement the details of it in her mind and commit every last word to memory. It was hard to believe it had happened. Stranger still to recall the sound of her daughter's soft London accent, clear as a bell. The voice she should know by heart, oddly alien to her. As she rounded the corner into Grove Square, she slowed down to avoid meeting Clare Barry, who was taking her time getting her shopping out of the boot of her car.

They'd almost been friends, once. Their girls went to the same primary school—Clare's two were a few years older than Carmel. The women sometimes bumped into each other after school, walking home up Harold's Cross Road.

One Friday in summer, as they passed Mulcahy's sweet shop, they gave in to the kids pestering them for an ice cream.

"Go on, then," Clare said, handing fifty pence to her oldest girl. "Just this once. And get one for Carmel."

"Thanks, Clare," Joan said, with a grateful smile.

Once the girls had their choc ices, they walked together across the road to the park. The two women sat next to each other on a bench while the girls licked their ice creams and took turns on the swings. The outing hadn't been planned. It just happened.

Clare took off her cardigan and folded it over her arm. Then she leaned her head of thick red curls back against the bench and closed her eyes. Joan didn't feel relaxed enough in her company to do the same.

"Isn't it a gorgeous day?" Clare said. Her eyelids flickered under the bright afternoon light.

"Please God it keeps up," Joan replied.

"We should enjoy it while we can," Clare said, sitting up again. "Stop that, Frances," she called out to her little one, who was grabbing the swing and arguing about whose go it was next. She turned to Joan, shading her eyes from the sunlight with her hand. "So what did you do before you had Carmel, Joan?"

"I worked down at the yard."

"No, I mean before you were married."

Joan reddened. She didn't usually have to say much about her life before Martin anymore. The locals who didn't already know her were few and far between, and other people rarely inquired about her past. Martin said it was just as well. "I worked at the Royal Candy factory."

"In Accounts?" Clare said.

"No, no." Joan dropped her eyes to the folds of her cotton skirt. "On the assembly line."

Clare cocked her head, all ears now.

"I didn't get to finish school," Joan blurted.

"Ah, I see," Clare replied.

"What about you?" Joan asked, deflecting attention from herself.

"Oh, you know, I spent years studying for a law degree, and look where it got me," Clare said, nodding toward the swings. "Wiping a pair of snotty noses all day long and picking up after the man of the house." She gave a hollow laugh.

It wasn't until they stood up to leave that Joan noticed the purple bruise circling Clare's wrist. "What happened? she asked, pointing to it.

"It's nothing," Clare said, putting on her cardigan and pulling down the sleeve. "I tripped when I was playing doubles at the tennis club last week. Clumsy, really."

"Ah, right," Joan said.

They continued the walk home in silence. The girls ran on ahead of them when they turned into Grove Square.

"Daddy, Daddy!" Frances shrieked as her father pulled alongside in his BMW and wound down the window. He tipped his head to Joan in a wordless greeting. She noticed Clare stiffen.

"You're early, Donal," Clare said, a little flustered.

"I'll see you back at the house," he said, before rolling up the window and driving away.

Clare's pace quickened, and she strode ahead of Joan. "See you around sometime, Joan," she said over her shoulder.

After that, Clare made a point of not stopping to talk to Joan at the school gates.

When Joan mentioned to Martin how strange it was, he told her she should leave well enough alone. What went on in other people's marriages was none of their business. "Sure you're too busy for gossiping with friends anyway," he said.

Now, Joan slipped past Clare unnoticed, hurrying up the driveway before letting herself into the house.

After dinner, she left Martin downstairs watching the nine o'clock news on television. They'd barely said a word to each other all evening. Upstairs in their bedroom, she opened the bottom drawer where the blouses and jumpers she didn't get much wear out of were neatly folded, and reached deep into the back corner, feeling for the small package she'd hidden there. Her heart gave a tiny jolt of relief as her fingertips brushed the corner of the box. She had clearly been worried it wouldn't be there—and had no idea why.

She sat on the bed she'd shared with Martin for thirty years, holding the small, faded package in her hands. Then she tugged on the black ribbon, undoing the knot, then peeled back the paper and took out the blue-velvet box. She inched it open. It had been so long since she'd bought the locket, she'd forgotten what it looked like. Now, seeing the tiny diamond, she remembered exactly what had compelled her to buy it.

She'd been cutting through Johnson's Court, from Grafton Street to George's Street on her way to catch the bus, when the locket in Appleby's window caught her eye. It was heart-shaped and had the birthstone for April, a diamond, in the center. She had surprised herself by pushing the door open, stepping inside the jeweler's darkened interior, and asking to see the locket. And she'd been shocked when, without missing a beat, she calmly told the assistant, "It's for my eldest daughter. She's eighteen next week."

"She's a lucky girl," the assistant said, with a polite smile.

"She doesn't want a party," Joan lied effortlessly, "so I thought I'd get her something special, something she'll always have."

"Well, this is a lovely keepsake," the assistant said, easing the two halves of the locket apart to show Joan the inside. "You see, you can put a picture of yourself on one side and her on the other."

Joan said nothing.

"Will I gift wrap it for you?"

"Yes, please. That would be lovely," Joan said, opening her purse to take out the money Martin had given her to pay the electricity bill. She'd slipped the box into her handbag and hadn't opened it again until now. Not even to show Martin. Not even when she reminded him about April's eighteenth birthday.

Martin had been sitting at his desk, cheese sandwich in one hand, cup of tea in the other. Joan was perched on the side of the desk, her cup cradled in both hands. "She's eighteen today," she said, searching his face. He frowned, not sure what she was talking about. She watched his expression change as the penny dropped.

He stopped chewing and swallowed hard before glancing at the calendar on his desk. Joan reached across and flipped the page over. "April first."

Martin shook his head. "When are you going to let it go, Joan? You can't keep living in the past."

Joan put her mug down with a sigh. "She might come looking for us, Martin. Now that she's eighteen." Panic flitted across his face. "We have to be prepared for that. And don't you think Carmel has a right to know?"

His eyes flashed. "I'm warning you, Joan. Don't you dare breathe a word of this to her. She has her mock exams next week, and I'm not having you upset her."

Joan blinked but stood her ground. "We'll have to tell her one day."

He pushed his chair back from the desk, standing up to his full height, and towered over her. She saw his surly bottom lip and the thunderous look in his eyes as his face came close to hers. "Not if I have anything to do with it!" he threatened, through gritted teeth. "Carmel can never know about what went on back then. Do you hear me?" For a moment Joan thought he might hit her. She was too terrified to do anything but nod. He'd never reacted like this before on the odd occasion the subject of April was raised. She'd never seen him so spooked about the prospect of having her back in their lives.

"Good," Martin said, sitting back down and picking up his sandwich.

Joan wished she had stood up to him back then. She'd believed if she bided her time, he would come around. Now, she traced the smooth edge of the polished silver with her fingertip and wondered which two photos her eldest daughter would have cut into tiny heart shapes to place inside. She had always tried to banish thoughts of her daughter's adoptive parents from her mind, but she couldn't help thinking of them now. She hoped they'd given her a decent life, worried that they hadn't.

Something else niggled. She couldn't put her finger on it, but the timing of Emma's letter didn't quite fit. She would have known who her birth parents were for years. So why was she only contacting them now? Joan snapped the box shut, wrapped it up again, and put it back in its hiding place. She would know the answer to her question soon enough.

Her head was splitting when she woke the following Monday. Even her usual hour of peace and quiet in the conservatory didn't help. She rubbed her temples and willed the fog to clear, but it was pointless. She kept going over her one phone call with Emma. The unfamiliar English accent had thrown her—in her heart she still imagined the daughter she'd given up as hers. The sound of Emma's voice, so foreign to Joan, was evidence that they no longer belonged to each other.

She was in no mood for a cozy family breakfast with Martin and his mother. Martin was sitting at the table prattling on like a big shot to Molly about the contract he'd won the day before. Joan filled the sink with hot water and a squirt of Fairy Liquid—she might as well make a start on the washing up.

"Joan!" Molly shouted in her direction. "You only gave me one bit of toast with my egg!"

Joan gritted her teeth, scrubbed harder at the frying pan, and began counting to ten in her head.

"Joan," Martin called over his shoulder. "Can you stick another bit of toast in for Mother while you're there?" No please or thank you.

Joan ripped off the rubber gloves and flung them into the sink. Soapy water splashed onto the floor as they met their target. "Do it yourself," she said, pushing past the table.

"That's no way to talk to your husband," Molly said.

Joan didn't trust herself to answer. She snatched her coat and handbag from the hall and opened the door.

"Joan?" Martin called, coming into the hall just as she was leaving. "Where are you going?"

"I'm going to open up at the yard with Carmel."

"And what about my hair appointment?" Molly shrieked from the kitchen.

"What about it?" Joan snapped.

Martin frowned, looking at her like she was speaking double Dutch. "You're supposed to take her in an hour."

"You take her. She's *your* mother!" Joan closed the front door behind her and marched down the driveway toward the yard without looking back. Let Martin deal with Molly for a change.

CHAPTER 17

When Carmel flipped the sign on the door of the builders' yard from *Closed* to *Open*, men were already dotted around the courtyard. Some leaned against their vans, arms folded across their chests. Others huddled in pairs, gratefully sucking the nicotine from their first cigarette of the day into their lungs. She glanced at her watch to make sure she wasn't late. No, half seven, bang on time. Her customers were just eager today.

"Morning, gents," she said, smiling, holding the door open to let the first customers of the day into the shop. It was always men at this hour of the morning—stubble-faced, in cement-speckled jeans, flecks of yesterday's paint in their hair. Ready to load up their Hiace vans with supplies: tins of gloss paint, boxes of screws, freshly cut lengths of two-by-four . . . whatever was needed for the job they were on that day.

In winter, they'd wait in their vans with the engines running, heaters on full blast, studying betting odds in newspapers draped across their dashboards and drinking cups of tea from the flasks their wives or mothers had filled for them. On a gorgeous day like today, they were outside, cursing to each other over the football results or the hassle they were having with some auld wan or other who was never satisfied with the work no matter what they did.

They would scan the sky for clouds, glad of the fine day because they had the outside of a house over in Ballsbridge or Foxrock to finish before they could get paid at the end of the week. The money would come in handy to buy new schoolbooks for the kids. "Christ, I could build a fuckin' school for what I have to fork out on books and uniforms for the three of them," Gerry Davy grumbled to John Paul, his apprentice, as they walked across the car park.

But it wasn't a customer who was first in line that day. Des Ryan, the postman, was at the head of the queue, waving the small stack of letters in his hand.

"I'll be with you in a minute, Des."

"No rush," the postman replied, his eyes darting around. "I can see you have your hands full. Your father not with you today?"

Carmel hadn't noticed her mother arriving until Mam stepped out from behind the line of customers waiting to get inside. She held her hand out for the letters. "Let me take those from you, Des."

The postman sniffed, reluctantly handing her the envelopes. "Good job I know where you are," he said, pointing to the address on the envelope at the top of the pile. "Because they certainly don't." Someone at Hurley's, the accountant's, had mistyped their address: Egan & Son Builders Merchants & Suppliers, 202 Ardeer Avenue, Dublin 6, instead of 20–22 Ardeer Avenue. It was the kind of mistake Des delighted in.

"Thanks, Des. What would we do without you to keep us right?" Mam said, a little too sweetly, from behind the counter. Carmel knew her mother didn't have much time for Des—or his gossip for that matter. She went into the tiny office with the letters. It had shrunk every year as the business expanded and they needed more shelf space on the shop floor.

Within minutes she was back by Carmel's side. "Now, who's next?" Mam said. "What can I get you, Larry?"

Some customers were already walking up and down the aisles lined with shelves full of hardware supplies, grabbing what they needed. Many of them knew the layout of the yard almost as well as Carmel did. Almost. Nobody knew every inch of Egans' like her. She'd grown up in the warehouse with sawdust in her hair and paint fumes in her nostrils. The yard was in her blood. Whenever she tried to imagine a life without it, she failed. The business was just too big a part of her.

"Got everything you need, Gerry?" she asked the man balancing a length of wood, two tins of undercoat, paintbrushes, and a packet of wallpaper paste in his arms.

He stepped forward. "I think so, Carmel. I've got to hit the road before the traffic gets bad. I'm on a job all the way out in Castle-knock for a professor from Trinity." He shook his head as he checked his watch. "Bloody Dublin Corporation, they'd want to do some-thing about those roads. They're a bloody disgrace."

There was a chorus of agreement in the queue behind him. Gerry hoisted the wood over his shoulder with one hand, pressing crumpled notes into Carmel's hand with the other.

"I hear you, Gerry," she said. "Here's your change, thanks."

With her mother beside her, they made short work of the queue of customers. This was them at their best, Carmel thought, working in harmony, shoulder to shoulder in a way they could never quite manage face-to-face.

"Fancy a cuppa, Mam?" she asked, when things quietened down.

"Love one."

When Carmel came back from the kitchen, she handed Mam a milky tea in the mug she'd given her last Mother's Day. The words *I'm Glad You're My Mum* were printed in cursive black writing across the front.

Carmel would never forget the night she'd bought it. She was in Eason's the evening before Mother's Day, with the fellas who always left things to the last minute, idly spinning the card rack waiting for inspiration to strike. The mug was perched on a display next to the cash register. It caught Carmel's eye as she was paying for the card she'd chosen. She was only looking. She hadn't meant to reach for it.

"It's gorgeous, isn't it?" the girl behind the counter gushed. "Your ma will be delighted with it. Want me to wrap it for you?"

Carmel couldn't take her eyes off the words. She was struck by the fact that she'd never said them to her mother. She couldn't even remember thinking them. Not once. Not ever. And standing there at Eason's checkout she wondered if she ever would. The shop assistant was waiting—her palm outstretched, jaws working the gum in her mouth—for Carmel to hand the mug over so she could ring it up. "No need to wrap it," she said, passing it to her. "I'll take it as it is."

She had been taken aback by her mother's tears when she opened the present the following morning. Not floods of distressed tears or shining tears of joy. Just two fat tears that rolled unchecked down her cheeks to her chin before she brushed them away with the back of her hand. "Thank you," she said, without looking up. Those silent tears still baffled her. It was the closest they would probably ever come to saying "I love you."

For as long as Carmel could remember, there had been this distance between them. It was as if an invisible wall had built up, brick by brick, and neither of them had a clue how to begin either scaling or dismantling it. Sometimes she wondered how to bridge the divide, but it would take two of them to rebuild the relationship, and her mother seemed content with things as they were.

Mam was sitting at the desk in the office, sipping her tea. She picked up one of the letters from the desk and turned the envelope over in her hand. "When will your father ever get around to changing the business name? I've told him umpteen times since you started working here. But there it is, still, in black and white. Egan & Son."

Carmel shook her head. "You're not still on about that, are you,

Mam? What difference does it make whether the sign over the door says Egan & Son or Egan & Daughter?"

"He should give credit where credit is due, Carmel. That's all I'm saying." Carmel opened the filing cabinet and began slotting receipts into files in alphabetical order. "I know it'll all go to you one day when we're gone, but . . ." Mam's voice trailed off.

Carmel stopped what she was doing and turned to her. "Don't start going on about how much money I'll have when you've all kicked the bucket," she said, jokingly. "I get enough of that from Granny. What good will money be to me without family?"

Mam stood, grabbing her mug from the desk. "Don't you ever underestimate the privilege of your independence, young lady," she snapped. "Not everyone has the freedom to thumb their nose at security."

Carmel gave her a quizzical look. "Now you've lost me." Her mother tutted, shaking her head, before leaving the room.

Carmel watched her go, mulling over the last moments of the conversation in her mind. What did she do wrong? What did she say? Why the hell couldn't they get along for more than five minutes? She slammed the drawer of the filing cabinet shut. "I give up!" she declared to no one but the magpie sitting alone on the tree outside the window of the empty office.

CHAPTER 18

Martin sauntered through the front of the yard after lunch. "Sorry I'm late," he said to Carmel. "I got delayed at the hairdresser's with your granny, and then I had my meeting." He eyed Joan as he came behind the counter. "Anyway, how's my two favorite girls?" He was acting as if Joan's outburst that morning had never happened.

"If the look on your face is anything to go by, Da, I'd say we won that contract," Carmel said.

"And you'd be right. They want us to supply everything from nails to wallpaper for the entire apartment block. That's us set up for next year!"

"That's great news, isn't it, Mam?" Carmel said, glancing at Joan.

Joan didn't say a word. She turned on her heel and walked away toward the office without looking at either of them. To hell with Martin, carrying on as if all was right with the world, crowing about raking in more money.

"What's wrong with Mam?" she heard Carmel ask as she left.

Martin followed her into the office, shutting the door behind him. He paced around in circles like a man possessed. "When are you going to stop acting like this?" he complained.

"Like what, Martin?"

"Like a kid who's been told Christmas is canceled."

"Oh, right! I'm supposed to just ignore my own daughter. Pretend she never happened, deny her existence," Joan fumed.

"Well, you've had plenty of practice. You never had any trouble ignoring the one that was right under your nose all these years!" Martin shot back.

His words knocked the wind out of Joan. She stiffened, color rising in her cheeks. The quiet resentment smoldering between them for years had erupted in his venomous words. He could never take them back. "That was below the belt, Martin. Even for you," she said, already making for the door.

"Wait, Joan! I'm sorry."

She stopped before opening it. "I'm going to meet her this weekend," she said, her back still to him. "It's not too late to change your mind if you want to come with me." She closed the office door, pausing to lean against it for a moment before continuing down the corridor. She listened for Martin's footsteps, but he didn't follow her. That was him all over. Hoping if he laid low and ignored things she'd just move on. Joan was sick and tired of just moving on.

She passed the entrance to the shop on her way out the back to get some fresh air. Carmel was speaking to a customer who was choosing paint colors for her bathroom.

"I'm not sure if I should go rose white or apple white. What do you think, Carmel?"

Joan slowed down to listen. She could see Carmel, head on one side, holding the color chart, giving this stranger her undivided attention. *She is the kindest person I know,* Joan thought, her eyes filling with tears. She deserved a mother who would have told her that.

It was just the two of them now, at the end of the day. From the office, the only sound Joan could hear was the clink of coins as Carmel cashed up. Martin had gone to do a delivery. The men from the warehouse were off home to their wives and kids.

She got the urge to go to her daughter—just as she'd often done after Carmel had gone to bed at night when she was small. Joan would creep into her bedroom and watch the steady rise and fall of her daughter's chest while she slept, sprawled like a stranded starfish in pink flannel pajamas, and promise herself she'd do better tomorrow.

Now Joan wandered out into the passage between the office and the shop and stood, watching her daughter stacking coins on the counter. Carmel, sensing someone was behind her, turned to face her. "What?" she said, a frown creasing her forehead.

Joan hesitated. "Did we have a good day, then?" she asked, nodding to the neat stacks of coins.

Carmel took a second to answer. "Not bad for a Monday." A moment of silent understanding passed between them. They both knew Joan hadn't been thinking about the day's takings. Carmel closed the drawer of the register and took a step toward her. "Mam, are you okay?"

Joan was instantly on her guard. "I'm fine. Everything's fine. Why do you ask?"

Carmel shook her head. "Oh, no reason. It's just you and Dad have been a bit funny with each other these past few days. I wondered if something was up."

This was her chance. She could sit Carmel down, right here and now, and tell her everything. Who could stop her? She hesitated, looking away, so Carmel wouldn't see the anguish in her eyes. "Did you ask your father?"

Carmel was quiet.

"Of course you did. And what did he say?"

"Just that it would blow over."

"Did he now?"

Carmel took a step back, raising her right hand as if she was about to swear an oath on the Bible. "Look, Mam, I don't want to come between you. It's just—"

"You wouldn't understand. How could you?" Joan could hear the blame in her voice, rising with every word. She had Carmel's full attention now.

"What do you mean, 'How could I?' You haven't given me a chance!"

Carmel's words stung Joan like a slap. It was true. She hadn't ever given Carmel a chance. Not since day one. She'd built an impenetrable wall around herself so solid it didn't even let the people she loved in. She hesitated for a second but then started backing away before the tears came. She didn't know what to say, couldn't get the words out. There was simply too much ground to cover.

She shook her head. "I can't . . . I'm sorry, Carmel. For everything. All of it." And she bolted out the door.

CHAPTER 19

It was the morning of her meeting with Emma. Joan's nerves were already at her, and she hadn't even made it out of the house. The bed was littered with the different combinations of skirts and blouses she'd tried on and discarded. She wanted to make a good first impression, but nothing felt right. Was it any wonder her stomach was in knots? It wasn't every day you met your daughter for the first time in thirty years. More than anything she wanted Emma to at least like her. That would be a good start.

Was Emma feeling the same way as she got ready in her hotel room? Would she be trying to convince herself that the right scarf, earrings, or shade of lipstick would somehow make her feel like she was putting her best foot forward? Like everything else about her daughter that remained a mystery to her, Joan had no way of knowing.

THEY'D AGREED TO MEET OUTSIDE BEWLEY'S café on Grafton Street, so neither of them would have to go in alone. Looking lost while you scanned the sea of faces chatting over their cups of Breakfast Blend and cherry buns was a surefire way to draw attention to yourself. That was the last thing Joan wanted. She recognized Emma immediately—not just because she'd inherited her dark hair and green eyes from Joan's side of the family. The way she stood against the café window, anxiously scanning the street left and right, like a newly arrived stranger out of place in an unfamiliar city, gave her away.

Joan stopped for a second at a safe distance to compose herself before approaching and tapping Emma lightly on the shoulder. "Hello, love."

Emma started and then, turning, half smiled. "Hello, eh . . . Joan?"

There was an awkward moment when they couldn't decide whether to hug. But the moment passed.

"Let me look at you," Joan said, taking a step back and briefly taking Emma's cold hands in hers. Her eyes filled, and she blinked the tears away. *Don't start, Joan. Don't you dare cry. Don't make a show of yourself in public.* "Will we go in and get a table before they get too busy?"

Inside, Bewley's was all soft jazz and the clinking of spoons in cups, mellow light through stained glass, the heady smell of coffee roasting. The waitress showed them to a quiet corner table she'd just cleared after the breakfast rush. The early risers had begun to head off, and the staff were regrouping before the morning-coffee crowd arrived.

Neither of them was hungry, but they went through the motions of looking at the menu to occupy those first difficult minutes and ordered fruit scones with their tea anyway. They must have looked like any other mother and daughter out for a day's shopping in the city.

Joan filled the awkward silences with small talk. She unzipped her handbag and took out the photos she'd brought to show Emma, sliding them sheepishly across the table like a bad hand of cards she wasn't sure she wanted to show.

"That's a picture of your father in the garden taken a couple of summers ago." She watched Emma studying the images in front of her. "And this is Carmel—your . . . sister. We only had one more child in the end." Joan pointed to the picture of her daughter taken on the bank-holiday weekend they'd all spent in Kerry two years before. It had lashed rain the entire time, and this was one of the few photos they'd been able to take on the only dry afternoon. Carmel in her blue anorak, walking barefoot on Inch Beach, glancing back over her shoulder and smiling at them.

Emma leaned forward and picked up the photo. "You didn't want any more children, then? After Carmel, I mean?" she said, looking up.

"We couldn't have any more."

Emma replaced the photo on the table between them. "She doesn't know. Does she?"

Joan shook her head and lowered her eyes. "There never seemed to be the right time."

Emma nodded slowly. But said nothing more.

"This place hasn't changed in years," Joan said, taking in the room, but she trailed off when she noticed Emma staring into the cup she held between her hands. *Easy does it*, she thought. *Don't expect miracles. Give the girl a chance.*

Still, she hadn't imagined Emma would have so little to say, so little to ask. Joan had a million and one unanswered questions she hoped might span the space and time that lay uneasily between them. What had Emma's life growing up in England been like? Had her parents loved her? How did she get on at school? Who were her friends? How had she met her husband? Joan had forgotten his name. She wanted to know all of it in good time. Deep down, there was only one question she wanted to know the answer to now. Was Emma happy? Had she been happy all these years?

Joan was ready for the one question she was sure Emma would ask her: Why? When she started rehearsing her answer, after their first phone call, she realized she didn't have to rehearse at all. She'd been going over and over it in her mind for years. She was prepared and ready to explain, to justify her actions.

To her surprise Emma never asked that question. Instead, she said something Joan wasn't expecting. "I wasn't completely honest with you in my letter, Joan." Emma took a sip of tea. Joan waited, heart quickening. "I've known I was adopted for years. I've had access to my records since I was eighteen."

Joan's mouth was suddenly dry. She lifted the empty cup to her lips.

"Can I get you another pot?" the waitress asked, right on cue.

"Yes, yes . . . please," Joan said, as the waitress picked up the empty teapot and began weaving her way through the tables.

Joan thought about all the times Emma might have walked into their lives over the past dozen years. The lost Christmases and birthdays they could have had together. She could have reached out to them years ago, yet she'd done nothing. Not a damn thing.

Joan didn't know why she was suddenly fearful, then furious. She tried to keep the irritation from her voice. "Why didn't you get in touch back then?"

"Because I couldn't risk it—the rejection," Emma said, looking away. "I guess I didn't trust you not to do that to me again. I didn't want to give you the chance."

Joan wanted to run from these words, but she sat bolt upright instead, perfectly still. Emma's eyes met hers. "When you first find out you're adopted, all sorts of things go through your mind. You flip back and forth between possible stories to own, each one more terrible than the last. Did my mother die in childbirth? Was I the result of a one-night stand or, worse, a violent crime?"

She ran her index finger around the rim of her teacup. "It was easier to live with the way things were than to go in search of a happy ending."

Joan opened her mouth to speak and then closed it again.

"Every scenario I dreamed up was about all the reasons why you couldn't possibly keep me. When I eventually discovered you and Martin were still together—that you got married—well, that wasn't a story I had bargained for." Emma kept her eyes on her plate, picking at a raisin in the scone she hadn't touched.

"Nothing prepared me for discovering that you could have . . . that the two of you were happily married and prosperous, getting on with your lives together as if I'd never happened. Somehow that made everything worse." Emma's voice was beginning to crack. She took another sip from her cup.

Joan couldn't look at her.

"I always believed you had no choice, took comfort from it, I suppose. But knowing Martin stood by you, that you just moved on, came back here, and lived happily ever after, as if I never existed, hurt more than anything I could have imagined."

Joan swallowed and reached a hand across the table. "Emma . . ." she began.

Emma slid her hands out of Joan's reach and placed them on her lap. She stared down at them, and her eyes filled with tears. "It's okay. You don't have to explain. I'm sure you had your reasons. None of it matters now anyway, in the scheme of things."

"What do you mean? Of course it matters. You're entitled to—"

"I mean your reasons. They're not important. The only thing I care about now is Ben." Emma looked up and saw the question in Joan's eyes. She reached into her bag. "You have a grandson, Joan. This is Ben." She handed over a photo.

Joan held the photograph, but she couldn't make Ben out through her tears. She blinked hard. The boy with the blond fringe in the photo was about three or four. He grinned from the seat of his yellow trike next to an enormous Christmas tree swathed in tinsel. "He's gorgeous, Emma," Joan finally managed. "So full of life."

Emma shook her head. "He's got leukemia, Joan. He's dying."

Joan dropped the photo on the table. "No," she whispered.

"I need your help. He needs a bone marrow transplant, and neither Matt nor I are a match. The hospital has thousands of potential donors on its database, and none are compatible. Neither are Matt's family. But there's a chance that you"—she hesitated before going on—"Martin, or maybe even Carmel might be. I didn't want to come, Joan, but when the doctors told us there was nothing more they could do . . . You might be his last chance."

CHAPTER 20

Martin sat on the edge of the bed, his back to Joan, taking his boots off. His slouched shoulders gave him the look of a man who'd had a long hard day he wished would come to an end. From where she stood at the bedroom door, Joan could see sawdust in his hair.

The memory of the tousled blond man who made love to her, there, on that bed, all those years ago came back to her, and she had the impulse to go to him. She wanted to be held by him again—the way he held her when they were in love. She wanted to turn back the clock, to a time when she never doubted him.

"Well?" he said, without turning to look at her.

She walked around the bed and sat next to him. The mattress dipped under their weight. He gave her a sideways glance, and she placed her hand on his knee and left it there. What was the sense in arguing now? There was too much at stake. Their grandson's life was on the line.

"You'd like her," she whispered, her fingers making small circles on his knee. Martin was rigid. "She looks nothing like Carmel," she continued.

"Stop. Just stop it, Joan. That's enough," he said, pushing her hand away.

"Martin, she needs our help."

He turned to look at Joan now, a frown knitting his eyebrows, their faces so close she could feel his breath. "What kind of help?" he sneered.

God, he sounds just like his mother, Joan thought. This was the kind of twisted assumption Molly would make: that people were only after whatever they could get. But she couldn't afford to antagonize Martin, not now. What he needed was reassurance, as he always did, that his good name and all he'd built were safe.

"It's not what you think. She's not after your money."

"What else could she possibly want after all this time?"

"She's got a little boy. He's sick. She asked if we'd have a bone marrow test," Joan blurted. She stopped and waited for him to speak. The silence hung heavy in the air between them.

"There must be hundreds of people who could be a match," Martin said at last, shaking his head. "Probably thousands."

"They've searched. They've tried everything. She's only contacting us as a last resort. The doctors normally prefer donors a bit younger than us." Joan stood and began pacing the room, her arms folded tight across her chest. "But they're running out of time."

Martin turned away again. "What did you tell her?"

"I said I'd get tested." She waited. "And that I'd ask you."

He let out a defeated sigh, hands slapping his thighs. "Why did you do that? You know how I feel about this."

Joan froze. "Because I thought this . . . he . . . Ben"—the words caught in her throat—"changed things." Martin chewed on his thumbnail. She could see his mind working overtime. "Please, Martin. We could keep it to ourselves. Nobody would have to know." His brow furrowed. He was wavering. He would give in. She was sure of it.

He got up and pulled his favorite blue-checked shirt from the neatly folded pile in the drawer, then turned to face her, steely-eyed.

"You couldn't leave well enough alone, could you?" he said. "Well, you can do what you want, Joan. But don't drag me into it." He moved to the wardrobe to choose a jumper. "I have enough on my plate. I warned you. I told you I wanted nothing to do with this."

"I can't believe you'd put your reputation before a little boy's life. This is your grandson we're talking about."

"I've had a bellyful of this!" Martin said, snatching his clean clothes off the bed. "I'm going to have a shower."

Joan shook her head as he brushed past her. "I haven't a clue who you are anymore, Martin," she said to his back as he slammed the door shut behind him.

THE FOLLOWING MONDAY, JOAN TOOK the bus to the Blackrock Clinic, where she'd arranged to have her blood taken—far from the prying eyes and ears of Dr. McBride's surgery in Harold's Cross. The receptionist at the clinic was all polite efficiency, and Joan was glad of the absence of chitchat. The less she had to say the better. She took a seat in the waiting room and filled out the health questionnaire, giving a false name and address, ticking all the yes/no boxes on the form and disclosing only bare-bones details about her previous history.

The television was on, a daytime show—distraction for the disgruntled who'd been kept waiting beyond their appointment time and for the anxious waiting to be tested. A toddler crawled on hands and knees around Joan's chair, choo-chooing a wooden train.

"I'm sorry," his mother apologized.

"Don't be." Joan smiled. "How old is he?"

"Three next month."

"Same age as my grandson," she heard herself say.

"Into everything," the mother said with a smile and a roll of her eyes.

Joan smiled back. What would she know? She didn't have a clue what Ben was like. That was what killed her more than anything else: what could have been—no, what *should* have been, if only she'd had the guts to follow her heart.

Emma's words kept rattling around in her head. The hurt in them. Joan couldn't stand it. Why hadn't she realized how hard it would be for her daughter to find out that she and Martin were still together? Well, today was the first step to making things right. Things would be different once Ben was well again. Then they'd all have a second chance.

The nurse called the fake name Joan had given, and she waved goodbye to the little boy. Inside the windowless white room, she peeled off her cardigan and politely answered the nurse. Yes, a friend's child in London was sick. They were investigating all avenues. She just wanted to help. No harm trying. It amazed her how easily the lies came, one after the other. *Isn't that just the story of your life, Joan?* she thought. Telling people what they want to hear. She inched her backside onto the examination table, leaving her feet dangling in midair. The doctor washed his hands at the sink in the corner with his back to her. "It's a very kind thing you're doing for your friend, Mrs. Clemence."

"It's the least I could do," Joan said, averting her eyes.

He came over, wrapped a tourniquet around Joan's arm, then snapped on his latex gloves. "Sit still for me, now. That's right, look away. A quick sting." Joan felt the needle pierce her skin. She didn't flinch. Just welcomed the pain. What must little Ben be going through over in London? She tried to remember his face from the photo Emma had shown her. She couldn't. Why hadn't she asked to keep it? Maybe if she'd been able to show it to Martin he'd be here now too.

"You're doing great, just a few more seconds," the doctor said, pulling on the syringe. She held her breath and closed her eyes. What did all those maybes she'd been depending on for years add up to now? Nothing.

"All done!" the doctor said cheerily, upending the small vial of blood between his thumb and forefinger, then dropping his latex gloves into the bin next to his feet. He stood with his back to her, washing his hands again. "That wasn't so bad, was it? We'll phone you with the results by the end of the week."

"Can I call you here at the clinic instead?"

"Yes, I'm sure that will be fine. Just check with the receptionist on your way out."

"Thank you," Joan said, trying to hide her relief. "So what happens if I'm not a match?"

"They'll keep your friend on the register and continue looking. You know, it's a long shot because you're not a blood relative."

Joan's cheeks grew hot. "Yes, yes, I know . . . And, er, what are the chances of matching to blood relatives? A grandad, say, or an auntie?"

"Well, obviously the odds are greater if it's a brother or sister. But any blood relative is a better bet than a complete stranger," he said, dropping a paper towel in the bin. "They'd have tested all the relatives before moving on to friends like yourself, Mrs. Clemence. It's very good of you to do it, although you do know we prefer donors to be younger if possible."

"Yes. But it's worth a try. It's the least I could do."

"Anyway, give us a call on Friday. As I said, we'll have the results for you then."

"Thank you," Joan said, shrugging her shoulders back into her cardigan. Friday. It seemed like an eternity.

She rode home on the upper deck of the number 8 bus; the air was thick with hacking coughs and the smell of damp coats. She rubbed a small peephole in the condensation on the window with her fingertips, and, as she watched pedestrians wrestling umbrellas at the zebra crossing below, her worst fears began to invade her thoughts. What if she wasn't a match? That was a definite possibility. What would she do then? What about Carmel? From what the doctor had told her, there was a reasonable chance Carmel could be a match.

Martin had made his feelings as plain as day, but he couldn't speak for Carmel. It would mean they'd have to tell her the truth, and there was no way Martin would allow that to happen. The bus came to a standstill in Parnell Square. All around Joan passengers gathered up umbrellas and shopping bags. "Last stop! This is the last stop," the driver shouted. Joan hadn't noticed where they were. She gripped the handrail as she followed the others down the stairs. "Miserable fuckin' day, wha'," grumbled the old man in front of her to no one in particular, turning up his coat collar.

Joan found a phone box near the bus terminus. She'd call Emma as arranged and let her know how everything had gone. The call connected and her coins slid into the bowels of the phone. She held her breath, waiting for someone to pick up at the other end. All she wanted was to hear Emma's voice.

CHAPTER 21

It felt good to be outside, even if it was only to take in the washing. Emma put down the empty laundry basket, then tilted her chin to the sky. Her eyes followed the contrails of a low-flying jet overhead. She tried to remember the last time she'd been out here kicking a ball around the garden with Ben. Gone were those normal days she'd taken for granted, and sometimes even resented. There was always a last request for another turn on the slide, one more push on the swing, a final bounce on the trampoline.

Emma reached for a pair of blue-striped socks on the washing line and sighed. What she wouldn't give now to be pestered by Ben for a few extra minutes of fun. What if those last times they'd played together in the garden really were "last times"? Squinting in the low afternoon sun, Emma unpegged and folded Ben's pajamas, then tossed them into the laundry basket. She'd drive herself crazy if she didn't stop thinking like this. Hefting the full basket onto her hip, she headed back inside. There was still time to iron Ben's things before she left for the hospital.

Emma had a good feeling about Joan being a match. What were the chances of her agreeing to meet and be tested so soon? She was surprised at how sympathetic Joan seemed. How concerned and, dare she say it, kind she sounded. Emma had steeled herself for a wall of silence and the sting of further rejection. But Joan was bending over backwards to do what she could to help. It was like all the good omens were stacking up in their favor. Organizing the next steps would be the easy part. She smiled to herself. Emma the Planner, Emma the List-Maker, always prepared, ready for every eventuality—except this one. She was used to taking things one day at a time now. So much so, she hadn't thought past what would happen if Joan wasn't a match.

As she unwound the cord of the iron and plugged it in, her mind was on Joan over in Dublin. She'd promised to let Emma know how the blood test had gone. Not that she'd have any real news. Emma just wanted to make sure it had been done, to keep the lines of communication open. She hoped Martin would take the test too, but since Joan hadn't brought up him or the prospect of that happening, she didn't want to force things. That was something else she'd learned recently. Patience.

She smoothed Ben's pajama bottoms onto the ironing board, gliding the hot iron along each leg. The smell of clean laundry infused the air around her. She worked steadily through the ironing, folding each item before placing it on the pile ready to take to the hospital that night.

Even though she was expecting Joan's call, she jumped when the phone's ringing shattered the silence. She unplugged the iron, leaving the cord dangling, and made a dash for the hall. "Hello? Joan?" Emma heard the rush of traffic in the background. Sounds she didn't recognize from their first call—a busier street, a new location. Joan must be calling from a different phone box. "How did it go?"

"Well. Well. It went well. I should know by Friday, please God," Joan said.

"Thanks for doing this, Joan." Emma wound the telephone cord tightly around her finger, so tight the blood pooled in her fingertip.

"It's the least I could do. I wish . . ." Joan hesitated.

What did she wish? Emma wondered. That she could turn back the clock? How far back would she need to turn it to have lived a life with no regrets? "Joan, I'm sorry. I need to go. Matt's holding the fort at the hospital."

"Right, right, of course. I'll let you go."

"I'm staying with Ben tonight."

"Give him . . ." Joan began, but changed course. "I'll be in touch," she said.

"Bye, Joan. And thanks." Emma heard the click of the receiver being replaced at the other end. Friday would be here before they knew it. They'd waited this long for better news; they could handle another few days. She leaned her back against the wall, and, for the first time, she thought about what it must be like for Joan. Doing all this, presumably in secret. It was unlikely her family and friends knew about the illegitimate daughter she'd given birth to in the sixties. Would Emma still be classed as illegitimate if her birth parents were married? What did it matter in this day and age? Why the hell had it ever mattered?

Back in the kitchen, Emma grabbed a packet of Jaffa Cakes, Ben's favorite, from the pantry, just in case she could persuade him to eat something, and put them into her overnight bag with the freshly pressed laundry. She should give her mother a call to let her know what was happening before relieving Matt at the hospital. No, that wouldn't work: it was her parents' bridge night, and they'd have friends over.

Even though they'd just gone back to Scotland after their visit, she missed them. She wished she could hop in the car and drive across the city to see them at the vicarage like she used to. Dumfries hadn't seemed that far away when they retired, but now, in the middle of this crisis, Emma felt cut off from the two people she needed most. As she drove to the hospital, part of her longed to take a detour and go back to her childhood home, the rambling vicarage at the edge of Waltham Forest in northeast London—and back to a time before she knew anything about birth parents or leukemia.

It hadn't been perfect, but it wasn't the worst place in the world to grow up. Dad was the vicar at St. Andrew's. Mum was forever in the kitchen baking scones and slices, laying everything out on doilies ready for visitors, who often arrived without notice. Their door was always open, and Emma's mother joked that they should have a revolving one installed for the constant stream of committee members, parishioners, and church elders who passed through. Emma wondered how it would have worked, given that they spent the entire winter battling the drafts that snuck under doors and through gaps in the window frames of the crumbling parish house. It wasn't just the adults of the parish who landed on their doorstep. The children came too, to play in the garden with its ancient oak trees to climb and a creaky five-bar wooden gate to swing on. Emma was happy to have playmates, but as an only child she hated sharing her mum and dad with everyone.

The first time she suspected she was partly a secret, she was sitting on her parents' bed watching her mother outline her lips in ruby red. "Mum, how come I have black hair and green eyes?" she asked, head on one side.

Her mother froze, as though caught out, unprepared. Their eyes met in the mirror, and she lowered the lipstick. "Why do you ask, Emmy?"

"Well, all my friends match their mummies and daddies." Emma held her mother's gaze, in the way only a seven-year-old with a nose for a flustered adult can. "Felicity has brown hair, just like her mummy. James has blue eyes, and his daddy does too."

Mum pulled a tissue from the box on the dressing table.

"You don't have black hair like me," Emma continued. "And neither does Daddy."

Her mother gave a little cough. "With so many colors to choose from, why would God limit himself to only creating people who matched?" She folded the tissue in half and placed it between her lips.

The conviction of Mum's words didn't match the hesitation in her voice. It wobbled and wavered. She sounded less like she was explaining and more like she was pleading with Emma to believe her. Mum scrunched the tissue and dropped it into the wastepaper basket next to her dressing table.

"So, some families match and others don't?" Emma quizzed.

"Yes, yes, that's it exactly." Mum was smiling now.

"Okay," Emma said, bouncing up and down on the bed.

"But," Mum said, turning to her, "just because they don't match on the outside doesn't mean they don't match on the inside."

"Oh?" Emma stopped bouncing, her dark pigtails landing on her shoulders.

"Yes, there's always a perfectly shaped place in the mummy's and daddy's hearts that matches a place in their child's heart."

"Sort of like a jigsaw puzzle you can't see?"

"That's it! Just like an invisible jigsaw puzzle."

Emma nodded and began to bounce again.

Poor Mum, who had tried so hard to prepare Emma for a soft landing when they finally broke the news of Emma's adoption to her. Instead she'd given her parents a rough ride, constantly nagging for a little sister and then imploding when she finally discovered the truth. About a month after her thirteenth birthday, Mum and Dad were out at yet another parish meeting. Now that Emma was older, she didn't mind. She enjoyed her own company, and it was Thursday, which meant *Top of the Pops* was on television. She could dance around the living room singing at the top of her lungs as Jimmy Savile counted down the Top Thirty.

Emma shrieked and jumped up and down on the sofa when he announced that Blondie's "Sunday Girl" was number one that week. Then she hopped off the sofa and sat cross-legged on the floor, nose inches from the television screen, admiring Blondie's heavily lined and shimmer-shadowed eyes. God, she wished she could bleach her hair just like Debbie Harry's.

There was no way her parents would let her touch her long black hair. If only she'd inherited their fair coloring, but she looked nothing like them. There it was: that uncomfortable cold feeling in the pit of her stomach. The same feeling she'd had in biology class last term when they were studying genetics and the words "I'm nothing like them" kept popping into her head.

When the song finished, Emma reached over to switch the television off. Then she stood up and wandered through the rooms of the house. First the kitchen, then back to the living room, before finding herself at the door to her father's study, a room she never went into. Not because it was explicitly forbidden, just because it was Dad's space.

She twirled in the swivel chair behind the rosewood desk, drumming her fingers on the armrests. Then, despite knowing she shouldn't go poking around in Dad's things, she opened one of the wooden drawers on the right-hand side of the desk. In it, she found a neat pile of the blue Basildon Bond writing paper and envelopes Dad always used next to a strip of stamps and a small tin of paper clips.

Emma worked her way through the drawers one by one. When she got to the last one, it wouldn't open. There must be a key somewhere. Yes, of course, she'd already come across one in the corner of the top drawer underneath the paper clips. A tiny brass key. Her heart thumped in her chest. She knew she shouldn't be snooping around in Dad's desk, but she couldn't stop. Something was telling her to keep looking.

The bottom drawer didn't glide open like the others had done. It was stiff and stuck. She leaned back, pulling on it with both hands, until it finally budged. Inside smelled musty, like an abandoned room neglected for a long time. There was a single cardboard file box labeled

OFFICIAL DOCUMENTS written in thick black marker in her father's precise hand.

Emma glanced toward the curtained window in front of her. She mustn't worry too much about getting caught. The car's headlights would warn her that her parents were home when they drove up the narrow driveway. She lifted the lid of the box and began riffling through it. She found Mum and Dad's wedding certificate. A copy of Dad's degree in divinity from the University of Edinburgh. And an envelope marked *EMMA*, again written in her dad's clear hand with Parker blue-black ink. It wasn't sealed.

She tipped the contents onto the desk. A yellowed birth certificate for an April Egan, born at the City of London Maternity Hospital to Martin Egan and Joan Quinn. *Who was April Egan?* She noticed the date: April 1st. That was odd. She and April shared the same birthday. The hair stood up on the back of Emma's neck as the truth dawned on her. This was *her* birth certificate.

It took exactly five minutes more to find the rest of the documents that would upend her world. The papers signed by her mother consenting to her adoption. Her case file from the adoption agency. Letters between a convent, the agency, and her new parents. It was all there. Emma couldn't think. She didn't know what to do. She just sat there trembling, with the adoption file in her lap.

In an instant all the pieces of the puzzle came together. The answers to the unanswered questions tumbled over each other. Why her parents had waited so long to have her. Why she bore no resemblance to them. Why she had no brothers and sisters. It all made sense. Why hadn't she seen it before now? The rattle of the study door handle made her jump. Mum was standing on the threshold, still in her mackintosh, hand over her mouth. Their eyes met. Mum stepped toward her. "Emma—" she began.

"Why? Why didn't you tell me?" Emma shouted. Mum kept walking across the room, one arm outstretched, as if she were trying to save someone from drowning.

"I'm sorry, Emma," she said, hesitating before going on. "We were waiting for the right time. When you were older," she continued in a low, calm voice. "So you could understand the whole story."

Emma flashed her mother a furious look and stuck her chin defiantly in the air. "How old did you think I needed to be to know my own story?"

"Old enough to understand that your mother had no choice."

Emma scoffed.

"Old enough to know that we chose you, and that you were wanted. Very, very much."

Emma was on her feet now, pacing back and forth in front of Mum like a caged animal. "And when exactly would have been the right time to tell me that I don't belong to you? That my real mother gave me away? That I was a mistake you and Dad were landed with—like the steak knives no one wanted in the raffle at the church fête?" She was shaking. She stopped to draw breath.

Then Mum was beside her. "That's not true, Emma. We wanted you more than anything in the world."

Emma stood, rigid, arms bolted to her sides. The minute Mum hugged her, her fury evaporated and the hot tears she'd been fighting fell.

Later that night, on the way to the toilet, she overheard her mother whispering to her father as she passed their bedroom door. "It'll be all right. She'll come back to us with more questions when she's ready."

But Emma never did. Whenever either of her parents tried to steer the conversation in the direction of her adoption, she shut them down. It was too painful to think about why her mother hadn't wanted her. No matter what they said or did, no matter how hard they tried, she kept the topic off-limits. Even on the morning after her eighteenth birthday party.

She had been half asleep and didn't notice the box file as she sat down at the table. It had been set next to her place, tied with a black satin ribbon. "What's this?" she asked. "Not another present?!" Mum laid the frying pan down on the stove, then walked over and pulled out the chair next to her.

"It's your story, love," she said. Emma's brow creased, and her eyes darkened. "We could take a look through everything together if you like."

Emma's chair made a scraping noise on the old terra-cotta tiles as she pushed away from the table. "*This* is not my story." She jabbed an accusing finger at the file. "You, me, and Dad. The time we've spent together. The memories we've made. *That's* my story."

Mum started to get up to go to her. "Ah, Emma, but—"

Emma took another step back. "*That*," she said, pointing again, "is just biology." She paused to consider her final words with care. "It is not the making of me," she said, eyes on the floor. "So can we drop it, Mum? Please? I know you're trying to do what you think is right. But surely that's my call now."

"Yes, yes, it is," Mum answered.

Emma walked over to her and squeezed her shoulder. "I couldn't care less about what's inside that box. None of it matters."

"Okay. But you know where it is if you ever change your mind."

EMMA PARKED AT THE HOSPITAL, peering up at the windows above where her little boy was lying, fighting for his life. She'd been so self-righteous at eighteen. Utterly determined in her refusal to acknowledge her roots and in her belief that blood was no thicker than water. Now the universe had played a nasty trick on her, showing her in no uncertain terms just how wrong she was.

CHAPTER 22

Matt was lying on the hospital bed next to Ben, his stockinged feet crossed at the ankles, reading a bedtime story. If it weren't for the drip attached to Ben's arm, Emma might have imagined they were back home on an ordinary evening after bath time. Matt was at the part in the story where Max, the little boy, was sailing back home over a year. He turned the last page and closed the book. "You missed the part where the Wild Things gnashed their terrible teeth," Ben said.

"So I did," Matt replied. "That must mean I owe you another story." How Emma wished they could all sail back over a year like Max.

Once Ben was asleep, they walked hand in hand to the lifts.

"Are you sure you don't want me to stay?" Matt asked as he pressed the button for the lift.

"You'll be back here soon enough," Emma said, laughing. "Remember when we used to say we practically lived here?" Matt nodded. "Well, now we do."

She hadn't meant to cry.

"Aw, babe," Matt said, holding her close.

"It's okay. I'm okay." She sniffed.

"Is it the call with Joan?" Matt asked.

"No, not really. There's nothing new there. She won't know until Friday." Emma pressed her cheek to his chest and thought about it for a moment. "I guess it's just every time I hear her voice I'm reminded of how different things could have been."

"I know." Matt stroked her hair.

"And I don't know whether to be mad or sad."

"It's bound to be hard for you, Em. But right now, we've got to stay positive—for Ben's sake."

Emma took a step back so she could look into his eyes.

"And remember: Joan isn't the end of the line. Your sister—"

Emma shook her head. "One step at a time, love. Okay?"

"You're right," Matt said, holding the tips of her fingers to his lips.

The lift doors opened in front of them.

"Now, go get some shut-eye before your shift tomorrow." Emma pushed Matt into the lift, keeping hold of his hand until the final moment before the door closed. She smiled to herself as she walked back to the ward, thinking about him. If she hadn't made up her mind to become a midwife, they'd never have met.

Her teachers kept telling her she was bright enough to do medicine. But she told them she wanted to go into a profession that was more about life than death. She'd sailed through her training, and when she qualified she landed several job offers. She decided to go for one a little farther from home, at St. Thomas's Hospital.

One Monday morning, in the small hours, she'd bleeped the junior doctor on call to put up a drip for a post-op patient who couldn't keep anything down, and Matt Hudson, shirt crumpled, tie askew, fair hair standing on end, had walked down the corridor and into her life.

"Looks like you've had a weekend of it," she joked.

"Yeah, sorry." He made a face and tugged at his shirt. "If it looks like I've slept in my clothes, it's because I have."

Emma laughed. "Hang in there. Only four hours to go until the handover."

"Then it's breakfast, a long hot shower, and twelve hours of uninterrupted sleep for me. In that order," he said.

"I don't blame you," Emma replied, rubbing her eyes. "Sounds like a dream."

"Why don't you join me?"

Emma's eyes widened. "Excuse me?"

"Oh, God, I meant just for breakfast, of course," Matt clarified, his face coloring. "If you're not doing anything after work, that is."

"Funnily enough, this is the one time I didn't put anything in the diary for first thing Monday morning after a week of night shifts," Emma teased.

"Great, great." Matt smiled back at her. "Will we meet outside the canteen and take it from there?"

As always on a Monday morning after a busy weekend, there were slim pickings in the staff canteen. Matt made a face as they both peered into the bain-maries. "Ugh, I don't much fancy dry bacon and cold toast, do you?"

"Nope," Emma said, shaking her head.

"Well . . ."—Matt hesitated—"I could whip us up some scrambled eggs on toast at my place if you like?"

"You have fresh bread and eggs in your fridge after a weekend on call?" Emma said, raising an eyebrow. "Lead the way." She wasn't sure how she ended up joining Matt for a hot shower after breakfast, then wrapped around him in his bed afterwards, where sleep was the last thing on their minds. That evening, she lay naked in the crook of his arm.

"Do you usually seduce women into your bed on the first date?" she joked, brushing her fingers across his chest.

"Only the eager ones," Matt teased.

"Hey! You got lucky!" Emma laughed and pinched his nipple.

"Caught me in a moment of weakness and extreme exhaustion." Matt scooted away, laughing.

When they were quiet again, he rolled to face her.

"Don't think I don't know it," he said, pushing her fringe out of her eyes.

He proposed to her the following spring on a weekend trip to Paris, and they had a winter wedding a year later. Their friends joked that their romance was a cliché. "All you need now is the 2.4 children and roses around the door." They didn't care.

She was pregnant within months. Emma could still see Matt's anxious face breaking into a grin when she came out of the toilet waving the pregnancy test. The pair of them gaping at the two faint blue lines showing in the small square window. He'd picked her up and spun her around, both of them giddy already.

It wasn't until six or seven months into her pregnancy that she began thinking about her birth mother. "I wonder what it was like for her?" she said to Matt one evening as she lay, head in his lap, on the sofa, hands joined over her belly, waiting to feel the next kick.

"It can't have been easy for a young woman on her own back then, Em. I mean, they didn't even have contraception in Ireland."

"I guess. But she wasn't the only one. Why didn't she tell the father?"

"You could find her and ask."

"No, Matt. No way," Emma said, sitting up to face him. "You know I made up my mind years ago not to go poking around in all that."

"I know, but that was before the baby. I wondered if being pregnant might change things," he said, placing his hand back on her belly.

"Why would it? She's never been here for me. Why would she want to be now?"

Matt stroked the back of her hand with his thumb. "I wasn't

thinking about what *she'd* want, love. I was thinking about what *you* need."

"I've done all right without her up until now," Emma said, turning her head to kiss him gently on the lips.

"She'd be dead proud of you, Em."

"She'd have no right to be."

As her belly grew bigger, Emma found it harder and harder to understand Joan Quinn. And on the day Ben was finally delivered into her arms, two weeks late, she knew for sure that she never would.

They'd named him Benjamin, but from day one he'd just been Ben. Their perfectly happy and healthy little boy, who slept in a room under luminous stars glued to the ceiling, surrounded by storybooks, stuffed animals, and love. He picked up the usual coughs and colds when he started nursery school and began mixing with other kids. Emma was lucky to be working part-time so she could juggle shifts around his snotty noses. But then there was a month when he was sick more often than he was well. He was pale, uncharacteristically listless, and he just didn't seem to be getting better. The antibiotics weren't working.

Emma and Matt stood in the door of his bedroom one night after they'd read him a "last, last" Kipper story before turning out the lights. Matt put his arm around her shoulder, and Emma leaned in.

"I don't know, Em. I don't like the look of him."

"What do you mean?" Emma said, her eyes widening, heart accelerating. "It's just a cold. He'll get over it."

"But it isn't just one. He's had one after the other."

"Him and every other kid at nursery," she said.

"No, Em. This isn't normal. Something doesn't feel right."

"What do you mean?"

"I mean I think it's time we asked for some tests to see what's going on."

Matt drove them to their doctor's surgery the following day. He carried Ben into the waiting room in his arms.

"No harm in doing a few extra tests," Dr. Sadiq said, removing his stethoscope from his ears. "It's always best to be on the safe side. His chest sounds clear," he continued, in a reassuring tone.

Emma flinched when Ben struggled against Matt's hold as the tip of the needle pierced the delicate skin of his arm. It was one thing watching a doctor inserting a needle into a baby who needed treatment at work—that was part of her job—but it was quite another seeing her own child suffer. She wanted to cover her ears against his cries. Instead, she came close, planting small kisses on his forehead and whispering to him, "It's all right, baby. Brave boy. Nearly done."

The blood tests confirmed what they'd known in their hearts but hadn't dared admit. This disease that could have afflicted countless other families had cursed theirs.

"Is there someone with you?" the nurse on the other end of the line had asked when she called to deliver the results.

"Yes, my husband's upstairs with my son," Emma replied, blood rushing to her ears as she backed into the staircase and forced her knees to bend.

"Who was it?" Matt said when he saw her sitting, slumped, on the bottom stair. She couldn't speak. She didn't have to. Her tear-stained face told Matt everything he needed to know.

"They want to admit him right away," she said.

"Of course," Matt said, putting his arm around her. He sat next to her on the stairs, their heads touching, and they cried together. "We'll get through this," he said.

She sniffled. "What choice do we have?"

Later, Emma dialed her parents' number from the pay phone in the hospital foyer and stood with a finger in her ear waiting for one of them to pick up.

"Hi, Mum, it's me," she said, turning to face the wall, her back to the people streaming past on their way to the lifts. "Is Dad there? Good. It's just . . . we've had a bit of bad news. It's Ben." She could hear the panic in her mother's voice.

"No, no, don't do that. Don't come down yet. It's too early to say. They're running some more tests over the next couple of days. Listen, I've got to go, but I'll keep in touch. Thanks, love you too."

Their worry grew with the number of bruises on Ben's arms.

"The prognosis is good if the chemotherapy works, especially for this type of leukemia," Dr. George, the consultant physician, reassured them. "But then you already know that," she said. "The curse of knowledge." She patted Matt on the back as she left the room. "We'll do everything we can for him."

And they had. But nothing so far had worked. Now, a successful bone marrow transplant was the only hope. The day they got the results confirming that neither she nor Matt was a match, Emma wailed in the shower, smashing her fists against the tiled walls. Their families and friends tested negative too. The UK donor databases had also drawn a blank.

The evening that particular piece of bad news was broken to them, they stood shoulder to shoulder, staring out of Ben's hospital room window at the gray rain clouds skimming the roofs of the office buildings opposite.

"What now?" Emma said.

"They'll keep looking. But . . ." Matt hesitated. "There's one thing we haven't tried. I mean, one thing you could do."

"Yes." She nodded. "There is."

"I know it won't be easy," he said quickly.

"Nothing could be worse than this," Emma replied, glancing at their son, who was propped up on pillows in the bed behind them. "Nothing."

Her father had picked up on the first ring. They'd arranged for Emma to call with an update at the same time every evening. "Hello? Emma?" he said without waiting for his daughter to speak.

"Dad, can you come? And can you bring my box with you?" Emma finally had a reason to find her mother.

As she sifted through the paperwork, stored in the documents box, Emma was thankful her parents were such good record keepers. They were used to paying attention to the details of people's lives, knowing who had married whom, who was sick, who was dead or dying. These things had often been the topic of conversation at the dinner table when Emma was growing up. Dad had explained that it was part of his job to attend to every tiny detail of parishioners' lives. Now she was grateful for his fastidiousness.

She sat next to her parents at the kitchen table scanning the documents they'd kept safe for her all these years. "Ah, so we know her name, that she was Irish, and that she wasn't married. That explains a lot," Emma said.

"Yes, it does," Mum agreed.

"It can't have been easy for her, whatever the circumstances," Dad said.

"I know."

On Monday, Emma called the adoption agency, and within a few days she had all the information she needed to track down her birth mother.

"You're not going to believe this," she told Matt that evening at dinner.

"Try me," he said.

"She married him."

"What?!" Matt's eyes widened.

"Or maybe I should say he married her. Same difference." Emma went on: "They stayed together when they went back to Dublin. For all I know, I have half a dozen Irish brothers and sisters who have no idea I exist."

"Whoa, wait a second," Matt said, scratching his head. "They left you here, traveled back to Ireland, then went ahead and got married—to each other?"

"Yep."

"That doesn't make any sense."

"Unless you have a swinging brick in your chest where your heart should be," Emma said bitterly.

Matt shook his head.

"I was beginning to feel sorry for her," Emma went on. "I needn't have bothered. She had more choices than most."

It was crystal clear to Emma that Joan hadn't wanted her enough to keep her. Her birth was a case of inconvenient timing. Her mother and father had been chronologically challenged, so they'd gotten rid of her.

Unwanted. The word popped into her head without warning and stayed there. This was how she'd felt all these years. Unwanted by the woman who carried her for nine months. That was why her instincts had protected her from contacting Joan before. What was the point? Emma would never understand her decision.

"I had this picture in my mind of a distraught girl of nineteen who hadn't known what to do. A frightened slip of a thing who traveled alone on the boat to England, wearing a thin coat, carrying a battered cardboard suitcase with a few meager possessions inside."

"Em, I'm so sorry," Matt said.

"I tried to imagine how lonely and terrified she'd have been. I'd almost fooled myself into thinking there would have been no way in the world for her to keep me." Her voice wavered. "But I was way off the mark. She's been doing just fine all these years, thank you very much."

Matt took her in his arms as the tears came. "I don't know what to say. Except that I love you. And I always will."

Emma raised her head from his shoulder and Matt wiped a tear from her chin with his thumb. "It doesn't matter. They're nothing to me. You and Ben, you're everything," she said, taking the frayed tissue from inside her sleeve, and blowing her nose. "I know there's no guarantee they'll get tested or be a match. But we have to try . . . right?"

"Right," Matt said.

"He's the only reason I'm contacting them."

"I know, love. I know," Matt said, holding her close.

Emma closed her eyes and breathed the familiar musk of his aftershave. The scent soothed her. She knew what she had to do.

CHAPTER 23

Back home, the house seemed to close in on Joan. She felt that if she exhaled her whole world might collapse. The rest of the day crawled by, just as she knew it would.

"Here's Carmel now," Molly said. She was sitting in her usual vantage point by the big bay window in the front room. "Get the door, will you, Joan?"

"She has a key," Joan snapped, without meaning to.

Carmel was coming for dinner, and, for her sake, Joan didn't want to spoil the evening. But the angry bruise under her sleeve where the needle had drawn blood two days before wasn't improving her mood. And she was tired. So bloody sick and tired of hiding the truth.

Carmel bounced up the front steps and let herself in. "Anyone home?" she called. It was a game she played with her grandmother since she moved out. Their ritual.

"In here, pet!" Molly called back.

Carmel settled herself in the armchair next to Molly.

"I'll just go and check on the chicken," Joan said.

"Where's Dad?" Carmel asked.

"He's tidying up a few leaves in the garden," Molly said.

Through the kitchen window, Joan could see Martin raking the leaves into neat piles on the lawn. His head was bowed in concentration, cheeks flushed with exertion. Steam rose, fogging the window as Joan strained boiling water off the vegetables, blocking her view of him.

Carmel's and Molly's voices carried down the hall. They were chatting easily, laughing at some private joke. It didn't seem right, all of them just getting on with their lives regardless. Joan knew she could soon wipe the smiles off their faces. She imagined herself casually dropping Ben into their cozy conversation as she passed the Bisto gravy across the dining table. "You have a great-grandson. He's dying." That would give Molly something to think about.

She finished setting the table. "Dinner's ready," she called out to Martin, shutting the door before he could respond.

Martin kicked his boots off at the back door, then joined Joan at the sink to wash his hands. "I'll finish the rest after dinner. Those flower beds need weeding this weekend."

He went to sit at the table, where Carmel and Molly were taking their places. Joan stayed put. Did he really think she gave a damn about his precious flower beds?

"Are you not coming to sit down, Mam?" Carmel said. "Your dinner is going cold."

"I'll be there in a minute. I just want to get these pots out of the way."

Truth was, she couldn't face Martin. She couldn't sit in her usual place opposite him and play happy families. She couldn't pretend anymore. But neither could she let on there was anything wrong, especially after the episode down in the yard the other day when she'd almost lost it. She wasn't sure what Martin would do if Carmel found out about Emma, or Ben. When she couldn't put it off any longer, she took her seat but avoided Martin's eye.

"Would you not think of planting some bulbs, Martin?" Molly said, between bites of mashed potato. "The flower beds are looking terrible bare."

Martin swallowed. "I could do, I suppose. Daffodils would add a lovely splash of color when spring comes around."

"They would," Molly said, with satisfaction.

Joan rolled her eyes. Typical. Martin had got to the stage where he did whatever his mother told him to. He didn't even stand up for himself anymore. Had he ever? She struggled to remember. Why had it taken her so long to realize her husband didn't have a mind of his own?

"Pass the gravy, would you, Joan?" Martin said. Joan handed the gravy boat across the table without looking at him. He took it without a word.

"A thank-you would be nice," Joan snapped.

Martin's eyes narrowed, but he avoided her stare. "Thanks," he muttered.

Carmel shifted in her chair, and Joan could feel Molly scowling at her. They were being pathetic, herself and Martin, making out their row was over something as trivial as table manners. Pretending the bad blood between them was as insignificant as a quarrel at all. With Carmel watching. Joan knew she should try harder.

After dinner, Martin went back outside to finish up and pack away the garden tools. Molly settled in front of the television to watch the news. Joan and Carmel worked side by side in the kitchen, in silence, washing and drying the dishes. They'd barely said a word to each other all evening. There was nothing new about that. Whenever Carmel was around, she was either entertaining her grandmother or being fawned over by her father.

As Joan stood arms deep in hot soapy water next to her daughter, a wave of sadness came over her. She blinked back the tears that were filling her eyes. "Are you happy, Carmel?" she said, out of the blue. She hadn't known she was about to speak the words.

Carmel put down the plate she was drying and wiped her hands on the tea towel. Her brows angled in a puzzled expression. "That's a funny question. Why do you ask?"

"Because I only just realized I never have," Joan said, with a sidelong glance. "I just presumed."

"I'm grand," Carmel said, turning to look at her. "Mam, there's nothing wrong, is there?"

Joan opened her mouth to speak.

"Nothing a nice cup of tea won't fix," Martin interrupted, wiping his feet on the doormat. "I think I've broken the back of it. Just the beds to dig and it should be sorted."

He walked across the kitchen to stand between mother and daughter. "Can I get in there for a second to wash my hands?" he said, reaching past Joan for the soap without waiting for a reply.

Joan moved aside. Just like always, she thought. Martin and Molly had been pushing past her and shoving her aside for years. She hadn't always been the mother she wanted to be to Carmel, especially in the first weeks and months of her life. By the time she'd been ready, it was too late. They'd squeezed her out of Carmel's life, and, like a fool, she'd let them. If they'd moved out of Grove Square long ago, things might have been different. Maybe now things could change for the better? Joan clung to the sliver of hope that she could save Ben and maybe even some tiny part of herself.

"Put the kettle on, would you, Carmel? There's a good girl," Martin said.

Carmel didn't move. She stood, tea towel in hand, looking from her father to her mother. "What's going on?" she asked.

"Nothing's going on. Your mother's just a bit tired," came

Martin's hasty reply. "Isn't that right, Joan?" he said, raising his eyebrows.

"Yes, that's right. I'm just a bit tired," Joan said, stepping back from the sink, peeling off first one yellow rubber glove, then the other. "I'm finished here." She turned and walked away down the hall without looking back at either of them.

CHAPTER 24

Carmel watched Mam traipsing along the hallway toward the stairs. "Something's not right, Dad," she said, turning to her father. "I'll go and talk to her."

"No! No, don't do that," he said, grasping her shoulder. "She probably just needs some peace and quiet."

Carmel took a step back. "I don't think that's it," she replied. "You keep saying she's tired. But the way she's been acting lately just isn't like her. There's something else she's not telling us."

"Now, Carmel, you know what she's like, how temperamental she can be. Surely you haven't forgotten how she was when you were growing up? She'll snap out of it. Doesn't she always? Now, let's get the rest of these dishes dried," her father said, smiling and holding the tea towel Carmel had discarded toward her.

Carmel brushed his hand aside. "Why are you talking about her like that? As if her feelings were no more than"—she struggled to find the right words—"an inconvenience."

"Ah now, that's not what I meant. Don't go putting words in my mouth."

Carmel's face flushed. "You're the one who's putting words in people's mouths."

"Just leave it, will you, Carmel?" Dad said, his jaw tightening.

"Why don't you let Mam speak for herself?"

A flash of anger she'd never seen directed at her before lit her father's eyes. "That's enough of your lip, young lady. I said drop it, and I meant it."

"Fine," Carmel shot back at him as she turned to go. "I'll leave you to it." She resisted the temptation to slam the door behind her. It started to rain as she reached her car. She sat behind the steering wheel, gripping it hard with both hands and shaking her head. She didn't buy what Dad said. In fact, the more she thought about the way he'd behaved that evening, the more she felt Mam wasn't the only one who was hiding something.

She peered through the rain-spattered windscreen at her parents' bedroom window. A knot of anxiety clenched her stomach, and she felt as if a dark cloud had settled over even the farthest reaches of her heart. As she turned the key in the ignition, she thought she saw the curtain at the upstairs window move. Her mother was standing behind the nets. There but not there, as always, beyond her grasp.

When she got home, Carmel dropped her keys on the table, then stooped to light the gas fire. She stood with her back as close as she could to the flame, allowing the heat to roast the backs of her calves. If Granny was here, she'd warn her about the risk of getting chilblains.

What a relief it was to be home! She shrugged out of her jumper as the room warmed up and plopped down on the sofa. The tension of the evening began to melt. The more time she spent at Grove Square, the less like home it felt, even though Dad still insisted on correcting her every time she referred to her flat as home. "This is your home," he'd say, pointing to the spot wherever he happened to be standing. And Carmel, who knew better than to make a big deal of things, would smile and say little else. Just like her mother usually did, she thought. Until today.

It was true there had always been friction between Mam and Granny. There was nothing new about the pair of them having the odd dig at each other across the dining table. Tonight was different, though. She'd never heard her mother speak to her father like that. It was as if she'd reached a breaking point. What Carmel had witnessed between them was no ordinary disagreement. And the way Dad had spoken about Mam just wasn't on. Then there was the weird conversation about her happiness while they were doing the dishes. Something was up for sure.

Carmel spotted the framed family photo on her bookcase and walked over to take a closer look. It had been taken in the side garden on the evening of her debs ball. She scoffed at the hideous blue satin off-the-shoulder number she'd chosen to wear. She'd thought she was gorgeous on the night, but she could see now that her eye makeup was too dark for her pale features. Hindsight was a wonderful thing.

Mam and Dad stood on either side of her. All smiles. She was already a head taller than her mother. *Nothing to see here*, she thought, replacing the frame on the shelf. There was an old Clarks shoebox full of photos somewhere, though. She remembered loading them into the car, one of the last things she'd taken from the house when she moved. Now where had she put them?

It didn't take her long to find them, on the floor at the back of her wardrobe, the green box held together with two big rubber bands. She returned to the kitchen, pulled out a stool, and tipped the photos onto the counter. There were the usual formal school and family photos. The ones they'd posed for on Christmases and birthdays. Her first communion. A holiday in Kerry. And Granny's seventieth. Carmel in the old Cortina she'd saved up for when she passed her driving test.

In every photo, they'd positioned themselves to capture the best camera angle, and had posed only for as long as they needed to crack dutiful smiles into it—the kind of smiles that would vanish as soon as the shutter clicked. There was a black-and-white photo of Mam and Dad cutting the cake on their wedding day. Mam was stunning in a simple white dress only the most beautiful woman could pull off. Dad looked so handsome and proud. They seemed happy—right for each other. What had happened from that day to this to change things between them?

Carmel knew that the lack of a brother or sister for her had been a huge sadness in her mother's life. It hadn't been spoken of directly. It was just another of the unsaid things that amounted to something bigger.

As she thumbed through a stack of photographs, she stopped at a small color one she hadn't seen for ages. It was at the bottom of the pile, the kind of photo that wouldn't be considered worthy of a frame. It was a shot of Carmel, taken by her mother when she was about seven or eight in the back garden at Grove Square. She wasn't looking at the camera. Her head was bent in concentration: tongue stuck between her teeth and a daisy-chain crown perched on her honey-blond hair. She held a strangled daisy in her fist.

Carmel remembered when the photo was taken. It was the summer holidays. One of Granny's relatives in Kilkenny died, and she and Dad went to the funeral. It was just Carmel and Mam left at home: the first and, she thought now, only time they ever spent a day and a night alone together.

It had lashed rain for a week, and Dad hadn't mown the lawn the weekend before. Now it was a carpet of daisies. When the sun finally came out on Sunday after Mass, Mam took Carmel into the garden. They knelt together on an old blanket spread on the damp grass, and Mam taught her how to make a daisy chain.

At first, Carmel picked the stems too short and selected the daisies only for the size of their flowers. Mam showed her how to pay attention to the underside of the flowers. The best daisies for threading were the ones with longer, thicker stems. They spent the entire morning there on the grass, splitting the stems with their thumbnails and threading flowers together. By lunchtime, they had green-stained fingernails and a daisy chain long enough to surround Carmel's bed. That night, when Mam tucked her in, she draped the daisy chain around Carmel's headboard before kissing her good night.

When Carmel woke in the morning, she found a string of wilted flowers dangling from her bed. She gathered them up and ran downstairs into the kitchen crying to her mother. "Can we save my flowers, Mammy?" she wailed.

"Oh, I'm sorry, darlin'. The flowers we pick aren't meant to last. They start to die as soon as we pick them. We just can't see it."

Carmel stared at the ruins of the once-beautiful wildflower garland in her hands. "But why?" she said, through her tears.

Mam crouched down so she was level with her. "Because once they're picked, they don't have what they need to survive." She took a tissue from inside her sleeve and held it up to Carmel's nose. "Here, blow, there's a good girl," she said. "They were beautiful while they lasted, though, weren't they?"

Carmel had nearly forgotten that day. It was as if Mam had lived on the fringes of her life since. Time alone with her mother had been fleeting, and it was eclipsed by the time she'd spent with Dad, who always seemed to be at the center of her universe. Her most vivid memories were of days by his side down at the yard, the smell of varnish and sawdust in her nostrils.

All through her childhood everyone said she was a "daddy's girl." Maybe that's why she hadn't noticed her mother's seeming indifference when she was small. The words "daddy's girl" were recited to her so often that Carmel took them as gospel. Dad had been the one to show her how to do things. He taught her how to count. On quiet weekday afternoons, he'd sit her on a high stool beside the counter and spill out a box of screws. He'd watch her count them into piles of ten with her chubby fingers, his smile wide with admiration and love. "That's it. Good girl."

When he was doing deliveries, he'd strap her next to him in the van, and off they'd go around the city dropping off paint, wood, and plumbing materials to customers.

"Fancy an ice cream?" he asked one midwinter afternoon when they'd done their last delivery. She bounced up and down in the passenger seat, clapping her hands. Dad did a U-turn in the middle of Rathmines Road.

"Where are we going?" Carmel wriggled in her seat.

"Wait and see," he said.

Instead of stopping off at McCarthy's, the local newsagents, to get a Cornetto from the freezer, he drove all the way to Sandymount to buy her a 99 from Mr. Ripple the ice cream man. They walked along the cold wet sand, laughing between licks—him with his trouser legs rolled up, carrying her shoes as well as his in one hand, their toes getting bluer by the minute.

When Carmel was old enough to reach, Dad taught her how to ring items up on the till. She'd been so proud the first time she served a customer, counting out the correct change.

"That's my girl!" Dad said, winking at Mr. Malone on the other side of the counter. And she thought her heart would burst.

Mam was a different kettle of fish. Carmel had no idea why her mother felt like a stranger to her. She was an outsider, a spectator on the outskirts of her life. It was as if there was a door into Carmel's world her mother didn't know how to unlock. As Carmel got older, she tried to look on the bright side. Maybe Mam's detachment was a good thing. Hadn't it made her into a fiercely independent child who insisted on doing everything for herself?

Like that morning when they were late for school. Carmel was sitting on the hall floor, wrestling with the buckles of her new patent-leather shoes.

"Let Mammy help you," Mam had coaxed.

"I can do it!" Carmel replied, gripping a shiny strap.

Mam sighed, looking at her watch. "Come on now, Carmel," she snapped, swatting Carmel's hand from the shoe. "We don't have all day. Let me do it."

"No!" Carmel screamed.

"Stop it now. Stop behaving like a spoiled brat!" Mam yelled, yanking her by the arm.

Her father came rushing down the stairs then, wiping shaving foam off his face with a towel. "What's going on, Joan?" he asked, as he bent to look Carmel in the eye. "Are you all right, pet?" he said, stroking her hair.

"She's perfectly fine," Mam said. "We're late and she won't do as she's told."

"You can't blame her the way you're shouting at her," Dad said. "She's only a child."

"I want Daddy to bring me to school," Carmel said, shaking free from her mother.

"I'm sorry, pet, I can't today. I have a meeting in town. But I'll pick you up afterwards and we'll go for a drive. Okay?"

Carmel sobbed as her mother pulled her down the driveway to the bus stop on Harold's Cross Road. Her face was plastered in snot and tears by the time they got to the school.

Was it any wonder then that she'd gravitated toward her father? Mam had no time for her, and, in the end, Carmel resolved to stop needing her. She navigated her childhood struggles—all of them, except periods, of course—from tying shoelaces to riding a bike, with Dad's help.

Then there was that awful day after a sleepover at her friend Rachel's, when Carmel had screamed those hateful words, "Why can't you be more like Rachel's mam?" She saw her mother flinch as if she'd inflicted a physical wound. She'd meant it, though. Rachel's mam didn't just bring them mugs of hot chocolate or ask them how the studying was going. She hugged and kissed Rachel. Held her close.

Mam never did any of that kind of stuff. She was more like an administrator in Carmel's life. She kept calendars, school stationery lists, and piles of folded navy blue knee socks in order, but she was the last person Carmel would think to go to for advice about wearing a bra, coping with period pain, or the heartache of discovering that the boy she'd fallen for fancied someone else.

She didn't invite Mam's opinion on anything, not even when she left school and was weighing up whether to take her place to study History of Art and Architecture at Trinity or to join the family business. Even though Mam was always around, Carmel felt like she had been little more than a shadow in her life.

And Mam seemed to keep Carmel at arm's length. Their conversations were about the practicalities of daily life. "Have you seen my PE kit?" "What time will you be home?" "When's dinner?" They never talked about the important stuff like life, the universe, love—especially not love, God forbid. Carmel sensed there was something missing between them, as if she and her mother were an unfinished jigsaw that could never be completed because a piece had gone astray. Whenever the feeling bubbled up unexpectedly as a tightness in her throat, she swallowed hard to make it go away.

The day after her fifteenth birthday, Carmel's friend Rachel was sitting in her stockinged feet on Carmel's bedroom floor, flicking through her album collection. "Not bad, not bad at all," Rachel declared. "The Police *and* Duran Duran. I'm impressed with your old pair—mine wouldn't have a clue what I liked. Couldn't care less either."

"Come on, that's a bit harsh," Carmel replied. "Your mam is great. At least you can talk to her. That must be nice."

"Well, it depends," Rachel said. "I mean, I hate when she goes on acting like she's my best friend." She rolled her eyes. "But she was great when I got my period."

"My mam is hopeless." Carmel sighed. "If you want your bed made with hospital corners and an apple a day in your lunch box, she's your woman, but don't go expecting a hug while she's at it."

"My ma's the opposite," Rachel said. "Have you seen the state of my uniform?" She pointed at the dried-in egg yolk on her school tie.

Carmel laughed. "Fair point, but aren't you big enough and ugly enough to do your own washing?"

"I'm allergic," Rachel said.

"To washing powder?"

"No, you eejit, to housework!"

Carmel lifted the arm on the record player and flipped the album over.

"Sting's a ride, isn't he?" Rachel said.

"He's not my type," Carmel replied. She was about to go on, but there was a knock on her bedroom door.

"Carmel, could you turn that racket down, please?" Mam said.

By the miserable face she had on her, Carmel could see that her mood hadn't improved since yesterday. "It's not even loud," she said, pushing back.

Mam sighed, closing her eyes. "Why can't you just do what you're told?"

"And why can't you just give me a break? You're always spoiling things."

Mam recoiled from her words, and Carmel felt her face flush. She knew she was going too far, but she couldn't stop. "Yesterday was the limit. You'd have thought you were at a funeral, not my fifteenth birthday party."

"That's enough, Carmel," Mam said, too quietly.

"Well, it's true. You—" Carmel glared at her mother, but something in Mam's eyes stopped her from saying another word. It wasn't fury, which Carmel could be indignant about. It was agony, and Carmel couldn't bear the sight of it. She turned back to Rachel, who was trying desperately to disappear into the wall behind her. "You'd better go, Rachel." Carmel grimaced.

"Sure. I'll see you tomorrow." Rachel shoved her feet into her shoes without opening the laces and slung her bag over her shoulder. "Thanks for having me, Mrs. Egan," she said, as she passed Mam in the hallway.

Carmel flopped back on her bed and punched her pillow. God, what an embarrassment Mam was. She couldn't even invite a friend around to listen to music. Why couldn't she ever be nice or just lighten up for once? Why was she always so bloody miserable?

Hugging her knees, Carmel turned to face the treetops outside her open window. She listened to the lazy breeze disturbing the leaves. And she made up her mind. As soon as she turned eighteen and was old enough to leave home, she'd be out of here.

Of course, she hadn't followed through on the vow she made during her teenage temper tantrums. Instead, she spent less time at home and more and more time at the yard, learning the ropes of running the business. Strangely, the yard became the place where she felt most at home, chatting to the tradesmen about the ins and outs of the jobs they were working on. The busyness of work was a balm.

If she'd learned one thing from her years talking to tradesmen, it was that there was no sense trying to fix a problem unless you could identify the root of it. And she knew that the root of this problem with her mother was buried beyond her reach. So, instead of trying to make sense of what was broken between her and Mam, she learned to live with it.

Carmel gathered up the photos spread out across the kitchen counter and put them back into the box. Except for the one of her and the daisy chain. That one she fixed to the fridge door with a couple of magnets. Somehow, it felt like a memory worth holding on to.

PART FOUR

CHAPTER 25

Dublin, 1965

The cold concrete floor numbed Joan's bare knees, and her brushed-nylon nightdress did little to protect her from the draft that blew through the gap under the toilet door. Another wave of nausea hit her, and she bent her head over the rim of the bowl. The retching tore at the insides of her empty stomach. She spat into the bowl and shivered, then sat back on her heels and wiped the clamminess from her forehead.

For the first time in her life she was glad of the outside toilet. It was a blessing to be able to hide her morning sickness from Da and Teresa, who were still asleep upstairs in the house and none the wiser. Martin had been gone a month, but he was never far from Joan's thoughts.

She felt exposed now that he was gone. Worn out. Weary with the worry of it all. It wasn't just the fear of her secret being discovered. She was petrified that once Martin was far away in London he would change his mind—that he would meet someone else or decide, in the end, that he was too young to be tied down.

Only weeks before she knew for certain she was pregnant, she'd found Esther Molloy in the same position: plastered in sweat, kneeling on the floor of the women's toilets in the factory. Esther's face was ashen. She looked like she'd seen the ghost of her future as she clung to the toilet bowl for dear life.

"Are you all right, Esther?" Joan had asked.

Esther's bottom lip trembled and she shook her head. "My da will bloody well kill me if he finds out, Joan. I don't know what to do." The first tears fell. "What'll happen to me?"

For a girl in Esther's predicament, her fate depended on everyone but her. On the fella who got her pregnant and how willing he was to own up to the fact. On how quickly the family could convince him to put a ring on her finger. A shotgun wedding, heads hanging, on the side altar down at St. Jude's if she was lucky. If that wasn't an option, the boat to England—if she could scrape together the fare. And if she wasn't so lucky? She might be sent away to some convent down the country, where the sisters could hide the mistakes of a girl in trouble and exploit her shame. It put the fear of God into Joan.

"You'll be all right," she lied, kneeling beside Esther and holding back her long auburn hair while Esther heaved into the toilet bowl and shook with small silent sobs. "It's all right," Joan kept saying, as if saying it would make it true.

Joan shuddered at the memory. Then she stood up and wiped her mouth with the back of her hand. No. She wasn't in the same predicament as Esther. Martin was standing by her. She *would* be all right. She made her way back to the house, walking barefoot through the dandelions that choked the overgrown patch of garden where her mother had once grown cabbages. Teresa would be up soon, and Joan didn't want to worry her. She had to make life go on as if nothing had changed—even though nothing would ever be the same again.

She washed her hands at the kitchen sink and thought about buttering the bread for the lunches. She found it hard to stomach the sight of food at this hour of the morning. Maybe she would be able to keep a bit of bread and butter down for breakfast. She'd try—she had the baby to think of now.

She wondered, not for the first time, if she should confide in Teresa. She hated keeping secrets from her sister. Should she tell her about the baby? About Martin? No. It would be foolish to say anything. Not just for her own sake, but for Teresa's too. One of these days, Da would come in from the pub shooting his mouth off, and Teresa wouldn't be able to hold her tongue.

She couldn't risk Da finding out or Teresa knowing anything if he did. He'd look for someone to blame, and she didn't want her sister in the firing line once she was gone. She'd tell Teresa everything one day, after the dust settled. She'd understand. She'd be happy for her big sister. And maybe once they were set up in London, Martin would agree to send for Teresa. Everything would work out—in time.

Joan sawed a slice of bread off yesterday's loaf, spread it with a thin layer of butter, then closed her eyes and took a cautious bite. Yes, she was doing the right thing. She placed the palm of her hand on her belly. She was only about three months gone, but it was getting harder to conceal the small swelling in her usually flat stomach. She couldn't afford to wait any longer.

It was time. Her ferry was leaving in the morning. Tonight, after work, she'd let Teresa and Da know about her plans to move to England. Da would be in good form because one of his drinking buddies had found him a few days' laboring work on a building site down on Westmoreland Street.

Joan waved Teresa off to work as usual. Now she just had Da

to contend with. He was drinking his tea in silence, elbows on the table in front of the window, framed by the yellowing net curtains. Joan came in from the hall, still wearing her nightdress and cardigan. When Da saw her, his face soured. "What's wrong with you?"

"I'll go in later today, Da. I'm feeling a bit under the weather this morning."

"Well, you'd want to be careful. Decent jobs don't grow on trees, you know." He put his mug down. "They could find someone to fill your shoes in a heartbeat."

"I know, Da." Joan didn't tell him she'd already arranged to collect her last pay packet from the factory at lunchtime.

He eyed the old clock on the mantelpiece, then pushed his chair back. "I'd better be off myself. Have the dinner ready for six."

As soon as the door slammed behind him, Joan was up the stairs like a light. She found the battered suitcase that once belonged to Granny Riley under Da's bed, next to the box of Ma's things, and carried it across the small square landing to her bedroom.

She was surprised at how calmly she sorted out the clothes she needed to pack, as if she'd done it a million times before. She folded her good green jumper and placed it on top of the slips and knickers, then laid the tickets Martin had given her before he left on top of the pile of clothes where she would be sure to remember them.

Joan had lost count of the number of times she'd secretly pulled those tickets from their hiding place beneath the newspaper that lined her drawer just to look at them: a one-way crossing from Dun Laoghaire to Holyhead and the connecting train from Holyhead to King's Cross. The tickets to her new life.

She snapped the worn metal clasps of the case shut and slid it under the bed, then straightened the bedspread. Tomorrow night, for the first time in her life, she wouldn't be sleeping in this bed next to her sister. There was a good chance she would never sleep under Da's roof again.

On the dot of twelve, Joan tied her headscarf under her chin and pulled the hall door closed behind her. She took her time walking down Ardeer Avenue, past the cramped rows of pebble-dashed houses that were so familiar to her she could name every one of the families who lived in them.

The estate was quiet at this hour of the day. The younger kids who didn't have school or work bounced balls or chalked on the footpath. Some kept the babies occupied while their mothers pegged the washing. There was a grand breeze out for drying.

Joan hadn't set foot in the factory office since the day, four years before, when she went to see about the job. Mrs. O'Leary handled the wages, and woe betide anyone who interrupted her on a Friday before the pay slips were tallied and ready. But today was Tuesday, and she nearly smiled at Joan when she knocked on the door. "Ah, there you are, Joan. I was expecting you."

"Thanks for settling everything up for me, Mrs. O'Leary."

"No bother at all, Joan," she said, putting on the glasses that hung from a silver chain around her neck. "And where did you say you were off to?"

Joan shuffled from one foot to the other, fiddling with the buttons on her coat. "Em, I've got the chance of work in London, so I thought I'd grab it with both hands."

The old woman peered over her glasses at her. "Oh . . . you're off to the bright lights of London? I didn't know." Did she imagine it or had Mrs. O'Leary shot a glance at her belly?

"I may as well have the adventure while I'm young." Joan smiled sweetly at her.

"You do right," the older woman said as she held out the small brown envelope. "Now, here's what's owed to you. Two weeks' wages. One in back pay. It's all explained on the slip inside."

"Thanks very much, Mrs. O'Leary," Joan said, and zipped the envelope into the inside pocket of her handbag.

"Have a safe journey now," Mrs. O'Leary said. She sat back down to attend to the columns of figures in front of her, and, without looking up, said, "Joan, will you shut that door behind you on the way out like a good girl?"

Joan closed the door and began walking toward the factory gates. She wanted to slip away, without a fuss. She'd already said her goodbyes the evening before to the couple of girls who might miss her when she didn't show up for work that week.

"Joan! Wait, Joan!"

Imelda, red-faced and breathless, caught up to her, then doubled over, hands on her hips. "Jesus, I need to give up those fags."

"I can't see that happening until Jesus himself comes down off the cross and takes them off you," Joan said.

"You're all set, then?"

"I am," Joan replied, patting her bag. "I'm loaded."

Imelda chuckled, then grew serious. "Did you hear about Esther?" she whispered, coming closer even though no one was within earshot.

"No, I didn't," Joan said warily. "What about her?"

"She's up the spout. Yer man's done a runner, and her auld fella kicked her out. Wants nothing to do with her. So I heard anyway."

"You're joking." The words caught in Joan's throat.

"No, her sister told me this morning," Imelda said, trying to meet Joan's eye. Joan looked away. "Poor cow."

"What'll happen to her?"

Imelda shook her head. "Don't know for sure. She had no choice but to go to the priest."

"No!" Joan gasped, hand over her mouth.

Imelda nodded gravely. "She'll probably be halfway down the country by now, God love her."

Joan's heart was going like the clappers, but she managed a look of calm concern. *There but for the grace of God go I,* she thought.

"Anyway, I'd better get back. Mind yourself, Joan. Send us a postcard from the Big Smoke." Imelda waved as she turned to go.

"I will," Joan lied. She watched her friend walking back toward the factory, not knowing when she might see her again.

CHAPTER 26

That evening, Joan tried to keep her hand steady as she ladled the stew into bowls. She would give herself away if she wasn't careful. "Here—make yourself useful and take these, will you?" she said to Teresa, rummaging in the cutlery drawer for spoons and handing them to her. She was glad she'd used some of the money from her last pay packet to buy a bit of meat to go with the potatoes. Anything that might soften Da up tonight would be worth it.

Joan chose her moment when the three of them were sitting down at the table with plates of steaming stew in front of them. Her cheeks were flushed from the heat of the stove, her voice falsely bright as her words tripped over each other.

"You'll never guess what?! One of the girls from the factory has an auntie in London who is looking for someone to work in her guesthouse in Islington." She was talking too fast. "It's good money, and she's offering digs and the fare over as well."

Teresa stopped chewing and stared at her. "So?"

"She's offered me the job," Joan went on.

Da's eyes narrowed.

Joan squirmed in her chair. "It's too good an opportunity to miss, Da. I didn't want to tell you until there was something definite." She knew how to handle Da: talk about more money, regular money, steady work, and envelopes with the few bob sent home. Then cast a few shadows. Sure you never knew where you were with the factory. They could lay people off any minute. London was the place to be.

Da put down his spoon. "And what about us? Who'll look after the house here?"

"There'll be one less mouth to feed, and I'll send money home as soon as I get on my feet."

Da reclined and folded his arms, as if weighing up his options.

"It could be the making of us, Da!" Joan said, her eyes shining.

Da was used to seeing the daughters and sons of the Cranmore estate come and go. You'd lose count of the numbers of young people who went over to England to find work. He picked up his spoon and finished his stew in silence. When the bowl was empty, he wiped his mouth with the back of his hand. "Just make sure you send the few bob home," he said, standing up. He left the room and his dirty dishes on the table without another word.

Teresa frowned and gave Joan the "you're not fooling me" look. Teresa knew her sister well enough to suspect that her story didn't add up. In bed that night, she sat up next to Joan, propping her pillow behind her. "What's going on, Joan? It isn't like you to make sudden moves."

Joan was glad the bedroom was shrouded in darkness, making it easier to hide her deception and her guilt over lying to her sister—though nothing could dull the ache of leaving her behind. She lay staring at the ceiling. "It's too good a chance to miss," she said. "Who knows, maybe I can find some work for you there?"

Teresa breathed a heavy sigh. Joan felt her body shift as the mattress sagged under them. "My life is here, Joan, for better or for worse."

Joan nodded, even though her sister couldn't see her in the dark.

"It's not a million miles away. I promise I'll write. And you can always visit." She tried to make her voice light.

Teresa was quiet. "I'll miss you, Joan," she said finally.

"I know. But it'll take more than the Irish Sea to come between you and me. We'll always have each other no matter what. Always. I promise." Joan wasn't sure how she got the words past the lump in her throat.

"Well, can I warm my cold feet on you while I still have the chance?" Teresa said, planting her frozen toes on Joan's thighs.

"Course you can. That's what sisters are for."

THE WIND DOWN AT DUN LAOGHAIRE Harbor was colder than it had any right to be for October; it went straight through her. Seagulls circled, wailing and scavenging for scraps. Joan got in line, along with all the other hopeful souls, to board the boat, her ferry ticket zipped into the back pocket of her handbag, along with a note from Teresa and the envelope containing her mother's wedding ring.

Her future with Martin was within her grasp. Handbag in one hand, battered suitcase in the other, Joan shuffled along the gangplank. Once on board, she found a place on the deck to stand, shoulder to shoulder with other passengers, looking out on the crowd there to see them off. The woman next to her was crying. Her loud sobs got on Joan's nerves—she couldn't deal with someone else's misery. Not today.

On impulse, she leaned over the rail and waved, pretending to say her last goodbyes to someone on the pier. She continued to wave frantically, grinning into the distance, as the boat edged away from the dock. The crowd thinned when passengers headed down to the lower deck, but Joan stayed, watching the green coastline diminish in the distance.

When at last her homeland was out of sight, she made her way belowdecks. Every available corner seemed to already be taken. Men, women, and children sat on suitcases or on the floor, and there was barely room to move. Joan squeezed herself in between a woman with two small children and an elderly couple.

"Excuse me, sorry," she said, when her case bumped their knees as she took a seat. The couple were off to visit their daughter in Birmingham, they said. Joan smiled politely, said little, and kept to herself. She unfolded the note from Teresa, which she'd found tucked into the handle of her suitcase that morning, along with a present: Teresa's favorite mohair scarf, the green one she'd bought on the never-never. Joan could only just make out her sister's handwriting.

I will miss you, Joan.
Mind yourself.
Love, T.

Joan's eyes filled, and she brushed the tears away with the sleeve of her coat. That morning, she'd stood alone in her childhood bedroom, imprinting it on her memory. The sun shone through the lace curtains, making the room appear less dreary than it was. Instead of seeing only the damp patch on the wall above the bed, Joan noticed the way the light filtered through the lace, creating delicate patterns on the pale pink walls—the color Ma had chosen to paint them.

Time seemed to have stood still in the room. Joan sighed, bending to straighten the ancient bedspread one last time. They might not have had much, but she and Teresa always had each other. Now she sat on her suitcase, alone on the crowded ferry, trying to ignore the smell of vomit that hung thick in the air.

Her stomach lurched. It wasn't just seasickness that had her in knots. She was nervous. What if Martin wasn't there to meet her? What would she do then? Where would she go? She shivered, and shook her head. Of course he'd be there. Soon enough they would be together.

She imagined Molly Egan telling anyone in Harold's Cross who would listen that Martin was over in London doing an accounting course, getting qualifications that would stand him in good stead when he took over the family business next year. If she knew that Joan, one of the unfortunate Quinn girls from the Cranmore estate, was about to join him, she'd have a heart attack. Joan allowed herself the briefest of smiles. Molly Egan would just have to get used to Joan Quinn. She wasn't going anywhere.

When they disembarked at Holyhead, Joan was swept along by the crowd. She was glad of the weight and warmth of her fellow travelers pressed against her as they shuffled toward the platform where they boarded the train to London. A guard with a clipped mustache and an accent to match walked up and down the carriages inspecting tickets. The afternoon sun shone onto the seat between herself and the woman traveling with the two toddlers.

The woman unpacked a biscuit tin filled with cheese sandwiches and a flask of tea. Joan's stomach rumbled, and, mortified, she looked out the window at the sheep grazing on the green hills of the Welsh countryside. A hand patted her knee, and she turned to see the woman holding the tin of sandwiches toward her. "Would you like one?"

Joan hesitated. The woman smiled reassuringly. "Go on, help yourself. This pair are too excited to eat anything. I don't know why I bother. They take a few bites and leave the crusts." Joan, starving and grateful in equal measure, reached into the tin, picked out a triangular wedge and held it in her lap.

"Thank you. It's my first trip away from home. I didn't know what to bring."

The woman gave a knowing nod and extended her hand. "Dolores. Pleased to meet you."

"Joan." She shook the outstretched hand, then settled back into her seat and bit into the sandwich. When Dolores held out a mug of tea, Joan accepted immediately. "Are you meeting your husband?" she asked.

Dolores brightened. "Yes, we are! We're meeting Daddy in London, aren't we?" she said to her children. The little girl burrowed behind her mother's arm. The boy just stared at Joan, wide-eyed. As Joan chewed, an unexpected lightness spread through her.

"Not long now," Dolores told her children, smiling at Joan. "We'll be there in no time," she said.

Joan wiped crumbs from her lips. "I'll be glad to get there," she said, knowing she could rest easy now. She'd be with Martin in a matter of hours.

She leaned her head against the window and allowed the rhythm of the train to lull her to sleep. Dolores shook her awake as the train pulled into King's Cross station, the last stop on the line. "We're here," she said, with a smile.

"Already?" Joan replied, rubbing her eyes.

"Hold hands now, you two," Dolores said, gathering up her little ones and their luggage. "Cheerio, Joan!" she called over her shoulder as she moved down the carriage. "Best of luck to you!"

Waving after them, Joan hoped she'd be as capable and kind a mother one day.

She stood at the door of the train, gaping at the hundreds of people milling around on the platform. The fear she'd let go of on the train gripped her again. How would she find Martin in this crowd? And what if he wasn't there to meet her? What if she found herself alone in this strange city with a baby on the way? She shuddered and forced herself to move.

As soon as she stepped onto the platform, she heard his voice ring out. "Joan! Joan!" She scanned the sea of faces, and then she saw him, big grin and unruly blond hair, handsome as ever, pushing his way through the crowds toward her. "There you are. You made it!"

He took her into his arms. Joan's cheek pressed against the rough wool of Martin's overcoat, and she breathed in the familiar scent of him. She felt weightless.

"Let me look at you." He grinned, holding her at arm's length.

"God, I missed you." He pulled her toward him and kissed her hard on the lips.

"Martin!" she said, coming up for air. "Not here!" She looked around self-consciously.

"We're not in Dublin now, Joan. This is London. We're as free as the birds! Here, give me that." He took the suitcase from her and spun her around. Joan had never seen him so happy. Like a kid on Christmas morning. He looked like a weight had been lifted from his young shoulders and he could finally stand tall for the first time in his life. His giddiness was infectious, and Joan felt a lightness in her step too. Her shoulders relaxed and she couldn't stop smiling. It was as though someone had removed an invisible rucksack she hadn't realized she'd been carrying.

CHAPTER 27

Martin pulled her through the crowds by the hand. "You'll love it here. I can't wait to show you. Wait until you see Buckingham Palace and Big Ben! As soon as we drop this bag off at your room, I'm taking you out to celebrate."

"You're the boss," Joan said, laughing. "I'm in your hands."

They caught the Victoria Line to Highbury and Islington. Joan gawked at the poker-faced strangers packed into the train carriage, marveling at a woman dressed from head to toe in a crimson-and-gold sari, a dozen gold bangles rattling on each arm. They climbed the steps from the depths of the Tube station out into the fresh autumn day. Martin swung Joan's suitcase in one hand and held tight to her with the other as they walked.

"This is it," he said, as they turned the corner into Bridge Road. Bare trees lined the street, a neat row of red-brick terraces, their chimney pots standing to attention against the darkening sky. "The guesthouse is just on the corner there."

Joan's stomach lurched as they neared the place she would call home for the next few months at least. "What's the landlady like?" she said.

"She seems nice enough," Martin said, squeezing her hand. "Come on." He took the steps up to the front door ahead of her, and then they stood together on the doorstep. "Ready?" he asked, about to lift the door knocker. Just as he did, the door opened, and a slight woman with a tidy gray perm and kind blue eyes stood before them.

"Ah, there you are," she said, stepping back from the door to let them into the hall. "You must be Joan." She held out her hand. "I'm Mrs. Clemence. Bit of a mouthful, so you can call me Mrs. C."

"Hello," Joan said, feeling she should say something else but failing to find the right words. Martin stood awkwardly next to her, her suitcase at his feet.

"Now, Martin," Mrs. C said, opening a door to the right of the hall, "you wait here in the parlor and I'll take Joan up to her room."

"Of course," Martin said in a polite voice Joan didn't recognize as he stepped obediently into the parlor.

"Joan, can you manage that suitcase up two flights of stairs?" Mrs. C asked.

"Yes, it's not too heavy," Joan replied.

"Good. Then follow me."

At the bottom of the stairs, Mrs. C pointed to a small cardboard sign pinned to a noticeboard. Joan had already spotted it. Written in thick red pen, it read *RESIDENTS ONLY. Strictly no visitors allowed upstairs.*

"This is a respectable boardinghouse," Mrs. C said.

Joan reddened. Her landlady, who was on the carpeted landing above, didn't notice. "You must be tired. You've had a long journey from home," Mrs. C said, studying the big bunch of keys in her hand looking for the right one.

"A bit," Joan said. "It'll be nice to get rid of the suitcase."

"Ah, there it is," Mrs. C said, turning the key in the lock and leading the way into the room. "This is you, Joan, the best room in the house. You'll have a lovely view of the cherry blossom in spring from here," she said, closing the tall sash window and drawing the curtains.

Joan placed her suitcase on the floor next to the black iron-framed single bed covered in a bright patchwork quilt.

"Now, you remember what I told you about there being no visitors allowed?"

Joan gave a solemn nod.

"There's only two more things that are any of my business," Mrs. C said. "You need to keep your room decent, and you must be reliable."

"Of course, Mrs. Clem—er, Mrs. C. That goes without saying."

"Now, Martin will have told you about our arrangement."

"Yes, he did," Joan said.

"Four hours of work a day will cover your room and board."

"Thank you," Joan replied. She'd never meant those words more.

"I'll leave you to get settled now," Mrs. C said, turning to the door. She stopped on the threshold, holding the door handle, and looked back over her shoulder. "You won't find me sticking my nose in where it isn't wanted. 'Ask me no questions and I'll tell you no lies' has always been my motto."

Joan gave her another grateful nod.

"If you need anything, you'll find me either in the kitchen or in my room along the other end of this corridor."

"Thank you" was all Joan could think to say as she closed the door behind her.

The springs squeaked under her weight as she sat on the bed, and exhaustion hit. She wanted to kick her shoes off, lie back, and close her eyes, but she couldn't keep Martin waiting downstairs. He was looking forward to taking her on their first proper date, one where they wouldn't have to go skulking around in the bushes just to be together.

The room was comfortable enough, she thought, looking around.

Its floral wallpaper and hissing hot-water pipes gave it a cozy feel. There wasn't a speck or a smudge anywhere. It wouldn't have mattered to Joan what it was like as long as she had a roof over her head, far away from the prying eyes of Harold's Cross, especially during the months that were ahead.

She looked for a mirror to freshen up her lipstick. There was one in the perfect spot on the tall chest of drawers, at just the right height. As she uncapped the tube of lipstick, she noticed the thoughtful touches of welcome around the room. An extra woolen blanket folded at the foot of the bed in case it got chilly in the night. A single white rose in a cut-glass vase on top of the dressing table. Joan sank her nose between the petals and breathed in the sweet smell of her new home. She tucked her hair behind her ears and took one last look in the mirror. "You'll have to do," she said, smiling at her reflection, before bounding down the stairs to Martin.

"Now, let's see. Where to first?" Martin said as they skipped down the steps into the street.

"I don't mind in the slightest!" Joan said, giving him her biggest smile. She was surprised at first to see so many people out and about this late in the evening but reminded herself that she was in London now—a long way from Harold's Cross. Couples on Vespas sputtered past them on the way to nightclubs in Camden. She couldn't get over the women riding pillion in their capri pants and knee-high PVC boots. "It's another world!" she said.

"Sure is," Martin replied, taking hold of her hand. They stopped at the Upper Street traffic lights, and while they waited for the lights to change, Martin took her in his arms and kissed her. A red double-decker stopped at the junction, and the young conductor hanging off the pole at the back wolf-whistled in their direction. They broke apart and gave him a wave. *"Another world" doesn't quite cover it*, Joan thought.

CHAPTER 28

Mrs. C had the radio on in the kitchen. "To keep us company while we work," she said. Joan already knew not to disturb her landlady while *The Archers* was on. It had taken her a week or so to get the hang of their daily routine. By late afternoon, she was in the kitchen helping to get dinner ready—peeling and chopping vegetables. Mrs. C set five places at the table. Her three other lodgers always knocked off work a bit early on a Friday.

"The foreman knows he's had his pound of flesh out of us come Friday lunchtime," Michael joked.

"Yeah, he wants us nice and rested for Monday morning, isn't that right, lads?" Joe chimed in.

The atmosphere around the dinner table at the end of the week was always full of good humor. Joe, Eddie, and Michael had their pay in their back pockets and the weekend ahead of them.

"You'll have that pattern scraped off my plates if you're not careful," Mrs. C joked, delighted to see them devouring the fish pie she'd made that afternoon.

"I was ready for that," Michael said, sitting back in his chair and patting his belly.

After dinner, Joan was at the sink scrubbing the pots when Eddie came to stand next to her. "Fancy coming down to the boozer with us for a drink tonight?" he asked.

Joan hesitated, glancing at Mrs. C, who was busy stacking the clean plates in the cupboard. She hadn't planned to meet Martin until Sunday because he was revising for exams the following week. Eddie could see her wavering. "Go on! It'll be a laugh, and you could do with getting out more," he said, nodding toward the pots and pans. "That's hardly what I'd call an evening's entertainment for a girl who's new to the bright lights of London."

"Are you sure I wouldn't be cramping your style?" Joan said, looking over her shoulder at Joe and Michael, who were still sitting at the table.

"Not at all. The more the merrier," Michael said. Joe grinned.

"Okay, you're on, then. Just let me finish up the pots and change, then I'll be right with you."

"So, WHERE ARE WE HEADED?" Joan asked, as they walked down Chatterton Road. The three lads towered above her.

"The Auld Triangle, of course!" Michael said. "Where else? It's a proper Irish boozer."

"They always have live music on a Friday evening, and it's great craic altogether," said Joe.

"Don't tell me you haven't been yet?!" Eddie said. "No self-respecting Irishwoman living in Islington would drink anywhere else."

"Not to mention that their beer is as cold as your girlfriend's heart, Ed," Joe teased.

The painted black façade of the pub jutted out into the junction, and the warm glow from its lights welcomed the weary in after a hard week's work. Joan recognized the familiar smell of Guinness mingled with cigarette smoke as soon as Eddie pushed the door open.

Inside, the rumble of conversation reverberated off the red flock-papered walls. "I'll find us a table," Eddie said, shouldering his way through the crowd. "Michael, you get them in."

"What are you having, Joan?" Michael asked.

"I'll have a white lemonade."

"You must be joking," Joe said. "That's not a proper drink."

"Honestly, a lemonade would be lovely." Joan blushed.

"Suit yourself." Michael shrugged as he took his place among the other men standing three deep at the bar holding their banknotes aloft. They sat around a high table perched on bar stools, and, when Michael came back with the drinks, the lads took the first deep swigs of their pints, smacked their lips, and exhaled.

"Ah, that hit the spot," Eddie said, admiring the contents of his glass before wiping the creamy foam from his lips with the back of his hand.

All around her Joan heard the familiar accents of home. There wasn't a Black or brown face in sight and only the odd Cockney lilt to be heard. This must be the place the Irish came to forget they lived in a multicultural metropolis now. A reminder of home. In the corner, a man with a Ronnie Drew beard began belting out the first few bars of "The Wild Rover" on a makeshift stage draped with the tricolor.

"So, what brings you to London, Joan?" Joe asked, innocently.

"Same as yourselves," Joan replied, her cheeks flushing.

"I hear you," Michael said. "There's nothing doing back home, is there?"

"We've landed on our feet with work here all right," Joe said.

"Do you miss it? Home, I mean?" Joan said, looking from one to the other.

"My ma's spuds definitely!" Eddie said. The other two were quiet, and Joan knew she'd hit a nerve. They avoided talking about home for good reason.

"I miss my sister," she said.

"How many have you?" Joe asked.

"Just the one. There were six of us, but when Ma died, Da couldn't cope, and the others were taken away."

"That's rough," Michael said, taking a swig of his pint. The others fidgeted and eyed the floor.

"How about yourselves?" Joan brightened, conscious that she was doing exactly what she'd promised herself she wouldn't do and putting a damper on their Friday night out.

"There's seven of us," Michael replied.

"I'm one of twelve," Eddie followed, puffing his chest out.

"Jesus!" Joan exclaimed.

"The eldest of nine," Joe said.

"Well, your mothers must be saints, that's all I can say."

The lads nodded in agreement as the crowd clapped for the bearded singer. An older man with a Cork accent called out across the bar. "Well, would you look at what the cat dragged in?! Eddie Leahy, what are you doing here?"

"Tony Brophy!" Eddie said, extending his hand. Tony came over and stood next to their table. "You know the lads. And this is Joan, who lives at our digs."

Joan held her hand out. "Pleased to meet you, Tony."

"Likewise, Joan. So, where are you from?" Tony pulled up a stool next to her.

"Dublin," Joan said.

"I know that," Tony said, rolling his eyes. "I meant what part?"

"Harold's Cross," Joan replied warily.

"Ah yeah, isn't that where the sweet factory is?"

"That's right," she said. "The Royal Candy. Do you know it?"

"That's the one. No, I don't, but I have a cousin who works there."

Joan's blood ran cold. "Oh, really? What's their name?" she asked.

"Jim. Jim Brophy." The room seemed to spin, and Joan had the urge to flee. "Do you know him?"

She frowned and stalled. "Er, the name doesn't ring a bell," she lied, as the vivid memory of Jim Brophy pinning her to the convent wall came flooding back.

"Will you have another one?" Tony offered, gesturing toward the empty glass on the table in front of her.

"No thanks, I'd best be off anyway," Joan replied, pretending to check the time on her watch.

"It's early yet," Joe said.

"The night is still young," Michael added.

"I have to be up early in the morning," Joan said, standing up and gathering her coat and bag from the seat. "Enjoy yourselves. I'll see you tomorrow. Nice to meet you, Tony."

Outside, she stood with her back to the pub wall. She closed her eyes and allowed the cool balm of the evening breeze to soothe her. "Never again," she said, glancing up at the Guinness sign swinging above the pub door. Her days of impromptu outings to places where her secret might be discovered and carried home were over.

CHAPTER 29

As the bells of Our Lady's church, half a mile away, were calling, Joan was buttering bread and peeling the thin brown shells off warm eggs for sandwiches. She'd made up her mind that she wouldn't be going to Sunday Mass. If her one night out at the Auld Triangle had taught her anything, it was that London wasn't far enough from home. What was that saying? All the world's a village. If that was the case, all of Ireland was a single street. Joan didn't want to have to answer the inevitable questions about whether she was from the north or south side of the city, what school she went to, and where her father grew up.

She wrapped the sandwiches in greaseproof paper and packed them in the wicker shopping basket Mrs. C had given her, adding a couple of apples for good measure. Then she tidied up, wiping the crumbs off the chopping board. The gray November sky she saw out the window didn't bode well for a picnic in the park, but that wouldn't matter, as long as she was with Martin. He'd be here any minute for their first Sunday outing in London together. She couldn't wait.

She picked up the basket and went to the hall, put on her coat and mohair scarf, and waited. He wouldn't be more than a few minutes away. Through the glass leadlight at the side of the door, she caught sight of Martin opening the gate and walking up the path. He wore the collar of his gray wool coat up around his ears, like a film star—hands buried in his pockets, broad shoulders hunched against the cold.

Then he rang the doorbell, and Joan's heart soared. He was already grinning when she opened the door.

"Ready?"

"All set," Joan replied.

As they walked to the bus stop at the bottom of the street where they'd catch the bus to Hampstead Heath, Martin took her hand. Out of habit, she pulled it away, but then she remembered.

"Our days of skulking around are over, Joan," Martin said. "Why should we have to hide how we feel about each other?"

Joan gave his hand a gentle squeeze. She'd never heard him sound so defiant. When they reached the bus stop, he took the basket from her and put it on the ground, then wrapped her in his arms. "I still can't believe you're here," he whispered.

"Where else would I go, Martin?"

He kissed her long and slow. She closed her eyes and never wanted to open them again.

They sat on the top deck of the bus, and Martin pointed out landmarks they hadn't yet visited in the distance. "I'll take you there one day," he kept saying, over and over, though they never strayed far from Islington. Joan was so happy just to be with him she barely took any notice. When they got to the park, they walked hand in hand on the tree-lined path, stopping next to the playing fields for a few minutes to watch a football match between two groups of boys who'd thrown their jumpers on the grass to mark the goals.

One of the smallest boys made a break for it, dribbling the ball toward the goal. The goalie stood his ground but dived left instead of right, and the ball flew past him into the back of the imaginary net and beyond.

"GOAL!" the striker's teammates chorused.

The football stopped squarely at Joan's feet. "Hey, goalie!" she called out, kicking the ball to the boy standing between the two piles of jumpers. She turned to see Martin smiling at her. "What?" she said, catching up to him.

He reached out and took her hand. "You'll make a brilliant mother."

Joan stood rooted to the patch of grass. "Do you really think so?" she said, her eyes searching his face. She hadn't known until that moment how much she wanted those words to be true.

"I know so," he said, with a cocky grin.

Her heart swelled with the compliment, but she dismissed it. "Well, let's find a seat and see how my egg sandwiches measure up, then." She let go of his hand and ran on ahead of him.

Mrs. C's place was beginning to feel like home. Within a couple of weeks, Joan had her morning routine set. She was up, dressed, and on her knees cleaning out the fire in the dining room by the time Mrs. C came down. Joe, Michael, and Eddie had already left for work. Mrs. C and Joan sat at the red Formica kitchen table drinking tea from willow-patterned cups and eating toast spread with home-made marmalade.

"It's nice to have a bit of company, Joan. It can get lonely here in this big old house, even when it's full of people. At the end of the day, when I shut that bedroom door, it's just me, the radio, and the BBC."

"My granny was just the same after Granda died, even though she had all of us," Joan said.

"Old age: it's a curse and no mistake," Mrs. C grumbled good-naturedly. "What about you, Joan? How are you settling in?"

"I can't tell you how grateful I am to be here," Joan said, tears in her eyes.

Mrs. C reached across the table and patted her hand. "When are you due?"

Joan gave her a startled look. Her free hand went to the small bulge in her belly. Up until then, the baby had never been mentioned—not to or by anyone. Joan hadn't lied to Mrs. C; she'd just skirted around the truth. Now her question made the fact that Joan would soon become a mother all the more real.

"How did you know?" she stammered.

"You learn to recognize the signs. A young lad knocking on your door looking for digs for his Irish girl, who happens to be coming alone on the boat."

Joan lowered her eyes. "I'm sorry. I should have been up front. I meant to tell you as soon as I got here."

"It's all right. You won't be the first girl in this predicament who's lived under my roof, and you won't be the last."

"I'm due at the end of March . . . I think."

"You haven't seen a doctor yet, then?"

Joan's eyes widened as she shook her head. "No. Not back home. There's no way, unless . . ." She trailed off.

"I have the address of a doctor a few of the girls who've stayed here have been to. I saved it somewhere. Let me find it for you." She stood, pushing her chair back from the table, and took a well-thumbed brown-leather address book down from its place on the shelf among her cookery books. She began flicking through the pages. "Here we go," she said, running her finger along the name she'd written in blue ink. "Dr. Marshall." She wrote the address on a slip of paper torn from the notebook she kept handy to write her shopping lists, then passed it to Joan.

"Thank you," Joan said, clutching the small piece of paper.

"And will the boy stand by you?"

"Oh, yes!" Joan answered, too quickly. "He gave me the ticket to come here and everything." She met Mrs. C's wise blue eyes.

"Good, that's good," Mrs. C said. They were both quiet for a moment, and then Mrs. C broke the spell, stacking the cups and plates. "Look at the time! All this sitting around isn't getting the work done, is it?!"

That afternoon, Joan was rubbing Brasso off the letterbox when the telegram boy stopped outside the gate and leaned his bike up against the garden wall. She frowned. Unless there was a wedding in the household, telegrams spelled bad news. "Telegram for a Mrs. Clemence," the pimply lad said officiously as he approached the steps to the door.

"Wait there," Joan told him, hurrying to the kitchen. She didn't want to frighten the life out of Mrs. C by shouting the news down the hall. "Mrs. C, there's a lad at the door with a telegram for you."

Mrs. C put down the rolling pin she'd been holding and rushed to the door, rubbing her palms on the front of her apron. Joan waited for her in the kitchen. "I hope it's not bad news," she said when Mrs. C returned holding the unfolded sheet of paper, knowing by the look on her landlady's face that it was.

"It's my sister in Devon. She's had another bad fall, and they're keeping her in hospital overnight for observation. She's asking for me."

"Oh, I'm sorry," Joan said. "Here, why don't you sit down?" She pulled out one of the chairs from under the kitchen table. But Mrs. C wasn't listening. She was busy rinsing her hands under the tap and already making plans for her mercy mission to Devon.

Half an hour later, they stood together on the street waiting for the taxi. "I don't like to leave you, Joan. You've only been here a few weeks. But I have to go."

"I'll be fine," Joan said. "It's only for a couple of nights. You're not to worry."

Mrs. C looked left, then right. "If this taxi doesn't get here soon, I'll miss my train," she said, pushing back her coat sleeve to check the time again. "Lucky for us it's not my busy time of year." She handed Joan the big bunch of keys that unlocked every room in the house, and Joan made a tight fist around them.

"Are you sure you'll manage now, love?" Mrs. C said.

"I'm sure. I'll be fine. Here's your taxi now," Joan said, pointing at a black cab driving toward them. Mrs. C picked up her overnight bag and started down the steps, glancing back at her as she went.

"Go on now," said Joan, waving her off. "You're not to worry. I'll see you on Sunday night." She returned to the kitchen and began wiping flour off the table. Mrs. C had planned a steak and kidney pudding for dinner, and Joe, Michael, and Eddie would still need to be fed when they got in from work. They would be out on the tear all weekend, and Joan wouldn't see much of them. She'd be left to her own devices until Mrs. C was back home again.

While Joan was assembling the pie, it dawned on her that she could sneak Martin into the house and up to her room that night. They could spend the weekend together, and Mrs. C would be none the wiser. The Cork boys would no doubt be too drunk to notice what Joan got up to. She hummed to herself as she rolled out a neat circle of pastry.

Once the kitchen was tidied, she caught the bus to the City Vocational College. She wanted to surprise Martin with the news that Mrs. C had been called away.

"What are you doing here?" Martin said with a smile, peeling away from his English classmates when he saw her standing at the bottom of the steps with her back to the wall. "This is a nice surprise."

"Well, I might have an even nicer one for you," Joan said, linking arms with him. "Come on."

"Where are we going?"

"Back to my place." She beamed at him. "I'll explain on the way."

MARTIN TRACED HIS INDEX FINGER from Joan's bare shoulder to her forearm and back again. "I wish we could stay here for good."

Joan laughed. "If Mrs. C catches you here, I'll be out on the street for good!" She threw the covers back in one swift move and sat shivering on the edge of the bed in her slip, rolling a stocking up one leg, then the other.

Martin lay on his side, propped up on his elbow and looking longingly at her. "Come back."

"Haven't you had enough for one day, Mr. Egan?"

"Never!" Martin said, making a grab for her arm and pulling her back into the bed. Joan laughed, remembering what she'd said to Esther. It *was* nice to be this close to someone you loved, someone who loved you.

They barely moved from the bed, never mind the room, for the rest of the weekend. Late on Sunday afternoon, Joan picked up their discarded clothes from the bedroom floor, opened the window to air the room, and made the bed. "Mrs. C can't ever know you were here. I feel awful about lying to her. She's been so kind to me."

"What she doesn't know won't hurt her," Martin said, as he pushed the tip of his belt through the buckle. "Now, how about going out for some dinner? I'm starving."

It was a cool, clear winter night by the time they left the house, the sky bright with stars. The smell of the coal fires, their smoke trailing skyward from the chimneys of the terraced houses, filled the air. Martin put a protective arm around Joan's shoulder as they strolled to the high street. On the way, they passed men in groups of twos and threes heading home from an afternoon in the pub, their steaming packets of fish and chips, wrapped in newspaper, tucked under their arms. "What do you fancy?" Joan asked.

"I'd kill for a cod and chips," Martin replied. "Will we go in?" he said, already pushing open the door of the fish-and-chip shop.

"What's it to be?" the stout Italian man behind the fryer called to them over the glass countertop.

"Whatever the lady wants," Martin replied, standing proud and pulling Joan into a hug. "Anything she wants."

CHAPTER 30

The shopping bags seemed to get heavier and heavier the closer Joan got to home. She hauled them up the steps before setting them down. She didn't want to break the eggs they needed to make the Yorkshire puddings for dinner. Now, where had she put her key? As soon as she unlocked the front door, Mrs. C called out from the kitchen, "There's a letter for you. I left it there on the hall table."

Joan put down the shopping and snatched the envelope. Her first letter from home, probably the first proper letter Teresa had ever written. She ran her thumb over the stamp her sister had stuck in the corner of the envelope—a map of Ireland, bordered by shamrocks. Reminders of home.

She imagined Teresa queuing at the post office in Harold's Cross to buy the stamp. Mrs. Ahearn who worked behind the counter would have asked how Joan was getting on in England, and Teresa would have relayed what she knew of Joan's life there—the little Joan had told her. She put the letter in her coat pocket and picked up the shopping bags again.

"It's a letter from my sister back home," she said, coming into the kitchen and starting to unpack the shopping onto the table. "They were already out of fresh bread. I said I'd come back later to see if they had another delivery."

She felt Mrs. C's hand on her shoulder. "You must miss her."

Joan gave her a grateful nod. "I do. Just as much as I thought I would. Maybe more."

Up in her bedroom, she opened the letter, making sure not to tear the paper. Anyone used to sending or receiving letters would call the single sheet of lined paper in Joan's hand a note. Like herself, Teresa had left school at fourteen and could only read and write enough to get by.

Dear Joan,

I hope things are going well for you in London and the work is not as bad as the factory. I am ok and Da is fine. He misses your dinners. I just miss you.

Write soon.

xx

T

Joan read and reread those few lines over and over. She imagined how long it had taken her sister to write them and felt the deep love the spare words couldn't convey. Da wasn't too pleased with Teresa's cooking. But he'd have to put up with it, given that he couldn't tell one end of a frying pan from the other. And she was sure Teresa missed having her there to warm her feet on at night now that winter had arrived.

What she wasn't sure of was how Da was treating Teresa now she wasn't there to keep him in check, and that worried her. There was no way to read between these few lines. She wished again, not for the first time, that she could somehow get her sister over to London.

There was so much she couldn't tell Teresa about her new life. In fact, she could tell her hardly any of it. Her doctor's appointments, Friday nights with Martin and his English friends from college at the

Crown, their Sunday walks. All of it was off-limits. She wondered how she would keep all of this from Teresa.

She had been picking at a small thread on the patchwork bedspread underneath her and, without thinking, pulled at it. The whole row of stitching unraveled, leaving a gaping hole. "Damn it!" Joan said aloud. She didn't have time to mend the bedspread now—there were a million and one other jobs to do around the place before the weekend. She folded her sister's letter back into the envelope then placed it in her bedside-table drawer.

That night, she and Martin sat in a corner of the Crown, waiting for his friends Dan and Oliver to arrive. Joan was unusually quiet. "What's up?" Martin asked, reaching for her hand. Joan hesitated. She didn't want to spoil his night out. He could have just met the lads on this own, but instead he'd invited her along. Still, he wanted to know.

"It's nothing much," she said, lowering her eyes. She didn't want him to think she had a single regret about being there with him. "It's just . . . I got a letter from Teresa today."

Martin stiffened. "She doesn't know anything, does she? You haven't told her about us . . . or anything, have you?"

"No, of course not," Joan said. "We agreed. But it's hard, Martin. She's not just my sister—she's my best friend. I don't like keeping things from her." She clasped her hands in her lap before going on. "She'll find out sooner or later. I'll have to tell her once the baby comes."

"We'll cross that bridge when we come to it," Martin said, looking past her toward the frosted-glass door of the bar, which opened and closed every few minutes, sending chill winter air down the back of Joan's neck. "Ah, there they are." He stood to wave and call out to his friends, "Over here, lads!"

Dan and Oliver were both from the English shipbuilding town Stockton-on-Tees. The Furness Shipbuilding Company was modernizing and needed young men with good heads for figures, so Dan and Oliver had been sent to London to brush up on the latest accounting practices.

It took a while for Martin to get his order in—three pints of pale ale and a lemonade for Joan. "Here you go, lads," he said, holding out the small circular tray to them when he reached the table.

"Don't mind if I do!" Dan said as he grabbed a pint, taking a swig before Martin sat down. "So, as I was saying, Joan, what red-blooded lad would say no to six months all expenses paid in the bright lights of London? We're having the time of our lives. Aren't we, Ollie?" He nudged his friend in the ribs.

"A girl in every port, that's you, Dan!" Martin said, laughing. Joan fidgeted in her seat and sipped her lemonade.

"Are you sure we can't get you anything stronger, Joan?" Dan said.

"No, thanks, I'm grand."

It was clear that Dan and Oliver knew nothing about the baby. Of course they didn't. You couldn't expect a respectable young college student like Martin to air his private life in public. No, he had done the right thing keeping their secret to himself.

Joan stood sideways, looking at herself in the full-length mirror. A draft blew between the gaps in the old sash windows, and she shivered in her nightdress, noticing that her belly now stretched the fabric. Soon it would be impossible to hide her pregnancy, even in loose clothes. She'd only gotten away with it for this long because she was tall. In the new year it would be obvious to everyone.

She thanked God every day that she didn't have to walk through Harold's Cross in this state, her belly straining against the buttons of her winter coat. To avoid going home for Christmas, she made excuses about money being tight. She'd posted a couple of small gifts—a shocking-pink chiffon scarf for Teresa and new gloves for

Da. She knew he wouldn't write as long as she kept sending him the few shillings Martin gave her.

Martin told his mother he couldn't come home because he had exams early in the new year—and anyway wouldn't he be home soon for good? Mrs. C was spending Christmas with her son in York, and the lads from Cork were getting the ferry back home. So this time there was no need to sneak Martin into the house.

They talked and kissed in bed, but there was an unspoken understanding between them that sex wasn't welcome now. They slept soundly, him spooned behind her, his arm draped over her belly. Joan woke on Christmas morning to Martin kissing her behind the ear.

"What time is it?" she said, still foggy with sleep.

"Just gone nine."

"I can't believe I slept this late," she said, rolling to face him.

"You must have needed it," he said, stroking her cheek. "Why don't you stay here and keep warm. I'll go down and light the fire."

"That would be lovely," Joan said, touching his arm. "I won't be long. Why don't we go for a walk after breakfast?"

"You're on!" he said, throwing back the covers.

Downstairs in the kitchen, Martin had set two places at the table. "Sit down," he said, pulling out a chair. Next to her place, Joan saw a flat package wrapped in white tissue paper tied with red string.

"What's this?" she asked, looking at him.

"Just something small," Martin replied. "I know we said no presents, but I wanted to get you something." He picked up the package and handed it to Joan. "Sit down and open it."

She sat and tugged on the string, then unfolded the tissue. Inside was a photo album. Its smooth cover smelled of new leather, and each page was separated by gauzy paper. "It's for our memories—to keep them safe," Martin said, looking down at her. "I remembered what you told me once about not having any photographs of your mother."

Tears welled in Joan's eyes. "Thank you," she whispered, standing now to hug him. "But I didn't get you anything."

"I've got everything I need right here," Martin said, kissing her forehead. "Well . . . apart from a decent fry-up."

"That I can definitely do," Joan said, as she folded the tissue paper around the album again.

After breakfast, they set out on a walk around the deserted London streets. "It's as if the city is all ours," Joan said, as they crossed Compton Road without looking left or right. Kids with new bicycles who had pestered their parents out of their cozy beds into the cold swerved up and down the icy footpaths. "Slow down, Robert!" a father yelled as he ran alongside a freckle-faced boy pedaling like the clappers.

"That'll be us before we know it," Joan remarked. Martin squeezed her hand. They walked arm in arm, like any other couple expecting their first child the following spring might have done, peering into the bay windows of the elegant houses on Gibson Square, where Christmas trees draped in fairy lights twinkled behind the glass. Joan imagined their life together, a proper family, here in London. All gathered around a real tree, stuffing themselves with mince pies and belting out carols without a care in the world. It was only a matter of time.

They had planned to see in the New Year at an old London pub that served pale ale and Cornish pasties, with Dan and Oliver and a couple of girls from Sheffield the boys had met. But Martin had second thoughts when he realized they could no longer hide Joan's pregnancy.

"It'll be lovely just the two of us," he soothed her. "Like old times."

Joan pouted. "Like old times when you had to hide me away, you mean," she said.

"No, not at all. You know I didn't mean it like that," Martin replied. "It's just . . . people ask too many questions. The less they know the better. Anyway, it's nobody's business but ours." He straightened to his full height so he was looking down on her. "Now, let that be an end to it." And so it was decided that they'd avoid people altogether, not just the Irish pubs like the Auld Triangle.

There was always the danger of meeting someone from home: a distant second cousin or a friend of a friend, someone's sister or so-and-so's nephew who went to school with yer man's brother. Anyone and everyone was a threat, a person who might ask whereabouts you were from, someone who remembered they knew Joan Quinn's family from way back or, worse, Martin Egan's. They played it safe, evading all but polite conversation with strangers.

"Only three more months," Martin told her. The weeks would fly in, and then all their worries would be over.

CHAPTER 31

In early January, Joan was on her way back from posting a letter home, taking care not to slip on the icy footpath, when something in the window of the wool shop on the corner of Cross Street caught her eye. There among the colorful display of wools and ribbons was a snow-white baby cardigan. Without giving it much thought, she found herself pushing the shop door open.

The bell above the door announced her arrival, and the shopkeeper came from out the back, holding her knitting, paused in the middle of a row. "You all right there, love? Can I help you?"

"I was wondering . . ."—Joan hesitated—"how much is that baby cardigan in the window?"

"Oh, that's just for display. We don't usually sell them."

"Ah, okay. Thanks anyway."

As Joan turned to leave, the woman called after her. "Tell you what, why don't you have it as a present for your little one? Can't be long now?"

"Three months to go," Joan replied. "Are you sure?"

"It'll be put to better use keeping the little 'un warm."

Joan couldn't stop thanking the woman as she folded the tiny garment, then wrapped it in tissue and brown paper. "We'll have you knitting yet!" the woman said.

"I'll be back," Joan said. "After the baby comes."

As she strolled along Islington High Street, Joan hugged the package. Back in her room, she unwrapped the cardigan and ran her fingers along the three pearly buttons. She held it to her cheek, closed her eyes, and imagined tucking tiny arms inside it. Then she folded it and placed it on top of her things for the hospital. A clean nightdress, knickers, sanitary pads, and a tin of Johnson's baby powder. She'd been turning the cap open every day for weeks just to smell it. With each day that passed she felt more ready for her baby to arrive.

That night she sat up in bed and rubbed her belly in small, slow circles with the palm of her hand, remembering the shopkeeper and smiling to herself. Maybe people would be kind to her and her baby after all.

ONE EVENING, AT THE END of January, Joan was standing up on the packed bus coming home from her doctor's appointment. Dr. Marshall told her everything was going according to plan. The baby was growing strong inside her. She couldn't have been happier. As she stood, lost in her thoughts, a silver-haired man tapped her on the shoulder. "Here, love, you sit yourself down there," he said, offering Joan his seat.

"That's very kind," she said, thanking him. The woman in the next seat glanced down at Joan's belly and then, for the briefest moment, at the bare ring finger of her left hand. She gave her a pitying smile, then turned to stare out the window. Joan's cheeks grew hot, and she pulled her coat across her middle. *I'm marked out, even here*, she thought.

That night, as she lay in the bath, looking at her belly rising above the level of the water, she remembered her mother's wedding ring. When she was in her dressing gown and back in her bedroom, she pulled open her bedside-table drawer. There, under the three letters and the Christmas card Teresa had sent her, was the envelope with the ring. Joan took it out and slid the worn gold band onto her finger. It wasn't a perfect fit—her fingers had swelled as the pregnancy progressed—but it was good enough.

Mrs. C noticed the ring as soon as they sat down to their cup of tea the following morning. Her gaze moved from Joan's finger to her face as she set the plate of toast down in front of her.

"It was my ma's," Joan blurted, rubbing her thumb against the thin gold.

Mrs. C stirred her tea. "I suppose you'll wait until after the baby is born to get married?"

The question, which Joan should have known the answer to, unsettled her. "I don't know," she whispered. "We haven't talked about it."

"Well, I'd say it's high time you did, Joan."

Martin knocked on the front door of the guesthouse that evening as usual. It was only five o'clock but already pitch-dark outside. It wasn't until they were seated at a small round table in the farthest corner of the pub that Martin noticed the ring. "Where did you get that?" he asked, pointing to Joan's finger.

"It was Ma's." Joan tried to read his expression. His hard-set jaw betrayed him. "Look at me, Martin," she demanded under her breath and placing a hand on her stomach. "I can't hide this any longer." The space between them seemed to expand like stretched elastic in the time it took him to react. He put down his pint and said nothing. "I know it's not Ireland, Martin," Joan said. "But you've no idea what it's like to walk around in public looking like I do. The pitying looks I get because I'm not married. The ring will just make life easier."

"Okay, right," Martin said, picking up his pint again, looking around the room.

"Besides, we can't go on ignoring the fact that the baby will be here before we know it."

"We're not ignoring the fact. How the hell can we?"

"You've changed your tune! What's wrong?" Joan said, trying to keep the panic from her voice. She'd never heard Martin speak about the baby like that before. Not in all the time they'd been in London. Not even when she first told him she was pregnant.

"Ah, it's nothing. It's not you," he said, tracing circles with his finger around the beer-ring stains on the table. "I had a call from my mother at my digs last night." He took a sip of his pint. "Paul, the warehouse supervisor, up and left yesterday without giving her any notice. I'd put money on it she said something to annoy him and he just walked out."

Joan sat bolt upright now, her pregnant belly sticking out all the more for it. "What else did she say?"

Martin's jaw clenched. "She thinks I should finish up the course early and come home now. Says she can't cope on her own."

"You can't—"

"Don't worry, I'm not going to," Martin interrupted, lifting his pint to his lips again. Joan was about to thank him but stopped herself. She wanted to hug him, but her bump came between them. "I wouldn't leave you here on your own," he said, with a fleeting smile. "But we might have to go back home sooner than I planned."

His words left Joan cold. She put a protective hand on her belly and tried to act normally, but she couldn't even return his smile. Surely once the baby arrived Martin would see that the only thing for it was for them to stay in London and forget about their old lives back home? Surely.

On Sunday, when Joan and Martin went out, a hard overnight frost still covered the ground, and the forecast was for snow. The entire park was blanketed white. Martin scraped the ice off a bench in the bandstand, and they sat blowing on their numb fingers. He was quieter than usual. Joan didn't know why his silence made her uneasy, but doubt churned in her stomach.

The baby would be here in a matter of weeks, and they were nowhere near ready. As she was thinking this, the baby kicked hard. On impulse, she took Martin's hand and placed it on her bump. "Feel!" she said, smiling at him. "We might have the next Bobby Charlton on our hands here. He'll make a great little footballer, that's for sure!"

Martin pulled his hand away, as if he'd been jolted by an electric current. Joan stared at him. His blue eyes were serious and sad. Joan's face flushed, and a cold dread crept into the pit of her stomach.

"We need to talk, Joan." Martin didn't have to say another word. He was having second thoughts. She knew—just by looking in his eyes. She knew. "I've been racking my brain looking for a way around this."

"A way *around* it? What do you mean, Martin?"

His eyes were downcast now, and he was concentrating hard on a crack in the bandstand floor between his feet. Joan's heart was pounding in her chest. He ran his fingers through his hair distractedly, a sign that he was working up to something he didn't want to say.

"Spit it out."

He turned to face her. Joan thought she read pity in his eyes.

"You know I love you, Joan, don't you?" She didn't answer. "But I don't see how we can keep the baby without causing a scandal back home."

Joan's insides froze. "I thought you . . ." She couldn't get the words out.

"Everyone would know. It could ruin us."

"What do you mean? I'm ruined already if you won't stand by me."

"I want to marry you, Joan. But not like this." He gestured toward her belly with a sigh.

She jumped to her feet. "Well, that's the first I've heard of it!" Her mind was racing. Did he have any idea what he was saying? Did he know her at all?

"This isn't how I planned for us to start our life together," Martin said, folding his arms across his chest, his eyes fixed on the frost-covered field beyond the bandstand. "It doesn't have to be like this. There are plenty of couples who would give their right arm for a baby." He stood and looked at her now, beseeching her to agree.

She tried to reason with him. "But this isn't *a* baby, Martin. It's *our* baby. We can't give it away just like that." She couldn't even look at him. "And then what? Go on as if it never existed?" Tears were blurring her vision as she fiddled with her mother's wedding ring, twisting it slowly one way then the other on her finger. Once the first ones fell, she couldn't stop them coming. This man she loved and trusted had knocked the feet right out from under her.

"Don't, Joan. Don't be like this. Don't cry," Martin said, trying to put his arm around her.

Joan pushed him away. "Don't touch me," she said through her tears. "Don't you dare touch me."

She let herself into the house without a sound that evening and went straight to her room. She couldn't face Mrs. C. Still in her coat, she sat on the edge of her bed. What was she going to do now? There would be no new life in London for the three of them. Martin had made that clear. He'd be returning home: a single, childless man with prospects, determined to take up his role at the helm of Egan & Son, and there was no way he could risk the whisper of a scandal reaching the ears of Egans' customers.

He wasn't asking Joan to marry him. He was telling her to choose. Respectability or ruin. Him or the baby. She couldn't have both.

Her thoughts were interrupted by Mrs. C's quiet knock on the door. "Joan, are you there? Dinner's ready."

Joan opened the door a crack. "Yes, I'm here. I'll be down in a minute."

"You're still in your coat. What's wrong?" Nothing much got past Mrs. C. She could probably see that Joan's eyes were red raw from crying. "Are you sure you're all right?" she asked.

"I will be," Joan replied.

She didn't sleep a wink that night, and the following morning she forced herself out of bed and through the motions of her routine. Michael, Joe, and Eddie sat around the table, in grubby work trousers, cracking jokes and moaning about their foreman. Joan sat opposite Mrs. C, silent and exhausted, feeling sick to her stomach.

"Here, you sit down there and let me do that," Eddie offered, stealing a glance at Joan's belly as she stood to clear the plates.

She gave him a weary smile. "You're all right, Eddie. It's good to have something to do." Out of the corner of her eye, she saw the lads giving each other a look. As she was stacking the plates next to the sink, she felt Eddie's big hand on her shoulder.

"Is there anything we can do?" he said, without meeting her eye.

"Not really, Eddie. But thanks for asking." Michael and Joe were draining the dregs of their mugs and pushing chairs back from the table. "Go on." Joan smiled at them. "You'd better get going or you'll be late."

Over the past few weeks, as her pregnancy progressed, Mrs. C had taken to giving her lighter jobs like tidying out the linen cupboard and folding the washing. She'd also started boiling an egg for Joan's breakfast. "You need to keep your strength up," she said every morning.

"Are you not eating your egg, Joan?" she asked now.

"I'm sorry. I'm not hungry today."

Mrs. C frowned and touched Joan's forehead with the back of

her wrinkled hand. "You do look a bit peaky. Maybe I should call the doctor."

"No, no, don't do that. I'm fine, honestly. It isn't that, Mrs. C. It's just . . ." She couldn't hold back the tears any longer.

Mrs. C put a bony arm around her. "What is it?"

"What am I going to do, Mrs. C? Martin doesn't want to keep the baby," Joan sobbed. "He says he still wants to marry me but it would be best for everyone if we had the baby adopted." Tears rolled unchecked down her cheeks.

Mrs. C was taken aback but recovered enough to say, "I see," through pursed lips. "And what do *you* want?" she asked, taking her freshly laundered hankie from her apron pocket and handing it to Joan.

"I don't want to have to choose," Joan said, blowing her nose. "I want the baby. How could I go back home and pretend it never happened? How can he expect me to do that?" She was sobbing hysterically now.

"Could you bring the baby back home with you?" Mrs. C offered. "Would your people help?"

Joan shook her head. "What kind of life could I give a baby there on my own with no money and my da coming home blind drunk every night?" She met Mrs. C's kind eyes, and an idea came to her. "Could we stay here, Mrs. C? Myself and the baby? I could still work for you. You know I'm a good worker. That's not going to change. And the baby wouldn't take up much room." She stopped to catch her breath now that she'd said her piece.

Mrs. C was quiet. Too quiet. "I'm sorry, Joan. I can't have a baby in the house, not at my age. I made a hard-and-fast rule when I started taking in pregnant girls not to get involved. I wish I could help, but there's just no way . . ." Her words trailed off.

No way. Of course, Joan could see that now. Mrs. C couldn't take on the problems of every other girl who landed on her doorstep. She couldn't be responsible for helping to raise a child. This place wasn't suitable for a baby who would grow into a toddler needing the freedom to run around before they knew it. She'd be fooling herself to think that things could be otherwise.

"I understand," Joan said. "Really I do. Don't worry, I'll sort something out." She tried to sound cheerful. "Who knows, Mrs. C. Maybe Martin will change his mind when he sees the baby. There's still time."

CHAPTER 32

The baby was six days late when Joan's waters broke in the middle of the night on the last day of March. She woke in a panic in soaked sheets before a wave of pain gripped her. She stuffed a hand towel into her knickers, then waddled along the landing to Mrs. C's room and knocked gently on the door.

"I'm sorry," she said, when a bleary-eyed Mrs. C opened the door a crack wearing rollers and a hairnet. "The baby's coming."

"Don't worry, love. I'll be right with you. Go back to your room, get dressed, and wait for me."

Joan did as she was told. "I'm sorry about the bed," she said, when Mrs. C arrived minutes later, a headscarf covering her rollers. She grimaced as another contraction gripped her.

Mrs. C picked up the small bag Joan had packed and repacked a dozen times. "Don't you give that a second thought. It's easily changed. We need to get you to the hospital now." Joan could only nod. "Careful on those stairs, Joan," Mrs. C said, as she guided her by the elbow toward the landing. Joan clung to the banister and took halting steps down toward the hall. At the bottom, Mrs. C helped her into her coat, which no longer buttoned across her middle, then they stepped out the front door and into the night.

The two women stood on the side of the path waiting for the taxi Mrs. C had called. "He's taking his time," Mrs. C said in exasperation, keeping an eye on Joan, who clutched her back as another contraction took hold. Finally, Mrs. C saw the cab on the other side of the road and stepped off the curb, waving her arms high above her head.

The cabbie did a U-turn and pulled up alongside them, then wound down his window. "Are you sure she's not going to drop that child in the back of my cab, missus?" he said.

Mrs. C reassured him that it was Joan's first baby and it would be hours before the child put in an appearance. Once they were in the back of the cab, she squeezed Joan's hand. "You all right, love?" Joan closed her eyes and nodded. How had her mother put herself through this half a dozen times?

The midwife on duty greeted them at the door of the maternity ward. The strong smell of hospital disinfectant turned Joan's stomach, making her even more nervous. "Let's get you examined and take a look at what's happening," the midwife said, pulling the green curtains around the small cubicle in a single swift move.

Joan lay back on the narrow metal hospital trolley and winced. Mrs. C put her bag on the floor of the cubicle. "Joan, I'm sorry, love, I can't stay," she said. "I've got the breakfasts to get for the others in a few hours." She placed her hand on Joan's shoulder. "You know how hopeless those young lads are. They might be able to build a house in a matter of weeks, but they couldn't boil an egg if their lives depended on it."

Joan bit her bottom lip.

"Don't worry. We'll take good care of her," the midwife said.

"Will you get word to Martin for me?" Joan asked.

"Of course. First thing in the morning I'll make sure he knows." Mrs. C gave Joan's hand another encouraging squeeze. "It'll all be over before you know it."

"Thanks for everything, Mrs. C. I'd be lost without you."

The day must have dawned, but Joan didn't know it. Time stood still as she lay there alone in the windowless labor ward, writhing in pain under the glaring fluorescent lights. There were so many unknowns she wasn't prepared for. How could she have been? The pain, of course, but also the fear of not knowing when it would end.

"How long? How much longer?" she kept asking the midwives, repeating the same question over and over without getting a straight answer. Between the waves of pain, she imagined Martin pacing the corridors outside. She heard the clatter of steel trolleys speeding past her curtained cubicle. The wails of other women. The sucking in of air. Rosary beads rustling somewhere in the near distance accompanied desperate prayers. *Holy Mary Mother of God. Pray for us sinners.* Newborns crying, protesting the harsh light.

The midwives, Helen and Sylvia, were tough and kind in equal measure. They weren't supposed to tell Joan their first names, but they broke the rules. "Just this once," they said. Joan wondered if it was because they felt sorry for her, a terrified creature, there all alone with no husband in sight. There was no mollycoddling, though—Helen and Sylvia made sure of that. They urged her on as you would a frightened friend. "I can see black hair. Two more pushes, and the baby will be here."

Joan's body took over, animal-like. In that moment, she knew exactly what to do. After the fearful months of powerlessness, this new sensation was liberating. She felt in control. She raised herself up on her elbows and gave one last push, letting out a long, low scream. Her body burned as though it might split in two.

And then it was all over.

Those first seconds of her baby's life happened in slow motion. Sylvia expertly balanced the baby on one hand while she rubbed it with a towel. Efficient voices hovered over Joan, mingling with the child's cries as she lay there waiting for them to announce her baby's arrival. The announcement never came.

"What is it?"

"It's a girl, Joan."

"Is she okay?"

"She's fine. Absolutely fine."

"Let me see her." Joan reached out, as if to take the baby from Sylvia. Helen and Sylvia exchanged a look. "Let's get you comfortable first, love. It looks like you're going to need a couple of stitches. And you'll need something for the pain."

They were just trying to do what was best. Joan knew that. Later, she'd remember how careful they had been only to refer to her child as "the baby," and never "your daughter." Of course, they'd have read Dr. Marshall's most recent note in her medical records. They were used to caring for unmarried mothers who could neither keep nor raise their babies.

"Please. I just want to see her."

Sylvia came around the side of the bed and placed Joan's little girl, wrapped in a pink blanket, in the crook of her arm. "There you go, love. Just a few minutes. We have to take her up to the nursery shortly and get her fed."

"But I'll be feeding her," Joan said, as she gazed down at her daughter. A defiant little red fist poked free from the swaddling. Joan could just make out the writing on the tiny pink-paper bracelet circling her wrist. *Quinn. 7 lbs 4 oz. 16:04, 1/4/1966.* A combination of seemingly random letters and numbers that would mean nothing to anyone else and everything to Joan in the years to come.

"Hello, you," Joan whispered, taking in every tiny detail of her daughter's face. "I thought her eyes would be closed," she said, to no one in particular. She pushed the blanket back from her feet to count her toes. Ten. There were definitely ten. She stroked the soft padding of her heels with her thumb. "You're perfect," she said, smiling and kissing the top of her baby's head, breathing in the smell of her.

The baby started to cry.

"Here, let me take her," Sylvia said. Joan shook her head, pressing the warmth of the small body closer to her breast. "Don't worry, we'll look after her," Sylvia said, hands outstretched. "Just while you have a bit of a sleep, Joan." The pethidine injection they'd given her was beginning to work its magic, and Joan lay back, exhausted, on fresh pillows. The baby was here and safe. She'd done it. She and her daughter had done it together.

"Tell them her name is April. For the month she was born," she heard herself call across the cubicle.

"We will. Now, you get some rest." The sound of Sylvia's voice seemed very far away now. The room swam, and Joan could hear her own heartbeat loud and slow in her ears. She felt as if she was observing the scene from somewhere far above the bed.

"Syl, hang on a second. I don't like Joan's color. Can you check her blood pressure?"

And that was the last Joan remembered.

WHEN JOAN WOKE AGAIN, SHE pulled at the oxygen mask covering her face.

"Hey, hey." Martin, who was sitting next to her bed, stood up and caught hold of her arm. "It's okay, Joan. You're all right. I'm here."

Joan tried to lift her head but slumped back against the pillows. She stared at the line in her arm, then followed the length of it up to the bag of dark-red blood dangling above her head. "What happened?" she whispered through parched lips.

"You lost a lot of blood, darlin'. You've been in here for a couple of days. The doctors said it was touch and go, and I thought I was going to lose you. I didn't know what to do, whether to send for Teresa, or your father."

Joan tried to sit up. "You didn't! Did you?"

"No, no. It's okay. Nobody knows. Our secret is still safe."

Their secret. Joan looked to her left and right. "Where is she? Where's our baby?"

"Don't worry, Joan. They're taking care of her in the nursery. She's doing well."

"We have a little girl. Did you see her, Martin? She's perfect."

He looked away, shaking his head.

"When can I see her, Martin?"

"Just you concentrate on getting better for now," he said. "Let me go tell the nurses you're back in the land of the living."

Two days later, Joan was transferred to a ward downstairs. Her body and her heart ached for April. She didn't touch the porridge and toast that were set in front of her. In the beds on either side of hers, women nursed their new babies.

Martin arrived at visiting time, trying to hide the strain on his face behind a bunch of daffodils. At that moment, he seemed, to Joan, like no more than a boy. He drew the curtains halfway round the bed, bent to kiss her on the forehead, then sat down on the plastic chair next to her. "How are you?"

Joan propped herself up higher on her pillows. "I asked the midwives about bringing April down from the nursery now that I'm better. They said you'd been talking to them about our plans. What plans exactly?"

Martin turned away and didn't look her in the eye. He couldn't.

His speech was halting. He sounded unsure, as if struggling to say the words trapped in his throat. "Remember . . . what we, er . . . agreed?" he mumbled. "What we said . . . would be . . . for the best?"

"We never agreed anything," Joan began, trying to sit forward so she could get him to face her. "Nothing was set in stone." She reached out and grabbed him by the arm, her heart pounding in her ears. "Please, Martin. Please." Panic threated to choke her. "If you saw her, I know you'd change your mind."

Martin stood, breaking free of her feeble grip. "We can't, Joan," he said, shaking his head and running his fingers through his hair. "*I* can't."

Joan tried to get up but found herself pulled back by the drip attached to her arm. "We'll work something out. You can get a job here. I can look after April. We'll be fine. I'll make it work," she pleaded, growing more desperate with every word.

Martin kept his gaze fixed on the blue bedspread covering Joan's legs. "We can't, Joan. Look at us! We're a pair of kids without a penny to our name or a roof over our heads. What kind of life could we give her?"

"We'd manage, Martin. People do."

"That's just it. I don't *want* to manage." Joan's mouth fell open, and her throat tightened. "I don't *want* to scrape by. I have a life and prospects waiting for me back home." He sat on the edge of the bed next to her and took her hand in his. "I want you to be part of it. There'll be more children, Joan. God willing, in time. When we're ready to look after them and give them a good life."

"But April needs our love now, both of us, together. We can give *her* a good life!"

Martin opened his mouth to speak, but there was nothing more to be said. His eyes told Joan everything she needed to know.

She covered her face with her hands. "Just go, Martin. Get out of here."

She kept the curtains drawn around her bed that night. The flimsy green fabric couldn't block out the sound of babies crying for their mothers all around her. She lay in a tight ball, her pillow damp with tears, staring into the distance as one by one the lights on the ward went out.

She went over every single option again and again, all through that sleepless night. She couldn't raise April on her own without money, especially in a city where she didn't know a soul. She couldn't take her illegitimate child home either, to live like a pauper under Da's roof, never knowing when he would blow up.

Joan remembered only too well what life had been like for Ma, how she'd been whispered about even though Da had done the decent thing. She'd never forget how the names she'd been called as a child wounded her as surely as if they had been sticks and stones. That was not the life she wanted for her little girl.

But Joan longed for her baby. Her sore breasts were hard with unsuckled milk, and her nipples tingled, leaving damp patches on her cotton nightdress. Even though moonlight seeped through the ward's high windows, still, the darkness pressed against her. She swung her legs out of the bed and stood up, then walked barefoot across the shiny green floor, pushing her drip alongside her. An exhausted new mother in the bed opposite fed her baby. The others slept soundly, their babies safely in cribs at the ends of their beds. Only Joan's baby was missing.

She would go upstairs to the nursery and look for April among the other newborns—she would know her immediately. Then she would march up to the midwives and tell them she'd changed her mind, say she was leaving and taking her baby with her.

Joan shuffled across the ward clinging to the drip stand; its wheels clacked next to her ankles, each step taking her closer to the double doors. She just had to get past the nurses' station and then she'd be able to go find April.

"Where are you off to at this hour, Joan, love?" The midwife at the desk was bathed in a halo of yellow light.

"I need to get to the nursery. I want my baby."

"You can't go up there now, Joan," the woman said, in a soothing voice. "It's the middle of the night. Why don't you go back to bed? Everything will look different in the morning."

Joan frowned at her. "But it will be too late by morning . . ." she began. She looked past the nurse to the corridor and the staircase beyond. What had she been thinking? Of course she wouldn't be allowed to roam the hospital at night. She went to the window instead and pressed her forehead against the cool glass, her eyes scanning the rooftops of the sleeping city she didn't know. The place that had once seemed new and exciting now looked as jaded as she felt.

During her fourth morning on the ward, Sister Patricia, who

found families for the illegitimate offspring of girls in trouble, came to visit Joan.

"I don't want to give her up, Sister," she said, through her tears. "Isn't there any other way?"

"Well, isn't that just it, Joan?" Sister Patricia sniffed. "There was another way nine months ago." She raised her eyebrows as if to underline the point. "But you chose otherwise. And now you're only thinking of yourself—not of the child at all." She folded her hands in her lap and scowled at Joan over the gold rims of her glasses. "Sure, what kind of life could you give her?"

It was a good question. One that Joan kept asking herself. What kind of life would it be? She stared blankly ahead, seeing nothing.

Sister Patricia rearranged her veil on her shoulders as she got up from her chair. "Good. I knew you'd see sense," she said.

Joan had no choice. She would have to sign the adoption papers. She would never proudly push her daughter in a Silver Cross pram around Harold's Cross, stopping to let every neighbor who passed look under the hood to admire her. Joan and Martin would not raise their child together. There would be no record of them as a family. No photographs. No reminders. No memories laid down. She had to let April go. She had no idea where her daughter would be going or who would take her. She didn't know who would hear April's first word or witness her first steps, only that it would not be her.

CHAPTER 33

In the days after she left the hospital, Joan moved like a ghost around the guesthouse. Nothing could have prepared her for how the loss of April would lodge in her body. A great lump behind her breastbone made it hard to swallow. She felt nothing except a heaviness in her limbs. The only thing that gave her any comfort was knowing she'd insisted that both she and Martin be named as April's parents on the birth certificate before she signed the adoption papers. She wanted her daughter to know she had not been ashamed to give birth to her and that her parents had loved each other, once.

She didn't care to wash or eat, and it was difficult to get out of bed. Mrs. C told her that Martin was worried. Let him worry. She couldn't care less about easing his concerns. She wasn't ready to see him, and she couldn't help herself from falling further into the hole her feelings had opened up. How could you grieve this much over a path you had chosen? A decision you had made, born of other decisions, made of your own free will. Nobody had held a gun to her head. This was all her own doing.

She woke in her bed on Easter morning to the sound of church bells and lay on her back staring up at the ceiling, her hand resting on her soft belly. Had it only been ten days since she'd become a mother?

Mrs. C's familiar footsteps shuffled along the landing and stopped outside her door. Then came two small taps of her knuckles. "Joan, are you sure you won't just have a boiled egg and a bit of toast?"

Joan coughed, clearing her throat to speak. "No, thanks, Mrs. C. Maybe later. I'm still a bit tired." She lay still, holding her breath, and waited for the sound of footsteps moving away and the creak of the first stair. Then she closed her eyes and pulled the covers over her head, blocking out the daylight and muffling the world she wished she could forget.

Listening to the rise and fall of her breathing under the covers, she remembered a time when she was very young, maybe only three years of age, when she was playing hide-and-seek with her mother. While Ma was making the beds, Joan hid in plain sight by covering herself with a blanket, thinking she was invisible. Now here she was, years later, still believing this was how she could make herself disappear.

She hadn't seen Martin since she left the hospital. He'd called to the door of the guesthouse a few times, but each time she'd asked Mrs. C to tell him she wasn't up to having visitors. Now, even in the dark beneath the blankets, the sound of her own breath was a cursed reminder that life would go on in spite of everything.

She threw off the covers again, swung her legs out of the bed, and went to the window. Unlike the view from the hospital, she couldn't see rooftops or the city skyline in the distance, but the cherry blossom was now in full bloom. Joan sighed. April would grow and thrive without her mother. And she . . . she would survive. They might have to be parted for now, but one day they would find each other again. She had to think so.

At lunchtime, Mrs. C knocked on her door again. "Martin is downstairs, Joan. Will you see him?" Joan stood, eyes closed, with her forehead against the door. Mrs. C waited. When Joan finally opened the door, they stood facing each other. "Why don't you give him a chance?" Mrs. C said, head on one side. Joan raised an eyebrow. "You're not being fair to the young lad," Mrs. C continued.

"Why do you say that?"

Mrs. C looked right at her. "I've seen a lot of girls in your predicament come and go over the years. I'm telling you straight: you're one of the lucky ones."

Joan opened her mouth to protest but bit her tongue. "What do you mean?" she said, frowning.

"It's not every young lad that stands by his girl, you know. I've had girls here without a penny to their name whose young men have washed their hands of them." She reached out and took Joan's cold hand in her warm one. "Martin loves you. He stood by you as best he could. He's prepared to give you a good life."

Joan cocked her head.

"Nothing can change how you feel about the baby," Mrs. C said. "But punishing Martin, and yourself into the bargain, isn't going to bring her back."

Joan was quiet.

"Will I tell him to leave, then?"

Joan hesitated. "Tell him to come back after dinner."

Mrs. C nodded, then closed the door, leaving her alone again. Joan went back to the window and saw Martin walk down the path, close the gate behind him, then disappear down the street under the canopy of pink blossom. She hoped she was doing the right thing.

Later, after toast and tea, Joan washed her face and wound her long dark hair into a tight bun at the back of her head, pinning it in place. She flicked through the three dresses in her wardrobe, none of which fit her properly now. She was neither the Joan before April was conceived nor the Joan who had carried her. She was caught somewhere in between body and soul.

She pulled a navy blue Crimplene maternity dress off its wire hanger. "This'll do," she said to herself, and slipped it over her head.

The loose fabric flowed over her hips. Before leaving the room, she glanced in the mirror. Her face was pale and drawn, but she couldn't be bothered to put on makeup to hide it. She pinched her cheeks between her thumb and forefinger, trying to bring some color back into them.

Mrs. C looked over at her and smiled when she came into the kitchen. When they heard Martin's knock on the door, at six o'clock on the dot, she said, "Don't forget to take a coat. It's cooler than it looks out there—that breeze is deceiving."

Joan took her coat from its hook in the hall and slung it over her arm before opening the door. Then she was face-to-face with Martin. He looked like he hadn't slept in days.

"There you are," he said, taking her hand. A sad smile masked his pained expression. "It's a lovely evening for a walk."

"It is," Joan said, withdrawing her hand. He seemed to know that he shouldn't take it again—like he'd always done whenever they walked down the street in London together. Before.

As they strolled to the park, Martin made small talk about finishing up at college. A group of children ran along the top of a grassy embankment, shrieking as they chased and caught each other.

"Let's sit down, Joan."

They sat on the bench overlooking the flower beds where red tulips, planted in tidy rows during winter, were in bloom.

"Where's your mother's ring?" Martin asked, taking hold of her left hand and rubbing the place where the ring had once been.

"No need for it now."

He reached into his inside coat pocket. "Well, will you wear mine instead?" He pulled out a small blue-velvet box and handed it to her. His hands were shaking. Joan tried not to show her surprise. She sat stock-still, holding the unopened box in her lap, wondering if it was too soon for new promises.

"Open it."

She eased the lid open. Inside was a ring the likes of which she had never seen. A large emerald flanked by two diamonds. She stared at it but didn't say a word. Then she snapped the box shut and straightened. She pulled her shoulders back, stuck her chin out, and looked Martin dead in the eye. "I will, if you promise me one thing. We're not going to forget April."

He opened his mouth to speak, but she cut him off with a raised hand. "Hear me out. You have to promise me that one day, when she comes looking for us, we will tell people back home everything."

He put his hand on hers. "Yes. Of course we will. I promise." He took the velvet box from her, removed the ring, and held it out. "Marry me, Joan."

Joan looked at it, and then at him, suddenly picturing the cherry blossom outside her window. Martin lifted her left hand and held the ring at the tip of her finger, raising an eyebrow. She nodded. He grinned, slid the ring over her knuckle, and kissed her.

"Now, let's get some fish and chips to celebrate," he said when the kiss was over, pulling her off the bench.

"I don't think so, Martin. I'm not that hungry," Joan replied flatly.

"Oh, all right, then," he said, with a frown. "Let's get you home, then."

They fell into step next to each other.

"Speaking of home," Joan said, "we should probably start making plans to go back sooner rather than later." Martin nodded. "We both have some letter writing to do in the meantime," she said.

THEY WERE SITTING IN THEIR quiet corner of the pub; Joan fiddled with her engagement ring. It still felt awkward and out of place on her small hand. "Did you write to your mother yet?" she asked, as soon as Martin sat down. "I sent my letter off to Da and Teresa last week. They'll have it by now."

"Yeah, posted it yesterday," Martin said, picking up his pint.

"You know she won't be best pleased about the baggage you're bringing home with you. And that's putting it mildly." Joan tried to shoot him a rueful smile, but her insides tightened. It wouldn't be easy for Mrs. Egan to accept a girl from the Cranmore estate as a daughter-in-law. There would be no doubt in her mind that her son could have done better.

Martin made a face but said nothing, stalling as he raised his pint to his lips.

"What did you tell her?"

He set down his glass, then sat straighter on his low bar stool, puffing out his chest. "I told her I met a gorgeous girl I knew from Harold's Cross in London. And that I want to come back home to marry her."

"Liar!" Joan laughed, giving him a good-natured thump on the shoulder. "Good idea to soften the blow, though, with the mention of coming home. She'll have missed you." She took a sip of her lemonade.

"I suppose," Martin said. Joan tried to read his expression, remembering the first time she'd gazed deep into his eyes and how she had fallen for him there and then. She hoped Molly Egan's disappointment in her would be tempered by the relief of having her son back home—safely settled and ready to take over the running of the family business, as had always been the plan. Maybe her heart would soften when she saw that Martin was happy. Isn't that all any mother would want for her child?

The final month in London flew by. The day before their return, there wasn't a breath of air, even though Joan had propped the bedroom window open as wide as it would go. If this was what summers in London were like you could keep them—she'd be glad of a bit of predictable Dublin drizzle. One by one, she pulled open her drawers and began folding the slips, knickers, and jumpers and placing them into her suitcase.

"How's it going, love?" Mrs. C called as she breezed past Joan's bedroom wielding a tin of Ajax on her way to the first-floor bathroom.

"Getting there," Joan replied.

"Let me know if you need a hand with that case. I'm just off downstairs to clean up after those three mucky pups."

Joan laughed. She'd miss her landlady, who had been like a mother to her these past few months. "I'll get the kettle on after I've finished this packing," she called down the stairs after Mrs. C.

It wasn't until she opened the bottom drawer that she remembered the empty photo album Martin had given her for Christmas and the baby things she'd brought to the hospital with her. The things she'd never used. There was the baby powder, the nappies and pins, and the tiny white cardigan the woman in the wool shop had given her.

She sat on the bed with a sigh. That afternoon seemed like a lifetime ago. She wasn't over losing April, but she was ready to be home again, to see her sister and to begin her new life with Martin, to find a way to move forward. Joan folded the arms of the baby cardigan across the row of pearl buttons, then smoothed her hand along it before wrapping it in tissue paper. She put it into her suitcase and closed the lid. She would never forget her daughter.

Down in the kitchen, she made the tea and sliced the scones she'd helped Mrs. C make that morning. Next to Mrs. C's plate she placed the bottle of 4711 perfume she'd wrapped with brown paper and string.

"What's all this?" Mrs. C said, sitting down in her chair at the head of the table.

"Just a little thank-you," Joan replied, her eyes shining.

"There was no need for that, Joan."

"I don't know what I'd have done without you, Mrs. C. I honestly haven't a clue." Joan leaned across the table and reached for the old lady's hand. She could see that Mrs. C was holding back tears.

Though they didn't say it, both women knew this would be the last time they spoke and that Joan would leave no forwarding address.

"I'll miss you, you know. But you need to be with your own people."

"I do," Joan heard herself say, and, right at that moment, deep in her bones, she felt her words to be true.

The journey home to Dublin was like a cassette tape being rewound, then recorded over, wiping it clean. They would begin again.

CHAPTER 34

Da couldn't shut up about his eldest daughter's engagement to the Egan lad. "Did you hear about our Joan?" he asked anyone and everyone who'd give him the time of day. He would be retelling this story around the streets of the estate and the pumps at O'Grady's for weeks to come.

It was a miserable morning, and the rain looked as if it was down for the day. Joan stood next to the window holding the jacket of her father's funeral suit up to the light. Her stomach was in knots. Today was the day she would introduce her family to Molly Egan up at the big house on Grove Square, and she hadn't dreaded anything more in a long while. Da and Teresa were getting ready upstairs. She inspected the jacket, brushing flakes of dandruff off the collar.

She heard Teresa taking the stairs down two at a time, which was good—it meant she wasn't wearing a mini or heels. She turned to look her as she entered the room. "Will I do?" Teresa said, twirling in front of her. Joan was relieved to see her dressed in a striped polo neck and the only below-the-knee skirt she possessed.

"Perfect," Joan said, with a grateful smile. She knew Teresa wasn't looking forward to this morning either.

"You don't look so bad yourself," Teresa said. Joan had dressed in a wide-collared white cotton blouse and navy corduroy skirt. Her hair was knotted at the nape of her neck in a neat bun. She looked like she was going to a job interview.

"Thanks, T."

Da came into the room behind them in his stockinged feet. A small square of toilet paper was stuck to his chin where he had cut himself shaving. "Where's my shoes?" he asked.

"On the hearth," Joan replied. "I gave them a polish for you. And here's your jacket." She held it out for him, and he shrugged into it, pulling at the ends of the sleeves.

"Right, we'll get going as soon as I've my shoes on," he said, picking the tissue off his chin.

"Looks like we'll need our coats and brollies too," Teresa said, glancing outside. "Another glorious summer's day in Dublin!"

They stepped out into the drizzle, Joan and Teresa sharing one umbrella and linking arms as they walked. Da followed behind.

"I hope Martin has that thing insured." Teresa pointed to Joan's engagement ring.

"Trust you!" Joan said, laughing.

"I'm bloody serious," Teresa said. "You mind yourself walking around here with that knuckleduster on your finger."

"You're right. I probably won't wear it much after the wedding, though," Joan said. "Best to keep it up for special occasions."

They bumped into Mrs. Hanlon from next door at the corner of Ashleaf Road.

"There you are, Joan. Congratulations! I heard the news."

"Thanks, Mrs. Hanlon."

"Givvus a look at your ring," she said. Joan held out her left hand. "Jesus, you'd knock your bleedin' eye out with that thing!" Joan smiled politely once more. It was hard to know what to say. "You've landed on your feet and no mistake. I'm delighted for yeh."

"Thanks, Mrs. Hanlon."

"If only your mother could be here to see it, Lord have mercy on her soul."

Joan gripped the umbrella in her right hand tighter.

Da cleared his throat. "We'd better get a move on, girls. We don't want to keep Mrs. Egan waiting."

"I'm sure we'll see you before the big day," Mrs. Hanlon said.

"You will," Joan replied. "Bye, Mrs. Hanlon."

When they reached the heavy wrought-iron gates leading up to Martin's house, Da gave a low whistle. Teresa dropped Joan's arm as they began walking up the path that divided the garden neatly in two. "Jesus, Joan," was all she could say, as she admired the handsome rose beds that lined the sweep of lawn to the left and right.

Joan thought she saw the twitch of a curtain at the wide bay window. Of course, Molly Egan would be up there looking down on them.

"Can I get you a drink, Mr. Quinn?" Molly said when they were all seated in the parlor. Da smacked his dry lips together, and Joan shot him a look.

"A cup of tea would be grand," he said, sticking a finger down the starched collar of his shirt. Teresa sat opposite Joan at the other end of the chintz sofa, balancing the china cup and saucer awkwardly on her knees. Joan kept her eyes on the delicate red rose pattern winding its way around the gilded rim of her saucer, wishing the morning was over.

Martin touched her on the shoulder as he passed. "Would you like a bit of Dundee cake, Mr. Quinn?" he asked, holding out the plate to Da. She knew by his careful movements that Martin was nervous too, and she felt as sorry for him as she did for herself.

"Of course, it's all a bit sudden to arrange a proper wedding," Molly sniffed as she sipped her tea. "You know what they say, 'Marry in haste . . .'" She trailed off, leaving her spiteful sentence suspended in midair. Teresa gave Joan a sideways look. "I still don't understand why the rush," Molly continued, looking pointedly at Joan's belly. Martin glared at her.

Joan was proud that he stood his ground, even if it was in his own way. She knew this was not the first time he had been quizzed about their courtship or the suddenness of their marriage. It was clear Molly suspected Joan had pursued her reluctant son. And she didn't believe Martin would marry her unless he had to.

"I suppose we'll have to make do," Molly sniped. Joan didn't think she was just talking about the wedding arrangements. Her words lingered in the awkward silence.

"Our Joan is a great girl for making do," Da began, his mouth still half-full of chewed fruit cake. "She's been managing the house since her mammy died, Lord rest her."

"That's just it, Mr. Quinn, we're not used to 'making do' around here," Molly said, her face arranged in a tortured expression. "It's all going to take some getting used to." She sighed. "More tea, anyone?"

"No, thank you," Teresa said in a clipped tone, covering the cup with her hand as Molly approached wielding the china teapot. "I've had more than enough already."

The only sound was the loud tick of the polished walnut clock on the mantel. Joan took another sip of lukewarm tea and looked out through the window at the rain lashing the lawn beyond. It was indeed a miserable day.

WILL YOU GET A MOVE ON, JOAN?" Teresa shouted up from the bottom of the stairs. "We want to get into town early before the buses get packed!"

"Coming!" Joan called back. It was a month before the wedding, and they were heading into town to go shopping for her dress. She pulled at the still-tight waistband of her skirt as she assessed her reflection in the bedroom mirror. Would the women in Arnotts' wedding-dress department figure out she'd had a baby?

She might be able to hide the scars on her wounded heart with her best bride-to-be smile, but would she be able to hide the telltale stretch marks when they were helping her into dresses? *Jesus, Joan*, she chastised herself. She wished to God she didn't care so much about the good opinion of total strangers. Well, worrying about it wasn't going to help. She shouldn't spoil the day she and Teresa had planned for themselves.

Teresa linked arms with her as they walked down Ardeer Avenue toward the bus stop. "I'm so glad you're home," she gushed. "I mean, what were the chances of meeting someone from around the corner in London, never mind the two of you falling in love? It's so romantic!"

Joan laughed. "Half of Dublin is over there looking for work, T. So I'd say the chances were pretty high." She had never dared admit to herself how much she'd missed Teresa while she was away in London. Now, as they walked down the sunny street together, she felt at peace for the first time in weeks.

In the shop, the sales assistant helped Joan narrow her choice down to two plain dresses, long-sleeved and A-line, matched with a short veil. "I don't want anything too showy," Joan said, as the woman pulled the various styles of dresses off the rails for the girls to inspect.

"Are you sure they're not a bit *too* plain? Don't you want something with an underskirt and a bit of lace?" Teresa asked. "Martin said you were to have whatever you wanted."

"It's just one day, T," Joan said. "I don't want to go overboard, and, besides, I won't have Mrs. Egan complaining that I broke the bank by buying an expensive dress."

"It's good of her all the same . . . to foot the bill, I mean," Teresa replied.

"What choice does she have? Da doesn't have the money for a

wedding, and she doesn't want us making a show of her son in front of the entire parish. Marrying me is bad enough!"

Teresa pulled a face.

Joan tilted her head to one side as she looked at her reflection in the mirror. White suited her dark features. She hadn't realized it until now. She liked the way the soft satin flowed over her hips and the scoop of the neckline elongated her neck. A simple string of pearls would work well with it. "What do you think?" she asked her sister.

"I think you'll knock him dead," Teresa said, her eyes shining. "Only you could pull off something as plain as that."

"I'll take this one," Joan said, with conviction. They chose a simple bridesmaid's dress in turquoise satin for Teresa. Once the dresses were wrapped and boxed, the sisters headed back down O'Connell Street to Bewley's café on Westmoreland Street. "My treat," Joan said, patting her handbag. The money left over from what Martin had given her to pay for the dresses would more than cover it. "Our last supper out together before I become an old married woman."

On the night before the wedding, the girls lay together in their childhood bed, unable to sleep. "How do you know when you've met 'the one,' Joan?" Teresa said into the darkness. "The one who would do anything for you?"

Joan didn't answer immediately, so Teresa propped herself up on her elbow just in time to see her sister hastily brushing tears from her eyes with the back of her hand. "What's the matter? Why are you crying?"

"Ah, it's nothing, T. Wedding nerves. I'm fine. I'll be fine." She couldn't tell her about April. Not now.

Teresa groped in the darkness for her sister's hand. "Are you sure you're okay?" she said, wide awake now.

Joan sat up in the bed next to her. "I'll be fine. I probably just need a good night's sleep," she said, patting her sister's hand. "You too!"

Teresa nodded, and they both lay down, back to back, next to each other.

"Teresa?" Joan said into the darkness.

"Yeah?"

"Will you promise me something?" Joan said, lowering her voice.

"What?"

"If someone ever tells you they'll do anything for you, don't mind them. That's not the kind of promise any of us is free to make, and only a fool would believe it."

"Okay," Teresa said, sounding puzzled.

The last sound Joan heard before dropping off to sleep was her sister's soft snores as she slept peacefully beside her.

The following afternoon, a fine September day, Joan's father walked her down the aisle of St. Jude's—delighted with himself. There was the prospect of a good party with plenty of free beer flowing to look forward to later. And Martin Egan was quite a catch. A man of means, with a family business to his name.

"You've done well," Da said to Joan as the wedding car approached the church. "You'll never want for anything." Joan regarded the posy of white lilies she held in her lap. Their pungent scent overpowered her. "Don't mind what anyone says about him being too good for you, Joan. The whole parish will be there to hear your vows."

He was right. Nothing could tear them asunder now.

CHAPTER 35

Some mornings, before Joan opened her eyes, April wasn't the first thought to enter her mind. She would feel the feather pillow beneath her head and the comforting weight of the blankets. Then she'd blink and see Martin lying next to her and remember what she'd given up to be here.

Their week on honeymoon in Dingle had been lovely—an escape in more ways than one because it was neither London nor Dublin. During the day, they walked hand in hand on wild deserted beaches bordered by green hills, and every night they lay naked in front of the fire in their rented cottage. It was all a world away from the imposing red-brick façade of the elegant Georgian house on Grove Square.

Martin couldn't get enough of her. "You'll always be as beautiful to me as the first time I saw you," he whispered, stroking her hair in the firelight. Joan knew in her heart that the girl Martin had fallen in love with was lost to both him and her, forever.

On their first night back, they sat down to dinner together, just the three of them. Molly had made an effort: not quite the fatted calf, but a roast chicken, plenty of potatoes, and an apple crumble for dessert. None of it for Joan's benefit, of course. Molly's iciness made it abundantly clear that she was less than pleased to have Joan under her roof, never mind as a daughter-in-law.

Molly emerged from the kitchen and handed Joan a plate of food. Anxious to please, Joan got stuck in. "This is delicious," she said, taking a mouthful of potato.

"It's good manners to wait until everyone is ready to eat before starting," Molly said through tight lips, as she took her seat at the head of the table. She looked over her glasses at Joan. "I suppose manners weren't something you bothered with on the estate."

The mashed potato turned to clay in her mouth. Joan swallowed and put down her fork. Her cheeks burned. "Of course" was all she could think to say. She lifted her eyes for the briefest of seconds to meet Martin's across the table. He gave her a sheepish smile but kept his mouth shut.

"Now, Martin, would you ever pass me the gravy before the dinner goes stone cold," Molly said, smiling at her son.

"She hates me!" Joan wailed in their bedroom after dinner.

"Give her time," Martin said. "It's all been a bit sudden. She'll come around."

Joan sighed. She was beginning to have her doubts.

A month after their wedding, Grove Square still felt nothing like home. Every night they slept in the bed where she'd seduced Martin on the weekend of the Kilkenny wedding. It seemed like a lifetime ago. Whenever he reached for her in the dark, she let him and lay still underneath him, staring at the ceiling, wondering if her mother-in-law was eavesdropping on their lovemaking in her bedroom below.

If she looked out their bedroom window, she could see the Royal Candy factory in the distance. And if she craned her neck, she could just make out the tiled rooftops of the Cranmore estate where she'd grown up. A place far enough away from the manicured lawns of Grove Square to be of no consequence or concern to the class of people who now called Joan their neighbor.

Her days were now about survival of a different kind. The things she had to worry about here were things she hadn't given a second thought to on the estate. Taking care to wipe her feet properly before coming into the house. A deep scratch she'd accidentally made in the parquet floor with a bit of gravel that got stuck in the sole of her shoe. Making sure she had receipts for every penny she spent from the money she was given—more money than she'd ever dreamed of, that was hers in name only. As it turned out, privilege and freedom were not the same things at all. Living in a fancy house with lush green lawns, surrounded by close-clipped hedging on all sides, didn't make you any freer than the next person.

She hadn't been prepared for the pretense of living back in Dublin. She was no longer sure where the lies ended and the truth began. The made-up stories she would need to remember and the real memories she'd have to forget were like a lead weight, always strapped to her.

JOAN SPOTTED TERESA WAITING UNDER Clerys Clock as soon as she stepped off the bus. She hitched a smile on her face and waved. Pretending had become second nature to her. She was brilliant at it now. Getting better by the day. Like an actress who'd been handed the wrong script, who was making it up as she went along.

They hugged each other briefly. "Is everything all right?" Joan asked, searching her sister's face.

"Yes. Why wouldn't it be?" Teresa said.

"I mean is Da behaving himself?"

"He's no worse than usual, if that's what you mean," Teresa replied. "Come on, let's walk. I'm freezing."

They started off down O'Connell Street together. It was hard to keep in step or in conversation as they dodged the throng of Christmas shoppers on the path. Joan had only seen Teresa once since the wedding. They were meeting in town today and going to Bewley's for tea—Joan's treat—so she could show Teresa the photographs.

Now that she was an Egan, it wouldn't do to walk the cracked footpaths down half a mile to the estate to visit her family. Of course, they were welcome to come to the house any time they wanted, Martin said. He hoped it went without saying. But Da and Teresa felt too out of place to make their way up the gravel driveway.

The reason they hadn't seen each other created an unfamiliar awkwardness between them. Joan hadn't reckoned on no longer belonging to the world of her past when she'd stepped over the threshold into the world of her future. She hadn't understood that it was impossible to belong in both.

Their conversation was stilted. It wasn't that they were out of the habit of being together. It was that they had less in common now.

"So, how's things, T? Anything new?"

"Just the usual, you know yourself."

"How's work?"

"Just the same . . . How's life up on Grove Square treating you?" Teresa said, avoiding Joan's eye while stirring the sugar that had already dissolved around and around in her teacup.

"Can't complain," Joan said. It seemed ridiculous to burden her sister by relaying the petty arguments she'd had with Molly. These were hardly what anyone living from pay packet to pay packet on the estate would call problems. And she couldn't breathe a word of the one thing she wanted to tell her sister about most of all.

"Good," Teresa said, reaching for the butter to spread on her scone. "Sounds like it's all working out for you."

Joan stayed quiet.

They fell into an uncomfortable silence, eating their scones and looking around the café at the comings and goings of the customers.

"Listen, T, I've been thinking about Christmas," Joan tried again.

"Go on," Teresa replied, head cocked.

"You and Da could come to us for Christmas dinner," Joan said. "I could ask Molly. There'd be plenty to go around."

"No, don't do that, Joan," Teresa said, looking alarmed. "Don't you know Da would be delighted to get stuck into Molly's drink cabinet?" She rolled her eyes. "It's your first Christmas as an Egan. The last thing you need is him making a show of you."

"But—" Joan began.

"And I don't want to be Auld Ma Egan's charity case," Teresa interrupted her.

"But I'm married to her son!" Joan protested.

"Doesn't make any difference. She still looks down her nose at us. You know that," Teresa said, making a face. "Maybe you can come over to us for a drink after your dinner."

Joan was doubtful. "Yeah, maybe."

"Did I tell you I met someone at the Metropole last weekend?" Teresa said, breaking the silence.

Joan put down her cup. "No, you did not tell me you'd met someone!" she said, smiling. "Is he from around here?"

Teresa blushed. "No. He's a garda. From Kinsale," she said, brushing crumbs from her mouth. "I said I'd meet him again this weekend."

"What's he like?"

"He's nice."

"Nice? Is that it?"

They laughed, eyes shining, cups of tea and the awkwardness forgotten for a moment. Joan checked her watch. "Listen, T, I have to go. I promised Molly I'd pick up some messages for her on the way home."

"Oh, right."

"This was nice. Let's do it again soon," Joan said, standing up to shrug into her jacket.

Teresa pushed her chair back and began winding her scarf around her neck. "Whatever suits you, Joan. You know where we live." She avoided her sister's eyes. "Oh, don't forget your photographs," she said, pointing to the bag containing the two wedding albums leaning against the table leg.

"I completely forgot to show you the photos!" Joan said, shaking her head. "I can't believe it!"

"There's always next time," Teresa reassured her.

The sisters parted ways at the door of the tea rooms with a small wave, not knowing that the next times would get further and further apart.

CHAPTER 36

"You're not thinking of wearing that to Mass?" Molly said, scowling at Joan as she came down the stairs.

Joan smoothed the skirt of her red winter dress with her hand. "What's wrong with it?"

"Do you not think it's a bit bright?" Molly replied, pulling on one brown leather glove, then the other.

Martin came over and touched Joan's elbow as if to steer her back up the stairs. "I'm sure you have something more suitable," he said. "It'll only take you a minute to change." And, to her surprise, she'd made her way obediently back up the stairs, pulling a navy jumper and green tartan skirt from her wardrobe and putting them on.

"I can't believe you let her speak to me like that," she said to Martin as she lay with her back to him in bed that night.

He propped himself up on one elbow and put the other arm around her. "I'm sorry, Joan. I just thought—"

Joan sat up, wrapping her arms around herself. "No, you didn't think. That's the problem. You have no idea what it's like for me living here, Martin, bowing and scraping under her roof. It's like . . ."

She fumbled for the right words. "It's like . . . I feel like a bloody prisoner."

Martin leaned over and kissed her on the lips. "I'm sorry," he said. "I promise it's not forever. Once we're on our feet with a few bob behind us we'll get a little place of our own."

Joan lost count of how many times he said that over the years. But whenever she broached the subject, he shut her down. A few months later, she saw a little terrace house for sale on Ashleaf Road. It needed work, but she didn't mind that. They could do it up over time. For once, Martin agreed, but after he mentioned it to Molly over dinner that night, she took to her bed for a week. Her angina, the doctor said.

"What's the sense in you buying your own place when I have all this space here?" Molly said. "And it's closer to the yard than Ashleaf Road." With great effort, she turned her head on the pillow and faced her son. "It'll all be yours eventually anyway," she said, pulling the sheet up around her neck. "Probably sooner than we thought."

"Don't talk like that, Mother," Martin said, sitting on the side of the bed.

"No, we have to face facts," Molly continued. "Dr. McBride said my heart could give out at any time." Her eyelids fluttered. "He doesn't think I'll make old bones. Just like your poor father, Lord have mercy on him."

"Well, maybe we'll wait until you're back on your feet," Martin said, glancing across the bed at Joan, who, without a word, was clattering the crockery as she cleared Molly's breakfast tray. From where she was standing it didn't look like Molly had the slightest intention of dying any time soon.

But there was no arguing with Molly Egan, so that was that. The house on Ashleaf Road went to another young couple.

The day Joan saw the *Sold* sign on her way back from the shops, she ran upstairs to their room, threw herself on the bed, and wept. When he came home from work that evening, Martin found her there, half-asleep, in crumpled clothes, her face still tear-stained. "What's the matter?" he said, concern in his eyes.

"I can't do this, Martin."

"Do what? What are you on about?"

"This!" Joan gestured around the room. "Stay cooped up here all day keeping your mother company. Why can't I come and work with you down at the yard?"

Martin sat beside her on the bed, rubbing the day's growth on his chin. "How would it look, my wife having to work?" he said.

Joan, sensing that he was wavering, knelt up beside him. "It's not like I *have* to, Martin. It's *your* business, and I'd be there by your side to support you. That's different from me having to go out to earn a wage because you can't provide. It's not the same thing at all."

Martin hesitated. Joan crossed her fingers behind her back and waited.

"I tell you what," he said. "We'll give you a trial, next week."

Joan gave him a grateful peck on the cheek. As she looked around the huge bedroom, with its picture window and view of the immaculate front lawn, a poisonous guilt crept through her. She knew how lucky she was. Any girl from the estate would trade places with her in a heartbeat. She leaned across, hooked her arms around Martin's neck, and kissed him.

The following morning, when she was on her way down to breakfast, Joan heard Martin and Molly talking in hushed voices in the kitchen. She stopped where she was, halfway down the stairs, to listen in.

"How will it look, Martin? What kind of man would let his wife work when they didn't need the money? She should be content to stay at home like other married women."

"It'll take her mind off other things," Martin replied.

"Well, it's not right, that's all I'm saying. It gives people the wrong impression."

Joan had heard enough. She continued on down the stairs,

gripping the banister hard as she went. Molly coughed when Joan came into the kitchen. "I was just saying—" she continued.

"I heard," Joan interrupted her.

"Leave it, Joan," Martin said, and his eyes flashed a warning from the other side of the room.

"Put the kettle on, will you, Joan? There's a good girl," Molly said, lowering two eggs into the pan of boiling water on the stove. "You'll have an egg, won't you, Martin?" she said, over her shoulder.

Joan held the kettle under the tap and bit her tongue. Why was Molly always sticking her nose in where it wasn't wanted? And when would Martin stand up to her?

One evening, when she was clearing the dinner plates, Joan noticed Molly's sideways glance at her belly.

"No news yet in the baby department?" Molly asked.

"No. No news," Joan said, banging cutlery and scraping the plates.

"Well, you don't take after your mother. I'm told she bred like a rabbit—popped out one after another with no trouble at all."

Joan felt the heat in her cheeks. She had the sudden urge to slap Molly hard across the face. Good job her arms were laden with dirty dinner dishes.

"That's enough now, Mother," Martin said, his eyes meeting Joan's across the table.

"I'm only saying."

Molly's reminders that time was marching on didn't help ease Joan's mounting fear. Every month her period came like clockwork—a bitter, bloody irony.

It was a blessed relief to be out of the house all day. To have something useful to do other than sit and listen to her mother-in-law taking down the world and everyone in it. The customers liked her, and she was good with them. And being at Martin's side, working together to build something while they waited for a baby, lightened her heart. Work was the only thing that took her mind off trying to get pregnant.

"Worrying isn't going to help," Martin said, over and over again. Then, finally, the following September, two years to the day they were married, following an early miscarriage and a novena to St. Colette, Joan's period didn't come.

Martin couldn't wait to tell his mother Joan was pregnant. They agreed to tell her at lunch, after Mass on Sunday. Joan came in from the kitchen carrying the freshly baked apple tart she'd made that morning.

Martin leaned back in his chair and cleared his throat. "Mother, we have a bit of good news for you." He looked at Joan as she came to stand next to him. He didn't reach for her hand. The awkwardness they always felt in Molly's presence had given rise to an unwritten rule never to touch unless they were alone. "Joan's expecting."

Molly blessed herself. "Thanks be to God," she said. "Not before time, mind you," she added. Joan slammed the tart in the middle of the table before taking her seat again. Was there no end to this woman's venomous nature?

"I've said it before, and I'll say it again," Molly lectured them over dessert. "It's high time Joan gave up working. It's not right."

Martin shifted in his seat. "Let's see how things go, Mother."

Joan stayed quiet until later that night when they'd escaped to their room. "Nothing I do will ever be good enough for your mother," she hissed at Martin, trying to keep her voice down.

"She's only trying to help," he said. "She wants what's best for us."

Joan sat bolt upright in the bed. "Trying to help?! Oh, come on, Martin, pull the other one. Your mother wouldn't piss on me if I was on fire."

"That's enough of your gutter talk, Joan!"

She couldn't see his face—the heavy curtains held the room in darkness—but she could feel his body tense next to her. "Aren't you sleeping here under her roof? Eating her food? Anyone would think you'd show more appreciation." With that, he turned on his side, his back to her.

If they'd been in their own place, Joan would have fought back, but knowing that Molly was probably listening to every sound from the bedroom below stopped her jumping out of the bed. Where would she run to anyway now that she was married and pregnant? She had nowhere else to go.

CHAPTER 37

The half-truths continued throughout Joan's pregnancy. She lied outright when the doctor asked if this was her first pregnancy. Suspicion was etched in his skeptical frown, the silver stretch marks on her belly a dead giveaway. His eyes narrowed, searching her face for the truth, and Joan knew he didn't believe her.

Memories of April came roaring back when she felt the first flutter of the baby kicking in her belly. Hormones ran amok, carousing around her body again, making her feel things, and remember things, she wanted to forget. In the small hours of the morning, when the baby's moving inside her made it impossible to sleep, she crept from the bed and groped in the dark for the baby cardigan given to her by the London shopkeeper, still tucked at the back of her bottom drawer. She pressed the soft wool to her cheek, consoling herself that in parting with April she'd done the right thing. It was better for her to be with a couple who were ready to rear a baby. Better to be wanted and welcomed. Better not to be branded a mistake, a sin. It was better for Joan to forget she was already a mother. Better all round.

Her waters broke early on the longest day of the year—21st June

1969—and a familiar, but until then forgotten pain took a hold of her. Wasn't childbirth supposed to be easier the second time around?

"You're doing great," lied Marie, the midwife, looking up as the blood pressure cuff around Joan's arm deflated.

Joan tried to smile. "How much longer?"

"It's hard to say, especially since it's your first," Marie replied, recording Joan's blood pressure on her chart. "I suppose the daddy wants a little boy?"

"No, he doesn't mind at all. It's me who wants a son," Joan said. The pethidine injection Marie had given her half an hour before had loosened her tongue. She'd never spoken those words to anyone, not even to Martin, even though they were true. She was not just hoping for a boy—she desperately wanted a son. A son would be a clean slate, the chance to stop wondering what kind of mother she'd have been to a daughter.

But hours later, after a difficult labor followed by an emergency forceps delivery, Marie greeted Joan's baby's arrival with the words, "It's a girl! You have a beautiful daughter, Joan."

"I know," Joan said, without even glancing in the baby's direction. "I already know."

She could barely remember those first days after her new daughter was born. She felt no flicker of recognition when the baby was placed in her arms. Her first thought was that this baby, with matching bruises on each temple from the forceps, could have been anybody's.

"Breast or bottle?" asked the nurse who admitted Joan to the ward.

"Bottle," she replied, without hesitation.

"You know breast is best for baby. Are you sure now?"

"I'm sure."

"Good for you," the woman in the bed next to her said under her breath when the nurse was gone. "Don't let them auld bitches tell you what to do, love. It's all right for them—spinsters, half of them. They haven't a feckin' clue what it's like to have one hangin' off your nipple, one nippin' at your bleedin' ankles, and another bun in the oven. Start out as you mean to go on."

Joan thanked her.

"Howya. I'm Angela. Call me Angie. This your first, is it?"

Joan had readied herself for the question. "Yeah. Yes, it is," she said with more conviction than she felt.

"Aw, God love you. You'll get used to it. Little Patrick here is my ninth. Not that I'm counting." She chuckled as she tossed the tiny bundle up onto her shoulder and began making small gentle circles on his back with the heel of her hand. "This is me annual holiday. A few days' rest in here away from the lot of them."

Joan could tell Angie didn't mean a word of it. In her eyes she saw what could only be described as out-and-out love. What did people see in *her* eyes when she looked at her daughter? Could they see the emptiness, the terror in her heart?

Martin doted on his daughter. Held her high in the crook of his arm, his face pressed close to hers. Whispering, cooing. His delighted eyes shining. Joan averted her own eyes, looking out through the dirty rain-splattered window at the cars passing on Parnell Square below. She'd wanted this—to be a mother again. This moment supposedly made everything, every precarious decision up to now, every sacrifice, worthwhile. So why did it feel so wrong?

That evening, just before the hospital visiting hours were coming to an end, she plucked up the courage to ask Martin the question that had been needling her all day. "Do you never think about April?"

The horror on Martin's face as he looked over his shoulder to see who might be listening told her all she needed to know.

"What's the use, Joan?" he said, adjusting the blanket the baby was wrapped in. "We did what we had to do. There's no use looking back."

Joan shook her head, letting his words sink in. "Oh right," she snapped. "I suppose you just want to move on?"

"We have to. We have Carmel to think of now."

"Carmel?"

"Yeah. What do you think? It was my grandmother's name. Mother would be over the moon if we named the baby after her. Carmel Molly Egan."

Joan didn't know what to say. She could only stare in silence at her knees, bent up under the bedclothes.

"It has a nice ring to it, don't you think?" Martin said.

Was he asking or telling her? What difference did it make what they called her? Let them have it their way. "Why not? Carmel it is, then," she said.

The nurse came, tinkling the bell that announced visiting hours were over. Martin handed the baby to Joan, and she held her awkwardly as he kissed them both on their heads. "I'll be back tomorrow to take my girls home."

As soon as he was gone, Joan called to the nurse. "It's my last night. Could you take her up to the nursery?" she pleaded. "Just for tonight?"

The nurse agreed. "Only because we're not that busy, mind you," she said, with a stern look of disapproval. "She won't rear herself when you're back home, you know."

"Thank you," Joan said, with a sigh of relief.

"I suppose you'll be wanting a sleeping tablet too?"

Joan shook her head.

That night, she lay on her back in the hospital bed, pretending to sleep. She wanted to think. To remember. She had committed every scant detail of each precious moment with her first child to her memory. And she would find her one day. "I haven't forgotten you, April. How could I?" she whispered in the darkness, even though nobody was listening.

CHAPTER 38

Joan peered into the pram at the puckered face of the crying baby. Carmel was dressed in the mauve cardigan Molly had crocheted for her. Her tiny fists pummeled the air in protest. It was two days since they'd brought her home, and Martin was back to work down at the yard. At first, Joan rocked the new Silver Cross pram up and down the garden, shushing the baby as she walked. The Miraculous Medal pinned to the pram's hood for the child's grace and protection bobbed from side to side, catching the early-morning sun.

Joan's grip on the pram handle tightened with every step. She began bouncing it back and forth on its spoked wheels. The squeak of the pram's suspension marked time with her heart as it beat faster and faster. The harder she shook the pram, the louder Carmel cried.

There was no use picking her up—she'd tried. The baby felt like a deadweight in her arms. It was as if all the tension leaked from Joan's rigid body into the soft folds of Carmel's skin as soon as she held her. When the crying got loud enough to be heard next door, and not a moment before, Molly appeared at Joan's side to intervene—and to gloat.

"Give her here to me," Molly said. "There now," she soothed, holding the baby to her.

And Carmel stopped crying.

The following day, Joan stood in the shadow of the high, ivy-covered garden wall, shaking the pram again. Her head ached and her hair, damp with sweat, stuck to the nape of her neck. She shivered, unable to get warm. "Shut up!" she hissed under her breath. Her words evaporated into the still summer air. She could feel her mother-in-law's eyes boring into her back from the kitchen window. And for once she was glad Molly was there—because she didn't know what she might do to the baby if she was left alone with her.

It wasn't just Joan's heart that seemed poisoned. Within days, she was back in hospital diagnosed with an infection. She wept as the doctor, flipping through her case notes, informed her that the damage to her fallopian tubes meant there was no guarantee she'd have more children.

Those first few months, Joan felt crushed by the burden of her sadness. Everyone else was in such high spirits that summer, the summer the Americans put a man on the moon. Anything seemed possible. Just watching the grainy black-and-white pictures of Neil Armstrong in his spacesuit bouncing around on their tellies gave everyone a spring in their step. Everyone except Joan. Carmel was almost a month old, but Joan was no happier. If a man could walk on the moon, she thought, why couldn't she love her own child?

The entire country stayed up into the small hours to watch RTÉ's broadcast of the Apollo 11 moon landing. The following morning, the papers were delayed, and the milk was late.

"Will you watch Carmel, Martin? I'm just nipping out for a pint of milk," Joan called up the stairs.

"Don't be long," he called back.

It was the first time she'd left the house without Carmel. She shut the gate behind her and glanced up at their bedroom window, where her husband would be getting dressed in his corduroy work trousers.

The scent of the roses blooming in Molly's flower beds should have lifted her spirits, but they had the opposite effect. Her heart felt ugly next to their beauty. She stepped out into Grove Square, but instead of turning toward the village and Ryan's grocery shop, she headed away from it, toward Ardeer Avenue and down the hill past the factory. Nothing, not even footsteps on the moon, stopped the furnaces firing in that place.

The farther she got down the hill, the quicker she walked. When she reached the bottom, she stood at the side of the road, busy now, with people late getting to where they were supposed to be. Packed buses trundled past in twos and threes, conductors hanging on to the poles at the back, glad of the cool breeze on a fine day.

Joan stood still near the bus stop, close to the edge of the path. Too close. Her toes inching over the curb. She gazed into the blackness of the new tarmacadam the corporation workers had poured a few days before, already softening in the heat of the morning. She wanted to melt into it. To disappear.

All she need do was step off the curb at the right moment, when the bus leaving the last stop was gathering speed, and it would all be over. Problem solved.

"Are you all right, love?" a woman in a sunny headscarf, pulling a shopping trolley behind her, asked, concern in her eyes. "What bus are you after? Where are you headed?"

"I don't know," Joan said, blinking. "I'm not sure where I'm supposed to be."

"Well, come away from there," the woman replied, with a gentle tug on Joan's sleeve. "Them buses would mow you down in a minute." She put her hand out to hail the bus she'd been waiting for. "Mind yourself, love. Do you hear me?"

The bus conductor helped the woman heave her shopping trolley on board, and she called back over her shoulder to Joan, "Mind yourself."

The words Ma used to say whenever the girls left the house

without her. The only thing that could have stopped Joan stepping off the curb at that moment was the memory of her mother.

JOAN FINISHED FOLDING THE FLOUR into the cake mixture, then poured the batter into the nine-inch round cake tins. It would make three tiers. That should be enough to feed the great and good who Molly had invited to Carmel's first birthday party the following day.

She licked the back of the spoon. She would have preferred a quiet family celebration, but Molly insisted on a big show. Still, it would be good to see Da again, even if Teresa couldn't make it. There was no sense inviting her old friends from the factory. Even if she'd stayed in touch with Imelda and the others who still lived on the estate, they'd never come. Joan knew exactly what they'd say. *We'd only be out of place, Joan. Grove Square isn't for the likes of us.* It was just as well, she thought, rinsing the spoon under the hot tap. She'd have enough to contend with tomorrow, keeping up appearances for Molly's sake.

It'd been a rough year, but Joan had made up her mind that Carmel's birthday would be a fresh start for both of them. She looked over at her daughter, sitting in her high chair, happily sucking on a crust of bread.

"Look, Carmel!" she said, holding up one of the cake tins. "This is for your party tomorrow."

Carmel babbled back at her, saliva dribbling down her chin and soaking her bib. Joan smiled, buoyed by their quiet moment together. Things could only get better. She put the cakes in the oven, set the timer, and sat down with a cup of tea to wait for them to rise.

Carmel dropped her crust on the floor and held her pudgy arms out to Joan. "Ma, Ma."

"All right, darlin', up you come," Joan said, standing to unclip her. She slid Carmel from the high chair, then swung her in the air. "Whee!"

Carmel rewarded her with a giggle. Joan propped her daughter on her hip. "Look," she said. "Look, Carmel. See the birds eating their breakfast?" She pointed at the window to the sparrows on the bird table in the garden. Carmel pointed too. Joan kissed the top of her head. She closed her eyes and breathed in the sweet baby smell of her little girl.

EVERYONE WHO WAS ANYONE WAS THERE to celebrate Joan's daughter's birthday the following day. Everyone except the two people in the world Joan's heart ached to see most.

Teresa had sent a birthday card, a rag doll with a fine head of yellow wool hair, and her apologies. She was sorry she couldn't get the time off work to make the trip up to Dublin for her niece's party. Even though it was only June, the bed-and-breakfast was already busy. The summer tourist season began early in Kinsale. She would try to visit them in the winter.

The hum of polite conversation among people sipping tea from Molly's best china filtered through from the front parlor to the kitchen. As she fumbled with a box of multicolored birthday candles, Joan realized her hands were shaking. She placed a single pink candle in the center of the cake, making sure not to smudge the letters of Carmel's name. She'd piped delicate shells in pink and white icing all around the edges.

"It's time," Martin said, coming into the kitchen, his camera at the ready. "Everyone's waiting."

Joan lit the candle. "Will it do?" she asked, pointing to the cake.

"It's fine," Martin said, and turned to head back to the parlor.

"Glad you like it," she replied, bristling.

"Ah, come on, Joan, don't be like that. There's a room full of important people next door. We can't keep busy men like Fergal Doyle waiting."

"Who is Fergal Doyle to us anyway, Martin?"

He sighed and swung around to face her again. "You know fine well who he is. He's the president of the Chamber of Commerce. Someone a local business owner like me needs to keep on the right side of."

"Oh, I see. It's just I thought we were celebrating our daughter's birthday. I had no idea we were conducting a business meeting."

Martin sighed. "In a small community like ours you don't get a second chance to make a good impression. You know that, Joan," he said, walking out the door.

She stood staring into the flame, watching the candle wax dribble onto the buttercream. She followed her husband down the dark hall with halting steps, shielding the candle with the palm of her hand, careful to keep her thumb from spoiling the icing.

When she appeared in the door with the cake, a chorus of "Happy birthday to you" rang out. Carmel was sitting on Molly's lap at the head of the mahogany dining table, legs going nineteen to the dozen. All the guests were gathered around them.

Joan walked in, holding the cake out in front of her like a peace offering, and set it down in front of Carmel and Molly. Carmel's eyes were wide with delight, and her blond curls bounced as she slapped her chubby hands on the table in front of her.

"Blow, Carmel. Like this. Watch Granny," Molly said.

Carmel made little breathy sounds with her lips, and everyone clapped, so she clapped too.

"Here, Joan, take this away before she gets the new dress I bought her covered in icing, would you?" Molly instructed, shoving the plate along the polished wood toward her. "And make sure all our guests get a slice."

Joan passed around plates of birthday cake and white paper napkins.

"Did you make it yourself?" Father Mac asked.

Joan smiled. Her face ached from smiling. Playing the part of doting wife and mother was exhausting. "I did, Father," she said, making sure she gave him a piece with extra icing on it.

Da stood near the bay window, nursing a cup of tea and a hangover. He was thinner than he'd been at Joan's wedding, his shoulders too slight for the suit jacket he wore and regularly pawned. He had the hunted look of a man who existed on the odd slice of buttered bread and a surplus of strong stout.

"Here, Da, have a piece," Joan said, bringing him a plate of cake.

"Have you nothing a bit stronger, love?" Da asked, holding out his cup and saucer, a hungry look in his eyes. The stench of last night's whiskey was still on his breath.

"No, Da! It's a child's birthday party." Joan was glad Molly had put her foot down and decided there'd be no drink at the party. Da could get awful maudlin with a few bevies in him, and she didn't have time for that, not today of all days.

He gestured around the room with his fork. "I wonder what your mother would have made of all this, eh?"

"She'd probably think it was daft. All this fuss over a baby's birthday. Wasn't she already pregnant with Teresa by the time I turned one?"

Da nodded, puffing his chest out and raising himself to his full five feet five inches. "She was indeed. Your ma was a born mother . . ." His sentence trailed off, and he cleared his throat. "I wish she was here to see how well you've done, Joan."

Joan's eyes filled.

"Maybe this time next year Carmel will have a little brother or sister to keep her company," Da said, winking. The blood rushed to Joan's face, threatening to betray her.

"You never know, Da," she said.

He had no idea that Carmel already had an older sister. She would be four years and eighty-two days old today.

Martin appeared again at her elbow, directing proceedings.

"Come on, let's have a family photo, the three of us together." Did he ever remember that they were four? Joan smiled for the camera, and for the room of acquaintances who had gathered to celebrate with them. People who, if they were honest, were there to show face, to keep in with the Egans for one reason or another.

Father Mac, to ensure that donations to the church roof fund kept flowing. Sadie Burke, to keep her husband's job at Egans' yard secure. Phil Farrell, to make sure Molly didn't switch to the new butcher who had opened up in the village. Joan didn't blame them. It was what she'd been doing all year. Showing her face.

She watched Carmel bouncing on Molly's knee.

"She's a real granny's girl, that one," Sadie groveled. "The image of her daddy."

Molly glowed.

And then it hit Joan. She had given Carmel up. By degrees, she'd made herself dispensable. Carmel wouldn't even notice if her mother disappeared from her life. Today was all the proof Joan needed. She sighed as she left the room and headed for the kitchen, where the dishes were waiting. Yesterday, standing in this very spot with Carmel in her arms, she'd fooled herself into thinking things could be different. Now, scraping cake crumbs off the dirty plates of guests she hadn't invited, she realized it would take more than her change of heart to make everything right.

PART FIVE

CHAPTER 39

Dublin, 1996

Joan never went to Mass on a weekday, but she did that Friday morning—the day she would get her results from the clinic. She'd gone from barely speaking to Martin to having nothing to say to him at all. They had been sleeping arms folded with their backs to each other since Sunday, and she'd have stopped sleeping in their bed and gone into the spare room if it wasn't for Molly knowing. *That's you all over, Joan. Hitch a smile on your face and pretend everything is hunky-dory.*

Without a soul to talk to, she had to get strength from somewhere. She scooted into the end of a pew halfway up the church behind a woman wearing a black lace mantilla. God, it was years since she'd seen a mantilla. She remembered back to the days when you couldn't go into the church without covering your head. Times had changed.

The other day, she heard the hat designer Philip Treacy on the radio, saying hats used to be a sign of conformity and submission.

Now, he said, a hat was a sign of rebellion—a way to stand out, not to fit in. As she bent her head in prayer, Joan couldn't help thinking how right he was and how much it was needed.

The doubts and fears that had been running through her head since she had the row with Martin on Sunday were a tangled mess of logic, but, despite sleeping badly, she had been surprisingly clear-headed when she woke that morning. If she wasn't a match for Ben, she reasoned, what were the chances Carmel would be, even if she agreed to be tested? If they hadn't found a match among all those people on the hospital database, surely Carmel was a long shot, too?

As she knelt, sunshine streaming through the stained-glass windows, Joan made up her mind. There was no sense trying to think her way out of the problem when her heart already knew what to do. If she wasn't a match, she would tell Carmel about Ben. It didn't matter how slim the odds or how Carmel might react over the great unraveling of their lives when the secrets she and Martin had guarded for years were exposed. She had to tell her.

After Mass, Joan deposited three coins into the collection box at the entrance to the church and lit three candles. One for Ben and one for both of her girls. Only faith that everything would work out in the end could get her through this.

The house was eerily quiet when she got home. It was Molly's morning at the senior citizens' club; Martin dropped her off on his way to work. Joan had the house to herself. Her hands were shaking as she dialed.

"Hello, Blackrock Clinic. Can you hold the line please?" Joan's heart was hammering. "Putting you through now."

"Ah, yes, Mrs. Clemence. I have your results here."

Joan held her breath.

"I'm sorry, your sample was incompatible."

"Sorry, what did you say? Does that mean . . . I'm not a match?"

"Yes, I'm afraid it does."

Joan's legs buckled. She dropped to her knees on the hall floor, still holding on to the receiver for dear life.

"Would you like to talk to the doctor?" the nurse offered.

"No, no, thank you," Joan said, her voice beginning to crack. She didn't wait for the nurse to say goodbye before replacing the receiver. *Damn it! Why did nothing ever work out as it should?* She collapsed onto the polished mahogany floorboards, head in her hands. She didn't recognize the sound that came out of her as hers. It was like the bellow of a wounded animal. When her sobbing slowed, she rocked back and forth, hugging herself, waiting for the dull ache in her chest to subside.

The ringing of the phone on the hall table startled her into silence. She sat up, trying to slow her breathing, while it rang out, then closed her eyes. It was probably Carmel calling from the yard, checking to see where she was. She couldn't face work. Not today. She needed to calm down before she phoned Emma.

Some fresh air—a walk in the park or down by the river—might help, but she'd be bound to bump into one of the neighbors, and she was in no mood for making polite conversation. She shuddered and roused herself, wiped her face, and changed into her slippers before making her way into the conservatory. Drawing her cardigan around her body, she stood staring at the birds pecking at the nuts and fat balls she'd left out for them.

She'd been positive she'd be a match, which was wishful thinking. Maybe she was desperate for a happy ending for her own selfish reasons. How would she break the news to Emma, whose heart she had already broken? And what now? She couldn't give up. This wasn't the end of the line. She'd ask Martin again about being tested. Surely once he knew she wasn't a match he'd agree to it. He had to. Even as the thought entered her mind, she shook her head. No. A man who'd forgotten how to listen to his heart would always take the line of least resistance.

On impulse, she decided to go out into the garden. Still wearing her slippers, she stepped out onto the damp grass. The quiet enveloped her. A bit of weeding might help clear her head. She found the trowel Martin had used to plant the bulbs for Molly in regimented rows along the flower beds. They'd be magnificent next spring, he'd said. How could he care so much about what lived and died in the garden yet so little about his own flesh and blood?

Joan knelt on the cool grass and began turning the soil with the steel tip of the trowel. It loosened easily against the blade. She worked slowly at first, carefully teasing the weeds out from between the plants, placing them in neat piles along the borders as she went. Blood pumped steadily through her veins with the exertion of the work, and sweat trickled between her shoulder blades to the small of her back. She worked faster, adjusting her grip on the trowel—grabbing it in her fist, jabbing between the plants at random.

An hour passed. She barely noticed. Rage smoldered then ignited inside her. One moment she was weeding, the next she was hacking at the flower beds, head bent, clawing at the soil with her bare hands, furiously uprooting every single bulb Martin had planted.

"We're back!" Betty called from the conservatory doorway, in her usual cheerful voice. It must be lunchtime already. Filthy and breathless, Joan sat back on her heels, shading her eyes from the sun with her hand. Betty looked horrified as she walked toward her. "Joan? Are you all right?"

It was only then that Joan registered the desecrated garden, the lawn strewn with clumps of dark soil and discarded bulbs. She saw the trowel in her hand and the brown earth drying under her fingernails and caking her palms. In a daze, she wiped them down the front of her sky-blue skirt.

Molly shrieked from inside the conservatory, "What do you think you're doing?!"

Joan straightened, standing on unbending stiff legs. She faced Betty, who stood gaping at her.

"Look at what you've done?!" Molly screamed, curling an accusing arthritic finger in her direction.

Joan walked calmly up the path.

"You'd better have that tidied up before Martin gets home," Molly continued as Joan stepped into the conservatory.

Joan stooped low until her face was level with Molly's. "Enough! You interfering old cow. If it wasn't for you . . ." Her hands balled into fists at her side as she spat the words. She witnessed the terror in Molly's eyes as she shrank back in her wheelchair.

Then she felt Betty's hand on her forearm, inching her away, creating distance between them. "It's all right, Joan. Why don't you go and get freshened up, and I'll put the kettle on?"

The warmth in Betty's voice broke the spell. Joan nodded and went upstairs to shower, trailing muck behind her.

Martin was home within the hour. "Betty called. She was afraid to leave you alone with Mother," he said. Joan was standing with her back to him, her hair dripping onto her dressing gown. "What the hell, Joan? We can't go on like this."

She turned to face him. "I tested negative, Martin."

He did that thing he always did when he was anxious or working out what to do next: he ran his fingers through his hair. "That's that, then," he said.

"No! Don't you see? It doesn't have to be. You could try. Martin, please?" She was begging him now, and she didn't care. "You wouldn't even have to meet them," she pleaded, her words falling over each other.

"If you're not a match, the chances of me being one are slim to nothing. I'm not risking everything I've worked for on odds like that."

Joan took a step toward him. Hands on hips, her spine straight and strong. "You selfish bastard! Always thinking of number one."

"Keep your bloody voice down, Joan. You'll upset my mother," he hissed, looking over his shoulder toward the bedroom door.

"To hell with your mother, and to hell with you too!"

Within seconds she was pulling open the wardrobe doors and drawers, yanking out the first items of clothing she could lay her hands on. She dressed in a hurry without caring what she wore. All she knew was that she had to get out of there.

"What are you doing?" Martin's voice sounded fearful. "Be reasonable."

The wild animal in her that had been howling in the hall earlier turned on him. "That's the last time you'll tell me what to do, Martin. Do you hear me?!" She stuffed her feet into her shoes and strode toward the door.

Martin was two steps behind her.

"Martin, Martin! What's all that racket?" Joan could hear Molly yelling from downstairs as she took the stairs two at a time.

Martin followed her. "Wait! What are you going to do?"

"What I should have done years ago, Martin," Joan said, slamming the hall door behind her.

She thought about going straight to Carmel's flat. But Carmel wouldn't be home from work yet. And something else was stopping her from heading straight to her daughter. She recognized it at once. Fear. It was easier than she'd imagined to walk out on Martin after years of being let down by him. It wouldn't be as easy to be shown the door by Carmel after she turned her world upside down.

She needed time to think.

So she walked. Down past the church, turning right at Harold's Cross Bridge. The daylight was fading, and cyclists on their commutes home passed her weaving between the cars, while the traffic crawled alongside.

Groups of people, pints in hand, gathered outside the Barge pub, laughing at the freedom of another week over. It was getting dark now, the air grew chill, and it started to rain. Joan's coat was still in the cupboard under the stairs back in Grove Square.

She walked the streets for hours—she didn't know exactly how long. Her head hurt. Her chest was burning. And she was wet through. If only it wasn't so late, she thought, as she passed a phone box. She could have called Teresa. But her sister would already be in bed with her alarm set for six in the morning. Anyway, in her hurry to leave, she'd forgotten her purse with the housekeeping money Martin had given her a couple of days ago zipped inside it.

A taxi slowed to a crawl as it passed her on the crest of Portobello Bridge, but she didn't turn her head to make eye contact with the driver, and he took off again along Rathmines Road, which was slick with rain.

Joan longed to see Teresa now. The longing was a physical ache behind her breastbone. When she reached the church, she sheltered for a few minutes against the railings under a giant sycamore tree, remembering that one time she visited Teresa and her family in Kinsale, alone.

She could count on the fingers of two hands the number of visits she, Martin, and Carmel had paid them over the years. These were only day trips for some occasion or other, a baptism, communion, or confirmation. Once or twice Joan suggested making a weekend of it, but Martin assured her that they couldn't afford the time away from the yard, not when they were so busy.

"I could go on my own," she'd said, looking up from the invoices she was checking in the office. "Take the train or the bus down." She peered over the top of her glasses to gauge his reaction.

"Where's the sense in that?" Martin said, without looking at her. "The bus takes four hours. You'd lose a day traveling. I'll take you in the car one Sunday; if we leave bright and early, we can be there and back before dark."

She'd accepted this, let it go, and the upshot was that she never got to spend any time alone with her sister. It was her fault they had grown apart.

There was that one long weekend, though, after Teresa's youngest son, David, was born, when Carmel was twelve and had just moved schools to St. Bridget's. Martin was up to his eyes in work and too busy to drive her to Kinsale, so she had taken the bus instead.

At first, when they spoke on the phone, Teresa seemed hesitant about her visit. "Are you sure you want to come down here to the madhouse?" she asked. "We're not exactly up for visitors. The place is a mess."

"I'm not coming with my white glove to inspect the surfaces, T. And I'm not a visitor. I'm family."

The other end of the phone line went quiet.

They had three precious days together. It was the closest she'd felt to Teresa since before she left on the boat for England. Teresa's husband, Ritchie, who was now a garda sergeant, collected Joan from the bus. "I'm working late shift tonight," he said. "Teresa will be glad of an extra pair of hands. James can be a bit of a handful, especially at bedtime."

"Four boys, Ritchie! I don't know how you do it," Joan said.

He checked his rearview mirror and smiled at her before backing out of the parking space. "Wouldn't be without one of them," he said.

Joan knew by the light in his eyes that he meant it.

Teresa was at the door before they were out of the car. They hugged each other close. Joan rested her head on her sister's shoulder, feeling the distance between them fall away.

"Careful," Teresa said, pointing to her chest. "You'll be drowned in breast milk before you know it."

"How's it going?" Joan asked.

"Oh, you know. I'm a bit sore still. It will pass soon enough."

That was the thing, Joan thought. She didn't know. She hadn't breastfed either of her daughters. A wave of guilt washed over her, but she chose to ignore it. This weekend wasn't about her. She was here for Teresa.

Later that evening, after she'd called home to speak to Carmel, Joan bathed the three older boys, read bedtime stories, and tucked them in, then came downstairs to the sitting room where Teresa was nursing the baby. "Can I get you anything? Tea, water?"

"Just sit down and talk to me, Joan," Teresa said, patting the cushion on the sofa next to her.

Joan sat. "Are you sure I can't do the ironing or something," she offered.

"You're only here for the weekend and the ironing will still be there long after you're gone."

"You're right," Joan said, reaching out to tickle her nephew's tiny toes. "He's perfect, T."

"He'll do," Teresa said, her face softening with love. "So, how've you been?"

"Grand," Joan said, swallowing a lump in her throat and keeping her eyes on the baby's feet. She looked up into her sister's face and registered a frown.

"What's up?" Teresa said, concern in her voice.

"Oh, it's nothing," Joan replied. "I just wish you lived closer." She hesitated. "I miss us," she said.

"Me too," Teresa said. "Me too."

It turned out to be an unforgettable weekend. The kind where you go nowhere and do nothing out of the ordinary, and, in doing so, delight in every moment. Joan wished she'd brought Carmel with her. She would have loved spending time with her younger cousins, who were no more than strangers to her since she saw so little of them. Seeing Teresa's boys together, she thought how lonely Carmel must have been growing up in Grove Square with only three adults for company.

Joan basked in her sister's contentedness. She could see how truly happy Teresa and Ritchie were together, and she in turn was happy for them.

On her last evening, return visits and more frequent calls were promised. Promises both sisters later broke with regret in the busyness of their lives.

Now, Joan stepped out from under the tree and kept walking, avoiding puddles along the path. It wasn't until she reached the Town Hall clock in Rathmines that she realized she was almost at Carmel's. It seemed like the only place to be.

CHAPTER 40

Carmel wasn't expecting anyone at that hour. She glanced at the kitchen clock. Almost eleven. Not even Lina from downstairs would ring her bell looking to borrow milk for a cuppa this late. She switched off the telly and stood, pulling the belt on her dressing gown tighter, before opening the apartment door and heading downstairs.

She half expected nobody to be there when she opened the front door. It was probably just young fellas messing about, playing knock-and-run on the way home from the pub. But as she opened the door a crack, she caught sight of her mother standing on the doorstep, silhouetted in the orange glow of the streetlight behind her.

"Mam? What on earth are you doing here? What's wrong?"

Her mother squinted against the light from the hallway. "Nothing," she said wearily. "Everything. Can I come in?"

"Of course!" Carmel stepped aside, opening the door wide. Mam came into the hall. Something was definitely up. Her mother had only visited her flat once since Carmel moved in. And she never went out alone at this time of night.

"You're soaked to the skin," Carmel said, as if she were chastising a small child.

"Yes, I'm sorry. I forgot my coat."

"Is Granny okay?" Carmel asked, scrambling to work out what emergency would have brought her here so late.

"Don't worry, your granny and your dad are fine," she said, shivering in the hallway. "I just had to talk to you."

"Come on up, then," Carmel said, touching her shoulder. They climbed the three narrow flights of stairs without a word, and then Carmel let them into her flat.

"Here, Mam," she said, handing her mother the towel that was hanging on a hook in the kitchen. She took the towel but just stood there holding it.

Carmel stole a glance at her as she lit the gas fire and put the kettle under the tap. "You'll need to get out of those clothes, or you'll catch pneumonia."

Mam tugged on a damp sleeve that stuck stubbornly to her skin.

"Here, let me help you," Carmel said, taking hold of her cardigan cuff. Her mother began to cry. "Aw, Mam!" Carmel put her arms around her. She smelled the familiar green-apple scent of her wet hair. Mam pressed her damp cheek against Carmel's dressing gown and sobbed while she held her.

When the kettle whistled behind them, she stepped back, leaving a smudge of mascara on Carmel's shoulder. "Oh, look what I've done to your dressing gown," she said, reaching across to rub at the black mark with her thumb.

"Never mind that," Carmel said, handing her a tissue. "Let's get you out of those clothes."

Ten minutes later, they were sitting next to each other on the small sofa. Her mother, dressed in one of Carmel's old tracksuits, cradled a mug of tea in her hands.

"Better?" Carmel said.

Mam nodded.

"Now, tell me what's wrong."

"It's all wrong. I've made a mess of everything, and I have no idea how to put it right."

Carmel leaned over and reached for her hand. "Why don't you start at the beginning?" she said.

CARMEL TURNED ON HER SIDE and thumped her pillow. The sofa-bed springs squeaked beneath her. This was pointless. There was no way she'd get any rest tonight. She was too wound up to sleep. She'd been lying awake for hours wondering who to blame. For the first time in her life, she understood what people meant when they talked about dropping a bombshell. That was what had just happened, this evening, right here in her flat on this very sofa. A secret had detonated, shattering Carmel's world.

As the hands crawled around the clock on the wall, the facts of the matter began to sink in. Mam had told her everything. Once she started talking she couldn't stop. The truth spilled out of her. Carmel had a sister in England who nobody knew existed. A nephew who was dying. A father she adored who she didn't know. And a mother who was falling apart. She was as mad as hell at the pair of them. How could they keep this from her, for her whole life? What kind of parents were they? What kind of people could abandon one child and deceive another—and not just for months or years but for decades? Was it any wonder she'd never been close to her mother? What kind of woman would deny her innate instinct to love her child?

The headlights from a passing car illuminated the room for a second. Carmel exhaled. Christ, she'd never have known any of this if her sister's son wasn't sick. She doubted her parents would have told her. They'd probably have gone to their graves and allowed their secret to die with them. How in God's name could they do this to her? Only now, this wasn't just about Carmel and her fractured family. A child's life was on the line. Somehow, she would have to put her fury aside and avoid adding to the problem. It wouldn't be easy, but she'd have to try. Take things one day at a time.

She sighed and threw back the covers, then got up, switched on the light, and walked across to her kitchenette to refill the kettle. The cool tiles under her feet grounded her and stilled her thoughts—or at least stopped them swirling like dark clouds in her mind. She took a chamomile tea bag from the open box on the counter and dropped it into a clean mug. Righteous indignation wouldn't get her anywhere, she told herself as she poured boiling water onto the tea bag.

She brought her tea to the sofa, blowing on it before taking a sip, and went over everything her mother had told her just a few hours before. To be fair to Mam, it couldn't have been easy. None of it. All of it. Not just tonight. Where would a girl in her predicament have turned, in the sixties, in a society where unmarried mothers were shamed or, worse, damned? What choices did they have back then when contraception was illegal? Imagine if she'd ended up in one of those awful mother-and-baby homes. Carmel shuddered.

She'd seen for herself this evening how hard it had been for her mother just to get her story out. What must it have been like to live with the shame and secrecy of that story for thirty years? She kept saying sorry to her, over and over again through her tears. A flood of tears that had shocked Carmel to her core. She'd barely seen her mother cry before tonight. Never in Carmel's entire life had Mam ever let her guard down.

"You must be furious with me," Mam said. "I wouldn't blame you."

For a minute, Carmel considered denying how she felt, but they might not get another chance to be completely honest with each other. It was time to tell the truth.

"You know, Mam, I've spent my whole life quietly resenting you without knowing why. I finally get it now. That's something, I suppose."

Her mother nodded then, as if she understood now, too. For years, Carmel had lived under the illusion that Mam was, at best, too pragmatic to show her feelings and, at worst, too cold to feel anything at all. Now she was beginning to see that her mother had been numbing herself all this time to avoid living with the pain of the past. She'd hidden behind the lie of a life she'd been forced to construct for herself. Just as Carmel had pretended not to mind the distance between them.

The sky was turning from blue-black to pink when Carmel finally yawned and closed her eyes. She wasn't going to make sense overnight of this situation that was thirty years in the making. No, not just thirty years, she thought. Generations. Generations of bad hands dealt to women like her mother who were not free to choose how to love or be loved.

She couldn't fix all of it, but she could try to put at least one thing right. How would they move forward afterwards? She wasn't sure. But she did have the answer to one of her questions. What kind of woman would deny her instinct to love her child? The kind of woman who had no other choice.

SUNLIGHT STREAMED THROUGH THE TALL WINDOW, warming the flat. Kiss FM was on the radio in the background—that latest Boyzone release they seemed to be playing day and night on repeat—and Carmel was cracking an egg into the pan when her mother appeared in the doorway in the tracksuit Carmel had given her the night before.

"How'd you sleep?" Carmel asked.

"On and off."

"You probably haven't slept in days."

"I have to admit it hasn't been easy," Mam said, rubbing her forehead. "You couldn't have got much sleep yourself on that sofa."

"I'm fine," Carmel lied. "Do you want an egg with your rasher?" She couldn't quite believe they were standing in her kitchen, talking about what to eat for breakfast the morning after her mother had upended her world.

"I'm not hungry, love."

"You need to eat something," Carmel insisted, handing her a mug of tea.

"Thanks," Mam said, and raised the mug to her lips. She caught sight of the old photograph of Carmel wearing her daisy-chain crown stuck to the fridge. "Where did you get that?" she asked, pointing to it.

"I found it at the bottom of a shoebox of old photos," Carmel said, glancing across.

"God, I'd forgotten," Mam whispered, half to herself, touching a corner of the photograph.

"Yeah, me too," Carmel replied, flipping the eggs. "Listen, I thought we could head over to the house after breakfast and get things sorted out with Dad."

Her mother gave her a grateful look. "I'm sorry, Carmel. I should have told you sooner."

Carmel switched off the gas under the pan and turned to her. "I wish you had. Everything would have made so much more sense if I'd known."

Mam blinked but didn't take her eyes off her. "What do you mean?" she said. "What kind of things?"

"Like why you were always so miserable on my birthday," Carmel said bluntly. Her mother opened her mouth and closed it again. "Like why I could never get close to you, no matter how hard I tried. Why we didn't hug. Why you felt like . . . like a stranger."

Mam lowered her eyes. "Carmel, I am so sorry. It was never you." She put her mug on the kitchen counter. "You did nothing wrong," she said, grabbing her gently by the shoulders. "Do you hear me? I wasn't the mother you deserved."

Carmel felt a single tear she didn't know she'd cried on her cheek and brushed it away impatiently with the heel of her hand. Mam put her arms around her. "I want nothing more than to tell you that I'll make everything up to you, love. That I'll be the mother you always wanted." Carmel sniffed, lifted her head off her mother's shoulder, and looked into her eyes. "But I can't promise you that." She kissed Carmel lightly on the forehead. "The only promise I can make you is that from here on in I'll be the mother *I* always wanted to be." She swallowed. "That's if you'll give me the chance."

When Carmel pulled into the driveway at Grove Square, they saw her father's van haphazardly parked at an odd angle inside the gates. He must have abandoned it there the evening before, after Betty's call. Carmel parked behind it. She switched off the ignition and turned to face her mother, who sat frozen in the passenger seat next to her. "Ready?"

Mam stared down at her hands clasped tightly in her lap. "Yes," she said.

Dad was already at the door before they began crunching across the gravel. "I was worried sick," he said, holding the door open. He looked from Mam to Carmel and back again, with anxious, bloodshot eyes.

Carmel was poker-faced. She couldn't work out if he was worried over Mam or more concerned about how much she'd told her. She spotted Granny sulking in the bay window. She probably still didn't have a clue what her parents had been arguing about yesterday.

"Dad, we need to talk," Carmel said.

Her father ran his hands through his hair and shook his head. "Leave it to your mother and me to sort things out," he said, avoiding her eye. "You should never have been dragged into this." He shot a filthy look over her shoulder toward her mother.

Carmel bristled. "This concerns me too."

He shuffled from one foot to another. "Let's not disturb your granny now," he said, ushering them to the kitchen. They followed him down the hallway. "Sit down," he said, motioning to the table.

Mam pulled out a chair. "I'm all right standing," Carmel said.

Nobody made a move to put the kettle on.

"I know everything, Dad," Carmel said, looking him squarely in the eye. "So we can all stop pretending." He was suddenly pale. Mam stayed quiet. "We don't have time to talk about the ins and outs of it now," she went on. "A little boy is dying, and we have to do what we can to help."

"Your mother and me have been over this, Carmel. It's none of our business."

Carmel fell silent and gaped at her father. "Are you saying you won't get tested?"

"I can't, Carmel. Think what it would do to your granny if word of this got out. The shock could be enough to kill her."

"Ah, yeah, here we go again." Her mother had found her voice.

Carmel put a hand on her arm. "Wait a second, Mam. You're not serious, are you, Dad?"

"Don't be like that, love, just hear me out," he said, taking a step toward her.

Carmel stood frowning, searching his face.

He was beside her now. "You don't understand, love."

"Oh, I understand all right. I understand you're not the father I thought you were." Her voice caught in her throat. "Come on, Mam," she said, walking toward the hall. "We have a call to make."

Her father stood in the doorway, arms wide, blocking their exit. "You have to see sense, Carmel. We can't risk losing our good name." He was begging now. "What about everything we've worked for?"

She shook her head. "Jesus, is that all you care about?" she said, pushing past him.

"See what you've done?!" he yelled at Mam, who'd got up to follow Carmel. Then he was down the hall after them. "Carmel, wait!" he called out, as they reached the front door. "What will I tell your poor granny?"

"Tell her I'm going to meet my sister!"

"You wouldn't do that to her! This isn't like you."

Carmel's eyes widened as she spun around to face him. "No? You mean I'm not your usual good little Carmel, trying to please everyone because she hasn't a clue why her mammy doesn't love her." Her father was taken aback.

"Ah, Carmel, that's not true—your mam has always loved you."

Carmel shook her head. "Maybe she could have, if you'd given her half a chance. But you didn't!" Now she'd got going she couldn't stop herself. "All those times when I thought you were in my corner, you were just driving a wedge between us."

He held up his hands. "No, listen. You're upset. You don't mean it."

Carmel heard the terror in his voice. It dawned on her that maybe she was the one other thing he was afraid of losing. "Come back in. We'll sort this out," he pleaded.

"You're dead right I'm upset. You've made your decision, Dad. Now leave me to make mine," Carmel said, turning her back on him. Her mother followed.

As they made their way down the steps to the driveway, they heard Granny calling out from the parlor. "When is someone going to tell me what's going on?"

"Why don't you mind your own business for once, Mother," her father said in disgust. *If only he'd had the guts to say those words thirty years ago*, Carmel thought, without looking back.

CHAPTER 41

That evening, Joan called Emma from the pay phone on the landing outside Carmel's flat. Her foot tapped on the worn carpet while she waited for someone to pick up at the other end.

Matt answered. "She's over at the hospital," he said. "Can I take a message or get her to call you back?"

"Could you just tell her Joan called? I'll try again tomorrow at six."

Carmel came and stood beside her. "It'll be all right," she said. "Let's start making plans anyway."

"I don't suppose it can do any harm," Joan replied, as they headed back inside. "You could take the blood test in town, or in Blackrock—that's where I went."

"Why don't we just go over and do it there instead?"

Joan frowned. "You mean to England?"

"Yes. It makes sense, doesn't it? If I'm a match we can get everything under way."

Joan hesitated.

"I'd like to meet Emma as well," Carmel admitted. "And be there for her if I can."

"Of course you would," Joan said. "I'll have to talk to her first, but, all right, let's see if we can make it work."

They sat side by side on the sofa, and Carmel flattened the pages of her A4 diary with her hand. "Now, let's see. Where are we?"

Joan could see several reminders of upcoming work appointments, neatly penciled in Carmel's handwriting. "What about work?" she said. "How will Dad manage without you?"

"I'm sure Egans' will still be standing when we get back, Mam," Carmel said. "The lads will hold the fort. Besides, what's more important than this?" She left the question hanging in the air as she met her mother's eyes.

"Thank you" was all Joan could manage. She couldn't believe how well Carmel was taking the news about Emma. Maybe she was still in shock and the fallout would come later? Either way, she was proud of how her daughter stood up to Martin. That couldn't have been easy for a girl who was the apple of her daddy's eye, and he of hers. Joan knew the crush of such a disappointment.

"Right," Carmel said. "I'll get these flights booked. I'd say Aer Lingus will be our best bet for flying into Heathrow."

"We should probably book one-way tickets since we don't know how things will go," Joan replied.

"Good idea," Carmel said, scribbling notes on the page. "Once you confirm the dates with Emma I'll head down to the travel agents and get everything sorted." Joan nodded in agreement. "Time for a cuppa," Carmel said, closing her diary. Joan watched as she crossed the room, sliding open kitchen drawers, banging cupboard doors shut. She opened her mouth to say something, but hesitated. She was so unaccustomed to speaking to Carmel about anything other than the practicalities of work and life, she didn't know how to begin. She took a deep breath. "Carmel."

"Yeah?" Carmel said, standing on tiptoe to reach for clean mugs at the back of the cupboard.

"I can't get over how you stood up to your dad," Joan said. "It can't have been easy for you."

Carmel turned toward her holding two empty mugs in one hand and a packet of Fig Rolls in the other. "And I can't believe he's prepared to just sit there and do nothing," she replied.

Joan left the sofa and came to where Carmel stood. She took her gently by the shoulders. "I'm so proud of you. I should have said that more when you were growing up." She looked deep into her daughter's eyes.

"Well, you have now, and now is as good a time as any to start," Carmel replied, her eyes shining.

Joan didn't know what she would have done without Carmel in the days that followed. Bright, capable, loving Carmel who was beside her in the hall when she broke the news to Emma that she wasn't a match and told her Carmel wanted to be tested. Carmel booked the flights to London and organized a place near the hospital for them to stay. Carmel had gone back with her to Grove Square to pack the few things Joan would need for the trip. She'd slept on the sofa, put mugs of sweet tea into Joan's hands, and held down the fort at the yard.

"Only one more night," she said to Joan as she handed her a bowl of soup the evening before they were due to fly to London. "Do you remember you used to say that to me when I was small, when you tucked me into bed in the lead-up to Christmas? Only this many nights, you'd say, counting them out on my fingers."

Joan shook her head. "I wish we had more happy memories like that from when you were growing up." She sighed.

"What are you on about, Mam? It's not as if we were at each other's throats all the time."

"No, I suppose not," Joan said, cupping her hands around the warm soup bowl. "What I meant was I wish there'd been more times when it was just you and me."

"Yeah, well, we can't change any of that now," Carmel said, passing her mother the bread.

"Thanks," she said, taking the basket. They took the first mouthfuls of soup in silence. "Carmel," said Joan.

Carmel looked up from her bowl. "Yeah?"

"I'm sorry."

"I know you are," Carmel replied.

BOTH OF THEIR SMALL SUITCASES were packed and ready at the end of the bed. Carmel had the tickets and the sterling notes they'd need when they got to London zipped into the front pocket of her backpack next to the cases.

Joan tossed and turned all night, watching every hour that passed on the clock until she heard Carmel getting up to put on the kettle in the room next door.

"You awake?" Carmel said, opening the bedroom door a crack.

"I'll get up now," Joan said.

"No rush, we have plenty of time. Will you have a piece of toast?"

"No thanks, love. I don't think I could keep anything down."

In the taxi on the way to the airport, Carmel double-checked the tickets. Joan felt like a child being brought on a strange yet scary adventure she wasn't quite sure she wanted to have.

The taxi driver was all chat. He had plenty to say about the state of the roads, the bloody traffic, and the price of petrol. Joan was grateful that Carmel was there to do the talking. They got through airport security without too much hassle. It was always quieter on weekdays, or so the fella checking their tickets told them.

It wasn't until they were at the gate waiting to board that it dawned on Carmel this was the first time Joan had ever flown in an airplane.

"Why didn't you and Dad ever make the trip back?"

Joan shrugged. "It was like everything else: it never seemed to be the right time. We had all these plans to travel—maybe even to visit New York or Paris one day." She looked at Carmel. "I suppose we just got very good at making promises to each other that we had no intention of keeping."

Their flight was called. "Passengers for flight EI158 to London Heathrow, please get ready to board at gate number ten."

"That's us," Carmel said, gathering up her jacket and the copy of *Hello!* magazine she'd picked up at the newsagents. "Got everything?" she asked, looking over her shoulder at her mother.

"I think so," Joan said, with a nervous smile. "I have my Milky Mints all ready for takeoff."

"You're quite the seasoned traveler already, Mam." Carmel laughed as they shuffled into the line of passengers waiting to board.

"Why don't you take the window," she offered, when they reached their seats.

"Are you sure?"

"Positive. Maybe you'll get a good view of the city as we come in to land."

Joan scooted across, and they fastened their seat belts and settled back. She reached for her daughter's hand as the plane began to gather speed on the runway, and Carmel gave her a reassuring smile. "I can't believe we'll be there in an hour and a half," Joan said, looking out the window.

"I know! It would have taken you an entire day to get there all those years ago." Joan nodded. "You were only a kid, really. It must have been terrifying doing that journey on your own."

"It was. But I was one of the lucky ones."

"How'd you mean?" Carmel said.

"I mean there were plenty of girls who didn't have the money to take the boat or someone waiting for them and a place to stay when they arrived."

"I can't imagine what that must have been like."

"I know. It was hard enough, even with your dad."

"I wish you could have kept her," Carmel said. "I hated being an only child."

"Me too. I always wanted you to have a brother or sister," Joan said, fiddling with the emergency landing instructions card in the seat pocket in front of her. "I lost count of the times I stood watching you playing or walking down the driveway to catch the bus to school, imagining what it would have been like if she'd been there with you."

"I suppose it was easier for me because I knew nothing about her," Carmel said.

"Maybe?" Joan replied, turning to face the window and her regrets, as the clouds breezed by.

They took the Piccadilly Line to their hotel, and once they'd checked into their room Joan started to relax a little.

"I told Emma I'd give her a ring when we got here."

"Good idea. Better give her our room number and check what time we're meeting her at the hospital tomorrow," Carmel replied.

After the call, Joan came and sat on the bed next to Carmel. "She'll see us there at ten. Ben's doctor will be on standby once they've taken your blood, and then it's just a waiting game."

"Fingers crossed," Carmel said.

It struck Joan that while Carmel had been busy taking care of her, nobody had been looking out for Carmel. "Are you sure you're all right?" she asked, taking hold of Carmel's arm.

"I'm fine, Mam. Really. I'll be glad to get tomorrow over, though. You know how much I hate needles."

They both laughed. "Yes! I remember your teacher complaining about the fuss you made at school when the nurse came to give the BCG injections."

"I know, and that was after I ate half of the barley sugar sweets they bribed us with!"

"I'll stay with you tomorrow," Joan said, leaning to give her daughter a hug.

"I know you will."

Later, when they turned out the lights and climbed into the narrow twin beds, Joan finally dozed off listening to the steady rise and fall of Carmel's breathing.

CHAPTER 42

Vanilla-scented steam rose, circling Emma as she watched the bubbles spread out across the surface of the bath. She sat on the side of the tub while it filled, inhaling the moist air. Ben's rubber ducks stood guard around the rim, exactly where he'd left them the last time he was home. She dipped a hand into the water, testing the temperature, then opened the cold tap.

With the tips of her fingers, she traced a figure eight in the foam. Or maybe it wasn't an eight at all. Maybe it was the curves of a lemniscate, the symbol for infinity she'd learned in geometry lessons a lifetime ago. The midafternoon bath was an attempt to relax. She raised her shoulders to her ears, then forced them back down. The tension across her back, which seemed to be the only thing holding her together these days, remained.

And then the phone rang.

She was an expert by now at dashing downstairs, arms outstretched toward the walls on either side of the staircase, almost flying. Her wet hands left their mark on the paintwork before making a grab for the receiver at the bottom.

"Hello, love, it's me. Just checking to see how you're doing?"

"Hi, Mum, I'm running a bath. You know, I thought it might help me to relax."

"Good idea, darling. Tomorrow's a big day for you." Her mother hesitated, and Emma could tell she was weighing up what to say next. "For all of you," she finished.

"Yeah, I suppose. They'll be nervous about meeting too—not just the tests."

Emma imagined her mother nodding on the other end of the line.

"It's only natural for them to be thinking beyond getting Ben well again."

"Well, all I care about is Ben," Emma snapped. She shouldn't take her stress out on her mother. She closed her eyes and breathed deeply. "Sorry, Mum."

"It's okay. I know this isn't easy for you, Emma."

"No." Emma sighed. "And . . . I've been thinking."

"Go on."

"If I'm honest, I *do* want to hear Joan's side of the story. I'm beginning to see that not knowing the truth doesn't help anyone, least of all me."

"So, you'll talk to her?"

"Yes, I think so, Mum," Emma said. "Perhaps I need to stop passing judgment and try listening for a change."

"It might help both of you, darling."

"Maybe." Emma let her mother's words sink in. "Thanks, Mum."

"What for? I didn't do anything."

"For always being here," Emma said, swallowing hard. "I'd better go."

"Bye, darling. Talk to you soon."

It wasn't until she replaced the receiver that Emma realized she'd left the bath running.

THEY WERE EARLY. EMMA SAW Joan pacing the hospital foyer as soon as the lift doors opened. She exhaled and straightened, trying to rid herself of the pessimism that accompanied weeks of bad news and very little sleep. Today there was hope. More than they'd had in a long time.

Joan spotted her as soon as she stepped out of the lift and gave her a small wave.

"You're here. Thanks for coming, Joan," Emma said, hesitating before walking toward her. She scanned the foyer, looking for Carmel, trying to place the blond girl in the blue anorak from the photo she'd seen in Dublin.

Carmel, who'd been sitting in the waiting area flicking through an ancient *Reader's Digest*, jumped up and walked toward them, hand outstretched. Emma took it.

"Hiya, I'm Carmel."

Emma blinked, and they stared at each other.

"Hi," Emma whispered, searching Carmel's face. She could see her doing the same. She let go of her hand.

"It's so nice to . . ." Carmel began but stopped midsentence when Emma started speaking at the same time.

"Thanks, Carmel," she said, "for coming. And for agreeing to do this."

"You're . . . welcome. I wanted to. It's important. I hope it works."

Emma nodded. "Me too." This—meeting her sister—was the strangest experience she'd ever had in her life. An unexpected relief flooded through her. Like that feeling you get when you find something precious you thought you'd lost long ago and had given up hope of ever seeing again.

"How's he doing?" Carmel said.

Emma grimaced. "So-so," she said. "But he's a fighter." She lifted her head to look Carmel in the eye.

Joan stood a few feet away, watching them and hanging on every word. Of course, Emma realized, it must be a strange feeling for Joan too: seeing both of her daughters together for the first time.

"Could we see him, do you think?" Joan said.

Emma looked away. "I'm sorry, Joan," she said. "Matt and I talked about that. It isn't the right time. Ben's just not well enough."

"Of course, of course. I shouldn't have asked," Joan said, shaking her head. "Now isn't the time."

"It's okay," Emma replied, placing a hand at Joan's back. "Will we go?"

Their feet squeaked on the smooth floor tiles as the three women navigated the maze of hospital corridors.

"It's a good job you know where you're going," Carmel said, too brightly, attempting small talk. "We'd be lost otherwise!"

"I know. One corridor looks like the next in this place," Emma replied. "But we're here now," she said, stopping in front of a set of double fire doors painted gunmetal gray. She pointed in the direction of the doors. "You'll be in good hands. I'd better get back up to Ben."

"Don't worry about us. We'll be fine," Carmel said.

"Will we see you later?" Joan asked.

"Can we play it by ear?"

"Of course. We'll let you know if we hear anything," Joan said as Emma walked away back up the corridor toward the lifts.

Matt was waiting for her in Ben's room up on the ward.

"Come here," he said, folding her into his arms. Emma exhaled, her ear pressed close to his chest, listening to the reassuring *thud, thud* of his heartbeat.

"You okay?" Matt whispered into her hair. She nodded. "Well, what was Carmel like?"

Emma took a step back to look at him. "Nice. Friendly. I liked her."

Matt smiled. "Well, you always were one for relying on first impressions," he said. "It took you all of five seconds to make your mind up about me."

Emma reached up to stroke his cheek. "What can I say? I'm just a good judge of character, I guess."

He took her hand and kissed her fingertips. "Still, it must have been weird—meeting Carmel, I mean, for the first time."

Emma sighed. "It was. I guess things would be easier if we were meeting under different circumstances."

"Yeah, it's a shame it had to happen like this," Matt said, glancing over at Ben, who was sleeping soundly.

"He looks a lot like her, you know," Emma said.

Matt frowned. "Who? Carmel?"

"Yeah. Maybe it's the fair coloring, but he could pass as hers." They fell silent for a moment, watching their son's chest expand and contract.

"Maybe that's a good omen," Matt said. "The likeness, I mean."

Emma stroked his hand. "Let's hope so," she said.

CHAPTER 43

Carmel sat next to Joan on the molded plastic seats in the hospital corridor. "She was nice," she said. This was all the conversation they managed before the nurse called Carmel's name.

"This way, please," she said. Carmel stood up and started to follow her.

"Can I come in with her?" Joan asked, getting up as well.

"Of course," the nurse replied, gesturing toward one of the rooms. "After you."

She drew a curtain around the cubicle with a flick of her wrist. "Carmel, would you take a seat and roll up your sleeve, please?"

Joan waited on one of the two chairs outside the curtain listening to the familiar script that had been recited to her in Blackrock Clinic when she'd been tested. She heard the nurse peeling the paper off the syringe, and Carmel's voice, cheerful despite the discomfort, then the vials of blood being dropped into a collection tray.

She couldn't help thinking about what little Ben was going through just a few floors above them. And what Emma said about it not being a good time to see him. She could kick herself for her impatience. Of course this wasn't the right time to meet him. All she needed to do now was to slow down. To give Emma some space. There'd be plenty of opportunities for visits with each other once Ben was well, please God. She had waited this long to unite her daughters and have her eldest back in her life; she would wait as long as it took for things to right themselves again.

"All done!" the nurse announced. Joan saw Carmel's feet slide into her shoes under the bottom of the curtain, and then she appeared from behind it.

"Okay?" Joan asked.

"I'm grand," Carmel said. "Nothing to it."

"We're marking this one urgent," the nurse said, labeling a vial of Carmel's blood. "We'll be in touch in a day or two."

They walked through the hospital's automatic doors and were met by bright sunshine.

"Now what?" Carmel said, smiling. "We have a couple of days to kill. Why don't you give me the tour of your old stomping ground?"

"You mean Islington?"

"Yeah, why not? I'd like you to show me while we're here. Would that be okay?"

"I'd like that too," Joan said.

Their first stop was Highbury and Islington. It was only half a dozen stops away on the Victoria Line.

"I don't know how many times we walked around this park when we were here," Joan said. "They've planted a few more trees, but not a lot has changed."

"What was Dad like back then?" Carmel asked.

Joan stood still for a moment, remembering. "Drop-dead gorgeous." She smiled. "Full of big plans. Scared stiff about what he'd let himself in for."

"It's hard to imagine you both here in the swinging sixties with your whole lives ahead of you. You were both so young."

"Too young," Joan replied. "But you're right, we thought we could take on the world together back then."

"Did you love him?" Carmel asked, looking at her.

"Oh, yes, I loved him all right. With every bone in my body. I would have done anything for him." She began walking again. "Maybe that was the problem. Perhaps I thought too much of him and too little of myself."

They had lunch at the Crown, where Joan and Martin used to meet after his classes. "We came here all the time until I got so big we couldn't hide the pregnancy," Joan said.

Carmel frowned. "You mean you couldn't let on even here in London that you were an unmarried mother?"

"Well, things were a lot more relaxed here than back home, but your father still worried about word getting back to your granny. He thought the less people knew the better."

Carmel took a sip of her Coke. "That must have been awful for you—feeling like you had to be hidden away."

Joan scrunched her paper napkin and dropped it on her plate. "It was. I hadn't bargained for how your father would feel once I started showing." She looked over at the bar, remembering the boy who had stood there once, ordering her a white lemonade and promising her the world. "What can I say, Carmel. They were different times."

After lunch, they walked up the street to Mrs. C's old guesthouse. Joan stood at the front gate, looking up at the freshly painted door. "This is it—the place I called home," she said. "Looks like it's been bought and done up by some yuppie banker working in the City."

"It'd be worth a fortune now," Carmel said.

"Of course, Mrs. Clemence, my old landlady, wouldn't have seen it. She'd be dead and buried years ago."

"Did you not keep in touch with her?"

"No. It was too risky. You know what it's like back home. A letter from England when you had no relatives there would have been enough to set tongues wagging the length and breadth of Harold's Cross. Des Ryan would have had a field day!"

Carmel nodded. "It's a pity."

"It is," Joan said. "She was like a mother to me back then. I had no one."

"You must have been petrified."

"Not in the beginning. I thought we'd make a go of it. Me, your dad, and the baby," Joan said, shaking her head. "I conned myself into thinking he'd leave the business and we'd make a fresh start here. More fool me."

"You didn't have much say in the matter."

"Still, there are things I'd do differently if I had my time again."

"Such as?"

"I would have been stronger. Pushed harder to keep her. And"—Joan turned to Carmel—"I'd have been a better mother to you."

"You were still only a girl. It must have been hard to know what to do for the best."

"What I did do wasn't enough. Not by a long chalk."

Carmel put her arms around Joan. "Well, it's not too late for us to put things right."

Out of the corner of her eye Joan caught a glimpse of a cleaner in the grand house peering out at them from behind the Laura Ashley curtains. She looked as though she might come out to tell the two women embracing at the front gate to move along. *Just you try it*, Joan thought. God help anyone who tried to break the spell of this moment with her daughter.

THEY HADN'T AGREED TO WAIT by the phone for the hospital to call the following day. It had just happened that way. They kept inventing reasons to stay put. The miserable weather. Their tired feet. The truth was that neither of them had the heart to leave the hotel room until they knew. When the phone on the bedside table rang, they both dived for it.

Carmel got there first. "Hello!" she said. "Yes, that's me. Uh-huh." She nodded. Joan frowned, meeting Carmel's eyes with a question. Carmel covered the mouthpiece. "The results—they have them. They just wanted to confirm it was me. I'm on hold."

Joan stood and began pacing the room, arms folded across her body, as if she was trying to stop her heart beating its way out of her chest. She came to sit next to Carmel on the bed. Carmel tilted the phone away from her, and Joan put her ear against the receiver. They listened, heads touching.

"Are you sure? Oh my God! Right, okay. Yes, okay. Yes. I'll see you bright and early tomorrow morning, then. Thank you. Thanks again!"

By the time Carmel put the phone down, they were clinging to each other, weeping.

"It's a miracle," Joan said at last, wiping her eyes. "Do you want to call Emma and let her know?"

"No, Mam. You call her. We wouldn't be here if it wasn't for you."

CHAPTER 44

Joan's hands shook as she sat on the edge of the bed in their hotel room and dialed Emma's number. She knew it by heart now. Emma picked up after only a couple of rings.

"Hello!"

She'd obviously been sitting right beside the phone. Waiting.

"Hello, Emma. It's Joan."

"Yes?" Emma said, in a voice so small Joan barely heard the word.

"It's . . ." Joan faltered and then started to sob.

"Joan, are you still there?"

Carmel took the phone and sat by Joan, holding the handset between them. Joan leaned her head closer. "Hiya, Emma. It's Carmel."

"Carmel?"

"It's good news. I'm—"

"Good news? You mean?"

"Yes. I'm a preliminary match."

"You're sure? They're sure?"

"That's what they said. Anyway . . ."—Carmel couldn't stop grinning—"they said I should come in early tomorrow morning to get the ball rolling on the rest of the tests."

"So they told you there will be more tests and it might be a few weeks before the donation can go ahead, all being well?"

"They did. I'm sure they'll fill me in on everything tomorrow. And Emma, just so you know, I'll do whatever it takes."

"Thank you. Thank you," Emma repeated, over and over again.

"Now. You'd better get off this phone and go and tell Matt the good news."

"Carmel . . . I . . ." Emma said, through her tears.

"Go on!" Carmel said. "We'll talk again tomorrow." She replaced the handset and grinned at Joan. "Here," she said, passing her a tissue.

"Thanks, love," Joan said, wiping her eyes. "I know we were all hoping against hope, but . . ." She couldn't go on.

Carmel patted her back, as if she were the child. "I know, Mam. I know," she whispered.

"I was thinking, I'd better phone Dad and let him know we'll be staying on for a bit."

"Yes, you should. We don't want your granny worrying either."

"I'll call him tomorrow morning once I've got my head straight. Look, my hands are still shaking," Carmel said, holding them up for her mother.

"No wonder!" Joan said. "Tell me, what else did the nurse say? I couldn't concentrate with all the excitement."

"Just that it'll be a couple of weeks before we know for definite if I'm a suitable donor."

"Oh, as long as that," Joan said. "Do you want to go home in the meantime, once they've finished the last of the tests tomorrow?"

Carmel took a moment to answer. "You know what, I think we should just stay here. That way I'm around if the hospital needs me." She stood, walking back and forth in front of the window. "And besides, the pair of us won't be much use back home with all this up in the air. So, I'm for staying put. What do you think?"

"I think that's a good idea," Joan said, her face breaking into a wide smile. "Mind you, it'll be a miracle if either of us gets a wink of sleep tonight!"

"I know," Carmel replied, sitting down again next to her. "Just imagine how Emma and Matt are feeling right now."

"In one way, I think I can," Joan said, leaning her head on her daughter's shoulder and staring out the hotel window at the new moon rising in the sky beyond.

THE TWO WEEKS, WHICH SHOULD have felt like an eternity, flew. When they didn't need to be at the hospital for Carmel's remaining tests, Joan and Carmel took the Tube to a new corner of the city to explore the sights Joan hadn't got around to visiting with Martin thirty years before. One day they saw the changing of the guard at Buckingham Palace; the next, they wandered Camden Market. They strolled along a section of the River Thames between Tower Bridge and Big Ben, counting the enormous cranes swinging against the changing skyline. In the evenings they rested and rubbed their tired feet, waiting for Emma to call from the hospital pay phone to let them know how Ben was doing. On the day they got the news the transplant could go ahead, Matt came on the phone to thank them both for what they were doing for his son. With each passing day Joan felt more like a mother to her girls than she ever believed possible.

WHEN THE PHONE RANG IN their hotel room on the evening before the bone marrow donation procedure, Joan picked it up.

"Hello, Joan. I'm still at the hospital. I just called to make arrangements for tomorrow," Emma said. Joan heard her take a breath. "And to ask if you'd like to meet for a cup of tea while Carmel's in theater."

"I'd love to!" Joan said. It was hard to contain her excitement.

"Where? At what time?" When the arrangement was made, Joan passed the phone to Carmel. "It's Emma."

The girls agreed to meet in the hospital foyer the next morning and said their goodbyes. "I suppose I'd better get a few things together for tomorrow. We have an early start," Carmel said.

"You won't need much," Joan replied, "just toiletries and overnight things."

As Carmel began sorting out what to pack in her overnight bag, Joan remembered the locket. Tomorrow might be as good a time as any to give it to Emma. She'd wedged the small box down the side of her suitcase in Dublin.

"What are you looking for?" Carmel asked when she saw Joan rummaging in her case.

Joan hesitated, unsure if she should tell Carmel about the present she'd bought for Emma long ago. But they had turned a corner together. She could be honest with Carmel now. "It's something I bought for Emma's eighteenth birthday. I thought I'd give it to her tomorrow. No sense in hanging on to it, is there?"

"Can I see it?" Carmel said.

"Of course. Open it," Joan said, unwrapping the box and handing it to her.

Carmel lifted the lid gingerly. "It's beautiful. Is that a diamond?" she asked.

"Yes, it's her birthstone," Joan replied. "That's why I bought it."

Carmel closed the box and gave it back to Joan. "And you've had it all this time, since I was what, fourteen, going on fifteen?"

Joan nodded. "I wasn't planning to buy her anything. I mean, why would I? She wasn't part of our lives," she said, looking down at the box in her hand. "But I spotted it in Appleby's window on the way to get the bus home from town and . . ." She stopped to think for a second. Carmel waited. "I suppose I just wanted to pretend I was still her mother." She looked over at her daughter, across the open suitcase that lay on the bed between them. "And I was saving my mammy's wedding ring to give to you on your eighteenth."

"Oh, Mam," Carmel said, coming around the bed and putting an arm around her shoulder.

"Anyway, you're the first person to see it," Joan said.

"You mean you didn't show it to Dad?"

"No. He went ballistic when I reminded him she was turning eighteen and might get in touch any day." Joan turned to look her daughter in the eye. "He was terrified you'd find out. He warned me not to tell you."

Carmel shook her head. "I can't believe it."

"Me neither. I can't believe I went along with it for all those years."

"I think Emma will love it," Carmel said, rubbing her shoulder.

"I hope so," Joan replied. "I just want her to know that she was never forgotten. That I'm sorry I couldn't be there for her." Her eyes were bright with tears. "I've got a lot of making up for lost time to do," she said, reaching for Carmel's hand.

"We all have," Carmel agreed. "And we will."

THEY BOTH WOKE EARLY the next morning. Since Carmel was fasting for the procedure, Joan didn't bother with breakfast at the hotel either. It was a small act of solidarity. They asked the hotel receptionist to call them a taxi and waited, distracting themselves by scanning the headlines in the morning newspapers in Reception.

"There'll be nothing but this royal divorce in the news from here until Christmas," Joan said, glancing at the photos of Charles and Di with the two young princes in supposedly happier times. "I wonder if she'll be able to make a go of it after all these years of putting a brave face on things."

"There's our taxi," Carmel said, picking up her bag as the black cab pulled up outside the revolving door.

They were both quiet in the back of the cab.

"Okay?" Joan asked.

"I'm grand," Carmel said.

As soon as they walked through the automatic doors of the hospital foyer, Emma rushed over and threw her arms around Carmel. "Thank you," she whispered into her sister's ear. "I don't know what else to say."

"I'm just delighted things are a bit more hopeful now," Carmel said.

The three of them took the lift up to the hematology ward together.

"Make sure you look after her," Emma said to Matt's friend Hannah, who was the doctor on duty. "She's family."

"Don't worry, she's in good hands," Hannah replied.

"I'd better get back to Ben," Emma said. "Will you be all right?"

"We'll be fine," Joan said, and she meant it.

"I'll see you later then, Joan. Is about an hour from now okay?" Emma asked, looking at her watch.

"Yes. I'll see you in an hour."

Later, as Joan walked beside the trolley wheeling Carmel to the theater, her stomach was a knot of nerves.

The hospital porter cracked jokes as the trolley's wheels squeaked along the glossy green floor, like a comedian playing his part, only his job was to put anxious patients and relatives at their ease. "Love the headgear," he said, grinning at Carmel and pointing to the blue hairnet covering her head. "I can see you wearing that going clubbing on Saturday. It'll be all the rage."

Carmel smiled lazily back at him, glassy-eyed. The diazepam tablet they'd given her was kicking in. "Are you asking me out?" She giggled.

"If only!" he said, holding up his left hand and wiggling his ring finger. "I think the missus would have something to say about that."

They were still laughing as they reached the doors to the theater.

"This is where we have to love you and leave you," the porter said, turning to Joan.

She bent to kiss Carmel on the cheek. "You mind yourself," she whispered, squeezing her daughter's shoulder.

"See you later, Mam," Carmel slurred.

"Right, we're off!" the porter declared, putting his weight behind the trolley before shoving it against the doors and out of sight.

Joan retraced her steps through the maze of basement corridors, passing worried relatives faking brightness as they too walked alongside loved ones on their way to the operating theaters.

She found the stairs leading to the canteen by following the different-colored arrows painted on the walls. Emma was already there. Sitting with her elbows on a Formica table overlooking the staff car park. She stood and waved when she saw Joan arriving.

"What can I get you?" she asked, reaching for her handbag slung on the back of the chair.

"A cup of tea would be lovely, thanks," Joan said, pulling out the other chair.

"Two teas then," Emma replied, weaving her way to the counter at the front of the canteen.

She made a face as she arrived back at the table where Joan was sitting, carrying a plastic tray. "This is all they had." She gestured at the two tired pieces of cling-wrapped fruit cake. "Probably been there since last week."

"It'll be fine," Joan said. "I'm sure neither of us is very hungry."

"I haven't been able to eat properly for weeks," Emma said as she sat down.

"No wonder, love."

"Today, though, it feels like we're turning a corner," Emma said, passing Joan a mug of weak-looking tea. "Thanks to you and Carmel."

"Please God," Joan said, taking a sip.

They sat in silence, not because they didn't know what to say but because they didn't seem to need words. It was as comfortable a silence as Joan had ever known.

"Oh," Joan said. "Before I forget. I've got something for you." Emma put her mug on the table and leaned forward, frowning. "It's something I've been meaning to give you." Joan took the familiar box tied with black ribbon from her bag and handed it to her daughter.

"What's this?" Emma said. "You shouldn't have."

"I wanted to. I always wanted to. Now I can," Joan replied. She leaned back, watching as Emma loosened the ribbon and snapped the blue-velvet box open.

"Oh, it's beautiful," Emma said, unhooking the chain from the velvet backing. "It's my birthstone."

"That's right," Joan said. "I bought it for your eighteenth birthday."

Emma looked up, her eyes brimming with tears.

"I wish I could have given it to you sooner."

Emma leaned across the table and kissed Joan on the cheek. "Thank you," she whispered. "I love it."

"I'm sorry." Joan fumbled for the right words. "I wish things had been different. I wish I'd—"

"You did what you had to do," Emma said, reaching for her hand.

Joan shook her head. "No. I did what was easiest to do. There's a difference."

"No. You thought you were doing what was best. That's all any of us can do."

Joan sighed. "It wasn't what I wanted. Not then. Not ever," she said, trying to steady her voice. "You need to know: even though I wasn't with you, you were in my heart and my thoughts every single day."

"I do now," Emma said.

They were quiet for a moment.

"Can you put it on for me?" Emma asked, holding the locket out to Joan.

Joan stood wordlessly behind her daughter and moved her long dark hair aside before fastening the clasp at the back of her neck. "It was made for you," she said, smiling through her tears, as she sat back down to admire the necklace.

"It's perfect," Emma said, feeling the smooth outline of the locket against her collarbone with her fingertips. "Joan? I know I said now wasn't the right time to meet Ben. But I was wondering if you and Carmel would like to meet Matt before you go home?"

"I'd like that," Joan said, smiling.

"You could come to dinner at our place," Emma went on. "Nothing flash, just a chance to get together. We've barely seen the outside of the hospital walls for weeks."

"That'd be lovely." It was more than Joan had hoped for on this first visit. The chance of a glimpse into Emma's life. "Carmel will be delighted."

"That's settled, then." Emma was rummaging around in her bag, looking for a piece of paper and a pen to jot down the address. "I have everything but the kitchen sink in here." She laughed. She scribbled the address and pressed it into Joan's hand. "Let's say seven o'clock on Thursday evening. That gives Carmel a few days to recover and Matt time to get home and make a start on the dinner."

Joan clung to the precious note. It was something she'd have given her eyeteeth for just a few months ago, and now here she was holding it in her hand.

Emma was slipping her bag over her shoulder. "I should go, Joan. They'll be getting Ben ready up on the ward shortly."

"Of course. Can I walk up with you?"

Emma hesitated. "Sure, why not?"

They waited for the lift, catching snippets of conversation between visitors and day patients about which floor they needed or the way to the X-ray department. Then they rode the lift to the pediatric floor in silence. As the doors pinged open, the doors of the lift opposite opened too, and a porter and a theater nurse wheeled Ben's bed out into the corridor.

"Ben!" Emma cried, rushing over to them.

"Ah, there you are, Emma," the nurse said. "We left a message on the ward for you. All set?"

The porter turned the bed, and from where she was standing Joan could see a pale, balding boy, his bleary blue eyes searching in the direction of his mother's voice.

"He's a superstar, aren't you, Ben?" the nurse said from behind her paper mask.

Emma glanced back at Joan with anxious eyes.

"Go on. You go. I'll be fine," Joan said.

"Thanks," Emma replied, turning away. "I'm here now, love," she said, walking alongside the bed with her hand stretched out toward her son. "Mummy's here now."

CHAPTER 45

Carmel had them booked on a flight home from Heathrow that weekend. Joan opened the small wardrobe in their hotel room and began slipping her blouses off hangers and putting them into the case lying open on the bed. She looked out the window at rain falling on the city rooftops, remembering back to the last time she'd been getting ready to leave London. And the things she'd packed to take with her, like the white baby cardigan that was never worn. Again, even now—especially now—something was willing her not to go.

"You all right, Mam?" Carmel interrupted her thoughts. She was coming out of the bathroom, zipping her makeup bag.

Joan nodded absent-mindedly, holding the blouse she was going to wear to dinner that night in her hands. "You look nice," she said. "Are you sure you're up to this? Didn't the doctor say it could take a week to recover?"

"Thanks," Carmel replied, adjusting her hair in the mirror. "I'm fine, Mam. Just a bit of an ache in my hip, nothing a couple of paracetamol can't handle. And besides, I wouldn't want to miss this evening. It was nice of them to invite us."

"It was," Joan said. "I'd better get a move on, or we'll be late."

The street where Emma and Matt lived wasn't far from their hotel, and since the rain had cleared they decided to walk.

"I think this is the one," Joan said, glancing from the address on the piece of paper in her hand to the number on the red door in the middle of a small row of terraces.

"Don't look so worried," Carmel said, as she pressed the doorbell. "It'll be fine."

Emma opened the door. "Come in, come in," she said, smiling. Carmel handed her the sunflowers and the bottle of wine she'd bought that afternoon. "They're beautiful! Thank you. They'll really cheer the place up," Emma said, leading the way into the kitchen where Matt was bending down to look into the oven, his back to them.

He turned as they came into the room. "This is Matt," Emma said, with a smile, going to her husband. "Matt, this is Joan and Carmel."

They stood awkwardly for a split second, just feet from each other in the narrow kitchen, all of them lost for words. Matt was the first to recover. He took a step toward them, hand extended. "Lovely to meet you both. I've heard a lot about you." His words reminded Joan that there was so much more for all of them to get to know.

"What will you have to drink?" Emma asked.

"I'd love a glass of red, please," Carmel replied. Joan's shoulders relaxed a little. This was a moment she would have given anything for before. She should enjoy it now.

"I'm sorry it's just a Marks & Spencer ready meal," Matt apologized, when they were all seated in the cozy dining room. "Cooking hasn't been top of our list of priorities around here since the little guy got sick."

"It's perfect," Joan said. "Thanks for having us."

Carmel and Emma chatted easily over dinner about work, travel, and life in London. Joan didn't say much. She wanted to savor the moment, to commit this scene, of her girls around the table, laughing together, candlelight dancing in their eyes, to her memory.

"Let me help you with the washing up," Carmel said, rolling up her sleeves, as Matt began clearing the table.

"I won't say no," Matt replied.

Emma and Joan sat in a comfortable silence at the table. "Would you like to see some of our old photos?" Emma asked.

"I'd love to," Joan said.

Emma stood on tiptoe to reach the photo albums on the top of the bookcase. She wiped the dust off them with the back of her sleeve. "It's been ages since we got them out," she said, handing them to Joan. "You forget."

Joan leafed through the stack of albums on the table, taking her time, while the girls and Matt tidied up around her. All the moments she'd missed, stuck between these pages. At least she'd always have tonight, she reminded herself, as she watched her girls helping Matt with the washing up.

She went back to the photos. Emma looked happy. That was the important thing. In yellow wellies, stomping in puddles. Singing in the school choir. Smiling gap-toothed in front of the tree on Christmas morning. Dancing on her wedding day. An overjoyed Emma with Ben in her arms, hours after he was born. Ben's proud grandmother cradling him, while her husband peered protectively over her shoulder. Emma's adoptive parents. The people who Joan knew, in that moment, would always be her mum and dad.

She studied the photo for a long time. The short balding man with kind eyes behind gold-rimmed glasses and the fair woman with rosy cheeks and a wide smile. They looked as if they belonged together—like a family.

"Let me take those," Emma said, touching Joan on the shoulder and interrupting her thoughts. Joan hadn't even noticed her coming up behind her. "Would you like a couple of photos to take with you?" Joan gave her a grateful nod. "I'm sure we have some more recent ones," Emma said, sitting next to her.

"You look like such a happy child," Joan said.

"I'm sure I had my moments." Emma laughed. "I guess the ones where I was having a tantrum over an ice cream I was denied didn't make it into the albums." She turned toward Joan with a knowing look in her eyes. "I *was* happy. They gave me a good life."

"I'm glad," Joan said. "That's all I needed to know." And it was true. The past could no longer haunt her, now she had the years ahead to look forward to.

"What a lovely fella," Carmel said as they walked back to their hotel after dinner.

"He is, isn't he? They're good together, aren't they?"

"Yes, they seem to be made for each other," Carmel said.

"Did you enjoy yourself?" Joan asked.

"Yes. It was a lovely evening."

"The first of many, I hope."

"I hope so too," Carmel agreed. "It was good to see you enjoying yourself."

It had been a great evening, all things considered. And things could only get better once Ben was well and life returned to normal for Emma. Joan was determined not to dwell on the years she'd missed by imagining what might have been. Tonight felt like a new beginning, not just for her and Emma, but for all three of them.

"Are you sure you're able to walk?" Joan asked.

"I'm grand. It's only down the road. Stop worrying."

They passed a corner shop at the end of the street. The shop owner was packing up, wheeling boxes of onions, garlic, and lemons inside. "Good night," he said, nodding to them.

"Good night," they replied in unison. Their heels hitting the path in sync echoed around the empty street. Joan reached for Carmel's arm and linked it with hers.

The doorman tipped his hat as they climbed the steps to the hotel.

"I could get used to this." Joan laughed.

"Might as well finish my packing," Carmel said, flicking on the light as she let them into their room. Ten minutes later, she was wrestling with her small suitcase on the bed. "Why is it impossible to repack an unpacked suitcase?" She grunted, leaning on the lid of her case as she struggled with the zip.

Joan came across from the bathroom. "Here, let me help you," she said, taking hold of the zip and inching the two sides together. "There!"

"Maybe we could come back for another visit," Carmel said. "Spend some time with Emma and the family when Ben is better."

"Wouldn't that be great?"

"And I wouldn't mind exploring outside central London as well," Carmel went on, sitting down next to her case on the bed. "Especially the gentrified areas. It's brilliant the way they're restoring run-down homes and breathing life into areas of the city that were neglected for years." She leaned against the suitcase. "I'd love to do something like that back home."

Joan sat on the bed next to her. "Would you really?" she asked. She felt as if she was just getting to know Carmel.

"I would, Mam. I want to build something I can call my own. Something nobody can say was handed to me."

"I understand that," Joan said.

Carmel smiled at her. "I think I know why now," she said. "You never really had anything of your own, did you? Not since you married Dad."

Joan shook her head and sighed. "That's just the way things were when we got married. I was one of the lucky ones, you know."

"How do you mean?" Carmel said. "Weren't you relying on Dad for money?"

"I was. But at least I could work in the business. A lot of women had to abide by the Marriage Bar. They had no choice but to give up their jobs when they got married."

Carmel frowned. "That's ridiculous!"

"I know!" Joan said, rubbing the back of her neck. "We just accepted it at the time. I'm glad you're going to create something for yourself, Carmel. So you want to get into the building game?"

"Yes. I'd love to make beautiful homes for people," Carmel said, her eyes shining.

"And you don't fancy 'settling down,' as they say?" Joan asked.

"No, not yet anyway. People keep reminding me that my biological clock is ticking and not to leave it too late. But I don't want to be on the lookout for Mr. Right just for the sake of having kids to please everyone else."

"You do what's right for you, Carmel."

"So you wouldn't be disappointed if I didn't give you a rake of grandchildren?"

"Not in the slightest. I'm proud of you for being true to yourself."

"Thanks, Mam." Carmel smiled. "And what about you? What will you do?"

"I don't know," Joan said, shaking her head. "There's only one thing I know I can't do."

Carmel knew what was coming next.

"I can't go back to your father. Not now. Not after Ben."

"I know," Carmel said. "I don't blame you."

Joan gave her a tight smile. "Oh, there's plenty of people who will," she said.

"Feck the lot of them!" Carmel said, standing now to face her mother with her hands on her hips. "It's your life. And nobody has the right to tell you how to live it."

"That's my girl!" Joan said.

CHAPTER 46

Emma turned over in the bed and drew the duvet under her chin. She'd just checked the clock for the tenth time that night. She kept going over what she would say to Joan later when she dropped her and Carmel at the airport. The last thing she wanted was for them to feel let down or, worse, used. She knew what it was like to think you'd been discarded.

Matt stirred in the bed beside her, sensing her restlessness. "What's up?" he murmured. It was their first night alone together since Ben got sick. A night off would do them all good, the ward sister said. Emma hadn't meant to waste this precious time with Matt by worrying.

"Nothing. Go back to sleep," she soothed. He turned on his side, spooning into her back, laying a protective arm around her waist. His slow, steady breath was warm on her neck and she felt inexplicably calm. She had to do what was best for her family right now: for Matt and for Ben. They needed some normality in their lives again. She hoped Joan and Carmel would understand.

Emma was up and showered before Matt.

"At least have a piece of toast and a coffee before you go," he pleaded, holding a mug out to her as she dashed from the kitchen.

"No time, love," she said, looking at her watch. "I want to get going before the worst of the traffic."

"Good call," Matt replied, following her down the hall.

"Meet in the canteen for lunch?" she asked, grabbing her keys from the hall table.

"See you there," Matt said, giving her a quick peck on the lips.

Carmel and Joan wanted to be at the airport early, in plenty of time for their flight. Emma had arranged to meet them outside the hotel and didn't want to be late. She was glad she'd offered them a lift, and pleased she'd invited them to dinner the night before. She'd been nervous about it, but the evening had gone better than she'd hoped. Way better. For a few hours, at least, they'd almost felt like a normal family.

It had been good to spend some time with Joan. She was surprised at how at ease she was in her company. Of course they weren't going to make up for thirty years overnight, but they'd begun to nurture the small shoots of something like an understanding. It felt good. Emma suspected there were still things they had to sort out back home with Martin. It was odd that neither Joan nor Carmel had mentioned him since they'd arrived. That was another reason they needed to give each other space. It wasn't that Emma didn't want her Irish family in her life, just that she couldn't afford to get involved in the emotional drama. Not right now.

As she pulled out of the driveway, Emma caught sight of Ben's swing hanging from the cherry blossom tree. She smiled to herself. She had so many things to be glad about at this very moment now there was hope for Ben.

She switched on the car radio and indicated left onto the main road. The traffic wasn't as bad as she'd expected. At the lights she pulled up next to an electrician's van. The words *Bright Sparks* were emblazoned on the side in luminous orange letters, and a Spice Girls song blared out the van's open window. Emma turned toward the sound and caught the driver's eye. He blew her a kiss as the lights turned green.

"Cheeky sod!" She laughed as she joined the line of traffic in front of her. It was good to feel happy again, like she was coming alive after weeks of not knowing how she would go on if Ben didn't make it.

Joan and Carmel were waiting for her on the hotel steps. She pulled in and popped the boot, and they loaded their cases before jumping into the back seat.

"Morning!" Emma smiled into the rearview mirror. "Traffic's not too bad at all. We should be there in plenty of time."

"Thanks, Emma," Carmel said, adjusting her seat belt. Joan was quiet.

An uneasy silence descended in the car on the journey to the airport. The joyful mood from the night before had faded. Nobody likes goodbyes, Emma thought, but this one would be especially hard. They'd only just begun to make up for lost time.

"Just drop us at Departures," Carmel said.

"No," said Emma. "I'd like to come in to say a proper goodbye."

Their flight was on time, and they checked their bags in and got their boarding passes. Emma walked with them right up to security. "Well, I guess this is the end of the line for me," she said, smiling and stepping forward to give Joan a hug.

"I'll call you," Joan said, holding back tears.

"Would you mind if you didn't, just for a bit?" Emma said. "It's just . . . with everything up in the air with Ben, it's not the best timing. I hope you understand." She could tell Joan hadn't been expecting this.

"I thought . . ." Joan couldn't finish the sentence. Carmel came to stand next to her.

"It might just be a matter of time," Emma said. "But I don't want to make promises I can't keep. My family needs me."

Joan's tears fell. She opened her mouth to speak but couldn't seem to form the words. All she could do was nod.

"We'll be here when you're ready," Carmel said, kissing Emma on the cheek. "You know where I am if you need me."

"Thanks, Carmel."

Emma leaned across and kissed Joan on the cheek one last time, then waved as they joined the line of people waiting to go through security. She stood watching them shuffle forward, before they got lost in the crowd. Joan turned to wave back, and then they disappeared among their fellow travelers waiting to make the journey home.

CHAPTER 47

When Carmel let herself back into the flat, her mother was up and in the shower. She'd been out to the Centra on the corner for the *Independent* and a small sliced loaf. Mam wanted to start looking in the classified ads for flats. They'd talked it over the night before.

"There's no rush to move out. You're welcome to stay here as long as you like," Carmel reassured her. "We've only been back a few days."

"I know, love. And I appreciate the offer. But you need your space," Mam said. "Besides, this sofa bed will have your back broken," she continued, patting the seat cushion next to her. Carmel had to admit that this much was true.

They'd hardly spoken about Emma since the flight home. Several times Mam went to the pay phone on the landing outside Carmel's flat and dialed her number but put the receiver down before the call connected. Emma had Carmel's number. She'd call when she was ready.

Carmel had been in touch with her father to let him know they were back in Dublin. But Mam made it clear to her that she wouldn't be going back to live in Grove Square. And Carmel had decided it was time to make her break with Egans' yard.

Her mother appeared at the bathroom door wearing Carmel's dressing gown.

"I picked up the paper for you," Carmel said.

"Thanks, love. I'll take a look as soon as I'm dressed."

"One slice or two?" Carmel asked, unhooking the plastic clip from the bread.

"Just tea for me, please."

"Will you be okay while I drop into the yard this morning?" Carmel asked, popping a slice of bread in the toaster.

"Of course. Did you let your dad know you're coming in to talk to him?"

"Actually, I'm not. Not really." Carmel stooped to open the fridge. "I just want to clear out my desk and pick up a few things."

"Are you sure, Carmel? Maybe you need more time to think things over?"

"I'm positive, Mam. Talking won't change anything. It's what we do that matters."

"I'm with you there," her mother said.

CARMEL STOOD WITH HER CAR KEYS in her hand and tilted her face to the sky. It didn't look like rain. So why not walk down to the yard instead? She didn't have much to collect. Besides, the walk would do her good. She'd take her time, maybe stop at the Kenilworth Café on the way.

At the bus stop on Harold's Cross Road, a small group of commuters heading into town lined up at the edge of the path as a full 16A sped past them without stopping. "Feck that," the silver-haired man at the front of the line said, withdrawing the hand he'd used to hail the bus. The others behind him groaned, retreating to the bus shelter to grumble about how the CIÉ bosses, who were paid a small fortune, ought to be hung, drawn, and quartered for the excuse of a bus service they presided over. Some things never change, Carmel thought.

In the end, she decided not to stop for a coffee. Better to get things over and done with before the day ran away from her. She was dreading seeing her dad face-to-face. Fearful of the look in his eyes she knew only too well. The pleading expression that in the past could make her cave in or change her plans.

"How's it goin', Carmel?" a man's voice called to her as she crossed the car park outside the yard. She turned to see Noel Carmody securing freshly cut lengths of timber to his roof rack. "It's well for some, sauntering into work whenever they feel like it," he teased.

She laughed. "Actually, I'm off today, Noel. I just came to collect a few things."

"Oh, right." He slammed his boot shut. "No rest for the wicked, I'm afraid," he said, climbing into his van and turning the key in the ignition.

When Carmel walked through the door to the shop, she saw young Enda, one of the lads from the warehouse, dwarfed in a blue shop coat, ringing up items for customers queuing at the counter. Dad must be out the back. She slipped behind the counter and headed for the office, where she caught a glimpse of her father through the window, buried under a mountain of paperwork. She tapped a knuckle on the open door before walking into the room.

Her father jumped up when he saw her, knocking his knee against the desk. The milky tea next to him slopped over the edge of his mug onto the table. They both ignored the spill. "Carmel! I'm glad you're here. It's good to have you back," he said.

"Dad, I just came to collect my things," she said, meeting his eye.

"Look, I know we have a few things still to sort out. Why don't you sit down?" he said, motioning to the chair opposite.

"Like I said. I can't stay," she replied, swallowing the lump in her throat.

"Ah, Carmel. You don't mean that. You know this place would be lost without you," he said, plastering a smile on his face. "You're the oil that greases the engine." She was silent. "We need you!" He sounded frightened and frantic all at once.

"What about what I need?"

Her father frowned. "Listen, I got a quote from the signwriter's to repaint the sign outside."

"Don't, Dad," Carmel said, shaking her head.

Enda came in from out front and knocked on the door behind them. "'Scuse me, Mr. Egan, could you give us a hand? There's a line out the door."

"I'll be there in a minute," her father snapped, glancing in her direction as he reluctantly left the room.

Carmel walked over to her desk at the other side of the office and began opening drawers, examining their contents. She packed a few things into her leather shoulder bag. The silver Parker pen her mother had given her when she got her exam results. A glass paperweight she'd treated herself to on a Sunday outing to the National Gallery.

She shuffled through the papers on her desk before unpinning the notices and cards she'd once tacked onto the corkboard next to her. A postcard with the Chrysler Building on the front, from Aisling and Linda in New York. She turned it over and smiled. They were forever inviting her to come visit them. Maybe she would.

Next to the phone on her desk was the framed black-and-white photo of her and Dad, taken when she was about five. He wore fashionably long seventies sideburns and a proud smile. Her blond plaits skimmed her shoulders as she sat on the counter gazing up at him, the pair of them too wrapped up in each other to notice the camera. Carmel couldn't remember who had taken the picture. Probably her mother, who was always there, either in the background or behind the lens.

She stared at the photograph as if seeing it for the first time—

a mirage of a life that had belonged to her once. Then she replaced it on the desk and picked up her bag.

The queue really was out the door, she noticed, as she walked back through the shop. Her father was behind her before she began descending the steps. "Carmel? Please?" She turned, registering his tortured expression, and realized he hadn't even asked how the child was.

"I'll call you sometime," she said.

"Let's make time now," Dad said, his arms spread wide. "I'll clear the decks here and we'll go for a drive to Sandymount. It'll be like old times."

"It's not old times, though, is it?" Carmel said, searching his face. She saw the remnants of regret in his eyes and blinked back tears. He knew as well as she did nothing could be the same again.

"Ah, don't be like that, Carmel," Dad said, taking a step toward her.

Carmel raised a hand to stop him coming closer. "Don't, Dad. Please don't. You're not making this any easier on either of us."

He nodded.

"I just need some time," she said, turning to go.

She sensed his eyes on her all the way to the end of the street. But she didn't look back even though she wouldn't have seen him through her tears.

CHAPTER 48

Later, Joan called Martin at work after Carmel got back from the yard. "I'll be around to the house to collect a few things tomorrow morning," she said. "I just thought I'd let you know."

"What time?" Martin asked.

"Some time after ten," Joan said. "Is that okay?" She kicked herself for falling into the trap of asking for his permission. Like she'd always done. She waited for his response.

"Listen, Joan, can we talk?"

"I'll see you tomorrow, Martin," she said, hanging up without another word.

She considered getting a taxi to Grove Square the following morning, but Carmel wouldn't hear of it. "I'll bring you, Mam. It's no trouble," she reassured her. "Do you want me to come in with you? It might help," Carmel said, as she drove along Leinster Road.

"Nothing will help, love. It's my mess to sort out, not yours. I'll be fine. Unless you want to go in and speak to your father."

Carmel shook her head. "No, I said what I had to say to him yesterday. He knows how I feel."

Joan patted her knee. "I'm sorry," she said. "It can't have been easy on you, all this. What did he say when you told him you weren't coming back to the yard?"

Carmel shrugged and shifted into third gear. "I got the impression he thought I'd change my mind."

"Head in the sand as usual," Joan said. "He doesn't know about your own plans, then?"

Carmel smiled. "No, Sonas Developments is our little secret. For now, anyway," she said, pulling into the driveway. "I'll wait here for you."

"Thanks, love. I won't be long."

Molly watched from the front window as Joan let herself into the hall. She seemed relieved to see Joan, in spite of herself. "I see you're back," she called out.

Martin came out from the kitchen, drying his hands on a tea towel. "Joan, there you are. Can I get you a cup of tea?"

"No, thanks, Martin. I'm just here to pick up my things, then I'll be out of your hair." She brushed past him, her foot on the first stair.

"Please, Joan, let's at least talk about it."

"I'm done talking. I've been wasting my breath for years," she said before climbing the stairs.

As she moved around the bedroom, opening and closing drawers, she was surprised by how little she owned that she wanted to take. What had she to show for more than half her life lived in this place? What part of that life did she want to hold on to?

She stood on a chair and pulled one of the suitcases they'd barely used from the top of the wardrobe, then laid it on the unmade bed. The air in the room was still and stale. Stifling. Why had she not noticed before that she could hardly breathe in this house?

Joan yanked her skirts, blouses, and dresses off their hangers and flung them into the case. She knelt to open the bottom drawer in the chest of drawers. Yes, she'd need a couple of warm jumpers. But the thing she had to bring with her was at the back of the drawer.

The snow-white baby cardigan with the pearl buttons, still wrapped in yellowing tissue paper. She tucked the cardigan in the corner of the case and closed the lid.

There was only one more thing she had to do. She sat on the side of the bed and began turning her wedding ring, working it loose with her right thumb and forefinger. This ring, and the promises that went with it, were all she'd wanted when she stood wearing a red dress in this very room one summer Saturday, long ago. She hadn't taken it off since the day Martin slid it on. At first it wouldn't budge, but millimeter by millimeter she got it to her knuckle and then with one last tug it was free.

She placed it on the bedside table, in the middle of a faded tea ring Martin's mug had made there once. Then she rubbed her bare finger and exhaled before standing to leave. There was nothing more she wanted from this place.

Molly and Martin were waiting for her as she hauled her suitcase down the stairs. Even though she'd played this scene out in her mind for days, Joan was not prepared for the venom in Molly's words.

"You will not drag my son's good name, and the name of this family, through the mud, Joan. We have no way of knowing if this child of yours is his. None at all."

"She's his all right, Molly. But more to the point, she's mine, and I'm not going to give her up a second time—not for love or money."

"Watch what you're saying, Joan." Molly's eyes held hers. "If a word of this gets out, even a whisper, I will cut you off without a penny. You'll be back in the gutter my son dragged you from. Do you hear me?"

"That's enough, Mother," Martin said. "She doesn't mean it, Joan."

Joan felt her fingernails digging into the flesh of her palms. It wasn't the first time in thirty years she'd wanted to slap Molly Egan across the face. But it would be the last. She picked up her suitcase and crossed the hall. "Do your worst, Molly," she said. "It won't be a patch on the harm you've inflicted on your own family."

She took her house keys from her pocket and placed them on the hall table.

"Joan, don't go," Martin pleaded. "At least give me a chance."

"A chance to do what?" Joan asked.

Martin took a moment too long to speak. "A chance to show you I can change."

"How can a man capable of denying his own flesh and blood change?" Joan asked, turning the latch on the door without waiting for a response.

When she opened the door, Joan was surprised to see Des Ryan standing on the doorstep, rocking on the balls of his feet, a sheaf of envelopes in his hand. She had no idea how long he'd been there. Long enough, she supposed. But for once she didn't care. "Anything interesting for us today, Des?" she said cheerily, looking right at him.

He flushed. "I don't think so, Joan. Just the usual."

Carmel got out of the car to meet her as she walked down the stone steps and across the gravel driveway. "Let me take your bag," she said. Joan got into the passenger seat and pulled the car door shut behind her with a satisfying *thunk*.

"Where to?" Carmel asked.

Joan looked at her blankly. "Maybe we could take a drive around the Cranmore estate?" she suggested. She hadn't been back in God knows how long. She'd had no reason to, not since Da died and Teresa left.

"If that's what you want," Carmel said, turning the key in the ignition. It was only when Carmel leaned over the steering wheel that Joan noticed her mother's thin gold wedding band, hanging from a new chain around her daughter's neck.

As Carmel's Mini drove under the chestnut tree that marked the entrance to the estate, Joan wound down her window and craned to get a better look. She barely recognized the place; the pebble-dashed houses were freshly painted, their gardens neatly planted. These might be the same streets where she grew up, but they were different now, changed almost beyond recognition.

They drove along in silence, a lazy breeze blowing in through the open window. Joan could see how much had altered about the fabric and character of the place. Half a dozen girls on their midterm school holiday stood on the path outside a corner house, a length of skipping rope stretched between two of them. They turned their wrists in unison, and the rope formed a perfect arc above them as they recited a rhyme she remembered from her childhood. *All in together, girls. In this fine weather, girls.* As the friends lined up to take turns jumping the rope, Joan sensed how different the lives of the children who were raised here now would be, and she smiled to herself before winding up the window.

"I've been thinking," she said, as they stopped at the junction. "How would you like to take a trip down to Kinsale to see your auntie Teresa?"

Carmel turned her head briefly to smile at her. "I'd love that."

"Me too," Joan replied. And because nothing more needed to be said, she laid her head back against the cushion of the headrest and closed her eyes, glad to no longer be living in the shadow of her secret. Then Carmel indicated right, and they drove down the familiar road. Together.

ACKNOWLEDGMENTS

Every creative project is an act of faith and love. This novel is one such project. It was made possible because of the faith and love of a group of extraordinary women. I am grateful to know and work with every one of them.

Thank you, Kimberley Kessler, for holding my hand from the very beginning. Thanks, Liz Hudson, for helping me stay true to the story's roots and making it better. Thank you, Gráinne Fox, lover of Irish stories, for being a fearless champion from day one. Thanks, too, to the rest of the team at Fletcher & Company. A huge thank-you to my courageous editors in both the northern and southern hemispheres, Maya Ziv and Beverley Cousins, for believing in Joan's story.

I am grateful to the talented illustrator Spiros Halaris for his ideas, and designers Kaitlin Kall, Christopher Lin, and Elke Sigal for the gorgeous book you hold in your hands. And to the editorial and marketing teams at Dutton, USA, and Penguin Random House, Australia, including Lexy Cassola, Janice Barral, Chandra Wohleber, Noreen McAuliffe, Emily Canders, and Katie Taylor, who have worked tirelessly behind the scenes to bring the novel to readers.

Thanks to my friends and first readers Kelly Exeter and Reese Spykerman, who told me to keep going, and Seth Godin for showing me how to start. Thank you to Catherine Oliver, who planted the seed about writing fiction.

I owe much more than I can express here to my dear friend Christine for trusting me with her story. And to my mam and dad for keeping our family legends alive around the kitchen table. Last but never least, thank you to my husband, Moyez, and our sons, Adam, Kieran, and Matthew, whose faith and love lift me up, always.

ABOUT THE AUTHOR

Bernadette Jiwa was born into a house with no books and a home full of stories, in Dublin, Ireland. She migrated to the UK in the 1980s, raised three sons with her husband, and now lives in Melbourne, Australia. She discovered she was a writer in her mid-forties when she started blogging and writing nonfiction. Almost a decade later, she began writing *The Making of Her*, which is her first novel.